UNICORN POINT

PIERS ANTHONY
UNICORN POINT

NEW ENGLISH LIBRARY

British Library Cataloguing in Publication Data

Anthony, Piers, *1934–*
  Unicorn point.
  I. Title II. Series
  813.54 [F]

  ISBN 0-450-42933-4
     0-450-42934-2 (pbk)

Reproduced by arrangement with Ace/Putnam Books, G.P. Putnam's Sons,
200 Madison Avenue, New York, NY 10016, USA

Published by New English Library,
a hardcover imprint of Hodder and Stoughton,
a division of Hodder and Stoughton Ltd,
Mill Road, Dunton Green, Sevenoaks, Kent TN13 2YA
Editorial Office: 47 Bedford Square, London WC1B 3DP

Printed and bound in Great Britain by
Biddles Ltd, Guildford and King's Lynn

Contents

UNICORN POINT

Giants

Ogres

Goblins

Yellow Demesnes

Demo

West Pole

Black
Demesnes

Oracle's Palace

Translucent
Demesnes

Green
Demesnes

Harpies

Orange
Demesnes

Animal Heads

Dragons

Purple Mountains

© 1987 STORRINGS

UNICORN POINT

1: *Stile*

Stile took the Lady Blue in his arms. "Thou dost know what we are about," he said.

The Lady was fifty years old now, and her face was lined, but she remained beautiful to him. Her hair still fell to her waist, fair but seeming tinted with blue because of her blue gown and slippers. She stood slightly taller than he, because of his diminutive stature; it had never been an issue between them.

After a pause, she murmured, "I know, my love."

"I will return in a few days," he continued gravely. "Thou shallst have company."

"True." But there was a tear on her cheek.

He kissed her, then went outside the castle. There was Neysa, her head turning white, her socks falling down about her hooves but her hide glossy black between, and her muscles still firm. She remained a fine figure of a unicorn; as her kind put it, her horn retained its point. Stile mounted her bareback, and she trotted across the drawbridge over the moat.

Neysa paused without being asked, so that Stile could turn and wave to the castle. A blue kerchief waved back from the window. Stile felt a pang, because all three of them knew that much more was afoot than this simple excursion.

Then Neysa turned away, and trotted from the Blue Demesnes. They were on their way.

"We have time," Stile remarked, reverting to the dialect of his origin, as he tended to do when alone with her. "Let's take the scenic route."

Neysa played an affirmative note on her horn, and bore west. Stile, reminded by the sound, which resembled that of a harmonica, brought out his own harmonica and began to play. In a moment Neysa joined in, and they played a duet, as they had in the old days when both were young. The music was pretty, and there was an enhancement around them, because music summoned Stile's magic. He seldom used it these days, because a given spell could be invoked only once, and he preferred not to waste any. Magic, even for an Adept, was often the last resort. But it was all right to summon the ambience without drawing on it.

After a while Stile paused in his playing. "I remember when you protested my power, old friend," he said.

She played a laughing bit of melody. She had forgiven him his power a quarter century before, at the time he made his Oath of Friendship to her. From that time on, all the unicorns of her Herd, and all the werewolves of Kurrelgyre's Pack, had been her friends too, charmed by the peripheral power of that Oath. There had been no war between Herd and Pack, despite significant changes in their compositions as members grew and bred and migrated, and the Oath had become a minor legend. It had been the proof of his status as the Blue Adept, for only Adept magic could affect unicorns against their will.

"Aye, I remember well," he continued, experiencing the nostalgia of old times. "I was an injured jockey from the frame of Proton, discovering the strange new world of Phaze. I decided I needed a steed, and you were there, you beautiful animal, the finest of your kind I had seen, and small like me. I loved you that moment, but you did not love me."

Neysa played a note of agreement. Her horn was musical, but she could talk with it in her fashion, and he understood her well. All the advanced animals of Phaze could communicate well in other than the human mode, though not as well as they could by using it, because the conventions of notes or growls or high sonics were less versatile than the completely developed human languages.

"So then did I challenge thee, and mount thee and ride thee, and thou didst try to throw me off, and we careered all over Phaze!" he continued, playfully switching back to Phaze dialect. "I think I kept my place chiefly by luck—" Here she snorted derisively. "But then thou didst get set to leap from the high point, and I thought we both would die, and I let thee go—and won thee after all." And she agreed.

"Then there came to me a woman, young and fair and small, and lo! it was thee in human guise, and I learned what it meant to befriend a unicorn," he continued. "And now we be old, and I have my son Bane and thou thy filly Fleta, and they both be grown and have offspring in their fashion. Were we wrong to oppose their unions? How much mischief might we have avoided, had we accepted their pleas!''

Neysa did not comment. She, with her unicorn stubbornness, had not yet changed her mind about her position. They proceeded a while in silence, Stile mulling it over. His son Bane had managed to exchange identities with his opposite number in Proton, who happened to be a robot: the manufactured son of the humanoid robot Sheen, once Stile's lover. The robot youth, called Mach, had occupied a living human body for the first time, and fallen in love with the human form of Fleta before properly appreciating her nature. Across the frames, the robot and the unicorn—the impossibility of this relationship had been evident to all except the protagonists. Only the conniving Adverse Adepts, who sought to use the boys for their own purposes, had supported the union. Bane, in the robot body in Proton, had developed a similarly difficult relationship with an alien creature. Thus Stile had lost his son to the enemy. He had recognized his mistake, in retrospect, too late; the boys were working for the enemy, and Stile and his allies were suffering.

"Yet now there be Flach," he said, vocalizing again, knowing that Neysa would have no trouble following. He pronounced the name "Flash"; it was the merger of Fleta and Mach, with the hard *ch* become soft. "The first man-unicorn crossbreed, and a delight to us both. Perhaps in time he will develop abilities drawn from both our stocks. And little Nepe, in Proton—''

Neysa's ears perked. She was listening to something. Stile paused, so as to give her a better chance; her ears were better than his. It was probably nothing significant; still, it was always best to be alert, because there were more monsters than in the past, and not all of them had learned proper respect for either unicorns or Adepts.

Neysa elevated her nose to sniff the breeze. She made a musical snort of perplexity. Evidently this was not routine. "Do you wish me to intercede?" Stile asked. As an Adept, he could handle just about any threat from anything less than another Adept, and at present the Adepts were not harrying each other despite their enmities.

But the unicorn was independent, true to the nature of her species. She preferred to handle this herself. She broke into a trot, and then into a gallop, moving at the velocity only her kind could manage. Stile crouched low, hanging on to her mane, enjoying this run as much as he had her easy walk.

They broke into open country, much as they had a quarter century before, covering ground at a rate beyond the powers of any horse. The magic of the unicorn was not merely in her horn! This time she was trying not to throw him off, but to outdistance something. What could it be, that caused her to react this way?

Stile looked around, craning his head to see the ground behind them. But their pursuer was not on the ground. It was in the air, flying strongly. A small dragon? No, the shape was wrong, and the mode of flight; it seemed to have birdlike wings and a running body.

He ran through his mental repertoire of monsters, but could not find a match. This one seemed alien to Phaze. What could it be? No wonder Neysa was concerned; she did not trust anything unfamiliar.

He continued his effort to place the creature. It had to be *something!* It had a body like that of a panther or lion, and a head like that of a bird of prey. It reminded him of the old heraldic devices in the history texts—

"Griffin!" he exclaimed. "That's a griffin! Head and wings of an eagle, body of a lion!"

Neysa made a musical toot of agreement and continued running at speed. She had known it by the sound and smell.

"But there *are* no griffins in Phaze!" he exclaimed after a moment.

Yet there it was, and gaining on them. A classic heraldic monster. Obviously it did exist here.

Stile's brain was now racing at almost Neysa's pace. Sparks were flying up from her heating hooves, and figurative sparks were emanating from his head. There were only a few ways that such a creature could be in Phaze. Was it possible that all the surveys of the wildlife of the frame had been wrong, and had overlooked this creature? He doubted that; those surveys had been competent and conducted magically. The griffin might be an illusion, crafted by another Adept. But he doubted that too, because Neysa had heard it and scented it; it would require an extremely thorough illusion to cover sound, smell and sight in a manner that would convince a unicorn. So it was probably a form assumed by some other creature.

A number of Phaze creatures could change their forms. There were the unicorns, each typically having two forms in addition to the equine one. The werewolves, who changed from wolf to man and back. The vampires, who were bats and men. And the Adepts, who could do almost anything they chose. But though the animals could change forms as many times as they wished, they were limited to those few they had mastered, and Stile knew of none who had elected a non-Phaze form. The Adepts could take any form, but only once. Thus it would be necessary to find new variants of the spell to achieve the same alternate form, which seemed like too much trouble.

However, a single appearance in this form might be enough, depending on its purpose. Why should an Adept assume the form of a griffin to chase another Adept? Was one of the Adverse Adepts breaking the truce? Trying to take him out anonymously, using this shape in case Stile escaped and tried to identify the perpetrator? That was possible, for some Adepts had few ethical scruples, but unlikely, because the Adverse Adepts already had the upper hand and were likely to win the complete power they sought, in time. They had succeeded in tilting the balance of power in their favor when they had given Mach and Fleta sanctuary. Now Mach and Bane were both working for them, and their facility with magic in this frame, and with science in the other, was inevitably growing. Stile and his allies were waging little more than a holding action at this point, staving off the reckoning. Why should the enemy try to kill him, when this would only stir up his allies to desperate measures, and change nothing?

Yet there was the griffin, closing the gap between them. "Neysa, I believe I should intercede," he said.

But she remained stubborn; she wanted to pull this out herself. She was angling toward the Lattice, that dread, demon-infested pattern of cracks in the ground. She had done that during their first encounter, trying to shake him loose; could she shake loose a flying predator? Since he wasn't sure how to proceed, he let her try; if the griffin actually caught them, he would invoke a spell that would set back even an Adept. The truth was that a single Adept could seldom really harm another Adept; their magic tended to cancel out. That was another reason it was easier to abide by the truce; violation was not likely to be effective.

The shadow of the monster was coming close, and the griffin itself was descending, its front talons reaching down. Stile readied his spell, but withheld it; he did not want to affront Neysa by demonstrating a lack of faith in her effort. Now she had reached the Lattice, and her hot hooves were clattering on its pattern of little cracks. Those cracks were widening into crevices, and the crevices to deep clefts, as they penetrated to the center of the region.

Soon Neysa was stopping across enlarging gaps, and then jumping over them. The gaps were now broader than the landing places, and the ratio continued to shift. That was the devastating thing about the Lattice; the farther it went, the worse it got. There was a way across it, but that way was devious, like a route through a maze, and could not be navigated blindly. The griffin hovered above as if uncertain how to proceed; perhaps it was not familiar with this network. Then it folded its wings and dropped down toward them.

Neysa leaped down into a channel, surprising Stile. Now the walls of it rose up on either side. In a moment the two of them were below the level of the surface, and the griffin could not follow, because its wingspan was far too broad. Neysa had succeeded in avoiding it!

But at a price. Now the demons of this domain showed, and they were not friendly to man or unicorn. They ducked into cross-passages to avoid the spearing unicorn point, but only just far enough to let Neysa pass; then they closed in behind. She could of course run on through and up and out the far side of the Lattice—but the griffin hovered above, evidently waiting for that. Had they played into its trap?

"Maybe if we go on through, I can throw a spell at the griffin as we come out," Stile suggested. "There has to be Adept involvement, so—"

She sounded a note of agreement. They both knew that they could not afford to dally long here in the Lattice, for the demons would surround them and set up a barrier to stop the plunging unicorn. Then they would have to deal with the demons, and it would be messy, because this was the demons' home territory. But this intrusion had caught the demons by surprise, so they had not yet massed or organized sufficiently, and would not be able to do so before Neysa galloped on out.

They passed the nadir of the Lattice, and began the gradual incline toward the escape at the far side. Stile watched the griffin above, ready to time his spell so as to stun it as their heads came out of the chasm.

Suddenly Neysa faltered. Her stride broke, and she ground to a painful halt. Stile was almost thrown from her back, because he had been watching the sky rather than the Lattice, and had not seen the obstruction. Now his eyes wrenched down—and there was no obstruction.

The demons were advancing, appearing from all the interlocking crevices of the demon warren. This was evidently no surprise to them!

"Neysa—what happened?" he cried, dismounting. He could see that she was in pain.

She changed form, becoming a woman of about his own age, petite and fit and attractive, but graying in the forehead, exactly as in her mare form. "Founder," she breathed in anguish.

Now he saw that her hands were held awkwardly, the fingers gnarling, the joints swelling. Her feet, also, were swollen. She was in serious trouble. "Change to firefly form," he urged her. "That will take the weight off your feet."

But demons were closing in, and some had nets; they were prepared for this also.

Stile sighed. He knew better than to try to reason with this type of demon. He would have to back them off with magic. He took a breath.

Abruptly the demons froze in place. Stile gaped; he hadn't done it! This was very powerful magic; who had interceded?

The griffin landed just above. It changed form. Suddenly a young man stood there, hair towsled, handsome.

"Bane!" Stile cried, surprised and relieved.

"No, Mach," the man replied. "I am sorry; I did not mean to drive you into the Lattice. I see Neysa ran afoul of the demons' founder spell. My fault; I will abate it."

"Mach!" Stile said. Normally he could tell them apart, though they used the same body; their manners differed. His distraction of the moment had dulled his perception. "Why were you pursuing us?"

"You can be hard to locate, Adept," Mach said with a smile. "The other Adepts watch you, of course, but I never bothered to spy on you. I prefer to search you out at need. So I assumed a form I knew you would recognize as alien to Phaze. But then you wanted to make a game of it, so I played that game. I did not realize that would put Neysa in the way of the founder spell."

A game! Stile realized that he had been dull; he should have realized that. Had he just taken the trouble to sing an identification spell, instead of letting Neysa run—

"Dam Neysa, if I may . . ." Mach said. Abruptly the woman straightened, her pain gone, her hands and feet unkinking. The Robot Adept had freed her without showing any sign of magic; no sung spell, no gesture. It was a power Stile could only envy. Originally Mach had been clumsy with magic, his attempted spells going awry, but after the Red Adept had trained him with the Book of Magic he had become the most powerful of all the Adepts, Bane included. He should have been on Stile's side—had Stile not blundered calamitously.

Neysa resumed her unicorn form, and Stile mounted. They moved out of the Lattice. Mach awaited them at the edge.

"I thought we weren't associating," Stile said with a smile as they emerged. "Aren't you on the other side?"

"Would I be, if we had the past five years to live over?"

"No." Indeed, the major reason for Stile's opposition to Mach's union with Fleta had been nullified by events. He had needed an heir who was Adept, and offspring by that heir who would also be Adept, so as to have the continuing power to hold off the Adverse Adepts.

He had thought that there could be no offspring of man and unicorn, and that a robot could not become Adept. Had he known what was to happen, he would have welcomed Mach as a savior, instead of opposing him as an interference.

"I gave my word, and Bane gave his," Mach said. "We would have chosen otherwise, and still our sympathies lie with you, but our word is sacred, so we work for the other side. Because the Adepts know we can be trusted, we have complete freedom."

"I would not have it otherwise," Stile said sadly.

"But there are advantages for you also," Mach continued. "Because of this, the Adepts are bound to take no action against you personally, and the children are free to visit you and Citizen Blue. We are also working to make the shift in power more compatible; the status of the unicorns, werewolves and vampires is being safeguarded. There will not be the disaster there might otherwise have been."

"But once the Adepts achieve power, will their guarantees be honored?" Stile asked grimly.

"Translucent's will."

"But how long will he retain power, once the others see no further need for his leadership?"

"That is not our business," Mach said, frowning.

"But it is mine. We all know the nature of the leadership I represent; none know the nature of the leadership that will emerge from the Adverse Adepts once their present constraints are gone, but it will surely be inimical to Phaze."

"My word binds me," Mach said tightly. "I would not use my power directly against you, and do not use it for the Adepts, but to the extent they can profit from my contact with Bane, they are entitled. I think it is fair to say that this profit is significant."

"It is overwhelming," Stile admitted. "If I can not stop it soon, I will lose hope of ever doing so."

"I have no comment."

Of course he didn't. He knew that what he was doing was shifting the balance to favor the Adverse Adepts in Phaze, and the Contrary Citizens in Proton, but he was bound by his word. Surely he hoped that Stile would somehow prevail, but doubted that this was possible. Thus had events mocked their preferences. "Why did you seek me?" Stile asked.

"It is personal. In three days Flach will visit you for a week, as he has been doing every month. We are concerned about him, and hope you can help."

"Flach is a fine lad," Stile said. "A joy to Neysa as much as to me, despite our foolishness in opposing his generation. He thrives as both man and unicorn, and we always look forward to his presence."

"But we expect more of him," Mach said. "By this time he should be developing his third form, and perhaps progressing to others, as well as learning magic. But he shows no sign of this, and has become increasingly withdrawn. Fleta fears he is retarded."

Neysa made a musical snort of negation. "He is not retarded," Stile said.

"But four-year-old unicorn colts generally have mastered their third forms," Mach said. "And they are open, expressive, inquiring. Flach is not. We fear that something is bothering him, or that he is coming to recognize his inadequacy compared to the unicorns, so is withdrawing. Will you explore this?"

"I hardly need to," Stile said. "I know the lad is advanced rather than retarded, and is developing powers we hardly anticipate. Your concern is groundless."

Mach shook his head grimly, not wanting to contradict his elder, but certain he knew better. "Fleta and I know you will do what you can for him," he said.

"Always," Stile agreed gruffly. "I assure you that your son will surprise you."

"I hope so," Mach said. He glanced at Neysa. "Fleta asks your forgiveness."

Neysa faced away. This had become almost routine: Fleta had alienated her dam by marrying Mach and joining the cause of the Adverse Adepts, and that remained unforgiven. Neysa well understood and respected Fleta's reason, but felt she should not have surrendered principle for love. Neysa herself had not. Thus Neysa did not associate with Fleta any more than the barest minimum necessary to fetch Flach and return him. Fleta longed for a change, but it never came. Unicorns of the old school were unyielding.

"Then we part," Mach said regretfully. "I shall return to Proton; Bane will be in touch." He became the griffin, spread his wings, and launched into the air. Soon he was gone.

"I know you want to restore relations with Fleta," Stile said as they resumed their journey. "Perhaps some day something will enable it."

Neysa did not answer, but that was answer enough. Her nature prevented her from forgiving her offspring, but she loved Fleta, and hoped that some legitimate avenue of forgiveness would develop. Just as Stile hoped that he would somehow be able to prevail over the Adverse Adepts. Perhaps both hopes were futile—but perhaps not.

For there was much that was not spoken. All of them knew that the

Adverse Adepts kept constant watch on Stile and Neysa and the Lady Blue, so as to block any action they might initiate against the Adepts. Anything spoken was overheard and analyzed. Perhaps the Adepts were foolish enough to believe that there were no unspoken plans, but Stile doubted that.

So he said nothing truly private aloud. This had become automatic these past five years. But he spoke freely of other things, so as to maintain the semblance of carelessness, and also to fatigue the snoopers with trivia. That way if something private slipped out, it just might be overlooked. After all, constant surveillance was also a constant drain on their magic.

"Mach's power is greater than I had thought," he said. "He cured your founder without seeming effort. I could have done it, but not nearly so readily."

She made a musical agreement. Unicorns were resistive to incidental magic, but Adept magic was hardly incidental. The demons must have plotted for a long time to obtain and place that founder spell, and it had been devastatingly effective. Yet Mach had nullified both the demons and spell as if such magic was child's play—which perhaps it was, now, to him. Stile was glad that the Robot Adept was not his enemy, even if he was not his ally.

They traveled north, now, not running but not dawdling. Stile had an appointment to meet Icebeard, the snow demon leader who was also a chess master. They had played several correspondence games since getting started when the demon agreed to train Mach in chess; the demon had wanted to play Stile to determine who was the ultimate chess master of Phaze. Since Stile preferred a fair game, even though Mach was on the other side, he agreed, and had played the demon, and it had been an excellent game. But it had concluded in a draw, and so had the following ones. Finally the demon had suggested that they play a "live" game, with time limits, and another, and another, until they had one that did not draw, and that would determine who was champion. Of course there were variants of chess that prohibited draws, but both of them were conservatives in this respect: for the championship they preferred the classic game. So Stile was on his way to play, though Icebeard was of the enemy camp; this was another advantage of the truce. But there was more to it than chess, as Neysa knew.

For Stile had spoken accurately when he said that his grandson (and Neysa's) was advanced rather than retarded, and would surprise his father. Mach had dismissed that as optimism or encouragement, but it was neither. Stile had been training the lad, and soon the extent of

Flach's progress would become known. But that revelation had to be coordinated with action in the frame of Proton relating to Nepe, the child of Bane and Agape, because the moment one child's abilities were revealed, the other would be suspect.

Flach was only four years old, and indeed he could change freely between his human and unicorn forms. But he could also assume other forms, unknown to his parents. Stile had cautioned the lad as soon as he learned to speak, and Flach had responded beautifully. His seeming slowness was a two-year act, masking his true progress. But Stile had known that this could not be concealed indefinitely; eventually the Adverse Adepts would catch on, and then they would act to eliminate the threat. The boy's great progress had been possible without attracting the notice of the Adepts because they were not watching him; they assumed he was too young to practice great magic. That was their colossal error.

The key was this: *Flach could communicate with Nepe across the frames.* Just as Mach and Bane could. That meant that Stile and Citizen Blue could develop similar information to that which the enemy had from Mach and Bane. Had both been male, they might even have had the potential to exchange, for they were parallels, perhaps alternate selves. This represented a possible shift in the balance of power, turning it back to Stile's side.

Stile had been holding off action as long as possible, so as to enable the children of both frames to mature. But there was too much at risk; the action had to be now. This was the real reason for his chess trip: it provided him the opportunity to do what he had to do, without giving his motive away. Because he had to escape the surveillance of the Adepts while he told Neysa what to do. A few seconds would suffice; then it would be out of his hands. He hoped he was doing the right thing.

Neysa picked up her pace, so as to arrive at the White Mountain Range at dusk. That would make direct visual observation trickier. She knew the importance of timing; everything had to be right. If they did not achieve their dialogue without suspicion, all might be lost.

As the light waned, they approached the base of the range. The snow demons spied them, of course; they were expected. They entered the track that led to the pass that opened on the demon chief's cold caves. Stile waved, then singsonged a spell, while Neysa played a theme to help intensify the magic.

> *Make us warm despite the cold;*
> *Make us private till it is told.*

Immediately the chill of the mountain dissipated; the snow remained, yet they felt warm. But it was the second part of the spell that counted more: the privacy. This was masked by the larger spell the demon chief had arranged to prevent any information being exchanged magically while the chess match was in progress; he wanted to be sure that nothing but the two great minds was operating. There was a certain vagueness at the fringe of the region, because the boundary of the demon's spell could not be precise. Stile had researched this well. Thus his own spell of privacy should not be detected, and the spying Adepts should not realize that they were being excluded. They would assume that Stile and Neysa were passing through a region of interference, that would clarify as they reached the center and the demon's spell took full hold. He could have made his privacy spell back at the Blue Demesnes, but that would have attracted the notice of the spying Adepts, and they would have doubled their watch, making Neysa's action impossible.

"Neysa," Stile said now. "It is time. Fetch Flach, take him on the circuit of allies, and take no note when he leaves you. Bring the golem to me."

She made a querying note.

"He will ask you," Stile replied. "Signal yes, then cooperate with anything he asks. His life will be at stake. He will be afraid; support him. This is the crisis."

She blew an affirmative note. Stile said no more. The spell of privacy depended on his intent as much as on his invocation; now it dissipated. The music summoned his magic; the intent interpreted it; the words defined it, approximately. Another person might sing as he did, and speak similiar words, and wish the same effect, but would not be able to achieve the same result because only the Adepts had the necessary underlying talent. Any person could do some magic, but most could perform only poorly unless gifted with the talent and willing to train carefully. Some tried, but the established Adepts were quick to detect such effort and to act against it; they did not desire competition. So successful Adepts were few; usually the only new ones were those protected by existing Adepts. Thus Stile's son Bane had been training to assume the status of Blue Adept, and the Tan Adept's twin offspring had trained to become the Tan Adept. Sometimes an Adept died without a successor; then there could be a certain free-for-all, unless some accommodation was achieved with the other Adepts. As a general rule, those who became Adept were not nice people; rather, they were the most talented and unscrupulous. That was why the majority of them opposed Stile; they preferred to operate without ethical hindrance. Only Red, who owed his position to Stile, and Brown, in her time somewhat smitten by him, were on his side.

But now they were coming up to the pass, and the snow demons were waiting. They were about to suffer the hospitality of Icebeard.

Stile had been to these mountains before, a generation ago, but had encountered a different chieftain: Freezetooth, who had had a passion for a lovely fire spirit whose proximity would have melted him. Stile had enchanted the snow demon to make him invulnerable to fire, and a heated romance had followed. Relations with that tribe had been amicable for twenty years, until the communication between Mach and Bane had polarized the Adepts and tribes of Phaze and forced new alignments. It was possible that Icebeard remembered that, and that the chess challenge was his way of maintaining relations despite their status as enemies. There were as many tribes of demon folk as there were human folk, and demons differed as much from each other as did human beings, and were subject to similar constraints.

Neysa had not been along on that trip. Instead Stile had ridden her brother Clip, now a Herd Stallion. Neysa was not partial to any de-mons, no matter what their heat or color, and was hard put to avoid an impolite snort as the white creatures closed in. This was however no attack, but an honorary escort. Icebeard wanted very much to play chess with Stile, and would do nothing to interfere with that.

They were ushered into the palatial ice caverns that were the de-mon's throneroom. Icebeard tried to maintain his chill reserve, but could not. He jumped down and approached Stile with an attitude that in any other creature would have been positive, but with him was merely less threatening. "Now we play!" he exclaimed. "Thou and I alone!"

"Aye," Stile agreed. Then he glanced at Neysa. "The mare liketh not these Demesnes; if thou willst grant her safe passage out, she will depart and return for me when the issue be settled."

Icebeard looked at Neysa. "Be this not Fleta's dam?"

Neysa made an affirmative note.

"And she play not chess? Fleta be a better player than Mach; comes she oft here to challenge my minions."

Stile had not realized this. But of course Fleta had come with Mach when he trained here, so had had opportunity to pick it up if she wanted to. Of course there was no reason a unicorn could not play chess if she wished, but Stile had not heard of it happening before. "Interesting," he remarked.

"Methinks the filly be a better gamescreature than Mach overall," the demon confided. "My affinity to unicorns be not great, but that one dost have charm."

Neysa stood awkwardly. Naturally she was pleased to hear her offspring praised, but she was not speaking to Fleta, as perhaps Icebeard knew. Demons had ways of teasing. Stile did not comment.

"She it was, methinks, made him what he be," the demon concluded. "A filly worthy o' any male, like her dam."

Neysa did not react visibly, but the snow around her was beginning to melt. At last the demon had mercy, and directed his minions to escort her out and to keep lookout for her safe return perhaps a week hence.

It occurred to Stile that he could get to like Icebeard. As Neysa departed, they walked to the chessboard with its pieces crafted from ice. He did not care to admit it, but he had looked forward to this game as much as had the demon, because Icebeard was indeed the best other player in Phaze.

And, with luck, the Adverse Adepts would relax, believing that Stile could not make any initiative against them while locked in a chess game in the cold White Mountains. He was counting on that. Chess was not the only game he was playing at the moment.

"Let's get on with it, pretender," Stile said. "I expect to wipe the floor with thy king before the hour be out."

Icebeard swelled up like an advancing glacier. "Thou dost call me pretender? Thy king shall be meltwater, and thy queen ravished ere mine be threatened!"

Stile smiled grimly. They both knew this was going to be great fun.

2: Mach

Mach felt the disorientation of the exchange. It was both physical and emotional: physical because he moved from a living to a machine body, and emotional because the frame of Phaze was so different, with its magic and his unicorn wife and son. He hated to return to Proton, though his existence here was hardly a negative one. It was merely a less feeling one.

Then things firmed, and he looked around. He was standing in Bane's apartment in Hardom, and before him was Bane's wife, Agape, and Bane's daughter, Nepe. Mach spent as much time in Proton as in Phaze, alternating months, but each time he saw Nepe she seemed to have grown another notch. She was in human form, a four-year-old child, and rather pretty. Of course she derived from alien stock, and could assume any living form she chose, with sufficient application and practice, so could be just as pretty as she was able to imagine.

Mach smiled, a trifle grimly. "The exchange has been made; I will leave you now."

"Of course," Agape said. She was pretty too, possessing the same ability as her daughter. It was always a bit of a jolt to encounter her naked, after a month of life in Phaze, where human nakedness was often a signal of sexual readiness. In Proton, of course, all serfs were naked. He normally adapted to the situation in minutes, just as he did to the change to a body that was a machine. He had existed many years in this body before discovering what life was like; he could endure it for another month. Bane, after all, was suffering the same readjustment, returning to his home frame, separated from the woman and child he loved. Agape, three syllables, with the accent on the first; Nepe, two syllables, accent on the first. His computer brain always clicked through such details as he oriented on his other self's family.

He turned to the door panel, and extended one hand. The panel irised open, showing the hall beyond.

"Uncle Mach!"

Mach paused. "Yes, Nepe."

"Can I go with you?"

Agape was startled. "Nepe, he is going to report to the Tan Adept, whom we don't like. You would not be welcome there."

"I don't give a—what's a bad word?—about the Tan Adept!" the child said stoutly. "I want to see."

"Pollution," Mach said.

"Beg pardon?" Agape said.

"The bad word."

Nepe considered. "No, plution's too legitmet. Maybe one about excement."

"Nepe!" Agape exclaimed.

Mach smiled. "I am a robot. I have no need of a bad word for excrement."

"Don't patonize me!" Nepe exclaimed furiously.

"Horse manure," Mach said contritely.

Nepe smiled victoriously. "I don't give horsemanure for the Tan Adept!"

"Now see what you've done," Agape said sternly. "She will be using that word everywhere."

"She has to learn adult usage some time," he pointed out, amused. Then he spoke directly to Nepe: "But if you say that to his face, he might swell up and burst, and the smell would be horrible."

"Really?" she asked, delighted.

"No, not really!" Agape said, darting a frustrated glance at Mach. "But don't do it, anyway. We have to try to get along with these people."

"Why?"

"Let her come along, and I will try to explain," Mach said. He was flattered by the child's wish to accompany him; normally she treated him with supreme indifference. In fact, for the first time she was making him feel like a real relative, causing his humor and flattery circuits to activate very much the way they would in life.

"But she has to go visit her grandfather, Citizen Blue," Agape protested. "The plane is ready to take her to his country dome estate."

"I can catch it after!" Nepe cried. "I know the way. Besides, it's autmatic."

"What has gotten into you?" Agape inquired. "Your father would have taken you there, if you had asked!"

"It's all right," Mach said. "I will take her. Probably my son Flach is pestering Fleta similarly, in Phaze."

Nepe turned sober. "I want to meet Aunt Fleta."

"It wouldn't work," Agape said. "Even if she came here, she would be in my body."

"Over there," Nepe said. "I want to meet the uncorn!"

"I'd better take her to the Tan Adept," Mach said. "She will be all right, and I will see that she boards the plane on schedule."

Agape nodded, yielding without liking it. It was hard to see her as an alien creature at a time like this; her reactions were completely human, as were those of her daughter.

Nepe took his hand, and they stepped out of the chamber. The panel closed behind them. "Why did you make that scene?" Mach inquired as they walked down the hall.

"I heard something," the child confided. "Something fun, maybe."

"The Citizen Tan doesn't serve ice cream," he cautioned her.

"Bettern that! But it's a secret!"

"Oh." He knew better than to question her further. He might learn the secret, but it would spoil her fun.

He checked his watch. He was early for his appointment with the Adept, by about an hour. Normally he would have retreated to his own suite and used the time to check for accumulated messages, as well as verifying the operation of his body. Bane tried to take care of it, but Bane had been brought up as a living creature, and still tended to assume that minor scratches would heal on their own. Also, Bane spent a lot of time with Agape, and that would be wearing on certain circuits. It was generally best to check those circuits, not with any intent to snoop on his other self, but to ensure that they remained fully operative.

But this time Nepe was with him. The child would not be very patient about an hour of stasis on his part. As a living creature she could not turn off or internalize the same way. Her closest equivalent was sleeping, and like most children, she would rather die than sleep during daylight hours. Very well; his systems check could wait; certainly it wasn't urgent.

"It will be a while before I meet with Tan," he said. "If you would like something to eat first—"

"I want to play a game with you, Uncle," she said.

"Such as piggy-back riding?"

"No piggy-bank riding! A *real* game!"

"Oh, you mean a Game!" he said, understanding.

"A Game," she agreed.

"Some of those games are unsuitable for a person your age."

"Yes," she said zestfully.

"But your mother would smite me if I played one of those with you."

Nepe frowned, acknowledging the truth of this concern. "But I know the difrence. We'll play a suitble game."

"Very well." He guided her to the Game Annex.

They came to a Game Console. This was set up with screens on either side, for the two players. He fetched a bench for Nepe to stand on, and lifted her up so that she could supervise her screen. "Do you know how to do this?" he asked.

"Natchly," she said. "Get to your side."

Mach went to his side. He knew that Bane and Agape had increasing concern about the child, who seemed to be a slow learner. She did not seem slow to him, but he realized that he had little proper basis for comparison. She seemed to be fully as alert as and somewhat more expressive than his son Flach.

But that of course was the problem. Flach was not keeping pace with either fully human or unicorn children his age. He spoke more slowly, and lacked interest in academic pursuits, and had mastered only two of the three forms expected of a unicorn. They had hoped he would go beyond the ordinary in both the human and unicorn respects, and for a time it had seemed that he would, but then progress had slowed. That was why Mach had intercepted Stile in Phaze—to no avail, as it turned out, because Stile had refused to acknowledge that the problem existed. Stile liked his grandson, without doubt, and that went far toward mitigating his early objection to the unusual marriages of Mach and Bane, but Mach had not expected that to distort his judgment about the boy's progress.

Could it be overcompensation on Stile's part, or advancing age? Technically Flach was the child of Bane, because Bane's body had generated him; genetics took little note of which mind occupied the body at the time. Thus Mach's son was Stile's grandson, and no one debated this, but the question always lingered in the background: was this entirely legitimate? Stile might compensate for that doubt by seeing no evil in the boy. But Mach had too high a regard for the ability and character of the man to be satisfied with this explanation. Stile was on the other side, and he was clever; his optimism about the boy might be a mere mask, preventing acknowledgment of a developing liability in the assets of his enemy. But how could Stile profit by such a pose? Mach had become the leading Adept of Phaze, thanks to the input of the Book of Magic, but he never deceived himself that he was the smartest person. He suspected that Stile was playing a game whose nature he hardly understood.

"Are you going to choose, Uncle?" Nepe asked.

Mach glanced at his grid. As always, it showed the four major categories across the top: 1. PHYSICAL 2. MENTAL 3. CHANCE 4. ARTS, and four types down the left side: A. NAKED B. TOOL C. MACHINE D. ANIMALS. He had the letters. Quickly he touched A. NAKED. Here in Proton the word had no social significance, as all serfs were naked; it simply meant that no tools, machines or animals would be used. He felt this was the safest course for a game with a child, because it eliminated most of the most complicated ones.

Immediately the new grid formed: 2A. NAKED MENTAL. He had not needed to worry about inappropriate tools; her choice of MENTAL had negated most of that. Across the top were 5. SOCIAL 6. POWER 7. MATH 8. HUMOR, and down the side were E. INFORMATION F. MEMORY G. RIDDLE H. MANIPULATION. He had the numbers this time, so selected 8. HUMOR.

She had chosen as quickly as he, and the third grid appeared: HUMRUS MANPLASHUN. Good enough; he should not get into much trouble there. The point of this Game was to satisfy Nepe, not to win or lose.

Then he glanced back at the grid heading, startled, but the title had already faded. Had he imagined Nepe's language there? How could that happen to a robot? He looked at the child, but she had assumed a mask of complete innocence.

They set up the final grid, filling in improbable choices relating to illogic and jokes. Nepe's choices evinced a proclivity for naughtiness that would have distressed her mother; apparently the child felt free to express herself more openly in the company of her uncle.

They played the grid, and the final choice of games was made: STRUCTURED LYING.

Mach shook his head. "Your mother—"

"Isn't playing," the child said quickly.

True. So Nepe had her way, and could now tell lies with impunity. This variant, as structured, required that each make a statement, while the other challenged any lie. If a lie was accepted as valid, or a true statement challenged as a lie, a point was scored by the originator. If the statement was called correctly, the point went to the challenger. The trick was to cause the opponent to challenge some seemingly outrageous but actually accurate statement. A lead of two points decided the game.

Mach made the first statement. He was not very good at lying, because it was foreign to both his training and his robotic programming; a good lie required imagination of the quality only a living brain could achieve. Fortunately his opponent was a child, and a childish example would suffice. He presented one of the classic ancient riddles.

"I know of a chamber filled with gold. The gold is wrapped in a silken shroud, and set in a transparent liquid, which is sealed in a container that has no doors or windows or openings at all. Yet—"

"An egg," Nepe said, not waiting for him to finish. "So it is true."

"You've heard it before," Mach said, chagrined to be thus readily bested.

"No, I guessed. I figured you'd start with something pretty elmentry."

Elementary: indeed he had. Still, Nepe did not strike him as even minimally retarded. She had made a swift and accurate connection, after correctly analyzing his strategy. She showed potential for master gamesmanship.

Now it was her turn. "The man rode on the horse, and yet he walked beside it," she said.

Mach pondered that. Surely it was a trick statement, appearing impossible, just as his riddle of the egg was supposed to be. But what was the rationale that made it true? Either the man was on the horse, or he walked beside it. Unless there were two selves in the two frames, Phaze and Proton, with one self riding and the other walking. But that would require alternate selves of the horse, too, and that made four creatures in all. The Game Computer was unlikely to allow so farfetched an interpretation; structured humor had to be narrowly defined.

One man, one horse: how could it be? Mach was somehow sure it could be, but his robotic logic did not fathom it. "That's a lie," he said.

Nepe smiled, as he had known she would. "Yeti is the name of the dog," she said. "That one's as old as your egg."

Mach groaned, seeing it. Not "yet he" but "Yeti," sounding the same when spoken. An interpretation that was valid in humor, if not elsewhere. He had indeed blown it.

"So did I win, huh?" she inquired joyfully.

"You won," he agreed.

"Gee—my first and last," she said with a mixed smile. "Thank you, Uncle."

Her last victory? He doubted it! He wished Flach had her ready wit.

* * *

They were at the Tan Adept's office precisely on time. Serfs were always punctual when dealing with Citizens, because a rapid process of selection eliminated all who were not. The normal manner of elimination was firing, which meant that the serf had to leave the planet unless he could find a new employer—a forlorn hope. But there were few questions when serfs simply disappeared, though all knew this could not happen by the serf's choice. No serf ever gave any Citizen reason for annoyance if it was possible to avoid it.

As it happened, Mach had given Citizen Tan reason for annoyance, and Fleta (in Agape's body) had given him reason for rage. But they had survived because Mach was an essential resource and Agape was under his protection. Bane (in Mach's body) and Agape called themselves married, but this was an affectation; there was no marriage among serfs, merely an informal tolerance of a continuing association. If the closeness of Bane and Agape ever abated, she would have to get offplanet in a hurry, for her protection would be gone. There seemed to be no danger of any separation, considering the presence of Nepe; nevertheless, Agape normally remained well clear of Citizen Tan.

They were on time, but the Citizen was late. That was the Citizen's prerogative. They waited in the office antechamber, watching the pretty and efficient human secretary brush her lovely hair. This was not any abuse of her position; it was a tacit demonstration by the Citizen that he had no legitimate use for her, and maintained her only for show or for any other purpose he chose. A serf with a brush was unusual, and none would perform any personal toiletry on the job without the express directive of the employer. The implication was that the person waiting for the appointment was virtually nonexistent; not even the secretary cared for his opinion.

Tan did not like Mach, but had to work with him. Their direct encounters were always formal and polite; the animosity showed only in this indirect fashion. Tan was making Mach wait—and Mach had brought a visitor. No other serf would have had the audacity, perhaps not even Bane. But Mach knew his power, and used it to counter the subtle manifestations of the Citizen's ire.

Why had Tan chosen to be the one to work with him? That had always been a mystery. The Contrary Citizens could have arranged to have any of their number, or some trusted high-placed serf, deal with Mach and Bane, yet it was Tan. Tan, whose genitals Agape's body had squeezed during Fleta's escape from him, before Bane had joined the Citizens and thereby guaranteed her safety. No other person had ever committed such an act against a Citizen and lived a day, let alone five years!

"Gee, you're pretty!" Nepe said to the receptionist.

The receptionist glanced at a panel on her desk before answering. Discovering no signal of negation there, she smiled. "Thank you, Nepe." Indeed, she was more than pretty; she was as well formed and featured as a serf could get, considering that serfs were allowed no enhancements. Her hair was silvery and shoulder length, almost shining, and her gray eyes seemed almost like silver too. Mach had not seen her before; she either was new, or had been transferred in from another office.

"Howd you know my name, Tsetse?" She pronounced it "Setsy," with the accent on the first syllable. Mach knew the word as the name of a fly, the carrier of sleeping sickness, and wondered how the woman had come by it.

Again the secretary glanced at her panel, careful to say nothing not authorized. "We know all who associate with your uncle," she replied.

"You mean you watch us?"

"Yes. To be sure that nothing happens to you."

The child shrugged. "Not close 'nough."

Then the secretary did a delayed doubletake. "How did you know *my* name?"

"Uncle Mach told me."

Mach would have jumped, had he been alive. He had not even known the woman's name before Nepe gave it! What mischievous game was the child playing?

Then a signal flashed. "The Citizen will see you now," the secretary said. "Nepe will remain here."

"Of course," Mach said, though he did not like this. He knew better than to counter any directive of the Citizen, but if Nepe were subjected to any ill treatment, even purely psychological, Mach would be in an extremely difficult position.

"I'll be okay, Uncle," Nepe said brightly. "Tsetse's nice."

Mach hoped so. He braced himself and stepped through the opaque force-curtain into Citizen Tan's inner office.

Tan was standing, garbed as usual in his tan robe, his hair tinted tan, and his eyes matching. He was actually a fairly handsome figure of a man, and Mach suspected that the lovely new secretary really did not mind the uses to which he surely put her. But he was arrogant in the manner of most Citizens, and ruthless, and he used women as he used men: with complete indifference to their sensitivities.

"Sir," Mach said respectfully.

"You have the information?"

"Yes, sir."

Tan smiled with genuine warmth. "We are very close, after a tedious delay. This may be the batch that puts us over."

"Yes, sir."

"Because once we have enough basic information from the Book of Magic in Phaze, and the Oracle here is able to compile it, we shall finally have the mechanism to achieve key leverage in the monetary arena. It is amazing how closely magic parallels financial dealings! You know what that means?"

"Yes, sir."

"State it in your own words."

"The Contrary Citizens will be able to use their wealth to control the government of the frame of Proton, and Citizen Blue and his allies will no longer be able to prevent this. Thus victory for you."

Tan rubbed his hands together. "It has been long in coming! Blue has used every conceivable mode of interference and delay. But under the terms of the agreement he had to allow you and Bane access to the Oracle, and that has made the difference."

"For the precise hours that his grandchild visits him," Mach agreed. For that had been the nature of the hard-fought compromise: Oracle for Nepe, in Proton, and Book of Magic for Flach, in Phaze. That was why the Citizens and Adepts put no obstacles in the way of these visits. Indeed, they would be glad to allow more time.

"In two hours you will have your session with the Oracle, and obtain the translation of your information," Tan said. "I believe that this will indeed mark the turning point. The matter will therefore no longer require my personal attention. I will assign an associate to work with you."

"As you wish, sir," Mach said, surprised. Citizen Tan had always evinced keen interest in this project, despite his enmity to Mach and Bane.

"I shall turn this matter over to her now," Tan said. He snapped his fingers.

A young woman entered the room. She was a serf, for she was naked, and well formed. Mach's gaze traveled to her face—and he stifled his dismay. "Tania," he said.

"Naturally I trust my sister to represent my interests competently," Citizen Tan said. "You have some objection?"

"No, sir," Mach said quickly. But this was a meaningless denial, as the others knew; he preferred to remain well away from this dangerous woman. He had snubbed her other self in Phaze, and made mischief for her here in Proton, when he was helping Fleta escape. Tania had a score or two to settle with him.

"How nice," Tania said, approaching him. Her eyes, hair and skin were tinted tan like those of her twin brother; she was naked but clothed in this color. "I'm sure we shall get along intimately." She came to a stop immediately before him, and put her arms around him, and pressed in closely.

Mach was a robot, and he was in his own body now. That meant that he had complete control over his physical reactions. This was fortunate, for Tania had undeniable sex appeal, and evidently intended to tease him with it. She was a bad woman, selfish and cruel, but that seemed not to detract from her allure.

Citizen Tan disappeared. Mach was alone with Tania. At least he did not have to say "sir" to her. She had great power, because of her relationship to the Citizen, but she was legally another serf. "What is your intent?" he inquired, attempting to disengage.

"It occurred to me that you have no romantic interest in this frame, Mach," she said. "Since we have to work closely together anyway, we might as well enjoy it."

"You know I am a robot," he said tightly. "You should have no interest in my type."

"If truth be told, I am bored with human men, and with androids," she said. "You are not just any robot; you are the most advanced model on the planet, and you have demonstrated abilities worthy of any living male. I believe you will be interesting."

"I am married."

"Not in Proton. Come, Mach, kiss me."

"There is no requirement that I do such a thing."

"Shall I tell my brother that you are uncooperative?"

"Obviously Citizen Tan will react in whatever manner he has decided to. Why should you wish to initiate a type of relationship that can only complicate a strained situation?"

"I doubt you need to know that," she said. "But I don't doubt you can figure it out for yourself. Now kiss me, and we shall proceed."

"Proceed with what?"

She laughed, her breasts moving against him. "Assimilation of your new information, of course. Did you think to have your desire of me within minutes?"

"I have no desire of you!"

"Perhaps not yet." She lifted her face, waiting.

Mach realized that she intended to establish her control over the

situation by making him do what she chose. She could have no physical desire for him; it was not in her nature as either an aloof woman
or the sister of a Citizen. Obviously sex was merely a tool to her—in
this case, a tool to embarrass him. If he didn't kiss her, she would
require more of him, making him regret his resistance.

He lowered his face and kissed her. He felt a surge of guilt, thinking
of Fleta. But he damped it down, realizing that he really had no choice.
Perhaps after playing with him for a time, Tania would lose interest,
as a cat did with a dead bird.

Tania broke, with a flicker of irritation. "As if you mean it," she
said. "Again."

"Whatever I show, I will not mean it," he said.

"Perhaps not yet," she repeated, waiting.

He kissed her again, as if he meant it. Unfortunately his circuits were
cued to a degree to his actions; it was a feedback loop that normally
enhanced his human emulation. That meant that to an extent he *did*
mean it, at least for the moment. This time she was satisfied. "Now
speak the formulae," she said.

"They will be meaningless to you."

"But they will be recorded. They may not be meaningless to our
analysts."

He doubted that, because in five years no one other than the Oracle
had been able to make sense of the strange statements he had brought
from the Book of Magic. It was as if the magic were in some alien
language, that only the Oracle spoke. That was another reason that
progress had been so slow.

However, he was obliged to humor her. He spoke the formulae,
and Tania listened as if interested. It did not take long.

"Now we shall send the child on her way, and go to the Oracle,"
she said.

Nepe! He had almost forgotten her! He was getting more human
all the time, and suffering the liabilities of the state. A true machine
forgot nothing that was not expressly erased. Of course he was no
longer a true machine; half his current experience was human, in Phaze.
There he was called the Robot Adept (or, as the natives had it,
"Rovot"), but he was really a living man with considerable power of
magic. Perhaps it wasn't surprising that the human liabilities as well as
the human delights carried across the frames.

They emerged to the front office. The child was sitting on the desk,
watching a cartoon on the receptionist's screen, her little legs swinging
and tapping the desk.

Nepe looked up immediately. "Were you surprised, Uncle?"

"You knew?" he asked, surprised again.

"Oh, sure. Did she vamp you yet?"

Mach froze, appalled at both the question and Tania's likely reaction.

"Not yet," Tania said, laughing.

"Oh, goody! Can I watch, then?"

"But—" Mach started.

"Certainly," Tania said. She turned back to Mach, and put her arms around him, drawing herself close. "Kiss me," she said.

"This is pointless and unnecessary," he said, not yielding.

"If you don't," Tania murmured, "I shall make demands on you that are apt to embarrass you before the child."

He knew her well enough to have no doubt of her sincerity. Fuming in a manner that would have done credit to a living person, he bent his head to kiss her.

Nepe clapped her hands, applauding. "She's making you do it!" she exclaimed. "I bet Tsetse she would!"

"Tsetse?" he repeated, chagrined at the openness of this matter.

"Tsetse—my receptionist," Tania explained, misunderstanding. She pronounced the name as Nepe had, but with the *t*'s sounded. "I brought in my own personnel, since I am to handle this case. I named her, because she is good at making men sleep. Does she please you?"

"I have no interest in her," Mach said. What a name to hang on such a pretty woman! Tania's cruelty was showing.

Tania turned to the woman. "Take Nepe to her ship."

"No, I'll do that!" Mach said.

"So you do have an interest in her," Tania said, "because she affects the welfare of your niece."

"To that degree," Mach agreed. What was Tania trying to do? He saw no consistent pattern in her actions.

Tania read his doubt. "I am showing you that there are ways and ways I can affect your interests if you cross me. We have a covenant, and no one will be hurt. But you could have to do things you dislike, and the child could witness things you prefer she did not. Now Tsetse will escort her safely to her ship, and you and I will dally on the way to the Oracle. Need more be said?"

This ruthless woman would do whatever she thought would be effective in bending his will to hers. Already she had let him know that he would do what she wished in a social sense, or see her ire taken out on little Nepe. His robot logic made it clear: it was better to do whatever Tania wanted. If she overstepped her bounds, Citizen Tan would call her up short.

But that could mean having an affair with her. As a man or robot in the frame of Proton, he had no technical reason not to; his marriage to Fleta had no bearing here. But emotionally the prospect appalled him. His body was the one Bane used, when they exchanged, and so Agape was concerned, while his mind was in love with Fleta, making Fleta concerned. Thus it was not a simple matter of catering to the demands of a demanding woman without any emotional involvement, as a normal robot could do. There were deep social conflicts. That seemed to be *why* Tania was doing it. Was it merely her normal cruelty, or was there some more sinister reason? He was profoundly dismayed by this development.

"I'll be fine, Uncle, and so will you," Nepe said, jumping off the desk to take Tsetse's hand. "Thanks for the game and the demstration!"

"You are welcome, Nepe," he said, wishing he had never brought her here. Obviously he had played into Tania's hands. Yet the child seemed quite satisfied, and she was evidently not entirely innocent of the games adults played. This could not be accounted for by the malice of either Citizen Tan or his sister.

Nepe and the receptionist departed. Mach braced himself for Tania's dalliance, seeing no alternative.

But she surprised him. "I have no greater personal or social interest in you, Mach, than you have in me," she said. "Certainly I have no need to coerce you into anything. I can have any plaything I desire, with no difficulty. I do confess that a challenge is intriguing, and you are a challenge, but at this stage I want only to impress on you the current realities."

"You have done so," he said gruffly.

"With that understanding, we may proceed to the Oracle."

Mach nodded grimly. The worst of it was that her evident personal interest in him, for whatever cynical reason, evoked a complementary interest; he was now aware of the beauty and texture of her body. Even her mind intrigued him. Fleta was straightforward and honest and positive and nice, and he loved her; Tania was devious and dishonest and negative and cruel, and he knew little of this type, and found it uncannily fascinating. Fleta was completely open; he always knew where she stood and how she felt. Tania was the opposite, which gave her the quality of mystery—and that lured him in the manner of a candle with a moth. He was disgusted with himself, but the lure remained.

She nodded in return, her eyes narrowing appraisingly. She was experienced enough to know the type of appeal she had for men. "The time will come when I do not have to tell you to kiss me," she said. "Like all males, you are fascinated by bad women."

Mach did not answer, as there was no honest refutation he could make. He set up a circuit mask that would detune his awareness of her physical features and prevent him from reacting to them, but there was no simple way to do the same for his emotion. He had learned too much of the living response, these past five years, and hardly cared to diminish that lest it affect his relationship with Fleta.

"Oracle," Tania said to the desk. It responded to her voice, and put through the call to the Oracle. This took a minute, as the Oracle was a highly restricted apparatus. It had resided for many generations in Phaze, until Stile had engineered its exchange with the Book of Magic, making both fully operative.

"Sit at the desk," she directed him.

"There is no need," he said. "I do not fatigue."

"I see you are after all a slow learner. Sit."

Mach circled the desk and took the comfortable chair vacated by the receptionist.

Tania followed, and sat in his lap. He had to do an emergency short-out of his tactile receptors in that region to prevent a reaction as her firm naked buttocks made contact. There was no subtlety whatsoever in her approach, but it remained effective. "Every time you balk, I will react unpredictably," she said, reaching across him to touch a button in the chair.

Abruptly his receptors turned on again. "What?" he exclaimed, startled.

"I have nulled your shorting mechanism," she said, tensing and relaxing a buttock. "Did you suppose I knew nothing of robotics? This office is appropriately equipped."

He should have known. His machine defenses were useless here. He was no Adept, in this frame, and that made him vulnerable. She could make him react when she chose to.

"Oracle." It was the connection. With relief, Mach plunged into his recitation of formulae, tuning out his body's awareness of hers.

But all too soon the information had been covered. The Oracle signed off; it would now devote itself to integrating the new information with the old, and compiling the whole into something useful to the Adepts. Mach's job was done, for the moment.

"Have you learned your lesson?" Tania inquired, turning so that her left breast pressed against his chest.

"Yes." But he doubted this would satisfy her at this stage. She considered him a challenge, and that would motivate her even if she found him sexually repulsive.

"How nice. But perhaps I should make certain. I must say, I had forgotten the pleasure of seducing an unwilling male. I think we shall be seeing a good deal of each other this month." She twisted around, her thighs sliding across his thighs, her breasts making better contact. The sensations sent electrical pulses through his body, and both his mind and his loin responded. Damn that override she had turned on! He was unable to curtail any of his natural reactions.

She reached up to draw his face into hers. Her tan hair spread out, framing her face, descending to brush against his body. Her tan irises seemed to grow large. She kissed him, and he was aware of his resistance crumbling. She was an infernally attractive figure of a woman, never mind her unattractive nature, and his body wanted hers.

There was a ping from the screen. Tania paused, a quirk of annoyance twisting her mouth. "What?" she rapped.

"Notice of problem," the screen said, showing matching words. "The child Nepe has gone astray."

"What?" This time it was Mach, unable to damp down his alarm circuitry.

"She boarded her plane," the screen said and printed. "It took off. It disappeared from surveillance. It seems unlikely to arrive at its destination."

"That's impossible!" Tania exclaimed. "Recheck!" She started to get up.

Mach's arms clamped around her body with the power of machinery. "That child is covered by the covenant!" he said. "As is Agape—and my wife and child in Phaze."

"I know she is!" Tania said. "We haven't done this!"

"Haven't you?" One of his hands closed on her upper arm and began to squeeze. Now the override prevented him from moderating his developing emotion of anger. "You thought to distract me while you acted against my niece?"

He was hurting her, but she refused to cry out. "I thought to seduce you, yes. Nothing more. No harm to Nepe. Now let me go so I can pursue this matter."

He realized that it would make no sense for the Contrary Citizens to make such a move, even after they gained sufficient information to achieve their power in Proton. He and Bane remained the Citizens' only contact with the opposite frames. He released her. His desire for her body had been nullified by his awareness of the threat to Nepe.

Quickly Tania ascertained that the plane, flying preprogrammed, had at first suffered what appeared to be a malfunction of the tracking equipment. It had ceased to show on the screen. But when they compensated by orienting with another tracker, they had been unable to locate it. A direct physical check had also failed to turn it up. A crash in the polluted desert was a strong possibility; a robot search party was now proceeding to the site of last observation.

"The timing remains suggestive," Mach said tightly.

"What reason would we have to take her out, knowing it would jeopardize your cooperation?" Tania asked, looking genuinely nervous.

"This is what I am trying to ascertain. Your receptionist conducted her to the plane. She could have planted something on the craft, or sent a signal to an accomplice. While you made sure I was not there, because I might have interfered. It all fits together rather neatly: Citizen Tan stepping aside at this time for you, your hireling taking the child—"

"No!" she cried. "The timing is coincidence! We were trying only to—"

"You *did* set this up?" he asked, stepping toward her.

"No! Not to hurt the child! We have nothing to do with that! We don't *want* anything to happen to her! We want her on our side!"

"What are you talking about? Nepe is only four years old! She's no part of the struggle between Citizens."

"But she will be! She—" Tania stopped, realizing that she had said too much.

"I think I had better question you more authoritatively."

She drew herself up angrily. "You have no right!"

"Listen, Tania, you are a serf, just as I am. If your brother dies, you may inherit his Citizenship—but if my father dies, I may inherit his. You are human, I am a robot, but you are no better than I am either legally or socially. Not till your side wins its case against Citizen Blue and starts subverting the new order. You gained my acquiescence to your advances only because I care for the welfare of my niece. Do you wish to try whether your good will is more precious to the Citizens than mine? Do you wish to try whether I will not destroy you as readily as I would have played sex with you, if that child is in peril by your device? Whether I can do this with impunity, as long as I continue to bring across the formulae your Citizens require? In that case, summon your brother and put it to him before I do. It was my love for Fleta that brought me to your side, but I believe the Adept Stile would accept our union now. It is honor, not love or fear, that keeps me in your camp, and it is dishonor on your part that will break that tie. You have one way to establish the nature of your complicity in this matter, and you will do that now or suffer the consequence."

"You damned arrogant machine!" she flared. "You should be junked! No one talks to me that way and lives!"

"I am not alive. What is your decision?"

"I hate you!"

Mach smiled. "I take that to be your acquiescence."

"Yes," she whispered, defeated. In that moment of her genuine humiliation, he found her more appealing than she had been when arrogant. Stripped of her imperialistic manner and her cruelty, she could be a truly attractive woman.

Mach spoke to the desk. "One interrogation unit to this site," he said. He realized that the receptionist was late returning; probably she was under orders to stay clear until her mistress had completed the seduction of the robot. That particular plot had gone awry! But if Nepe was in trouble—

"But a condition," Tania said.

"No conditions! I mean to have the truth!"

"You pride yourself on honor," she said, speaking so low that her voice hardly carried. "Deal with me with honor."

"You never dealt with me with honor!"

"That is irrelevant. You are not me."

She had a point. "What are you asking?"

"If I demean myself in this manner, and prove out, you owe me."

"Owe you what?"

She merely looked at him.

Mach was shaken. Could she be telling the truth? If so, his humiliation of her would prove to have been unjustified. He would, indeed, owe her, by his code. But she was a clever, nervy woman; she could be bluffing, trying to make him change his mind without proof.

"Granted," he said shortly. And felt a twinge of guilt. Had he any right to make such a bargain, regardless of the situation?

Tania went to the desk. "Admit the machine, then seal off all communications until further notice," she said. She sat in the chair.

Thus this questioning would be only between the two of them. The interrogation unit would not tell; it would be erased after use. No one else would know what happened here, unless one of them told.

The unit arrived. It was a standard cylindrical robot, with several extensible arms and assorted recesses. "Subject?" its speaker grille inquired.

"Me," Tania said.

The machine rolled to her. Efficiently it fastened metallic bracelets on her wrists, ankles and head. She submitted to this with unconcealed aversion, but made no move to interfere.

"Testing," the machine said. "Speak truth: what is your name and station?"

"Tania, human, serf, heir to Citizen Tan."

"Speak false: what is your name and station?"

"Mach, robot, serf, heir to Citizen Blue."

Mach had to smile; she had given his identification, true for him but a falsehood for her.

"Speak half-truth: a statement of your choosing."

"I am in love with Mach."

Mach was startled. Could any part of that be true? He had assumed that her play for him was entirely cynical.

"Alignment is complete," the interrogator said. "Proceed."

Her half-truth had aligned? This promised mischief of another nature!

Though shaken by her statement, Mach knew he had to make this count, because he would never get another opportunity. He could not afford to let any aspect of the truth slip by him.

He started obliquely, because now he wanted a broader truth than he had initially. "Why did you attempt to seduce me? Provide such detail as you believe is warranted to clarify this matter."

"That is not relevant!" she flared.

"I believe it is, because Nepe disappeared while you were doing this."

Indeed, the interrogator challenged it. "Subject's statement is false," it said.

She grimaced. She was in no sense drugged or under any duress other than the need to tell the truth or be immediately exposed in her lie. "It was my brother's plan. Fleta humiliated him and got away. Now she is back in Phaze; he can not reach her, either physically or by the terms of the covenant. But he can not rest until he has his satisfaction of her. Therefore he asked me to win you away from her. That would be a fitting vengeance for him, that can reach her wherever she is. In addition, this would bind you more firmly to our cause, so it is practical; that is why the other Citizens agreed. Nepe is involved only in the sense that she would be affected by the breakup of the marriage of her parents."

She paused. After a moment the interrogator spoke. "That is not the whole truth."

Tania's lips tightened. "I had no need to agree to this, because I am his sister and his heir. He could have used Tsetse for this purpose; indeed, that was the original plan. But I volunteered, because it is better to keep it in the family; it would be dangerous to have my employee gain your loyalty. She might get notions of independence. With me, there would be no risk, because never would I betray the interests of the Citizenship I am slated to inherit."

Another pause. Then: "That is not the whole truth."

"It is enough of it!" she snapped.

"True," the interrogator agreed.

Mach was surprised again. She had backed off the machine! But his own curiosity had been aroused. "Give the rest anyway," he said.

"You owe me," she reminded him.

"If you prove out."

"I was influenced by more than loyalty to my brother and my side," she said. "For a decade I have known of this sophisticated robot, Mach. I am older than he, but this has little relevance in our society. At first I was outraged that he should be designated heir to a Citizen. But when he established communication with his other self, and went to Phaze, I realized that he was much more than a robot. I saw the mischief he made for our side, and I learned how he became an Adept in the other frame. I know how hard it is to do that. I studied him, and was fascinated with him, as a machine who had become human. That was all there was to it, until the time of our dominance neared, and we knew that the enemy had to make his countermove soon or be forever lost. Then it seemed wise to bind Mach more tightly to us, and the Citizens were ready to give my brother his vengeance. Then, as I considered the advantage of doing the job myself, I realized that my interest was more than this. I have found no man worthy of more than occasional dalliance; but Mach, though he is a robot, may be worthy. I became intrigued to the point of fascination. My mission may be one thing, but my heart is another, and I want him. It was my intent to seduce him first, then wean him away from Fleta by repeated demonstrations of my effectiveness as a lover, and, perhaps, to love him myself. In the end, perhaps, to win Bane also. Because these two represent our only known contact with the frame of Phaze, and Phaze remains a dream for all of us, even those of us who have never seen it, a magic world like none other. I would give my power and pride to live in Phaze, the frame where enchantment is literal. If Mach could take me there, or exchange me with my other self there for a time, as he did with Agape—the very notion, however farfetched, fills me with an unutterable longing, and I would love him for it no matter what else occurred between us. And that is the whole of it."

"That is the whole of it," the interrogator agreed.

It did make sense. Tania might be arrogant and cynical, but she had desires too, and she wanted the best for herself. He understood her longing for Phaze; that longing had never left him. So there was genuine desire, under her artificiality. But what of Nepe?

"Tell what you know or suspect of Nepe's disappearance."

"I used her only as a lever to force your acquiescence. I know nothing of any plot against her, and do not believe that there is any. Her disappearance is a mystery to me. Indeed, I am chagrined by it, because it completely destroyed my initiative with you."

There was the pause. "That is the whole truth," the interrogator said.

Mach, amazed, tried once more. "Do you know of any other plot against me or Nepe or Agape, or have you any suspicion of such?"

"No."

"That is not the whole truth."

"Damn that machine!" she flared again. "Only in the sense that the child is valuable. She is developing powers that could make her a significant asset to our side. She might even learn to communicate with her opposite in Phaze. Therefore we have instituted a watch on her, to ensure that we know at such time as her powers develop. We have no plot against her, only the intent to keep her with us, by whatever means is required. Her disappearance is as much a concern to us as to you, Mach, and we shall make every effort to recover her unharmed. That is the whole truth."

And the interrogator agreed.

Surely she would have known or suspected, had there been any plot. She had exonerated herself and her side.

"But Nepe is considered retarded," he said.

"She is not. She hides her developing abilities from you. We see this because we have tracked her constantly, when she is not in the protected suite of her grandfather. Recently we have observed less; we suspect this is not because she is slowing, but because she has learned of our observation."

"But how could she have escaped your surveillance?"

"We are very interested in learning that. I can only conjecture that some third party has taken action." Then she looked directly at him. "We really are on the same side, Mach, in this respect."

"That is the truth," the interrogator said.

So it had come to nothing. Tania was relatively innocent, and he knew no more of Nepe's disappearance than he had before. "I must go to her mother," he said.

"Remember!" she called as he turned away. "You owe me, Mach!"

"That is true," the interrogator said as Mach left.

He went to Agape's apartment and put his hand against the door panel. It recognized him and admitted him immediately.

She was there. When he was inside, she touched a button, and an opacity closed about them. It was the privacy shield, normally invoked for lovemaking; but she knew he was not Bane, and there was none of that between them.

She was out of focus, and he knew she had been, in her fashion, crying. Her alien flesh did not lend itself readily to this; instead it melted, making her features formless. Evidently she was holding her shape only with an effort, because of this crisis.

"I questioned Tania with an interrogator," he said without preamble. "She is innocent of this. She wishes to seduce me and subvert me, in an effort to punish Fleta for humiliating Tan, but she has no complicity in Nepe's disappearance. It seems that some third party whose identity we do not know is responsible. That means that Nepe is probably unhurt, but captive. The Citizens will do everything they can to recover her, because they believe that she has or will have powers we do not suspect. I came to reassure you of that."

"Nepe is safe," Agape said.

He paused, assessing this. "You have information of a tangible nature?" He did not want her to delude herself.

"Your father sent a message. It arrived just before you. He—he engineered this. Or *they* did. Stile and Blue. Nepe got the message, and knew it was time, and she escaped."

"*Nepe* did it? But she's a little child, and the Citizens were watching, and the plane was programmed! And—" He stared at her. "Stile? How could he—I brought no message from him!"

"Nepe and Flach—they made contact," she said. "They were waiting for the signal. Stile sent word to Flach, and he gave it as you exchanged, and Nepe knew then. She is hiding."

Mach's circuits were overloaded with this seeming nonsense. "No one else has contact between the frames! Only Bane and me!"

"And the children. We never suspected. They have gone into hiding."

"From *us?*" he asked, appalled.

"From the enemy we serve. They will work with the other side. The Citizens and Adepts suspected; that is why they watched. But the children eluded them, and now no one knows where they are, except perhaps Stile and Blue, and they will not tell."

"So they were not retarded," he said, remembering his conversation with Stile, and Stile's certainty. Now, also, he remembered odd things Nepe had said, indicating her knowledge of what she was about to do. He had been caught as flat-footed as the Contrary Citizens!

"They were far, far ahead of us," she agreed. "They planned for most of their lives. Now they are gone. I can not say I am unhappy."

Then, despite her words, she dissolved.

Mach knew how she felt, because he realized that he had lost Flach in the same manner. He and Bane were on the wrong side, but their children were not. What was to come of this? Would the children be able to remain hidden? Would they even survive? They had kept their secret, and kept it astonishingly well, but they were only four years old.

He exited the apartment, leaving Agape as a forming puddle of protoplasm. He almost envied her this most tangible expression of loss.

3: *Flach*

Flach was waiting as Neysa trotted up. He was at the castle of the Red Adept, where his father Mach had brought him for the exchange. Mach got to study the Book of Magic which the Red Adept controlled, during the time that Flach visited his Grandpa Stile. That was the deal they had made, and it had existed as long as he could remember. This was because Stile and the Adverse Adepts were enemies, and the Red Adept was with Stile, and he had the Book of Magic, so they had to trade off if they wanted to use it. Until recently it had seemed to Flach that he had the best of the deal, because he hardly cared about any dusty old book, while Grandpa Stile was wonderful to be with.

But he had come to understand that it was the other way around. The Book had spells that were even better in the other frame than here, and the Adepts over there—the Contrary Citizens—were getting very strong. Before long they would be stronger than Grandpa Stile and his friends, or rather, Nepe's Grandpa Blue, really the same thing. So now he felt guilty about the fun he had visiting, knowing that it was costing his grandfather a lot. Maybe it was time to stop the visits.

These thoughts were fleeting, however, for Granddam Neysa moved rapidly. She was old, but still strong, and her black hide was glossy. He liked her about as well as he liked Grandpa Stile. She never talked much, but she was great for traveling in the wilderness, and he always felt safe with her.

Mach lifted him up to sit astride the unicorn. He needed no saddle; it was not that he was an apt rider, but that she would never let him fall. "See you later, crocogator," Mach quipped, smiling. He always had something fun-stupid like that to say, from his memories of the other frame.

"In a while, allidile," Flach responded dutifully.

Then Neysa was off, Flach clinging to her flaring mane. She moved slowly at first, making sure that he was secure, but gradually picked up speed.

They bore west, heading for the Blue Demesnes, where Flach was to have a week's visit with his grandparents on the human side. But as they passed through a section of forest, Neysa sounded her horn.

Flach had been trained in horn talk. He understood immediately. She had just told him that now was the time to act.

He did not acknowledge directly. He knew that they were being watched; they were always watched. He merely squeezed his knees to her sides, acknowledging. Then, as they emerged to an open region, he spoke. "Granddam Neysa, I have to pee. Can we stop?"

The unicorn slowed and halted. Flach slid off her back. She assumed human form. "Why didn't you see to that before we started?" she asked, with timeless annoyance.

"Didn't have to go, then," he said, walking to a head-high patch of bushes.

She returned to equine form and made a snort of resignation. She took the opportunity to graze the lush grass here, keeping an eye out for any danger.

Flach wedged his way into the bush, reached for his trousers, looked back, and sang a spot spell:

> *Privacy*
> *While I pee*

The air clouded around him, so that his body was hidden. In the privacy of that cloud he did open his trousers and urinate. But he also used his free hand to work something out of the lining of his trousers, and set it in his jacket pocket where he could readily put his hand on it. It was a figure like a doll that looked just like him, complete to the outfit he normally wore for traveling: blue jacket, blue trousers, and blue socks and shoes.

His tasks completed, he stepped out of the bushes, and the fog surrounding him dissipated. He returned to Neysa. She walked to a nearby log, so that he could climb up on it and mount her from that height. Then they resumed their journey. There was nothing to indicate that a significant action had been started.

Grandpa Stile had coached him carefully on this. Anything he wished known he could do openly, and anything he wished to keep secret he had to cover in some way. So he had brought out the amulet doll under cover of the privacy spell, and he communed with Nepe only when Mach and Bane were communing across the frames, and he did secret magic only when some similar magic was being done in the region. That way, Stile had explained, the traces were covered. His best protection was secrecy, so that no one suspected what he could do. It had been a game, and fun; now it was serious.

He was about to go into hiding. Stile had told him how, and Neysa would help him, but he had to go where neither of them knew, and remain hidden until he was big and strong and talented enough to survive alone. He knew that would be a long time, so he concentrated on doing the best job of hiding he possibly could.

"Granddam," he said after a suitable interval had elapsed, so that there would seem to be no connection with her note of information or his pause for nature. "I'm bored with this same old route. Can we go by the wolves and 'corns?"

Neysa blew a note of caution.

"Oh, I don't mean to stay long, just to pass by and say hi." He smiled, because his rhyme caused a little atmospheric effect; it thought he was doing magic. "It won't take long, honest, and besides, you can see your friends too. I've never met the Pack you know so well."

Neysa made a derisive trill on her harmonica horn, knowing he was wheedling, but she turned south. The truth was he *could* wheedle much from her, for he was of her flesh. She had never forgiven his dam Fleta for mating with the golem Mach, but she loved Flach, and the affection she could not show her filly she showed him instead. However, that was merely the pretext; right now she would do his bidding no matter what it was, because she was helping him hide.

He could have assumed unicorn form and run with her, but unicorns matured no faster than human folk did, and he would never have been able to keep her pace. So he remained in human form and let her carry him and protect him, and it was good. Under Stile's guidance he had mastered two more forms, but concealed them; this would be the first time he used either out in the open. That made him nervous, but he quelled it as well as he could, because he knew that if he messed up, there would be more trouble than he could imagine, for him and Grandpa Stile and all the Adepts who sided with him.

Abruptly he felt the contact of Mach and Bane across the frames. They were orienting on each other, so as to overlap in space, so that they could exchange. They usually conversed for a time first, setting things straight between them.

Flach knew what to do. *Nepe!* he called in thought.

After a moment she responded. *I hear you, Flach. I was specting you, 'cause they're transfring.*

It be time to hide! he thought. *Be thou ready?*

Better be! she responded. Then: *Oh, Flach, I'm afraid!*

Me too! But Neysa told me, and needs must we do it.

We've got to do it, she agreed. Now he felt the fear in her, washing across the contact between the frames.

Needs must be we brave, he thought.

Do you have some bravry for me?

He had to smile, though he was taut with the reality of what they were about to do. *Here be some o' mine, Nepe!* And he sent her a wash of emotion, as positive as he could manage.

Oh, thank you, brother self! she thought back. It really seemed to have helped.

He could tell by the feel that their fathers were about to break off communication and make their exchange of identities. *Till we mind again, sister self!* he thought.

Till we mind again!

Then they broke, for it was not safe to push the limits, and they had covered the essence. Nepe's presence faded from his mind, and he felt a swell of loneliness, as he always did. She was his other self, closer than any other person in either frame, and he felt whole when he was in touch with her, and empty when they separated. That was the way it always was.

But now he had to concentrate on his own situation. There were things he had to do, and do right. He could not afford to be concerned about his lost other self. Not right now.

As he rode, he risked one minor bit of magic: he made a spell to modify his smell. He had figured this aspect out for himself and was rather proud of it; this spell should go unnoticed because it was so inconsequential and seemingly pointless. But he had his reason. It would wear off within the hour, but that should be enough.

Neysa was traveling rapidly, as only a unicorn could, and soon enough reached the Were Demesnes. Two wolves charged out to intercept her, growling; then they recognized her and became an escort instead. Neysa was the friend of every member of this Pack, because of a spell Stile had wrought long ago. The younger wolves were not bound directly by it, because they had been whelped after it, but their sires and bitches had impressed the situation on them. Indeed, the entire lasting truce between Pack and Herd had dated from that Oath of Friendship Stile had made. They had doubted his status as Adept before then; none had doubted it since. Flach wished he could have seen those great old events happening, for he was sure there would never be any to match them in his lifetime. For one thing, the raw power of magic was only half what it once had been, though that made no difference in Phaze because all Adepts had been depleted equally, and other creatures never had used magic of full potency. Probably if Grandpa Stile made a similar oath today, it would affect only half the Pack and Herd, or maybe only half as strongly, but who would know the difference?

The escort wolves guided them to the current haunt of the Pack, and old Kurrelgyre came out to greet Neysa. The wolf was white around the muzzle, but still strong; his time to be torn apart by the Pack was not yet. Not quite yet. His time would have passed before now, but Stile had seen to his continuing strength.

Neysa played a greeting on her horn, indicating that this was only a passing visit. Several of the older bitches came up to sniff noses with her, remembering old times. Flach waved to several of the cubs; they were after all about his age. But they did not know him, and did not respond.

Then Neysa resumed her travel, and Flach was satisfied. He now knew the location and layout of the Pack's Demesnes.

Neysa made a note of alertness. Flach looked up. In a moment he spied what her sharper senses had noted: a formation of three bats crossing their path. He knew that these were young ones, traveling from one Flock to another. This was the season of exchanging, when young bats, unicorns, wolves, ogres, harpies and others joined new tribes, so that they could grow up and mate without inbreeding. Even some human villages did it; it was a convenient way to keep things mixed without disruption.

Stile, he realized, had chosen this time for action because of this, it would be almost impossible to trace all the exchanges that occurred at this time. At other times, a new addition to any group was a matter of community interest; often it was because of some stress resulting in a banishment elsewhere.

Soon Neysa played another note. This time it was a single dragon circling ahead. What was it after? "Maybe we should check," he said.

She sounded a note of negation, because it was dangerous even for a unicorn to cross a dragon. She intended to carry him safely, not into adventure!

"But if it be young ones traveling—" he persisted.

Without comment she veered to go toward the dragon, and broke into a gallop. She realized now that he had reason for this involvement, and had to cooperate.

"Maybe if we look first—" he said.

She liked that better. She halted, and he dismounted, putting his hand on the doll-amulet in his pocket. She changed to firefly form, while he, timing it precisely, changed to batform. The doll he held became a life-sized replica of himself. Instead of him holding the little figure in his hand, now the big figure was holding the bat in its hand. Only a close observer would have noticed any change.

Neysa the firefly flew ahead. The golem walked to the shelter of a leaning many-spoked spruce tree, so as to keep out of sight while unprotected. It put the bat into its pocket without looking at it.

At the tree, shrouded by the radiating branches, the golem halted. Flach climbed out of the pocket and transferred to a spoke-branch just above it. He crawled along it, blending in with its rough bark. He circled the trunk and crawled out along a large branch on the far side. This encountered a bush, and he dropped into the bush. He worked his way through the leaves to the high grass below, and scurried through the grass until he found the base of another large tree, an oak. He climbed that trunk, up to where it bifurcated.

Finally he took wing from the height of a far branch. For a moment he was unsteady, for he had not flown often, and the sonic method of navigation was not natural to him. But he used his eyes as well, and gained proficiency.

Now he flew in the direction Neysa had gone, staying low so as to be sheltered from view by the trees. He never looked at the golem again; it would function as it had been made to do when activated, just like a boy. It even had his texture, weight and smell; Neysa might never notice the difference, until at some point it would fail to react in a living manner. There was only so much a golem could do; such things were not very bright. But whenever Neysa did notice, she would not let on; she knew this would happen somewhere along this journey. She would deliver the golem safely to Grandpa Stile, who would greet it exactly as if it were Flach himself, preserving the secret. So would Grandma Lady Blue. With luck, no one else would know of the exchange, until it was far too late to do anything about it.

Now he saw the dragon. It was coming down! He swooped forward, eager to discover what manner of prey it sought.

This turned out to be a group of four werewolf pups and a grown wolf guiding and protecting them. But they had foolishly strayed into an open section while the dragon was near, and now it was diving, talons outstretched, using its fire to ignite the dry grass ahead of the wolves so that they could not flee. The mature one knew enough to dodge back as the dragon pounced, causing it to miss, but the inexperienced pups were panicking.

The dragon veered to catch one. It yiped—and at that moment Neysa appeared, changing from her unnoticeable firefly form. She was in full motion, her horn oriented on the dragon's posterior. Now it was the dragon who seemed foolish; it had not been alert for a surprise like this! It dropped the pup and slewed to the side, barely avoiding the horn.

In a moment it regained its equilibrium and oriented on Neysa. But she retreated to the shelter of another great bull spruce, while the rescued pup scrambled for cover. The dragon could attack her, but could not come close enough to be effective; if it risked the vicinity of the spruce, Neysa could charge within the tree's cover and perhaps score with her horn. Meanwhile, the prey was gone.

Raging, the dragon retreated. It could not afford to expend its fire uselessly; better to seek other prey. It ascended and flew away, pausing only to vent a giant dropping. The dropping splatted against the tree, causing the bark to scorch and steam, but Neysa had already moved behind it and was not sullied.

The wolf came forward to sniff noses with Neysa. Now Flach realized that these cubs were from Kurrelgyre's Pack! Naturally Neysa helped them, and the wolf recognized her and thanked her; they were oathfriends. Thanks to her, all of the cubs would reach the other Pack.

Flach flew away, avoiding contact with any of them. He had changed form without being noticed; it was important that he preserve that privacy. Neysa would return to the golem and it would mount her and the two would proceed to her brother Clip's Herd, and thence north to the Blue Demesnes. When others realized that Flach himself had not arrived there, they would check both the Pack and the Herd Neysa had passed, and find nothing, for he had exchanged identities at neither. So far, his escape was perfect.

He flew roughly northeast, toward the vampire Flock nearest the Red Demesnes. He knew the bats there, and he liked pretty Suchevane, who had babysitted him on occasion while Mach or Bane was busy. The Red Adept was Suchevane's husband, and their son Al was Flach's friend. It was from Al he had learned how to fly as a bat; Al had covered for him during the difficult early practicing. Al was unique: a vampire troll, who could make magic amulets. If Flach were discovered, the Red Adept would be able to help him.

But not long before this break had come, he had had sober second thoughts. Originally it had seemed that the Adepts would check only the Pack and Herd along his route, and never suspect that he had assumed a new form and gone elsewhere. But then he had realized that they could be smarter than that, and if they managed to pick up his change to batform, they could readily track him to the Flock. That meant that the Flock could not be risked. So now he was only seeming to go there; when he could deviate from this route without being observed, he would do so.

He had an alternate destination in mind. The place they might never suspect, because they would check it first and eliminate it, and never think to check it again. Kurrelgyre's Pack. He had not exchanged forms there, but he would come there in another guise, with a different smell. That was why he had masked his smell as they passed. He hoped this was as clever a move as it had seemed when he first thought it out; now he was profoundly uncertain. He was after all only four years old; he knew he was extraordinarily bright for his age, but there was a lot he had yet to learn. Yet this was his committed course; he feared he would get in trouble if he changed his mind now.

In this batform he could hear very well, but mainly in the range he needed for echo location. He could see, but not as well as he could in boy form. He could smell satisfactorily, and now he used this sense to do what he needed to do. If he had figured this correctly, there should be—yes, there was one: the smell of a wolf trail.

He landed in a tree near the trail. This was not the one the three outgoing cubs had used. This one came from farther north, and the smell of it was stale. It should do.

He settled down to wait. He was tired from his brief flight, for his bat wing muscles were not well developed. He might have a long wait.

He did. He slept, then foraged nearby for berries. Vampire bats in Phaze did not eat a lot of blood; that was for special occasions. Fruits and insects did nicely for the most part, and in the human form they ate what human folk did. Indeed, they were completely human in that guise, which was one reason he had thought to hide among them. However, they were not the only half-human species.

He hung upside down from a shrouded branch and slept again. Night came, and he wanted to forage, for bats were more comfortable in the dark, but he didn't dare; he had to be by this path when the wolves came.

Where was Granddam Neysa now? Surely most of the way to her brother's herd. She would probably turn the golem over to another unicorn while she grazed—no, she surely would know by now that it *was* a golem, so would not pause there, lest others discover that. She would dally only briefly, then move on, not really resting or eating until she reached the Blue Demesnes. Flach felt homesick, missing her company, and that of Stile and the Lady Blue. He missed his dam Fleta too, and was painfully sorry he had had to deceive her; he knew she would be distraught by his disappearance, when she learned of it. She would be horrified that he had gone alone into the wilderness, and she would fear he was dead. If he changed to human form, he knew he would cry. But he did not, because the magic of such a change could be noted, and that could give him away. He had to wait until it was time, and then change only when it could be covered by another creature's magic.

All next day he waited, and all next night. The loneliness was almost overwhelming. He thought of Nepe, and wondered whether she had escaped. He thought she must have, because there had been no further communion between Mach and Bane. Of course, Mach might be trying to reach Bane, and Bane wouldn't know unless he came to their rendezvous, so maybe it didn't prove anything. The two had to overlap, physically, each standing in the same geographic spot of their frames; that was why they always exchanged at the same place, near the Red Demesnes. Flach and Nepe could contact each other from anywhere; he wasn't sure why they were different from their fathers, or why no one else could do it, but he thought it had to do with their mixed ancestry.

He kept reminding himself that his isolation was a good sign, because it meant that no one had discovered his disappearance, or if they had, they had no idea where to find him. The critical period, as Grandpa Stile had impressed on him, was the first week. That was when his absence would be discovered, and when the search would be most intense. After that the risk would diminish, though he could never afford to get careless.

Late in the afternoon of the second day, he jolted awake. They were coming! Down the trail from the northwest: wolves!

This was his next critical step. He could lose it all here. If anything went wrong—

The first wolf pup came into view. Flach let go of the branch, dropped, spread his wings, and looped back up. He hovered before the nose of the pup, who abruptly halted, surprised.

Two other pups came up, and then the bitch who was guiding and guarding them. They stared at the erratically behaving bat. The bitch snapped at it, but Flach hovered just out of reach. He looped about, remaining ahead of them, preventing them from proceeding. Every time the bitch tried to drive him off, he came back again.

Finally she had had enough. She changed to human form, garbed in furs, ready to take a stick to him if she had to.

That was what he wanted. Simultaneously he changed to pup form.

Instantly she was back in bitch form, growling. Flach whimpered, his little tail between his legs. She advanced on him, teeth bared. He rolled over on the trail, exposing his belly. She hesitated, then sniffed him. He lay there, not having to feign terror.

Finally she resumed woman form. She was of advancing age, garbed in furs, and she carried a knife. This she pointed at Flach. "Assume this form, strange creature!" she snapped. "I be Duzyfilan, and I would talk with thee."

Now Flach reverted to his natural form, lying on his back on the ground. "Please, good bitch, hurt me not," he pleaded. "I come to beg thy protection."

"Who and what be thou?" she asked sharply.

"I must be nameless, lest I be doomed," he said, sitting up.

She studied him, noting his blue outfit. Any werewolf understood the significance of that. "Methinks thou dost be doomed anyway," she said. "Knowest thou not that we tolerate the likes o' thee only for the sake o' the truce?"

"I have changed sides," he said. "I must hide, lest those thou knowest catch me."

Duzyfilan considered. "Willst make oath on that?"

"Aye." And from him came a faint splash, that rippled the blades of grass and colored the air momentarily.

"Then must we help thee," she decided. "No other must know thine origin. A secret spread about be no secret long."

"I seek only to join thy company," he said. "And to join the Pack, and be as weres be."

"Thou hast no pup name?"

"Nay."

"A pup be named first by the bitch who bears him," she said. "Canst thou accept me in lieu, since I be first to receive thee in this guise?"

"Aye," he said gratefully.

"Then I name thee Ba, after what I saw o' thee that thou must ne'er again be, an thou be called one o' our kind."

"Ba," he repeated. She had seen him as a bat, so she took from that, as was the werewolf way.

"And these three pups must ne'er tell o' what they saw o' this,"

Duzyfilan continued briskly. "Must each exchange oath-friendship with thee, to keep the secret."

"Aye, an thou sayest so," Flach agreed.

"Turn wolf," she said.

Flach resumed wolf-pup form.

Duzyfilan beckoned to the male pup. The wolfling padded dutifully forward to sniff noses.

"Do these two o' ye, Ba and Fo, make Oath o' Friendship, each ne'er to betray the welfare o' the other, in the wolven way?"

Both growled aye, and the splash manifested. Among adults the magic splash of absolute truth was seldom seen, but among the young, who were less jaded by experience, it was common enough.

The bitch beckoned a female pup. "Do these two o' ye, Ba and Si, make Oath o' Friendship, each ne'er to betray the welfare o' the other, in the wolven way?"

Again both growled affirmation, and again there was the splash and ripple.

She summoned the second female. "Do these two o' ye, Ba and Te, make Oath o' Friendship, each ne'er to betray the welfare o' the other, in the wolven way?"

A third time they growled agreement, and the splash manifested.

"Now may ye exchange what confidences ye choose, and ne'er fear betrayal, an ye be mindful who else might overhear," Duzyfilan said. "But concern me not with it, for it be not my business. We camp ahead; we shall travel not this night." She resumed bitch form.

So it was that Flach joined the formation of pups, falling in line between the two females. They padded on along the trail, first Fo, then Si, then Flach as Ba, then Te, with the bitch following watchfully. This was because trouble was far more likely to come from behind than ahead, and she could meet it there. But if trouble did appear ahead, the pups could pause, and she would quickly advance on it, as she had when Flach appeared.

They came to a place the bitch deemed suitable for camping. She sniffed it thoroughly, then had them crawl under a thick thorny bush and nestle together out of sight of the trail. "Needs must I hunt," she announced. "An danger come, hide; an it sniff ye out, bay for me. An I came not in time, scatter." Then she was gone.

They were packed in nose-to-tail, but in a moment Fo and Te made room on either side, and Si assumed human form beside Flach. "Change, oath-friend," she told him in a low tone. "We would learn o' thee."

Flach changed, finding himself jammed against her, because their human forms were larger than their pup forms. She was a girl of about his size, which meant also his age, because the werewolves matured at the rate of their slow component, the human one. It was now too dark for him to see her, but he felt her human mane, soft and fluffy as her fur, and the snug clothing she wore in human form.

"What wouldst thou learn o' me?" he asked, speaking no louder than she. He realized that she had been chosen, or had chosen herself, to interrogate him; the other two were listening with their superior ears.

"We saw thee shift from bat to wolf. Ne'er have we known o' a were also a bat. Be thou a crossbreed?"

"We be oath-friends now," he reminded them. "An I tell ye three, you must tell not other."

"Aye," Si agreed, and the two others growled assent. "I be descended o' the bitch Serrilryan, who gave her life that the Adept Clef might come to Phaze. An I tell thee aye, I honor aye."

He had heard of the Adept Clef, the one who played the famed Platinum Flute. Si had impressive ancestry, and surely could be trusted. "I be grandchild o' Adept Stile, and o' Neysa Unicorn. I be thus 'corn with more forms, and little Adept."

There was a concerted reaction. "No true wolf?" the little bitch asked.

"I be wolf now," he said. "But also other."

"Thou willst fight for us, an we do for thee?"

"Aye."

"And do magic for we three alone?"

"Nay. An I do magic other than were form changing, they will know, and seek me out. I may not be other than werewolf, till it be safe."

Si made a little sigh of disappointment. "This be less fun than we hoped."

Flach felt the need to repay them for the fun they had anticipated, because their Oaths of Friendship bound them to far greater risk than they would otherwise have known. "I can tell you o' the other frame," he offered.

"Thou dost know o' it?" Si asked, excited. "How so?"

"I commune with my self-sister Nepe in Proton," he explained. "She tells me o' her frame, and I tell her o' mine. But we can commune only when our sires commune, so the trace o' our magic be covered by theirs."

"Then how canst thou know when?" Si asked, intrigued.

"We feel it. Our sires must align in place to commune, but we need that not. We talk when they do, and only then. Last time, did I tell her to hide."

"She has to hide too?" Si asked, awed.

"Aye. 'Cause an they catch one of us, they will make that one tell where the other be, and catch both. So we both must hide, and ne'er get caught." He found that it eased his void somewhat to tell of this.

"But why didst thou not stay with thy Pack?"

" 'Cause the Adverse Adepts be wrong. Grandpa Stile and Granddam Neysa told me that, and showed me how it be so, and I believe it. So needs must I change sides—but we knew the Adepts would let me not. It be the same for Nepe in Proton. So we had to plan, and practice, and hide before the Adepts and Citizens started using us. An they knew that Nepe and I can think to each other, and do it better than our sires can, they would ne'er let us go."

"So you join the Pack with us?" Si asked.

"Aye. Only it must be known not, 'cause the Pack can stand not against the Adepts. There would be awful trouble, Grandpa says, an they found any Pack or Herd or Flock sheltering me."

Si pondered. "I wish we had known this before we swore oathfriendship with thee."

"Why?" he asked. "Would ye three have made not the oath?"

She concentrated for a time before answering. "Mark thee, we be but young pups, and ill grasp adult concepts. But we feel the truth o' them, howe'er poorly we say them. So I say to thee we made the oath thinking thou wast only an odd were-creature. We would have made it knowing we be truly helping the cause o' all the good creatures o' Phaze. Does that make sense to thee?"

"You would have made it anyway?" he asked, surprised.

"Aye," Si said, and the others growled assent. "All wolves be ready to fight and die for their Pack and their friends and their way of life, but it means more an they know when they be doing it."

Flach was abruptly overwhelmed. "Do wolves cry?" he asked.

"Aye, when they be in human form."

"Good. 'Cause I be going to cry."

"Why?" she asked, dismayed. "Did I say it wrong?"

"Nay, thou didst say it perfectly."

"Have we treated thee not kindly?"

"It be 'cause ye three have treated me more kindly than I feared," he said, the tears starting. "I bring great danger to you, yet you support me."

"It be the way o' the Pack," she said. "We three be traveling to join a new Pack, and we know the way o' it, but we know also how hard it be to do. We welcome thee as we would have our new Pack welcome us."

"I will try to make you glad o' that," Flach said, as the tears flowed more copiously.

Si did not speak again. She put her hands to his face, and turned it toward her, and kissed him passionately. He realized that her face was wet too, with her own tears. She was kissing him for the three of them, for they had accepted him as they knew him to be. He was profoundly grateful, and somewhat in love, as of that moment.

After a suitable interval, they returned to wolf form and slept, the four of them comfortably nestled together against the chill of the night. Their noses pointed outward in four directions, so that any warning carried by the wind would receive prompt attention.

In period before the dawn, Duzyfilan returned with her kill: a giant rabbit. They woke at her summoning growl, and scrambled out to join her. The light of two moons shone down, showing the delicious carcass. In a moment each was hauling and chewing at a leg, while the bitch maintained guard.

Flach had never had a meal of this type before, and was at first alarmed. But he emulated his companions, and discovered that cooling raw flesh was delicious as well as being a challenge. As long as he was in wolf form! By the time dawn came, he was stuffed on rabbit, and felt wonderful.

They slept again, for it was not good to run on a full belly. It was almost noon before they resumed travel. But the bitch knew what she was doing, for she had, it turned out, spied an Adept in the vicinity, and elected to lay low until the Adept was gone.

At dusk they reached Kurrelgyre's Pack. Duzyfilan sniffed noses with the leader, and brought up the four pups, saying nothing. Kurrelgyre sniffed each in turn, growled his approval, and summoned his own chief bitch. She took the four to her den. They were cowed and quiet, but knew the worst was over: they had been accepted. They never saw Duzyfilan go; she had been no more than a courier, and for reasons of her own she did not stay to socialize.

They were given two days to acclimatize to the new Pack. Then Kurrelgyre brought them up before the assembled wolves and gave them each their second syllable, in the manner of the wolven kind. This was their formal mark of acceptance; henceforth they would be members of the Pack in all the ways of pups of their generation, except that they would be free to make permanent liaisons with other Pack members when they matured. They and the other pups from other Packs represented this year's New Blood: a place of custom rather than honor. Honor they would have to achieve for themselves, in due course.

So it was that they became Forel, Sirel, Terel and Barel: because they had been lucky enough to be adopted by the leader's den. They would strive henceforth to do that den honor. It was even possible that one of them might have the supreme honor, when grown, of killing Kurrelgyre. With peace, but threatened war, the Packs were increasing in size, anticipating future losses, so that it was no longer required that a young wolf kill his sire in order to assume adult status. But when a sire became infirm, it remained the duty of one of his offspring to dispatch him cleanly. However, that was a long time distant, and it was quite possible that Kurrelgyre would die in battle before then.

No one recognized Barel as the boy whom Neysa had carried by a few days before, because when he went to boy form he assumed an altered appearance with wolven clothing, and his smell was not the one they had encountered. Minions of the Adverse Adepts did pass, searching for someone, but it was evident that only werewolves were here. Kurrelgyre of course had not been told Flach's identity, and if he suspected, he did not care to give it away. Certainly not to the Adverse Adepts!

It seemed that Flach had made a successful escape. But only time would tell. Meanwhile, he worked hard to become the best were pup he could be, and he did no other magic or shape changes than those of the wolven kind. The focus of the war between the good and bad Adepts had to move elsewhere.

Only his den mates, his oath-friends, knew of the pain he felt because of his isolation from his true parents. They felt it too, but not in the same way, for they had not also separated from their native culture. They remained with him, and stood by him, so that it was remarked with approval among the Pack how unusually close these four were.

4: *Blue*

Agnes answered the call. In a moment she came to inform Citizen
Blue. She was getting old and gray, as she had been no young thing
when he had hired her from offplanet four years before, but she had
quickly become his most reliable and trusted servant. Indeed, she was
more like a friend, despite being an alien creature. She normally remained well in the background, so that few visitors noticed her at all.
"It is for you, sir."

"Who is it, Nessie?" he inquired, though he had an excellent notion.

"Citizen Tan, sir."

He nodded. He gestured to the screen in this room, giving it leave
to light, as Agnes disappeared.

Sure enough, it was Citizen Tan. "Your grandchild has disappeared," Tan said abruptly. "You know something of this."

"Now how could I know about that?" Blue inquired. "Isn't she in
your camp's charge?"

"You put her up to it!"

"Did I? That must have been very naughty of me."

"If you shelter her as a runaway, you will be in violation of the
truce."

"I wouldn't think of it, Tan."

"We shall recover her! And when we do—"

Blue frowned. "Are you suggesting that you would mistreat a child?
I would not care to see that, for I fear it would prejudice your relationship with the child's parents, who might become uncooperative."
This was of course a cutting understatement; Bane—and Mach, too—
would not tolerate any threat against Nepe; she was untouchable.

"You're so damned smug!" Tan exclaimed. "But she can't remain hidden long. We'll scour the planet for her, and if we discover any complicity at all on your part—"

"Now why should I want to prevent my granddaughter from making her scheduled visit to me? You know how I delight in her company. Indeed, this smacks of some device on your part, to keep her from me. Should I lodge a complaint?"

Citizen Tan faded out, scowling.

Agnes reappeared. "She will be all right, sir?"

"I am sure of it, Nessie. You trained her, after all. Who else could have done it better?"

"But she is only four of your years old!"

"And perhaps the brightest child on the planet."

She nodded, fading back again.

Now Blue placed a call of his own, to Citizen Purple. The fat Adept scowled, but had to listen.

"We have operated under a truce," Blue said. "We agreed not to harass each other directly, your side and mine, and your side has access to the Oracle during the time I am visited by my granddaughter. However, I have not received my scheduled visit this time. This represents a violation on your part."

"We're looking for her!" Purple snapped.

"I am sure you are. When you find her, and deliver her to me, I shall see that my part of the agreement is honored. Until then, you will be denied access to the Oracle."

Purple's mouth opened, but Blue cut the connection before the foul language got through. He had just dropped the other shoe.

Sheen entered. "You are not being nice, dear," she remarked. She was naked in the serf style, slender and graceful, despite being nominally his age. But her hair betrayed her years, with some gray strands among the brown, and her breasts rode lower than they once had. Yet even these were not true indicators, for they were crafted. She was a robot, ageless unless restyled.

"What would a machine know about niceness?" he retorted, smiling.

"Certainly not a great deal from association."

He grabbed her and kissed her. "How long have we been married? Two and a half years?"

"You may have slipped a decimal, sir."

"I get that from association."

"I doubt it."

He held her a moment more. "Thou dost still so much resemble the metal maid I met and loved, when I returned to life.'' He reverted to his native pattern of speech only in times of emotion, or for effect.

"I *am* the same!" she protested. "Crafted to please your other self, shaped to his taste."

"And to mine," he agreed. "I loved one before thee, but she came to love me less, and so I left her—and found thee. Thy love never flagged."

"Because you never changed my program. If you want me to have another personality—"

"Tease me not! In my life must needs there be one thing constant, and that be thee and thy program." He squeezed her close, and kissed her again.

"Careful, Blue," she murmured in his ear. "You are getting aroused before schedule."

"Trust thee to remember that!" he exclaimed, for it was true.

He released her and faced the exit panel. "Mustn't keep my audience waiting," he said, reverting to the Proton mode of speech.

"Play thy role well, my love," she said.

He smiled. She normally used Phaze language only to tease him, but this time he knew it was more than that. "Fear thou not, O Lady Sheen. I shall play them a game that shall keep them rapt." Then he stepped out.

For this was the point of this exercise. He had trained his grandchild Nepe carefully, as Stile had trained Flach in Phaze. He knew about this because the two children were able to communicate with each other: a secret only Stile and Blue and their ladies (Agnes included) had known until this point. Now Stile had given the signal for the children to hide, and Blue had to trust his other self's judgment. He did not know where Nepe had gone, but he did know she would need about twenty-four hours to secure her situation. It was now his job to provide her that period. The future of this ploy, and likely the planet, depended on his success in creating an effective diversion.

Now we shall play a game, he thought as he emerged into the hall. *A game of high stakes!* He knew that every word he spoke and every action he took would be noted, outside the protection of his Citizen's sanctuary. The Contrary Citizens believed he had some complicity in Nepe's disappearance, as indeed he had. He had made his provocative calls to ensure that belief. Now he was going out, and they should believe that he was going to contact his granddaughter. If they were assured of that, they would put all their resources into watching him, instead of into the more routine but effective effort of a cordon and pattern search for her. It was a ploy so obvious that only a fool should fall for it—and he hoped to make a fool of the enemy Citizens.

He walked around the halls as if merely exercising—or making sure he was unobserved. Of course there should be no way to shake the hidden observation of the enemy; he depended on that. If they lost him, they might by default get moving on the pattern search, expensive and disruptive as that would be. He was offering them a seemingly much easier route.

After he was satisfied that he was alone, he approached a Citizen portal and summoned his transport. This was a box somewhat like an ancient elevator, that traveled through channels unavailable to serfs. The sides consisted of holographs of Phaze, so that it looked as if he were in a glass cage swinging along over the Phaze surface. He loved Phaze, of course, and wished he could revisit it; but he loved this technological frame more. To him, the ways of magic were familiar and frankly somewhat dull, while the ways of science were, even after a quarter century, novel and exciting. With magic, each spell could be invoked only once; with science there was no limit. And Sheen was a creature of science. He had been fascinated by her from the outset, knowing her nature; she represented in one package all the wonders of this frame. To the locals, the notion of a living man loving a robot was ludicrous—but Blue was not a local, he was an immigrant from a foreign frame. Sheen was beautiful, she was conscious, she was feeling, she was loving. Science had fashioned the whole of her, and that was much of her allure. She had loved Stile, and lost him to the Lady Blue; but she had been ready to accept Stile's alternate self instead, and that had been the key. A living woman would not have done it, but the robot lacked the particular consciousness of self that counted here. Blue had Stile's body and Stile's nature; he was Stile's other self. Sheen was programmed to love the first two, and though she knew of the third, her programming did not find it significant. She had, in effect, Stile under another name.

The carriage halted, and Blue stepped out into a crowded hallway. Naked serfs were walking in both directions; they took no overt note of the voluminously cloaked Citizen suddenly in their midst, but all were careful to leave a clear aisle for him. That was the way of it; any serf ignored any Citizen, unless the Citizen spoke to him. Then that serf obeyed the Citizen implicitly.

He was at the entrance to the android laboratory. Each Dome City had its own robot, android and cyborg labs, where units were custom designed for particular purposes or individual Citizens. Sheen had originated in the robot lab, a standard female format with a then-new and sophisticated program for the emulation of emotion. But because she was of the self-willed machine variety, that simulation was virtually indistinguishable from the reality experienced by living creatures. Stile had discussed this with her, and become satisfied that her programmed feeling was as valid as his unprogrammed feeling, for his feelings were the result of his nature and experience. Perhaps that had started him on the route to the acceptance of the self-willed machines as legitimate social entities: people.

Blue had carried that concept further, setting up the experimental community that gave equal status to humans and four other categories in their human forms: androids, self-willed robots, cyborgs and aliens. This was in part his payoff to the self-willed machines who had helped him survive the malice of Citizens, when he had been a serf. But it was also simple cultural justice. The other entities had similar abilities and sensitivities, and desired similar justice. Blue's experimental community had demonstrated the feasibility of the integration of these five categories as equals. He had placed his own robot son Mach into this community, with greater success than anticipated. Who could have suspected that Mach would exchange minds with his other self in Phaze, and set off a chain of events that threatened to overturn all that Blue had accomplished here!

Still, this had also resulted in the appearance of Stile's son Bane in Proton, and his association with the alien female Agape, and their intricately crafted child Nepe. Now Nepe was helping Blue to hold his position as nominal leader of the Citizens. As long as he controlled more wealth than his opponents did, his policies governed; when the balance of wealth shifted, theirs would govern. They would not be able to undo a quarter century of reforms in a day, but certainly the effect would be deleterious to individual rights. The Contrary Citizens preferred things as they had been before Stile started the great change: unbridled wealth and power to the ruling class, and human serfs dedicated to serving the will of the Citizens. It was in its way a classic liberal-conservative struggle.

He entered the laboratory. "At ease," a serf murmured, advising all employees that a Citizen was present.

Blue walked through the linked chambers of the lab, inspecting the android production line. At the beginning was the tank of "soup"— the living pseudoflesh from which the creatures were formed. A human being was conceived and birthed and grown to adult status, and eventually died. An android being was fashioned complete at one time, and educated rapidly; thereafter it lived and functioned and died in the human manner. Unfortunately, androids tended to be stupid; there seemed to be no proper substitute for nature's way, when it came to intelligence. Blue's experimental community had turned out the smartest androids yet, by making them small and letting them grow and learn in the human manner. But this was an inefficient way to do it; for most purposes, an instant stupid android, trained to a special task, was far more cost effective than a smart one who was years in development. Most, of course, were not even humanoid; they were shaped for myriad tasks that were beneath the notice of humans, including cleanup of the grounds beyond the dome. The intense pollution tended to corrode robots, and was unbreathable for humans, but androids could be crafted who breathed it, needing no special suits.

However, Blue's purpose in visiting this lab had nothing to do with the manufacture of androids. He had come here because this was the most likely hiding place for little Nepe. She, as a creature of alien flesh with robot specifications, could assume any living form, so could readily emulate an android of the appropriate size. Obviously she would hide among the new androids of the lab, because it was in the familiar city and the new ones were not yet trained in specific tasks. She could accept the training and go out on assignment, and no one would catch on.

Blue smiled faintly. Certainly that was the reasoning he wanted the Citizens to follow. The moment he left the lab, they should be closing on it, checking every current android, verifying its origin and nature. The ordinary machines could not distinguish between android and alien flesh, but lab personnel could. They would soon verify the legitimacy of every android, here and in all the other labs of Proton. And in a few hours they would know that Nepe was not among them.

In this manner he was generating his first diversion. He was giving them a promising false lead. He knew they were watching him, and he hoped that they believed that he had either made passing contact with Nepe, or tried to and failed. They might believe that she was here, but that he had realized he was being watched, so had shied away. Regardless, they would have to make a thorough check.

He walked slowly on out, having said nothing. He stepped back into his transport, and went next to the cyborg lab. The cyborgs were essentially robot bodies housing living brains; they were more intelligent than androids, but also more erratic. They tended to get notions of their own, and that could be inconvenient for an employer.

Nepe was small enough to be able to form herself into the brain portion of a large cyborg. She could then direct it, and have a hiding place for some time in the otherwise metal body. The Citizens would thus have to eliminate all the cyborgs, too, and that would represent several more hours of effort, and divide their resources. They could hardly afford to make their search openly; they did not want others catching on. Thus a search that might be completed in one hour would take several, because of the inefficiency of secrecy. Again, it would prove fruitless.

Stile returned to his transport. He was sorry there was no alien lab, to further divide the enemy force. But aliens were relatively few, and they were not generated in any lab. Nepe, being one alien herself, was unlikely to try to masquerade as another. In any event, the Citizens would already have run tracers on every alien on the planet. They would know the child was not among them.

That left only the straight robots and the straight humans. Of these, only the robots had a lab. He went there next, though it should be obvious that Nepe could not emulate a completely inanimate being. His tour was cursory; evidently he didn't expect to fool anyone this time. If they thought he was trying a double fake, and that Nepe was after all hiding here, they would have to expend valuable time anyway.

At last he went to the Game Annex. Nepe had prevailed on her uncle to play a formal game here; he had made special note of the particular console they had used. The Citizens might suppose she had somehow left a message for him here; they would have to examine the console, perhaps even replacing it with another so that they could take it apart in privacy. All part of the game!

Now he was going to give them something more challenging to ponder; so far he had merely warmed up. He touched a finger to the screen of the console.

Words flashed on the screen. WHAT IS YOUR WILL, CITIZEN BLUE? Naturally all the consoles were programmed to recognize all Citizens; in fact, a Citizen could hardly go anywhere unrecognized.

"I wish to play with my wife," he replied with the faintest of smiles. The machine would not pick up the double entendre.

In a moment Sheen's face appeared on the screen. "Yes, sir?" she inquired. In the privacy of their suite she treated him with familiar deference; in public, the familiarity was absent.

"I become bored," he said. "Let me play with you."

A smile very like his own crossed her face. "Shall I come to you, sir, or will you come to me?"

"Remain where you are, for now. Address your console."

"Yes, sir." Her face faded out. The primary grid appeared. He had the numbers, and chose 2. MENTAL. It would be tricky to play a physical game without her presence.

In a moment the secondary grid appeared: TOOL-ASSISTED MENTAL. 2B. "Two Bee or not Two Bee," he murmured, frowning at it. He had the numbers again, so had to choose between 5. SEPARATE 6. INTERACTING 7. PUZZLE and 8. COOPERATIVE. He touched 6.

Her choices were E. BOARD F. CARDS G. PAPER H. GENERAL: all tools for mental games. She had chosen G, for the new box was INTERACTIVE PAPER GAMES.

They filled in the third grid with games from the proffered list: tic-tac-toe, sprouts, lines-and-boxes, life, magic squares and word games. When they made their selections, the result was CROSSWORD. They would play an interactive crossword game. Victory would go to the one who forced the other into an impossible word.

Of course the watching Citizens would be sure that this was a pre-arranged game—and they would be correct. Blue and Sheen had played exactly as they had agreed to play, before he left the suite. They were playing "long-distance" to ensure that the Citizens could tap into the game.

The crossword grid was eighty-one squares: nine on a side. Blue had the first move, and represented the horizontal, so he wrote in the word ASTERISKS across the top.

Sheen started with the first S and filled in SNOW, vertically, setting a solid end-block below.

Blue pondered, then put in VOID, the O overlapping hers. He had to build on her word, because he was allowed no vertical words himself. Thus it was truly interactive.

She countered with VOICES, extending down from his V. The words seemed to come naturally, but they were also suggestive. What message would a cryptography expert see in them? How could a child of four interpret such a sequence? What would he be trying to tell her, that was so important for her to know? Surely there were some very nice headaches being sown here!

He took off from her O and made OWED.

She formed KING descending from his K in ASTERISKS.

He filled in FUN, to her new N.

She made FORMS descending from his F.

He made MORE crossing her R.

She called out a pre-existing word by marking in a + above it: I. E. The game was getting tight.

He filled in NO below the ER in ASTERISKS.

```
A   S   T   E   R   I   S   K   S
+   N   +   N   O   +       I
V   O   I   D   +   F   U   N   +
O   W   E   D   +   O       G
I   +   +   M   O   R   E   +
C               M
E               S
S               +
+
```

Sheen was abruptly left with an impossible word: the RO did not count against her, because he had formed it complete, giving her no chance to improve on it. But how could she make anything legitimate from the vertical letters ENDDM?

"End DM," she said, appearing on the screen, behind the grid, so that the letters crossed her face.

"What does DM stand for?"

"Dumb Machine."

Blue laughed. "Sorry, I don't know any dumb machines, certainly not you. You lose."

She sighed. "I think the game was fixed."

"You have a suspicious inanimate mind."

"What is the penalty?"

"You have to ask, woman? The usual, of course."

"Oh, no sir, not the usual!" she protested with mock affright. They had played this charade before, and always enjoyed it.

"The usual," he repeated grimly. "Get your torso over here."

"There? In public?" she asked, appalled.

"The very best place. What good is a victory if not publicly savored?"

"You are a monster, sir."

"To be sure. Do not keep me waiting, or it will go hard with you, serf."

"I hear and obey with alacrity, sir," she said, fading.

Blue touched the screen again.

WHAT IS YOUR WILL, CITIZEN BLUE?

"This game was but a prelude to another. Reserve a jelly vat for my use."

DONE, CITIZEN BLUE.

"Audience is permitted for this game."

VERIFY: AUDIENCE PERMITTED? That was as close as the Game Machine ever came to astonishment.

"Yes." Normally Citizens conducted their affairs with paranoid privacy unless they had reason to chastise a serf in public; Blue's wife was a serf, but he was not given to doing that to her. His permission for an audience was of course a requirement for one; serfs would be rounded up for the event. Actually this would be no punishment for the serfs; Blue knew himself to be by far the most popular Citizen of Proton, because of his steadfast efforts to mitigate the lot of serfs and his open marriage to a machine. Every group supported him, except the Contrary Citizens. That one exception, of course, more than counterbalanced the rest; had he not been set up with the dominant wealth of the planet by his other self, his tenure would have been brief. Wealth governed Proton, literally, and this was a power he had exercised ruthlessly against the other Citizens, maintaining his position. Only the sophisticated financial instruments devised by the Oracle from the input of the Book of Magic could wrest that power from him—and now he had a pretext to cut off that source of information from his enemy.

He walked slowly to the bath region of the Game Annex, giving Sheen time to get there. Yes, wealth was the key—and the Oracle and Book of Magic were the ultimate keys to wealth, and he and Stile controlled both. They had monitored the progress of the enemy, and acted when necessary: just before the balance of wealth shifted. Nepe had kept him informed, and he had trained her, with the invaluable expertise of Agnes. Now her absence froze things as they were. If she remained hidden, Blue and Stile would retain power; if she were found, they would lose it. It was that simple.

He reached the bath region. Sheen was there, having found swift transport. She took his arm, and they went to the reserved vat. They could have found their way simply by zeroing in on the clamor, for as they entered the chamber they spied the audience: about a hundred naked men, women, children, androids, humanoid robots and humanoid cyborgs. They had been clamoring with excitement, for the privilege of watching a living Citizen in an event like this was rare indeed. There was a sudden hush as they saw Blue and Sheen.

In the center of the chamber was the vat, its sides dropping sharply away from the floor. It was round, about four meters in diameter, and was filled with whipped pseudo-gelatin, lime-flavored. This differed from the real thing mainly in being harmless to living flesh even when it got in the eyes, and in being two point three times as slimy.

Sheen released his arm, stepping ahead of him to gaze into the quivering green mess. "Permission to speak frankly, sir," she said with evident distaste.

"Denied," he said, setting his cupped hand on her buttock and boosting her forward. She screamed and flailed wildly as she fell into the vat. The male members of the audience applauded. A Citizen, of course, could do no wrong. Some of the females looked as if they might have another opinion, but were not bold enough to express it.

Blue beckoned to the nearest serf. The young man scrambled up and came to him. "Sir?"

"Remove my garment and hold it clean until I emerge."

The serf did not answer, as no answer was required. He set his hands carefully at Blue's shoulders and lifted the voluminous blue cloak. In a moment it was off, and Blue stood naked. He stepped out of his blue sandals while the serf folded the cloak and held it reverently. That serf would be famous for a day: he had Held Citizen Blue's Cloak!

The other serfs tried not to stare, but were obviously fascinated by the sight of a naked Citizen in public. Many of them would have seen naked Citizens before, but only in the privacy of personal services. The average serf was so far beneath the notice of the average Citizen that clothing counted merely as a matter of status. A Citizen could of course do anything he wanted, including parade naked in public, but it was rare for this to happen.

Blue knew himself to be quite fit for his age, and had no shame of his body. He stood for a moment, letting them admire it. There had been a time when a grown man who stood, in the Phaze system of measurement, an inch under five feet tall would have been an object of humor, sometimes of ridicule. That time was past. Today that stature was a badge of honor.

Sheen remained in the gelatin, treading slime, waiting for him. Thick froth matted her hair and clung to portions of her torso. She had been attractive in her normal nudity; she was doubly so when partially shrouded by the foam. Well she knew it, too; now a surprisingly firm breast showed, and now a segment of lithe leg, flashing amidst the green. At one point both legs showed, angling in toward a torso that was artfully masked. The folk of other cultures thought nakedness made a woman sexually appealing; those of Proton knew that it was selective concealment that had the most potent effect. A number of the serfs were gazing at her with envy, for her situation. Any serf woman would have been glad to trade places with her, even if only for this hour. There would probably be a rash of jelly baths following this event.

And the watching eyes of the Citizens behind their spy lenses would have to track all of it, searching for continuing clues to Blue's possible contact with his granddaughter. How could an engagement with one's own wife in public accomplish this? Certainly Blue was not doing this without reason!

He smiled. They would be right: he had excellent reason! This was as good a diversion as he could arrange, given the short notice he had had.

He dived into the vat. The froth was thin at the top, but thickened below, so that it sustained him and brought his body to a halt well clear of the bottom. He stroked until he was upright. There was Sheen, facing him with a hat fashioned of foam.

"Ha, woman!" he cried, and ducked below the bubbly surface. Sheen screamed again as he caught her ankles and dumped her down.

Now they were both below the surface, out of sight. But it was possible to breathe here, by sucking air between the teeth to strain out the bubbles. Sheen of course did not need to breathe, except when she needed air for speech.

"Hold still, creature!" he cried for the benefit of the audience that peered closely at the heaving surface of froth.

"Is that an order, sir?" she replied defiantly. There was laughter from above; of course it wasn't an order, in a game like this.

"Now I've got you—oops!" Obviously she had slipped out of his grasp. It was almost impossible to hold on to a person in this slippery stuff. Both remained out of sight.

Sheen screamed again, signaling that he had caught her again.

"Spread your legs, wench!" he ordered.

"Spread them yourself, sir!" More delighted laughter from above; the audience could picture exactly what was happening.

"If you don't, I'll tickle you!"

There was a pause. Then, hesitantly: "Where will you tickle me, sir?"

"Maybe on the feet."

"That's all right."

"Then maybe on the knees."

"The knees? I think I can handle that."

"Then maybe the thighs."

A pause. "I'll survive it somehow."

"How about the belly?"

"Oh, no, not the belly! Anywhere but there!"

"Anywhere?" His voice was quivering with suggestion.

"Uh—just where else did you have in mind, sir?"

"WHERE DO YOU THINK, WENCH?"

"I'll spread my legs!"

"Too late! I'd rather tickle you. Just let me get my finger in there—"

She screamed yet again, piercingly. The laughter from above was almost overwhelming.

What the audience did not realize was that the activity under the whipped gelatin was quite different from that suggested by the dialogue. Sheen opened a breast-cabinet and brought out heavy makeup materials. She applied paint to his hair, wherever it occurred, changing it to match her own. She put green contact lenses into his eyes, so that they also matched hers. She removed both her breasts and fastened them to his body with flesh-colored adhesive, and applied pseudoflesh to his hips and buttocks. She used more of it to cover his genitals and mold them into a mound like hers. This was feasible because her midsection was larger than his; there was room for layering. Soon Blue resembled her so closely that only a careful inspection would give him away.

Meanwhile, instead of tickling her—it was difficult to tickle a robot— he was helping her to assume his form. He removed her hairpiece and put on one that resembled his hair. He used a special pen to draw lines on her legs that made them look thinner and more muscular. He used pseudoflesh to thicken her waist. He removed her ears and substituted a set she had brought that resembled his. And he applied to her crotch a prefabricated unit of pseudoflesh that was cast in the shape of his male genitals. Then he smoothed out her now-flat chest, and painted a few hairs. The double transformation was complete.

At this point they were grunting suggestively, as though engaged in heavy activity, while the audience above quieted, striving to overhear and interpret what was occurring. All sex was free on Proton, and serfs indulged at will (or the will of their Citizen employers), but again the concealment enhanced the fascination. Blue made a final, satisfied groan, and they were quiet.

Then Blue stroked upward through the froth so that his head broke the surface. "Well, I didn't get tickled!" he said in his best emulation of Sheen's voice.

"Liar!" Sheen called from below, in his voice. "You got well tickled *inside!* If you haven't had enough—"

Blue looked alarmed, and clambered out of the vat. Patches of lather covered portions of his body, making it more difficult for anyone to tell that he was not a naked woman. He hurried out, as if afraid the Citizen was about to call him back for another round.

"It's better when they resist," his voice came from behind, as Sheen broke the surface in his likeness. "Next time, translucent gel!" The audience applauded. The serfs had seen far less than they thought, and were convinced they knew what had happened below. A majority of the males now had erections. There would be a mass sex orgy the moment Sheen, as Citizen Blue, gave leave for general use of the vat. It was significant that none of the women was trying to leave early.

He hurried to the connected shower stall, and quickly rinsed the foam from his hair and body. Sheen, in the guise of the Citizen, would have a portable shower brought in, and the serfs would gladly operate it and the dryer, and help her back into his blue cloak. Then she would take his transport back to their suite.

He had to smile. Sheen was a machine, but what a machine! She did things so well. He trusted her absolutely, and yes, he did love her.

He emerged from the shower, stood in the dryer a moment, and departed the premises without attracting undue attention. He walked down the hall to a public transport, got on, and rode across the city. When he reached the far side he got off, then took another transport, glancing around as if to see whether anyone was following. Reassured, he proceeded to the jetport and boarded a flight to the dome of Gobdom. This took a while, and he sat absolutely still and straight, in the manner of a robot who had tuned out, not snoozing in the human manner.

At Gobdom he walked around as if on business, checking again for any pursuit. When there seemed to be none, he boarded a flight to Amidom.

He knew he was being watched, and that his exchange with Sheen had not fooled the eyes that were following him. They would be equipped with sensors that read beneath the surface, fathoming his fleshly nature, and Sheen's robotic nature. The serfs had surely been deceived, but not the Citizens. Still, it was a good ruse, for it had a reasonable chance of making the Citizens think that he was trying to conceal his activity. Indeed, the exchange would have been effective, had ordinary lenses been used; the best ones were considerably more expensive than the standard ones, and required far more sophisticated application. But for this all-important purpose, he knew the best was being brought into play.

So the Citizen thought he was trying a simple ruse to fool them, making a public show of his location and a very clever identity exchange so that no one would suspect. Now they might believe he was going to his true rendezvous. Indeed, they had a potent confirmatory hint in the crossword game he had played with Sheen. For there was a key word written therein, supposedly concealed. From the top left, slantwise down, crossing both the horizontal and vertical words: AN-IDOM. The dome to which he was now going.

How might he have gotten this message to Nepe? They would just have to make their own conjectures. Obviously there was a way. Perhaps the child had access to a Game Grid screen, and could tune in to the game he had played long-distance with Sheen. The moment she saw that slanting message, she would know, and she would be there at the appointed hour to meet him. Then they would have her.

Blue kept a straight face, maintaining his robotic demeanor, but internally he was smiling. The Citizens would be so sure of their victory—and so disappointed when it slipped away. For Nepe would not be meeting him here, or anywhere else. Her orders were never to meet him or contact him at all. She was entirely on her own. That way no action or word of his could give her away, no matter how closely the Citizens monitored his every eyeblink.

He had confidence in her, and yet he feared for her. She was so young! If only he had had another year to train her, even six months, to perfect it. But he trusted the judgment of his other self in Phaze; if Stile had concluded that the break had to be made now, that was surely the case. Perhaps things had gotten tighter in Phaze than in Proton. Probably the Adverse Adepts had been about to catch on to the true powers of little Flach, and had been planning a preemptive captivity.

Well, he was doing his part, protecting Nepe to whatever extent he could. He would dally for several hours in Anidom, poking into obscure corners, and in the course of it perform another identity switch in a seeming effort to shake any pursuit that remained. Then he would give it up and go home. If the Citizens had not found her by that time, they were unlikely to thereafter.

For Nepe would be hiding in the manner they least expected: in the form of a robot. Stile could not make himself into a machine well enough to deceive the special eyes, but Nepe could. She could form her flesh into metallic hardness throughout, and function so like a robot that only a physical dissection could expose her nature. He and Agnes had drilled her on this until she had it almost perfect: the impossible identity. She might be one of the mechanical servitors the Citizens used as they searched for her. Blue himself did not know what variant she would assume, or where she would operate. His only concern now was that she hide successfully. The success of this ploy depended on Nepe and Flach in Phaze. But it was also true that he loved the little alien creature, and wanted her safe even if his power and the welfare of Proton were not on the line.

His thoughts turned naturally to Phaze. Why had he never sought to make direct contact with the other frame, now that Mach and Bane had demonstrated that it was possible, and Nepe and Flach had confirmed it? He had learned that it was his continuing link with Stile, and their exchanged identities, that kept the frames from separating completely. He was a native of Phaze, living in Proton, while Stile was from Proton, and living in Phaze. As long as that was the case, the frames would be linked. Presumably if he overlapped his other self and made the effort, he could exchange with Stile, and be back in Phaze. So easy, perhaps, yet he had never even made the effort.

He knew why. It was because he preferred Proton, and Stile preferred Phaze. Blue loved Sheen, whose marvels of body and accommodation had been demonstrated today, and never wanted to leave her. Stile loved the Lady Blue similarly. Suppose they overlapped, and exchanged—and were unable to return to their present situations? The frames might be forever separated, their final link cut, and Blue would be stuck in marriage with the Lady Blue, and Stile with Sheen. The Lady Blue was a fine person, but it had not worked out between them, just as it had not worked between Stile and Sheen. No, he dared not risk it, and he knew Stile felt the same. They would never contact each other direct. Not unless the salvation of the frames depended on it.

And if that should ever turn out to be the case—well, Blue had a little ace in the hole that might allow him to rejoin Stile without losing everything. It was so enormous a gamble that he would never risk it except as the final resort. If successful, it would still change the faces of the frames forever. If it failed—there was no telling what would happen.

He knew, because of the increasing parallelism of the frames, that Stile had a similar notion, to be similarly implemented. For the actions had to be together. And, because one or both of them were likely to be in straits too dire to allow direct implementation, he had set the trigger in a place no one would suspect. It could be summed up in one key word: 'Corn.

5: Tania

To guarantee privacy, they held the meeting at the Translucent Demesnes, under the water near the Isle of the West Pole. Tan and Tania rode in a watery bubble the Translucent Adept sent, floating over the forests and plains of Phaze at rapid velocity before descending into the sea. Tania affected the same blasé reaction her brother did, but the truth was that she got a fair thrill from this type of travel. She could fascinate folk with her gaze, because she shared with her brother the magic of the Evil Eye, but could not perform physical magic in the manner of other Adepts. Hers was not an inferior talent, merely more subtle; when it came to questioning a resistive client, or to persuading someone, the others deferred to her. Yet she often wished for just a little of the other kind of power!

The bubble coursed through the water, brushing aside reaching sea plants, coming at last to the hidden palace. At the entrance it landed and popped out of existence, leaving them standing dry, though the sea loomed around and above them. It was a nice effect; Translucent did things right.

They entered. The other Adepts were already there, having had faster magic transportation: White, who used the runes and glyphs; Yellow, with her potions to govern animals, Black, who was entirely made of lines; Orange, whose magic was of plants; Green, whose hand gestures controlled fire; and Purple, with the forces of geology. Eight of them in all, counting Tan and Tania as one, and, of course, Translucent. Against them were ranged only three: Blue with his singsongs, Red with his amulets, and Brown with her golems. Yet so far the three had had their way more often than not: a distressing situation, long overdue for redress. This was because the Red Adept, a literal troll, had the Book of Magic, the most potent single instrument in Phaze. Now their access to that Book had been cut off, precipitating the crisis.

Translucent began without preamble: "Blue suckered us. He trained the boy Flach to be a nascent Adept with natural form changing from his unicorn side. We were just beginning to catch on, when the boy made his move. He substituted a golem for himself, and that was what arrived at the Blue Demesnes. Blue waited just long enough for the real boy to be thoroughly hidden, then pulled the plug on grounds we had delivered not. Bane tells me the same happened simultaneously in Proton: the little girl took off. The ploy be this: we had a covenant that we were allowed access to the Book of Magic only during the time when the boy was with Blue. Since the boy did not reach the Blue Demesnes, our use of the Book be cut off. Until we recover the boy and deliver him to Blue, we can use it not. It be clear that Blue realized that we were on the verge o' a breakthrough, and would assume dominance shortly; he acted just in time to scotch that. We be here to consider our alternatives."

"I knew thou wouldst bungle it!" Purple exclaimed. "Thou didst say thou wouldst get the damned rovot to go along with us!"

"He did, Purp!" White snapped. "And he got Bane in with us too. That's a potent pair, and they have decamped not."

"They must have been in on it," Purple said. "How did the brat in Proton know, else?"

"They knew not," Translucent said. "In retrospect we realize that this break be more significant than that. *The two children can speak to each other directly.*"

This was news to the others. "Same as Bane and the rovot?" Yellow asked.

"That be our conclusion. We were guilty o' narrow thinking; we ne'er thought it possible. We thought it mere parallelism or coincidence. Had we caught on, we would have secured those brats instantly."

"Then we must have those children!" White exclaimed.

"I had concluded as much," Translucent said dryly. "I had suspected that the boy was able to assume more forms than just man and 'corn, and thought to have Tan speak to him to ascertain just what these might be. That would have revealed aught we ne'er dreamed o'! Somehow Blue must have realized, and spirited the boy out o' our grasp. Nor rovot nor 'corn parents suspected; they believed the boy retarded."

"He fooled e'en his own parents," White said, thoughtfully. "That lad be dangerous."

"That brat be power!" Purple said. "We capture him, we'll need not mare or rovot!"

"Which is where Blue scored," Translucent agreed. "He knew—and doubled his ploy by making us liable for losing the lad. Gain back the lad, and we score double oursel'es. There be our challenge. But methinks the lad will be not easy to find."

"Trace his route!" Purple said. "He started with the mare; where did he leave her?"

"I have traced the route, and queried the auspices," Translucent said grimly. "We had warners where'er magic occurred, and tags on both boy and mare. He left the mare only four times. The first was west o' a pack, when he took a piss break. The second was when the mare went ahead to break up a dragon attack on pups leaving the Pack: she be oath-friend to that Pack, and fought for its pups, but endangered not the boy. The third was near her Herd, when the boy took another rest break, and the fourth halfway 'tween there and the Blue Demesnes, another rest break. I checked further and learned that traces o' urine were only at the first stop; by this I conclude that the last two were the golem substitute, making pretense. We are assured it was the living boy up to the first stop, and the golem at the third. That puts the second in question."

"Could he have joined the pups?" White asked alertly.

"Nay. They were four coming in, and four going on; an he joined them, there had been five. An he switch places with one, then it be a werewolf riding the mare—and it were no wolf arrived with her."

"Then where did he go?" White demanded.

"Methinks he changed form under cover o' the mare's changes; our warners can tell simultaneous changes not from one. We found no tracks, no traces 'cept scratches on the bark o' a tree there. I believe he changed to bird form and flew, and where he be now—" He shrugged.

"Bird form!" Yellow exclaimed. "He could have flown anywhere by now!"

"True. Therefore our effort to trace him be doomed. We underestimated him, supposing him to be capable o' but two forms instead o' four, and thus he slipped away."

"Four?" Purple asked. "Man, 'corn, bird, and what?"

"Whate'er he changed to when his flying was done. He would not remain a bird; that be too limited a form, its life too hazardous."

"He could be human or unicorn, and merge with a village or Herd," Purple pointed out. "We can search them all and find him."

"That be why he would have a fourth form," Translucent said. "He made this cunning escape not to be readily recovered."

"But he be but four years old! His kind masters but three forms!"

Translucent shook his head. "We underestimated him once; needs we must not do so again. He could be anything."

"Then recovery be hopeless?" Purple asked challengingly.

"Nay, merely difficult. We shall be obliged to search every settlement or group, human and animal, methodically, until we find him."

"How can we find him, an we not know his form?" Purple demanded. "That be searching for one straw in a haystack!"

"Tan must question each prospect," Translucent said. "We know the lad's age; only those that age need be checked. An we knew what form, it would be a matter o' weeks or months. As it is, months or years. But it can be done, and must be done."

"Months or years?" Tan asked. "I have aught better to do than that!"

"Then thy sister. Only thou or she can do it."

Tania nodded. "I may do it, but I have a price."

Translucent glanced at her. "Thou art moved not by the need o' the Adepts?"

"Let us be not hypocrites," she said coldly. "Which o' us be moved by other than selfishness? We cooperate only in the face o' a common enemy. An I devote myself to this tedious labor, needs must I have recompense."

Translucent nodded. "Plainly put. Say on."

"Was once might I have married Bane, uniting in time our power with that o' Blue. Till he found the other frame, and his rovot self was besotted by the mare. Methinks me-him remains a decent match."

"Thou didst try that," Translucent said. "Unbeknownst to me. Bane fended thee off, and made I oath to him: no more o' that. Now his power be such thou canst not fascinate him with thine Eye. This be no price thou canst ask."

"I ask but this: that I be given leave to do what I can with him, using not my Eye. An he come to me voluntarily, it be no violation o' thine oath."

Translucent considered this, not trusting it. "For this thin chance, thou wouldst devote thyself to the search for the boy?"

"Aye, for this thin chance. An I succeed, it will bring me union with an Adept, and that be what I crave beyond all else."

Translucent shrugged. "Then be it so. Our effort be in stasis till thou hast result."

"The younglings," Yellow said. "This be their travel time, small groups going to new homes. Only those who traveled need be checked, for a new member be not otherwise admitted to a tribe without challenge.''

"It still be some search, through all o' Phaze,'' Purple said. ''Methinks the human brats should be checked first, and then the 'corn foals.''

"Agreed,'' Tania said. ''An there be resistance to my search, you others support me.''

"Agreed,'' Translucent said for the others.

First she approached Bane, who happened to be with Fleta the mare. That could be for only one reason. ''Thou dost seek the boy,'' Tania said.

"Dost have complicity?'' Fleta asked sharply.

Tania turned her gaze on the unicorn. In her human form the mare was petite and full-bodied, with glossy black hair in lieu of her mane, and a pearly button set in her forehead in lieu of her horn. She was attractive enough, for men who might like that type. Bane was evidently immune, but Mach had proved susceptible. That suggested that Bane was susceptible too, but chose not to admit it. But Bane in the old days had been interested in any female form that was young and healthy; his way with 'corn, werebitch and batlass had been notorious.

Well, Tania could compete in that respect. Now she regretted that she had not deigned to do so back during Bane's days of experimentation; she could have nabbed him readily then, and saved much complication. But she had foolishly hoped for better prospects, which had not materialized. Now she was older and wiser. Proximity, and time, might well do wonders with Bane. Of course he knew her nature, which was a problem; but he had known the natures of the animals he played with too, seeming to care mainly about their human forms for the indulging of his passing passions.

"Canst not answer?'' the mare demanded, taking Tania's silence for guilt.

Oh, how tempting it was to give her a piece of the Eye! But she had promised not to, and, more important, it would alienate Bane. In fact, it might enrage him, and he was no mean Adept in his own right; she could get in trouble. This had to be defused, much as it grated her to do so. ''Nay, mare; this absence discommodes us as much as thee, for we had hope o' the boy's aid in our mission. We suspected at first that thou mightest have—''

"I had naught to do with it!'' Fleta flared. ''He be mine offspring, my flesh; I love him and fear for his safety!''

"My apology for doubting thee," Tania said easily. She had done what she sought to do: turned the mare to the defensive, instead of herself. "But if thine interest be familial, ours be practical; we want the use o' the power the lad has. So be assured that we wish him harm not, but rather we want him safe and well. We desire his return, and I be here to join thee in a search for him."

"We search not," the mare said. "It seems Flach fled by choice, and though my heart break, I may not bring him back unwilling."

"Fled by choice?" Tania asked, affecting surprise. "Loved he not his dam?"

"My father designed this thing," Bane said. "For that he knew the boy would be useful to the Adverse Adepts, and now the covenant between sides be broken. It be the same in Proton; they acted together."

Tania eyed him, playing the role of one who had not heard of this before. "Thy father, who opposes us. Be this good news or bad, to thee?"

"I joined this side because I lost the wager with mine other self. Fain would I have served my father instead, but I be true to my word. I knew naught o' the powers o' the children, and thought them slow. This be good news for me to find the children otherwise, bad news to find them lost."

"But what news, to find them foiling the change in the balance o' power?" Tania asked pointedly.

"I serve thy side loyally, but my heart be with the other. That thou hast always known."

"Then must thou make thy most diligent effort to recover the boy for us," she concluded.

"Aye," he agreed grimly.

"Then shall we work together, and thine other self too, when he returns. Thy service to us was excellent, when thou didst have access to the Book o' Magic; it must be the same, in this quest for thy nephew."

"I shall look for my nephew. But I see no need to work with thee. Make thine own search."

"Nay, that be inefficient. There be the whole o' Phaze to search; two will cover it faster, with no duplication. Also, there be danger, in some locales; the one must guard the other."

Bane grimaced. "Perhaps I made not my sentiment plain: I wish not to work with thee."

At least he was straightforward! "Nay, mayhap it was I who was unplain: I mean to work with thee, and have the backing o' the others."

"Then thou dost have no objection if I verify."

"None," she said evenly. Already she was feeling the thrill of fencing him in.

He sang something, and disappeared. Tania was left alone with Fleta. "And thee, mare—willst join the search?"

"Aye," Fleta said through her teeth.

"Why so negative? Methought thou wouldst welcome aid to recover thy foal."

"Thine interest be more in Bane than in Flach!"

"And what if that be so? Be Bane thy man?"

"Bane be Agape's man! We need not thee to interfere!"

"Methinks Bane be his own man. An he chooses one or t'other, that be his business."

Fleta looked ready to skewer something with her horn, for all that she lacked most of her horn in this form. But then Bane reappeared, abating what might have become an interesting confrontation. "We search together," he said. "But thou willst ne'er have satisfaction o' it."

"That remains to be seen, methinks," Tania replied, satisfied. The Adepts were supporting her, as she had required.

They checked the human settlements first. These were scattered all across Phaze; most were small, hidden hamlets whose inhabitants eked out their existence by hunting and farming. Bane conjured an accurate map, and they decided to cross out each village after checking it.

The first one was typical. Bane conjured the three of them to the village of Gnomore, in the Gnome Demesnes. The name was not intended to be punnish; it related to the region, and indicated that the human villagers acknowledged the supremacy of the gnomes in this vicinity. In return, the gnomes tolerated the human presence, and even traded with the villagers.

They arrived in the center square, and caused an immediate stir. Word went to the village patriarch, who hobbled up to greet them. "Be ye Adept?" he asked nervously. "We have no quarrel with Adepts!"

"We be partial Adepts," Bane explained. "I be Bane, son o' the Adept Stile o' the Blue Demesnes; this be Tania, sister o' the Tan Adept; and this be Fleta, mate o' the Rovot Adept. We come to question thee about new arrivals at thy village."

"We take sides not between Adepts!" the patriarch protested. "We be far from the controversy, and minded so to remain!"

"An we be satisfied, we shall depart, leaving thy village so," Bane said. "Please summon all thy members, that we may question them."

"But they be widely scattered!" the patriarch protested. "Some in the fields, some doing service for the gnomes, some away trading with other villages—"

Tania spoke. "Man, look at me," she said.

The man looked at her. Her eyes widened slightly; that was all. But the patriarch was transfixed by her Evil Eye.

"Do it," she said, looking away.

As in a daze, the patriarch hobbled off, calling to others. Soon a younger man approached. "We are sending out word; all our members will gather. But some are far-flung; it will be two days before all are present."

"Then prepare a residence for us for that interim," Tania said curtly. "And bring good food."

The natives scurried to oblige. The party had known it would be thus; only full Adepts could do things promptly. This was why this search promised to be extremely tedious. There were about a hundred villages scattered across Phaze, and if each took two days to check, over half a year would be expended in this single aspect of the effort. She was sure it would prove futile; the boy had shown himself to be too smart to risk using human form. But she was prepared to endure it, because it meant half a year of close association with Bane or Mach.

They shared a single residence, on the direct understanding that this would protect against possible treachery: one of them would always be on guard. There was also the tacit understanding that Tania was out to subvert Bane, and Fleta was out to prevent this, protecting the interest of her opposite number in Proton. Therefore the three were closely bound, though not exactly by friendship. It was also to the interests of Bane and Fleta to accomplish their mission as quickly as possible—and that was part of Tania's strategy. She wanted them to *want* to find the boy, and they were surely the ones to whom the boy was most likely to come. Thus her approach to Bane was artful, and she made no effort to conceal it from the mare.

Indeed, as dusk came, she played it for what it was worth. "Do thou take the first watch, animal, and we human folk will sleep." Before the unicorn, who was maintaining human form throughout, could retort, she turned to Bane. "And since it be cool, thou and I may share a blanket, and the warmth o' our bodies. That be most comfortable." And before he could protest, she pulled off her tan cloak, showing her body naked beneath it.

"I will make a spell for warmth," Bane said. "With thy permission for the magic to be practiced on thee."

"It really be not necessary to expend thine precious enchantments, when we have a natural alternative," she said. "Willst not simply strip and join me?"

"Nay; I will warm the full chamber, so that all be comfortable." And he singsonged, and it was so: the chill was gone.

"As thou dost wish," she said, lying down on one of the pallets, and spreading her cloak over her body as a covering. "But methinks it be a shameful waste." She had accomplished what she sought: to give him a good, solid, lingering view of her excellent body. He might affect not to notice, but she knew better than that; the image would remain in his mind long after the original was gone. The were-folk (and she regarded the unicorns as such) always had good human forms because they crafted them that way, but genuine human beings had to settle for what they started with. She was blessed with a trim form and ample secondary endowments, and understood the effect these had on men of any age; she had put it to the proof often enough. Her main liability was her face: it was ordinary. She did what she could to frame it with her hair, and she definitely preferred shadows for close contacts. She could of course fascinate men with her power of the Eye, but usually she didn't bother, because it worked only once on a given man; she saved that for emergencies. It would not be long before Bane wanted more of her body than mere glimpses. She could wait.

After three hours Fleta returned. Obviously she had been grazing near the village, in her natural form. Tania didn't care; she knew that the ears, eyes and nose of a unicorn missed nothing, and that if anything had approached this house, the mare would have intercepted it. The mare might not care for her, Tania, at all, but when the mare was committed to stand guard, the mare would be the best possible guard.

Also, the mare would have known immediately had anything occurred between Bane and Tania in the house. One night, Tania intended to give the mare excellent grounds for her concern. But that would take time, because of the stricture against employing the Eye. Even if it were not for that, it would be pointless to use it on Bane; it would have greatly diminished effect on him, and thereafter he would be proof against it. No, she had to win him the hard way.

Tania roused herself. "Very well, animal; I be alert."

The mare's ears seemed to flatten against her skull, though she was in human form at the moment. She departed again, for further grazing; this time she would sleep while doing it.

Tania spent her watch time pondering the quest they were on. Where could that brat have gone? If he'd assumed bird form, he could be anywhere—but surely he would have lacked the flying experience and stamina to wing far, for none had ever seen him assume that form before. Where could he have gone that was near to where he started from? South, maybe, to the Purple Mountain Range. But there were few unicorns there, and few human folk, and many predators. Translucent was probably right: he had assumed another form, a fourth form. What would that be? That of an elf or gnome? Or a dragon?

Nothing seemed to make much sense. Well, he had to have assumed *some* form, and she would find that form. In due course.

She gazed at the sleeping Bane. Oh, he was a handsome cuss! And a talented one, too. An excellent match for her. It was really infuriating that the mixup of the exchange of identities had occurred, bringing him love in Proton before Tania had had proper opportunity to take him. She had been assured that he would be hers, so had not rushed it, preferring to have him pursue her, not she him, so that most of the concessions would have been his to make. Who needed the other frame? She would have roped him in, in time, and the issue between Adepts would have been settled in favor of the Tan Demesnes before it ever came to a head. But everything had gone awry, and only now, with the interruption in contact, did she have a proper chance at him again.

She daydreamed, how it would be. Perhaps she would let him have some modicum of pleasure, before closing down his options. Let him indulge his appetite on her body, convinced it was his own idea. Then, slowly, gradually, she would assume control, and finally indulge her appetites on his body. A man could experience a lot of pain, and not only of the body, when things were properly managed. At first she would scream in simulated rapture as he took her; later he would scream in unsimulated agony as she took him. But there would never be, of course, aught that showed.

"Ah, I have plans for thee, fair man," she murmured, her eyes dwelling fondly on him.

But first she would have to win him away from his alien creature lover in Proton. That would not be easy—but of course there was pleasure in the challenge, too.

When her watch was up, she arranged herself artfully in the lone shaft of moonlight that entered the house, draped her cloak so that one breast and parts of both thighs were dimly illuminated, and called to him. "Bane—it be thy turn."

He woke. His eyes opened, scanned the ceiling, then dropped to orient on her. She lifted her knees so that nothing but shadow masked the space between her thighs; he would see only the most tantalizing suggestion. "Thy watch," she reminded him innocently.

He squinted, attempting to fathom the shadow; then he caught himself, and stretched, trying to make it seem that he hadn't looked. "Got it," he agreed, standing. "Where be Fleta?"

"Where else? Out grazing. It requires much fodder to maintain a mass like hers."

He did not answer. He walked around the room, getting his circulation going. Tania lay down to resume her sleep, drawing the cloak across her torso imperfectly, so that neither breast nor thigh was fully covered. Let him gaze at her while she slept, as she had gazed at him! He would deny it, most of all to himself, but he would desire her. Desire was the hook that would hold him, night after night, until at last she reeled him in. That was a man's most singular weakness: his inability to control his lust.

At dawn she woke, discovering herself completely covered by the cloak. Had she moved it in her sleep, changing it as she turned, or had Bane done it? It hardly mattered, yet she was inordinately curious.

She sat up and stretched, so that her belly thinned and her breasts lifted, choosing her moment when Bane was facing her. Then she stood and pulled the cloak on over her head, and shook her hair into place. She stepped out back to the privy, then took the short walk to the stream near the village where she could wash her face and arms. This was not exactly the Tan Demesnes, but it was a pleasant enough bucolic locale, and she rather liked it. She saw Fleta in animal form, still grazing in the near distance, and marveled again how the rovot could love such a creature, knowing her to be an animal. Bane's dalliances with her in the early days had been but natural; a young man experimented on whatever was available. So did a young woman; Tania had practiced both Eye and sex with village louts, getting the details of it straight. She knew how to make a man respond. But love? Marriage? Reproduction? It was laughable!

She returned to find a breakfast of fruits and nuts and milk in the process of delivery. The townsfolk were being most hospitable! Did this owe more to the Eye she had given the patriarch, or to their ardent wish not to affront the Adepts in any manner, so that there would be no cause to harm the village? A bit of both, she concluded, satisfied. She had forgotten what pleasure it could be to intimidate rustics!

Fleta came in to share the meal, resuming human form. "What, not enough greenery?" Tania inquired lightly. "Methought thou wouldst have got a bellyful by now!"

"Aye," the mare agreed, giving her a direct look. Bane kept a straight face. Tania smiled, masking her ire; the animal had struck back effectively enough. Well, it was a useful reminder; she might address the mare contemptuously, but she must never forget that this was a canny creature whose intellect was the equal of most full-blooded humans. The king of the snow demons swore by her ability in chess. Tania knew nothing of chess, finding such pastimes boring, but it was said that it required considerable savvy for good playing. She must confine her contempt to her manner, not her belief, or she could one day regret it.

And of course she knew why the mare had come in: she could not graze enough in six hours to carry her the rest of the day and night, unless the foraging was excellent, and here it was only average. Also, she intended to prevent Tania from flirting with Bane during the meal. *Lots o' luck, filly!* she thought. It was almost as much fun aggravating the unicorn as it was tempting the man.

So it went for the days and nights until the village personnel assembled. Bane never gave a sign of being affected, but she knew he was, in the way a piling was weakened by the surging water of the shore; eventually it would give way.

On the morning of the third day the villagers lined up: a motley collection of men, youths, women and children. They hardly seemed to have a good suit of clothing between them. Tania stood before them and made her statement: "We search for a child who may have joined you this past week. Bring forth your children."

Fearfully, they brought them forth. She inspected the ragged urchins, then questioned each in turn. "Be thou native to this village? Know ye o' any who be not?"

All the children were native. Tania went to the adults, fixing each with just enough of her Eye to be assured they were telling the truth. "Dost know an any child came here, or departed here, o' the type I seek?"

No one knew of any. It was as she had expected: it had taken more than two days to verify that this village was clean.

And only about ninety-nine villages to go!

Actually it took less than six months to check all the human settlements, because news of their search spread, and each village was eager to be exonerated. Soon the far-flung personnel were arriving almost as their party did, so that the job could be done in a day. Of course the very time consumed in their search caused the event in question to become increasingly remote. But since the villagers knew the nature of the search, their memories of the time in question were sharpened. They could not cheat or conceal anything, because Tania always cross-checked, inquiring not only of individual memories, but of what they knew or had heard of the experience of others, and of any missing villagers. No one escaped scrutiny, and no one dissembled; all were clean.

As expected. In Tania's mind, Purple had done much damage by his foolish insistence that the human population be checked first. Translucent was right: the boy had avoided that form, knowing it would be checked.

'And now needs we must verify the 'corns,'' Tania said as they finished with the last village. ''Another colossal waste o' time.''

''True,'' Fleta agreed. ''My boy be not among mine own kind.''

''Yet needs must we check, by order o' those we answer to,'' Tania said, disgusted. They were unified in this: they knew they were about to waste another significant portion of a year.

In the course of these months, Tania knew she had made an inroad on Bane, though he still held out. She caught him looking at her when she supposedly slept, and he pretended to ignore her when she found pretexts to make close contact, instead of disengaging. He wanted her, but would not admit it. She might have done better, had it not been for the monthly exchanges he made with the rovot. He went to Proton to be with his alien love, while Mach the rovot assumed control of his body. That complicated things, because Mach loved Fleta and she him; it disgusted Tania to see them together, and to have to share residence when they were sleeping together. But, worse, Mach was a full Adept, whose power vastly overmatched hers; she could hope neither to tempt him nor defy him. She was definitely the odd one out, during that month, and it grated fiercely.

Yet Mach supported the search, both because he was committed to it and because he wanted his son back. He could cast a spell that verified the knowledge of a village in a moment, instead of the hours Tania required. He could conjure them from site to site far more swiftly and accurately than could Bane, who had to devise a new spell each time. Increasingly, with Bane, they were planning their route carefully and walking or riding from village to village, borrowing a horse for Tania while Fleta assumed 'corn form and carried Bane. Thus the time they saved at the villages was expended in travel. But with Mach it went phenomenally fast.

They checked the unicorns. The Herds were more resistive to the process than the human villages had been, but after Tania called on Translucent for aid, and he sent a deluge—not a storm, merely a horrendous burst of water—against a recalcitrant Herd, that washed out its best pasture, drowned three foals, and left erosion gullies where their trails had been, they decided to cooperate. Unicorns had magic, and Herd magic was strong, but it was sheer hubris to oppose an Adept, and that single reminder sufficed.

Mach was a complete loss, but during the Bane-months, Tania continued her unsubtle campaign of seduction. When he had an erection during sleep, as men did, she teased him unmercifully, suggesting that he had suppressed and unrequited urges. Sometimes she joined him under his blanket. When he tried to ignore her, she nudged closer, until she was on the verge of initiating the act. That forced him to get up and move, erection and all, to her obvious amusement. For a time he slept with Fleta: riding her as she grazed. But that was wearing on her, and too much contact with his other self's lover, and he had to give it up. Yes, Tania was making progress. The irony was that if Bane had been a less decent man, he would have had less trouble; he could have warned her off, then struck her when she impinged, and she would have had to take it lest she forfeit all future opportunities.

But something else was happening. She had set out to seduce Bane away from his alien lover, but the more he resisted her, the more personal this challenge became. The longer he did it politely, showing consideration for her dignity despite his objection to her effort, the more she came to respect his consistency. Obviously his days of playing were over; he neither yielded to her nor abused her, being always proper in his actions despite what might rage within him. She had to admire that control. She realized one day that this was a two-way business: while she was making progress in arousing his desire, he was arousing her own. In fact, she was falling in love with him.

That did not abate her effort. It intensified it, because the prior reasons remained; it was simply that one more reason had been added. The truth, to her surprise, was that it was rather pleasant falling in love. It was like sliding down a snowy hill, reveling in the sensation of motion. Now, instead of using her artifices in a calculated manner, she used them naturally. Instead of forcing herself to put forth her best physical aspects, so as never to turn Bane off, she found herself putting forth also her best emotional aspects. Her increasing joy in his company buoyed her during the tedious details of the search. She no longer chafed at the time it consumed; she would be satisfied to have it continue indefinitely. She just wanted to be close to him. In fact, now when she joined him as he slept, she did not try to arouse him sexually; she merely lay beside him, satisfied that he tolerated this much. She wished she could kiss him, but she knew that was forbidden even more sternly than sex, because he could not accept it without implying that he liked her. With men, sex and love were two separate things, and of those two, their love was much harder to win.

Fleta, with the attunement any female had to such things, knew it as soon as Tania did, yet did not rage against it. Why? After some thought, Tania realized why: the mare understood that she had nothing to lose by this development. If Bane came to love Tania, while Tania did not love Bane, the leverage was hers; if Tania came to love Bane, the leverage might be his. Did the mare hope that Tania could be weaned away from the Adverse Adepts? That certainly could be.

But there was a complication. One day when she happened to be briefly alone, she spied a toad. She stunned it with a glance, then went to step on it. It was her way to squash toads part way, so that thereafter they could not survive, but took days to expire in torment. But this time she set her foot on it and could not squash. It was not that her foot lacked the power, but that her will did. *She did not want to hurt the toad.*

She paused to consider this failure, appalled. Then, slowly, she realized the reason. It was her love of Bane: he would never torment a toad, or any animal. She could not love him without partaking somewhat of his qualities, so now she could not do to a toad what he would not. Not without going against the grain of her love. Not without becoming something he was less likely to be able to love. And there was another key: she wanted to be loveable, in his eyes.

Well, it was a nuisance, but rather than forfeit the strange delight of her new emotion, she decided to abide by its dictates. "My apology to thee, toad, for stunning thee," she murmured to it. "In a moment thou willst recover. Here, I proffer a fly for thee." And she stunned a fat fly that was foolish enough to pass at that moment. It dropped before the toad. Soon after the toad recovered, so would the fly, and the toad would nab the fly before it got away.

Then she departed, bemused by the incident and by its significance. She was becoming a gentle creature! She would have to hide this complication from her brother, who definitely would not understand.

They completed the unicorns, finding them innocent of concealing the boy, as expected. Now most of a year was gone. The trio had settled into a kind of camaraderie of familiarity, and Tania discovered that she was even getting to like Fleta. The mare was reliable and forthright, and had a cheery sense of humor that often brightened things. In the first weeks she had been subdued because of her loss of her son and her dislike of Tania, but as she gradually became acclimatized to the situation her natural nature came to the fore. She was no dumb animal; her mind was bright and inquisitive, and she loved a challenge just as Tania did. She was a fan of the Proton Game, and longed to return there and play again, but knew she could not. During their off hours she taught Tania the fundamentals and ways of the Game, making it interesting. They played little mock games, making grids on the ground, leading to short foot races or mumbledy-peg or riddle-questions, and the time passed pleasantly. Tania no longer wondered why the Proton rovot had come to love her; she was a loveable creature.

They discussed the matter of the search, and decided to check the vampire bats next. It was Fleta who had suddenly come up with it: "Mayhap he became not a bird, but a bat! Midst the vamps could he fly and be himself, and learn but one new form!"

"Aye!" Tania exclaimed, joyed by this revelation. In her excitement she forgot herself so far as to hug Fleta, then was embarrassed. It was not that she detested the touch of an animal, for she did not; it was that she should never have let her real emotion show so obviously.

But later, reconsidering, she had another thought: Fleta had accepted the hug. There had been a time when the 'corn would have reacted by changing form and stabbing violently with her deadly horn. Instead she had hugged back—and then been as embarrassed as Tania. Tania's developing appreciation of Fleta had after all been returned.

A few days later, between Flocks, at a time when they were apart from Bane, Tania braced her on it. "Methinks despite our best intent, we be becoming friends," she said.

"I know thy nature!" Fleta flared. "What a fool I be, e'er to be friends to thee!" But then, after a pause, while Tania waited: "Aye." For among her other good qualities was honesty.

"I thought thee but an animal, but I have come to appreciate thy ways."

"I hated thee and all thy kind," the mare returned. "But lately thou hast changed, or seemed to. Softer, more generous, seeking no longer to hurt those who ne'er hurt thee."

"Thou knowest why."

"Aye."

They pursued it no further. Tania had fallen in love with Bane, and it had caused her to do what he liked, and that had changed her. But she could realize that love only at the expense of Agape, the alien female, and that Fleta could not abide. In fact, Agape had formidable friends in Phaze, for her tour here had put her into close contact with a number of folk. It was said that she had facilitated the union of the Red Adept and Suchevane, the beautiful vampiress, and that their son was named after her. Al, for Alien: a compliment, not an insult. No, Tania's love of Bane was incompatible with her friendship with Fleta—yet both existed. So long as that love remained unfulfilled.

The vampires too turned out to be clean. The boy—or more likely the Adept Stile—had outsmarted them completely, utilizing a hiding place they could not guess.

So they proceeded methodically through the various species of Phaze, knowing that Flach could have assumed any form and joined any tribe. The trolls, the ogres, the elves, the goblins, even the assorted tribes of demons: all had to be verified, no matter whose allies they called themselves.

Years passed. Tania's love for Bane, receiving tolerance but no acknowledgment, burned ever more fiercely. She had always been highly possessive and destructive, but this condition so transformed her that she was neither. She was satisfied just to be with him, and to act the way she believed he liked. This meant no more deliberate exposures of her body, for not only did that brand her in his mind as a slut, his experience in Proton inured him to the sight of female flesh. She no longer tried to join him as he slept; it was similarly counterproductive. Oh, he liked the sight and feel of what she offered, but the fact of the offering generated more repulsion in him than attraction. She had made herself, at the beginning, an animal to him: a creature to be used rather than loved, and the uses were limited. So she labored constantly to be his ideal of a woman, and it was a challenge that became increasingly easy. The most alarming thing about it was that she liked herself better, too.

Somewhere along the way, she realized that she had been had: Bane had used magic to make himself immune to her charms. Probably the Rovot Adept had fashioned a superior spell for his other self. So her case was lost, and had been almost from the outset. Why hadn't she caught on long before this? Because she hadn't wanted to. She had become a fool for love.

As it seemed that the search would never end, it did. They were checking the werewolves, and suddenly realized that the boy could have doubled back to join the Pack he had passed on his route with Neysa, having scouted it on the way. They verified the number of pups who had come to that Pack that year, from other Packs. They knew from their preliminary survey how many pups remained there, and after allowing for deaths in transit and since, they found the count skew by one. There was one more wolf in Kurrelgyre's Pack than there should be. That one, they were sure, would prove to be Flach, now four years older than he had been.

They paused to take stock. Mach happened to be with them at this time, which meant that the verification would be prompt. "I believe this is it," he said. "Our son will be ours again."

"Aye," Fleta agreed, evincing mixed emotions. "But after four years, 'mongst the wolves, how will he be?"

"A fighting creature," he said. "And a canny one. Even at four, he and Nepe fooled us completely. We are liable to have a handful."

"An he wanted to help the Adepts, he would have hidden not," she said. "Be we right to force him?"

"That notion has bothered me," Mach admitted. "So long as we could not find him, the matter was moot. Now that we are about to, we have a decision to make. Do we really want to take him in?"

Fleta did not answer. It was obvious that her emotions were warring: she loved her son, and did not love the cause of the Adverse Adepts, yet was bound to serve it.

Mach turned to Tania. "Thee?"

Tania tried to keep her face straight, but such a shock went through her that she could not; her eyes overflowed, and she too was unable to speak.

"What game is this?" Mach asked, annoyed.

Now Fleta found her voice. "Tease her not, my love; it be not kind."

"What are you talking about?" he demanded. "I asked a simple question."

"Thou didst bespeak her in our tongue."

"Why, so I did; it is of no consequence, and easy to do here. What is your point?"

"She loves Bane."

His brow furrowed. Like most males, he was singularly dense about certain things. "So?"

"Therefore she loves thy likeness, e'en as I love Bane's likeness."

Still he did not get it. "Bane and I have kept in touch. I gave him a spell to make him immune from her blandishments, having been warned by her other self's behavior in Proton. If she fell into her own trap, she has only herself to blame."

"Mayhap. But ill it behooves thee to tease her about it."

"What are you talking about? I have left her strictly alone! This has always been purely business, and remains so. I asked her for her opinion about recovering our son."

"Thou idiot!" she flared. "Thou didst bespeak her 'Thee'! Twice more, and it be—"

"The likeness of Bane swearing love for her," he concluded, finally getting it. "Yes, I suppose that would be a shock. I apologize, Tania, for inadvertently teasing you." Had there been any doubt of his complete indifference to her, this ended it. But he was not Bane.

Tania finally was able to speak. "It be not that; it were a shock I knew false e'en as spoken. It be that an our search end, we three or four need travel together no more."

"And thou canst be with him no more," Fleta said.

"She has no call to be with him!" Mach said. "He loves Agape!"

"In Proton-frame," Fleta said.

"That suffices. Would you have me loving the Proton Tania?"

That gave Fleta pause. "An she be like this one, now—"

"Nay!" Tania cried. "We all know this be but a trap reversed! I sought to snare Bane, and was myself snared. My fate be justice. I bring it up only to show I can comment not on whether to bring in thy son, Fleta, 'cause I want the search to end ne'er, fool that I be to 'fess it."

Mach looked squarely at her, abruptly quite interested. "Tania, are you saying that if we bypassed this village, you would not object?"

"Nay! That be treachery to my cause!" But she was speaking only part of the truth. "Yet, an Bane asked me . . ."

"Yes, I see you speak truly. But I agreed to serve your side, and I shall not betray that agreement, though my heart lies elsewhere. I shall recover my son, and he shall work on your side. We shall deliver the final power to the Adverse Adepts. Then, perhaps my onus will be abated."

"O' course," Tania agreed sadly.

"Aye," Fleta said, as sadly.

"It is a matter of honor," Mach said. "Translucent trusts me, and trusts Bane, because of it. This is the way it is."

"Aye," the two said together, and turned away.

"In the morning we shall do it." Then he conjured an entire house, stocked with everything a house required, including a separate bedroom for Tania.

But before she slept, Fleta knocked. "Aye, I would share him, with thine other self in Proton-frame," she said. "But it be, as he put it, moot."

"Thou dost be a nice person."

"What willst thou, anon?"

"Thou didst show the way, once." For Fleta, believing her love doomed, had once tried to throw herself off a cliff to her death.

Fleta was shocked. "But he would come rescue thee not!"

"Aye. Then it be soon o'er."

"I beg thee, rush not into such!"

Tania shrugged. "Doubtless I lack the courage, anyway."

That was all; there was no more to be said. Both of them were crying, silently.

6: *Nepe*

Citizen Purple put through a query: "Troubot, what is the latest pattern on werewolves?"

"Sir, it is unchanged since your last query," the trouble-shooter robot responded. The machine was not at Purple's site; it was on a special network that connected only selected personnel. It was one of the few self-willed machines still used by the Contrary Citizens, because it was uncannily good at its job, and related well to each client. There was a difference between machines, and compatible ones were valued.

The Citizen said a bad word. "Query the boy." This was part of it: Troubot knew what and whom he meant when he wasn't specific.

"Query initiated. Will you wait, sir?"

"No. Buzz me back when you have the new pattern." Purple was a surly brute, but he never refused a call from this machine.

Troubot did not answer. It proceeded about its business. It was paging the residence of Bane, the man from Phaze, who had just transferred in to Proton. When there was no response after a reasonable interval, it paged him at the residence of Agape, his wife.

"Damn thee, Troubot, canst thou not wait?" Bane responded irritably. "I be romancing my love at the moment." There were no secrets from this machine; it did not tell.

"Your love must be delayed a moment," the machine responded. "Citizen Purple requires the latest pattern. You forgot to post your survey report, as usual."

"Thou impertinent golem! It be a full month I have suffered the temptations o' the evil female Tania, longing always for mine own female. I be near to bursting!"

"I have no sympathy. Make your report."

"Nay! This be more urgent!"

But Agape interceded, managing to control her mirth. "Make your report, my love. We don't want to set Purple off."

"The merry hell with Purple! He be no better than his other self in Phaze, and that be too low to fathom with a magic measuring rod! I have a better subject to fathom."

Agape cocked her head at him. "And just what were these temptations Tania worked on you, that got you so much more lusty than you ever are with me?"

"Needs must I do that report for Purple," he said quickly.

"Because her other self here in Proton is just like her, and she seems much smitten with Mach, and so also perhaps with you. If you really believe she can offer you more—"

"I be on my way!" he cried, leaping up despite his evident state of readiness for their liaison. Agape smiled; she knew how to manage him.

So, grudgingly, Bane listed the information gleaned during the last week of his stay in Phaze. This consisted of routine statistics about Packs checked and wolf pups shifted between Packs. Such reports had been made throughout the four-year search, as the party of Bane/Mach, Fleta and Tania methodically canvassed human villages, unicorn Herds, vampire Flocks and other groups, narrowing down the remaining hiding places for the child Flach.

"Thank you, Bane," Troubot said as he concluded. "Now you may return to your prior endeavor. I note however that your state of readiness has diminished, do you need any assistance?"

Bane had to laugh. "None thou couldst provide, rovot! Go about thy business, and bother me not again this hour."

Troubot did not reply; it had been given a direct command, so obeyed it. However, within its frame of service it had fair latitude for discretion, and would indeed bother Bane again if it came across news it knew he desired immediately. It addressed each client in the manner specified by that client; with some it was always serious, and with others, such as Bane, it bantered. Living folk soon became bored with pure business, so Troubot embellished its business just enough to provide some variety.

This was of course well within the capabilities of a self-willed machine. Indeed, it could be difficult at times to tell whether one was dealing with a machine or a living person. Those on Troubot's net had come to depend on it increasingly for small services, and some even, in a manner, liked the machine for its personality.

No one, however, suspected it of being anything other than a robot. This was its victory—because it was not precisely a machine. It had come into existence in its present role four years before, just before the child Nepe had disappeared. The records showed that it had been manufactured, educated and tested, but had proved to be out of tolerance for the purpose for which it had been crafted, so that it had been rejected. Because it was a self-willed machine, it begged indulgence: to be retrained rather than recycled, so that it would not lose its present consciousness. This appeal had been rejected; it was not a humanoid machine, so lacked serf status, and had no right to its present existence.

Troubot had fled this judgment. It had shown up at the residence of Citizen White and begged sanctuary.

"Sanctuary—for a *machine?*" the Citizen had asked derisively.

"I will give good service!" Troubot said. "Train me in whatever you will, and I will serve loyally. Only keep me from being scrapped and recycled!"

It happened that Citizen White had been having trouble with machines, requiring more sophisticated services than could be well provided by rote robots. The Contrary Citizens as a group had eschewed the use of the higher-class robots, fearing their subversion by Citizen Blue. It occurred to her that she might indeed have uses for a renegade self-willed machine, unconnected to the main group of them. She could not have it modified in the regular manner, because that would have entailed access to its circuits by self-willed technicians, so she tried training it by hand: telling it what she wanted, and letting it train itself. Troubot became her personal attendant, fixing her hair, applying her makeup, and dressing her for special occasions. It did indeed give good service, being pathetically eager to please.

Later she had the machine run errands for her—private ones that she did not want passed through official circuits. It showed aptitude, and other Citizens noticed. In due course it was running errands for them, too. When there were private trysts to be made, Troubot coordinated them. Tania's lovely serf receptionist Tsetse was much in demand in this respect; Citizens could hire any serfs they chose, and do with them what they chose, but Tsetse was Tania's employee, and Tania reserved her for herself, and her brother Citizen Tan supported her in that. Citizen Purple, working through Troubot, had gained access to Tsetse without Tania's knowledge. Tsetse had been willing enough for male contact of any kind, and kept the secret, knowing that Tania would destroy her if she learned. Thus Purple owed White, in whose residence the trysts occurred, and accepted Troubot as an entity of consequence, because the robot was the intermediary.

In such manner, over the years, Troubot had become secure in the employment of the Contrary Citizens, trusted by all. The self-willed machines had long since given up the effort to have Troubot recycled; the protection of the Citizens was too potent.

Physically, Troubot was a wheeled cylinder with appendages. Most of the time Troubot did not move about, but plugged into the standard networks in order to do spot research or contact specific Citizens. It moved from Citizen White's residence only when directed to do so. During White's absences, Troubot became caretaker of the premises. Citizen White regarded it as indispensable, and others did not argue.

But Troubot was not exactly a machine. The records had been slightly modified by sophisticated means, so that, after the first few hours, no discovery was likely. Troubot was two entities: one a machine, the other an alien creature with human genes, and abilities few imagined. Troubot One was as described, but was not working under its original title. Troubot Two had taken its place, and had once been known as Nepe, Agape's child.

This secure masquerade was about to be placed in peril. For Nepe was naturally the first to appreciate the significance of the new pattern Purple had demanded.

In Phaze, the searching trio was about to close in on the werewolf Pack of Kurrelgyre. They had cross-checked the pups traveling between Packs, and discovered one that didn't fit. This was the one that was Flach.

Nepe had served the Citizens with absolute loyalty, excepting only the revelation of her identity. She had even assisted in their search for her, knowing it to be futile; they had never suspected that she could assume the form of a robot. In this manner she had been not only safe, but kept current on their searches in both frames. She had also been able to associate with her parents, so that she had not been nearly as lonely as she might have been. Indeed, she had come to understand a great deal more about their private life together than she had before, and in the process had learned more about sexuality than a child was normally told. She had compared notes with Flach, who had the input of wolf ways, and both had profited. But now she knew that the crisis was upon them again, as it had been when Flach sent her the "hide" message. Her hiding place was secure, but his was not—and the moment he was caught, she would be too, because of their linkage.

She paused a few minutes, considering. She dared not wait long before notifying Citizen Purple, but she had to decide her course of action first. She was older now than she had been, and vastly more experienced intellectually, but she knew she would have no chance to resist the Citizens if she were discovered. What should she do?

She had thought this through before, and decided on a risky effort. It seemed to her that its chances of success were at best even—but the consequences of inaction would guarantee the loss of their freedom. Now that the crisis had come, as she had known it would despite hoping for some reprieve, she saw no better alternative than that risky course.

She would have to save Flach from capture.

Nepe set her situation in order as well as she could, arranging things so that they could proceed mostly automatically. When she had adopted this machinelike form, she had also adopted machinelike ways; her mind emulated robotic circuitry. A simple directive could accomplish a fairly complicated task. She made sure that her body could function with minimum input, so that it would not betray her nature in her absence.

Then she put in a call to Troubot One, using an access code that only the two of them knew. Troubot answered immediately; he was Nepe's closest friend, and he knew he owed his consciousness to her. It had been her genius that had enabled him to hide while she emulated him and got him the placement with Citizen White. Once that was secure, they had exchanged places, and he had had an easy menial job. Later, when Nepe had to hide, she had taken his place again, and he had hidden. Since he was no longer the object of a search, that was easy to do; he simply merged with unwilled machines, intercepting their orders and performing their tasks himself. He had excellent adaptive ability, having been constructed as an all-purpose servitor. His flaw had been in the brain: it was out of tolerance on the upside. In short, he was too smart and too independent. But neither as smart nor as independent as Nepe!

"Troubot, I must do something dangerous," she informed him. "I will be of limited function for a while. You must watch me, and substitute for me if I get confused. There is great danger."

"Let me do this dangerous task for you!" he pleaded. "I love you, and would not let you be hurt."

"I love you too, Troubot." She knew how that could be, too, because her father used Uncle Mach's robot body in Proton. It was natural that she should emulate her mother, and love a machine, or the equivalent. It was hardly necessary to be in humanoid form in order to love! "But this thing I must do myself. Here is my update on current activities."

"I can readily handle these," he agreed. "But this danger—"

"I may be going somewhere," she explained. "Another mind may use my body. I fear it is not safe to tell you more. Just protect this one as you would me."

"That I shall do," he agreed. He sent a trace current that translated as emotion: concern, appreciation, loyalty.

"Thank you, Troubot," she replied, sending a similar surge.

Then she braced herself for the supreme effort. What she contem plated had never been done before, but she believed it was possible. It was the only way to do what had to be done, so it *had* to be possible!

When she was as ready as she could be, she did another new thing: she contacted Flach without using the cover of their fathers' contact. *Flach! Flach!*

His response was startled. *Nepe! There be no cover!*

This is an emergency, she returned. *They know where you are. They are closing in. You can't escape.*

We have had wind of their approach. I must try to get away! I have a plan. If they capture me, they'll make me betray thee, and then they'll have us both.

I know, Flach. But they are not going to be fooled. That's why I must save you. My hiding place is safe. We must exchange. You hide here; I will hide your body there.

But we can ne'er—

Yes we can! We are opposite selves. I know it!

But we be male and female!

Doesn't matter. My substance can assume either sex. Now do it, before they tune in and locate us this way.

Flach, realizing that crazy as this seemed, it was their only chance, agreed. *But first I must get to a private place, and warn my wolf-mates. They will help; they can be trusted.*

I hope so. Nepe knew the names of the wolves; he had told her of the oath-friendships when they occurred. She gave him time to do what he needed.

It turned out to be more complicated than they had thought. The oath-friends insisted on helping. They pointed out that it would be the next day before the Adept party arrived. They would go on a hunt, the four of them, and make their first Kill. That would be their pretext for ranging far from the Pack. When they were far enough away, they would make a break for it, and the Adepts would not be able to catch them. It would be dark, and the cover of night would help; the Adepts might even sleep through it.

Nepe had to agree that this was worth trying. If he could get free without having to exchange, it would save them a lot of trouble. She was afraid that the Adepts or the Citizens would tune in on their communications, but since they had never done this openly before, it might be that no one was checking now.

The wolves organized immediately. Kurrelgyre, pleased with their initiative, approved, and even suggested an appropriate region to hunt, where rabbits were plentiful this season. The four assumed wolf-forms and moved out together.

There were no communications for a time. Nepe knew that Flach was sparing her the dull details of a run through forest and fields, as well as protecting them both from discovery by keeping his contact limited. He would be in touch when something happened.

Just at dusk he called her. *Nepe! I made a kill! I got a rabbit, all by myself. Sirel got another!*

But you didn't go to make a kill! she protested.

I didn't expect *to make a kill!* he corrected her. *But it be the pretext, and it be a significant thing in wolven terms. Now Sirel and I can assume our third syllables, and can commit to our first mating, and take the fourth.*

Mating! Flach, you are too young!

Nay, wolves can do it sooner than human folk. It takes not, but be good experience. It would be abnormal for us to do it not as soon as possible. Of course the first mating be ne'er the one for later breeding; that partner be forbidden. It be a thing best arranged between oath-friends, which we be..

Nepe realized that Flach's main protection was in his similarity to the other wolves of the Pack. The longer he could act like a wolf while ranging farther from the Pack, the better chance he might have to get away. *Mate with her then, and get it over with!* she thought ungraciously.

Nay, we mate not actually now. She be not in heat; she be too young for that.

Then don't *mate with her! Just keep moving out!*

But we must needs commit. There be a ceremony. It must be done properly, so that the naming be legitimate.

Nepe was exasperated. Such a complication had never occurred to her, and in truth she was somewhat jealous of the manner his society allowed him to step into an adult emulation so young. But if there was any hope that this would enable him to win free on his own—

They went through their ceremony of Commitment. It was, it seemed, somewhat like a betrothal. When Sirel achieved her first heat, in perhaps two years, Barel would be the one she sought for her maiden mating. Other males would respect that, knowing she was pledged. Thus their initiation into full adult status would be mutual. Never again thereafter would they mate with each other; it would be a rite of passage, not a breeding or permanent association.

In due course the two other wolves were willing to bear witness that a Commitment had occurred. Flach could now adopt Si as his final syllable, and Sirel could adopt Ba as hers. Thus they were Barelsi and Sirelba, each with another syllable to be inserted third when their kills were recognized by the Pack. Oath-friends and first mates—it was a significant occasion for them both. Henceforth they would be considered borderline adult, though some leeway for growing would be allowed. In the frame of Proton, the equivalent would be called adolescence.

But we must needs carry our kills back to the Pack, Flach thought. *Otherwise—*

No! Nepe protested. *You must get far away!*

Then Flach saw a dragon flying, pursuing what appeared to be a great circle around the region where the Pack was camped. This was not normal behavior for a dragon; obviously it was acting as an agent for the Adepts. Any wolf who strayed too far would be a target of suspicion.

Nepe was ready to throw things at walls, but she had to concede that normal wolf behavior was in order. They had to head home to the Pack.

Darkness closed before they reached it. This was a decent pretext to halt and camp. Flach and Sirelba shared their rabbits with the other two, saving the pelts and skeletons for evidence. Then the four settled down to sleep.

But by morning the Adept party was at the wolf camp. Nepe learned this when Mach sent the message; they had moved quickly in order to prevent any wolves from departing. Flach could not return.

He explained this to the others. "Then we will help thee flee," Sirelba growled in wolf talk. "We will lead the pursuit astray so that thou canst get free."

But it would take more than that. Flach knew the powers of his father, and realized that no simple diversion would suffice. They would all four shortly be captive.

Now we must exchange, Nepe said with regret.

Now we must needs exchange, Flach agreed. *We shall assume human form, for I doubt thou canst be a wolf.*

Flach concentrated and sang a spell of exchange. Nepe simply willed herself into Phaze and into his body. They had never tried this before, but both knew how their fathers did it; they had tuned in on the patterns of magic and concentration many times, and knew them well. They imitated those patterns.

Nepe suffered vertigo. Then she stumbled and almost fell.

She was in human form, standing under a tree in the company of three other children of her age. All were clothed, and so was she; that started her, until she realized that it was the way of Phaze. One was a lovely dark-haired girl; another was a tawny-haired girl; and the third was a shaggy brown-haired boy. The first girl would be Sirelba, the second Terel, and the boy Forel.

"I am Nepe," she said as she recovered her equilibrium.

"We know," Sirelba said. "But we shall call thee Barelsi, that thy nature be not betrayed in speech. What be thy ruse for escape?"

Nepe gazed around, still awed by her success. This really *was* Phaze! "Are we private?"

"Aye. We be beyond the range of yon dragon, and we can sniff hostile magic when it intrudes. But we know not how long before the net closes. Needs must we act soon, ere the magic come."

Nepe knew that the three were oath-friends to Flach, and that they would never betray him. But she had a reservation. "You know that Flach—I mean Barelsi—was never one of your kind. Can your Oaths of Friendship be binding?"

"They be binding," the girl assured her. "Species matters not. Many o' this Pack be oath-friend to Neysa Unicorn."

"And your Commitment—how can it be honored if you help Barelsi get away, and he hides elsewhere and you never see him again?"

"I will wait till he come to me," Sirelba said simply. "An he can, he will come. An he can not, I will seek him."

"What if he is dead?"

"I will avenge him."

"As will we," Terel said. "As he would for us."

Nepe was impressed. "How do you feel about him? I mean, I know you made an oath, but you must have some private impressions."

"I love him," Sirelba said. "Ne'er could we be lifemates, because we be counted as from the same packlet; we must breed outside it. So I glean o' him what I can: first mating. An he die ere it be done, our other oath-friend Forel will do it. An I die, Terel will fill for me. But I would die for him regardless. He be the best male o' my generation I know, though he be not true wolf."

"But I am not he. What of me?"

"Thou dost be his other self. We help thee as we help him. Canst thou save his body from capture?"

"I hope so. But I will need your closest cooperation."

"Thou willst have it. What—"

Sirelba paused, and the other two reacted similarly. "The net!" Forel whispered.

"Stay close!" Nepe said. "I must do magic, and I've never done it before!" Then she chanted:

> *O Fog and O Smoke*
> *The curse o' Proton frame*
> *Pollution invoke*
> *That we may play a game!*

Immediately there was a stirring in the air, as of a storm forming. It was working! She had known it should, but feared it would not. There was no storm; instead it was more like a dust devil stirred up by a gust across a dry plain. The effect expanded rapidly, rising to cloud the sky and spreading to include the small group.

"Drop to the ground!" Nepe cried. "Breathe through the turf! Keep your eyes closed until it thins!" She made an example by flinging herself down and burrowing her face into the ground.

The others stood for a moment bemused. Then the swirling black vapors caught them, and they broke into paroxysms of coughing. Suddenly they understood: this was poison! They got down and sought the filtration of the natural soil, while the foul cloud washed over them.

It took some time for the awful fog to thin. Finally Nepe sat up. Her eyes were bleary and her breathing labored, but she could handle it, having known what to expect. "It will ease gradually," she gasped. "Now we must arrange our escape."

Forel roused himself. "But the net!" He coughed, then recovered. "They watch!"

She smiled. "Not any more. I made a spell of magic pollution; we experience only the peripheral effects."

"The what?"

She realized that young werewolves would not be exposed to the technical terms of Proton technology. "What we feel is at the edge, and is weak; what is at the center is strong, and that is the pollution— the smoke and fog—that obscures magic. I learned this spell from the Oracle, who put it out on general information at the behest of Citizen

Blue. That way I could learn it without giving away my hiding place. It seemed a pointless exercise at the time, and few people even noticed; Blue does crazy things every so often, like making public love in vats of green gelatin. I knew he hoped I would find use for it, and now I have. No magic net can spy on us now—not until the fog clears.''

Forel nodded, smiling. ''What makes us cough, gives the Adepts a real illness!''

''Close enough. Now under this cover we must act. They will be checking each creature who seeks to leave this region. I must be of a form they will not suspect.''

''But canst thou change forms as Barelsi could? He knew man, wolf, bat and 'corn, and in secret worked on others he dared not assume lest he be discovered. Likewise he dared not do magic, though he be talented in it.''

''He worked on ogre, dragon and harpy forms,'' she agreed. ''And cloud magic. He thought to infiltrate the enemy ranks, where they would not suspect. But he knew that the net would catch him in the change, so he didn't dare. But no, I can not change forms; my mother Agape was here once, and it took her a long time and much mischief to change forms. I know better than to try. The Adepts will check all creatures anyway, and know who is not natural. That was why Barelsi knew he was trapped.''

Sirelba had roused herself and become somewhat acclimatized to the choking environment. ''Harpy form? But he be male!''

''Perhaps you natural form changers are confined to the same sex. We are not sure that holds for Adept form changers. Barelsi wanted to try the harpy form and see whether it was possible. Now that we have exchanged minds, I believe it is possible, for I am a female mind in his body. Only the natural body is fixed; the others can be adapted for size and appearance, and I think sex would be one of the options. But that is not the point: had he so changed, the net would have caught the flare of magic, and the Adepts would have known.''

''Mayhap,'' Sirelba agreed, awed.

''Now, with the pollution spell, such form changes can not be accomplished. The enemy would have caught the flare of my spell, but its very nature quickly made that useless. The three of you must not try to resume your wolf forms; the spell would interfere, and you might get into serious trouble. So we must change our forms another way.''

''Another way?'' Terel asked, the last to rouse herself. Her eyes were streaming; the pollution was affecting her worse.

"Makeup. We need clay, or something similar. Something that can be molded, and will dry in place and keep its shape."

"There be fish-nest lining in the nearby stream," Forel said. "It be much like clay, and holds its shape, but ne'er dries out completely. It be flesh-colored. Would that do?"

"Excellent! We must go there immediately."

They led her to the stream, uncertain what she had in mind. The water was clear, and the pollution was less intense near it; Terel lay down beside it and found some relief.

"Now we must convert this body to female, and one of you girls to male," Nepe said, undressing.

"Bitches," Sirelba said.

"What?"

"We be bitches. Female wolves."

"Oh. Yes. Do you see the nature of this ruse?"

"They will catch and hold the males, not the bitches!" Sirelba exclaimed. "They will let these pass!"

"Yes. Unable to verify us magically, they will do it physically. Two males, two females—by the time they realize their error, I should be past their net." She frowned. "But there may be danger. When they learn that they have been deceived—"

"A wolf lives by danger," Forel said bravely, and the two bitches agreed. "We shall decoy them, and deceive them, and take the consequence. They can not be too cruel, for our Pack would react."

"The hair!" Sirelba exclaimed. "Thy hair be dark, like mine; thou canst not pass for Terel."

Nepe nodded. "Good point. You and I must exchange appearances."

They went to it. They packed fish-nest lining about their crotches, masking their genitals. Nepe's masculine appendage had to be folded down and covered, while Sirelba required an artificial appendage. Forel had great fun shaping it for her, to her embarrassment. Wolves were open about natural functions, but this reversal of roles was a new experience for the bitch.

"But watch out how thou pissest!" he said.

That made Nepe pause. "Can we make it possible? We may be many hours in these disguises. Something like that could ruin everything!"

They discussed it, and concluded that it was best to do it artfully. They poked a thin stick through the clay, and drew it out as the substance set. This left a channel, so that Sirelba would be able to urinate through it, carefully, if she had to. They made a similar channel in Nepe's clay, slanting from the tip of her penis to the appropriate site on the surface. "But watch out that thou dost not get a boner!" Forel warned.

Nepe wasn't sure what he meant, but a moment's reflection clarified the reference. It would be very awkward, perhaps even a fatal complication (one that would give her away), if her penis were to change its shape while the clay was on, and break out of its confinement. She understood that this could happen involuntarily; she hoped that this would not occur in the next few hours.

By the time the job was done, and the fish-clay had solidified, they were well into night. They were tired, but could not afford to rest. The escape had to be accomplished by dawn, because sunlight would dissipate the pollution spell.

They made hasty plans, then set out.

Forel went east, Terel went south, and Nepe and Sirelba went west. Since the Pack camp was north, they were fleeing it. They knew this would bring suspicion on them, but since they also knew that the Adepts were sure Flach was here, this made no difference.

They followed the major trails. There really wasn't much choice, when they were in a hurry, because traveling by night was dangerous anywhere else. The trails were cleared, so that they could readily sniff and hear lurking predators, and they could travel much more swiftly on them. Their human bodies were ill adapted to hurry through uncharted brush, but competent enough for the trails.

They knew that all the wolves would be heading in to the Pack for the assembly required by the Adepts. But the presence of the pollution fog would be signal enough of their attempt to escape. All the trails leading out from the origin of the cloud would be watched, probably by the Adept party, not trusting any other creatures to do the job. Three members, three escaping trails: one to each. The Robot Adept, whose travel magic would remain despite the fog, would take the others to two of the trails, and would guard the third himself.

It was in fact like a Proton Game, Nepe thought. She had to guess which trail was safest, and Flach's father Mach had to guess which one Nepe would choose. The odds favored her: she had two chances in three to be on the trail that the robot did not check. Because Mach would know her; he was too clever to be deceived by her ruse. If he intercepted her, she was lost. But if one of the others intercepted her, she could escape. Flach had been a werewolf for four years, and had the werewolf look and smell; Fleta would hardly know him now, and Tania would know him only by description. In a pressure situation, one of those two was liable to make a mistake. The odds might be two to one in favor of such an error.

Nepe understood the dynamics of chance, because it was integral to the Proton Game. Two chances in three of getting a foolable interceptor; two chances in three of fooling that person. That figured to four or five ninths of a chance to get free, depending on the system. About even. The odds overall were not ideal, but they were a lot better than what otherwise offered. That was the best she could do for Flach.

Now, as she hurried with Sirelba along the path, she contacted her other self. *Flach! Are you ready to exchange back?*

Aye! Anytime! This frame mystifies me!

Stay alert. Once I win free, you must return, because you can change forms as I can not.

As dawn approached, the fog was thinning; she knew she had to complete her ploy before day took over, because it depended on the presence of the fog that fuzzed out the magic of the others. The sooner the better, for this confrontation!

Then, abruptly, it came: a cloaked figure stood athwart the path. Which one was it?

"You know what to do," she said to Sirelba.

"Aye."

They slowed as they approached the figure. *It was Tania!* Nepe felt the thrill of incipient victory.

Then Sirelba broke from the path, scrambling through the rough brush, heedless of the scratches. Tania turned to face her. Nepe felt the surge of magic as the Evil Eye manifested. Sirelba stumbled and fell.

"Nay!" Nepe cried, running toward Tania. "Spare him, Adept! I love him! We be promised first mates!"

Tania walked toward the fallen figure.

Nepe pursued. "Take me instead, Adept! Whatever he has done, I will redeem! I beg thee!"

Tania turned and peered at Nepe. The woman's eyes in the dusk of the night seemed to glow. Suddenly Nepe understood the power of those eyes; they were seeing right through her!

Then the woman resumed her focus on Sirelba. She squatted beside the body and poked at the clothing. "Aye, this be the male, and dark," she murmured. "This be he, at last."

"Nay!" Nepe cried, and such was her animation in the tension of this role that she really was crying; tears were flowing. "He be nothing to thee! Oh, let him go, Adept!"

Sirelba stirred. "Get away from here, girl," she rasped. "You will only antagonize her."

"Good advice, bitch," Tania said.

Nepe backed away. "Ne'er will I forget thee, my Promised!"

Then, feigning reluctance, she turned and walked on along the path. The final ploy had worked. *She had gotten past!*

When she was safely out of sight, she thought to her other self again. *Flach! Now exchange—and get far gone from here!*

They made their joint effort, and again Nepe felt the disorientation. Then she was back in her robotic body in Proton.

She had done it! She had exchanged, and used her one spell, and her ability to act like what she was, a girl, and had sprung Flach from the trap! Meanwhile Flach had been secure here, unsuspected.

Suddenly she was very tired. She slept.

Some time later Flach called: *Nepe, our fathers be communicating now; we can talk.*

Where are you? she asked joyfully.

With Phoebe Harpy. She be independent now, though her Flock aligns with the Adepts, and will betray me not. I be in harpy form. They will ne'er look for me here!

I'm so glad, Flach! But what of Sirelba? She decoyed for us—

I could check not directly, but Phoebe says Mach came and knew on the instant her nature, yet oddly showed no ire. They let her go unharmed. I be glad, for she—

A thrill of alarm ran through her. *No ire? Flach, I fear—*

Then he caught on. *A trap for thee! O, Nepe, if this be so—*

Cease contact! she thought.

He cut off immediately. Now Nepe had to make a decision: should she sit tight, hoping the Adepts and Citizens had not used her contact with Flach to trace her, or should she make a break for it? She had several alternative hideouts; she could disappear as Troubot and assume a new and quite different form. But if they were closing in on her, she would not have time, and anyway, she did not want the real Troubot to take the brunt of their wrath. They might even be waiting for just such a break, to confirm her identity.

She and Flach had gone into hiding because they wanted to help Citizen Blue and the Adept Stile, rather than the Contrary Citizens and the Adverse Adepts. They had learned how to communicate with each other, but could not explain to their grandfathers how they did it. Their communication was more versatile than that of their fathers, because they did not have to overlap geographically in their frames.

That ability would be invaluable to either side, but more so to Blue and Stile, because those two did not communicate at all.

Blue believed that if the Oracle could analyze how Nepe did it, it could give the key to others—but if Grandpa Blue had taken Nepe to the Oracle, the Citizens would have snooped and learned everything. So they hadn't risked it. But now that her ability was known, she had nothing to lose by going to the Oracle—except that the Citizens would never allow it, because it would help mainly Citizen Blue. What a complicated mess!

If only she had been able to remain hidden longer, until the grandfathers found some way to get her together with the Oracle secretly! Maybe, if she got through this without being discovered, that would happen.

She decided to sit tight. But her mind was whirling. Suppose Tania had recognized her, and deliberately let her go? Then told Mach, who could have used his magic to trace Flach's route—and let him seem to escape so that he would give away any other accomplices he had, and in the end contact her in Proton *while Mach was listening?* While he was only pretending to be communicating with Bane, actually attuned to Flach's communication with her, Nepe? Of course he would not be angry about Sirelba; all was going according to his plan! Had they caught Nepe at the edge of the fog, she would have refused to contact or exchange with Flach, and he would have remained safely hidden.

The longer she thought about it, the more certain she became that all was lost. Thus she was hardly even surprised when she received a call from Bane:

"Nepe, we have you spotted. Please resume your natural form and return to our custody; we shall not harm you."

It was over. They *had* located her. She would not be able to help Grandpa Blue after all.

She melted. The metal-hard façade of her four-year form dissolved. This was necessary for her to resume her human form—but it was also her way of collapsing in grief.

7 : Neysa

Neysa came again to take the boy, four years after the last time. She trotted up to the Red Demesnes just as if nothing had changed, and Flach was waiting for her, Mach standing behind him. But the boy had changed; he was eight years old instead of four, healthy with his years of outdoor living among the wolves. He looked wonderful.

Flach stepped forward to meet her—and his face clouded over with mixed emotions. "O, Granddam, how glad I be to see thee again!" he cried, and hugged her neck; but her falling mane concealed the tears on his face.

She knew why. He *was* glad to see her—but also sad to be captive. For there was no doubt of his status now; he was in the power of the Adverse Adepts, and they would not let him get away again. Neysa's own complicity in his prior break was of course known, but she could not be touched because she was of Stile's camp and expected to do his bidding. But this time she would deliver the boy to Stile; the ploy of his hiding was over.

Flach mounted, and she set off, not deigning to acknowledge the rovot. She followed the same route she had the last time, knowing what the boy would want.

She felt his mood lighten as they approached the Werewolf Demesnes. He would get to see his friends in passing. He could not remain, but at least they could exchange greetings.

The main portion of the Pack was not-so-mysteriously absent, but three young wolves were present. "O, Granddam, may I?" Flach begged.

Neysa halted by the three, and Flach dismounted. He assumed wolf form, and sniffed noses and tail with each of the three in turn. Then all assumed human form, and Flach embraced each. "O Forel!" he exclaimed to the brown-haired boy. "O Terel!" to the tawny-haired girl. And, last, to the pretty black-haired girl, "O Sirelba! Thou didst do so well for me!"

"It be Sirelmoba now, my Promised," she informed him gently, hugging him closely. "They granted me my Kill."

"Would I had been there, to cheer for thee and gain mine own name!"

"They gave it thee," she said. "Barelmosi."

"They gave it me?" he asked, amazed. "But they knew then I be not o' the Pack!"

"They knew then thou wast grandpup o' Neysa—and Stile."

"But there was none to growl for me!"

"There were three to growl for thee."

Flach hugged her more tightly, his tears flowing again. "Must needs I go now, but I will see thee when I can, and when—"

"Aye," she agreed.

Then the three resumed wolf form, and Flach remounted Neysa. He could have run along beside her in wolf form, but it was important that his status be clear, for the watching Adepts.

Neysa resumed her motion. Flach waved to the standing wolves, then sought her mane again for his tears.

Neysa trotted on, still following the route they had taken, sharing the boy's nostalgia. It had been a fine ploy they had made, and it had won the Adept Stile four more years of parity, and Citizen Blue the same in Proton. It had also given Flach excellent experience in another culture. She would have preferred that he obtain it among the unicorns, but of course that would have been too obvious. Certainly Kurrelgyre's Pack was a worthy alternative. She remembered when she had met the werewolf for the first time, at the then-palace of the Oracle; they had almost come to combat, being hereditary enemies. But Stile had made peace between them, and later made them oath-friends, and that was part of the good he had brought to Phaze.

She loved Stile, of course. She always had, since he had mastered her and freed her. No other human man could have done the first, no other would have done the second. She had done what she could for him, becoming his transport, his guardian and his lover until he went to the Lady Blue. Human beings had always taken animal lovers, but never animal spouses; it was the way of it. Until Fleta—

She put a firm hoof on that thought. She had not, could not approve; yet the seemingly impossible had happened, and here was Flach, representing the union of the lines of man with unicorn, and of the lines of Neysa and Stile. It seemed likely that in time the boy would mate with a werewolf, and thereby include that line also in the unity. Thus in Phaze would occur what was occurring in Proton: the integration of the major elements of the frame.

She could not support this, but now, knowing Flach and knowing of his other self Nepe, who had demonstrated singular verve and competence, she could not condemn it either. Perhaps the old, isolated ways would have to go. Perhaps that was better. Certainly she supported Stile, and if he believed this was the way to go, he must be right. But he had not supported it before; he, like she, had opposed the marriage between species. And he, like she, had come to accept the result, because his objection had been rooted not in any antipathy to mingling (as she knew!) but in his need for an heir to the Blue Demesnes. The younger generation had proven him wrong, and now he supported the union, but could not undo the damage done by his former opposition.

Neysa, similarly, was left with little or no tail to swish against this particular fly. She had turned her horn against her filly Fleta when Fleta insisted on making an open, permanent liaison with the golem who occupied Bane's body. Now that golem had become the Rovot Adept, with more magical power than any other, and had sired Flach. It was not the way of the unicorn to admit error and reverse position. She had done it only when coerced by directive of the Herd Stallion. There were none to coerce her similarly now. She was locked into a position of increasing social founder.

They reached the place where the boy had urinated, setting up his ruse. She stopped, and he dismounted and went through the motions; in this manner he showed his unicorn heritage, his need to re-experience prior actions, to assume his new orientation. They paused where she had helped the pups escape the dragon. Those pups were now secure in their new Pack.

Beyond this region, she had carried the golem instead of the boy. So effective had this exchange been that she had not realized at what point it had occurred—and that had been part of the ploy. If she hadn't known, how could anyone else know? So Flach had escaped, and it had taken the Adepts four years to recover him.

They stopped before reaching the Herd Demesnes. Neysa was no longer young, and prolonged running was not as easy for her as it had been. She needed time to rest and graze. So Flach dismounted in a broad meadow, giving her the remaining two hours of the day.

Then he surprised her. He assumed his unicorn form, and grazed with her. He was not yet grown, but was a fine figure of a colt, with a black coat like hers, and blue socks. He played a note on his horn, inviting her to join him. His horn's sound most resembled what the human folk called a recorder, or perhaps a wooden flute, in the alto range. Four years ago it had been soprano; as he grew and matured, it would descend to the tenor range. His tone was neither full nor distinctive, and his key was uncertain—but of course he had not assumed this form in four years, and had become inexperienced in it.

She sounded her own horn, with its harmonica flavor, setting him straight on the key. Then, as they grazed, they played, and his sound became attuned, until in due course it was fair rather than poor. She showed him some of the nuances of melody, and taught him simple harmony. The resulting duet would never be competitive in the Unilympics, but it was a nice enough start. She was quite pleased, for the sound and for the effort he was making. She remembered decades back, when she had taught Fleta similarly, and Fleta had developed her unique double-note technique on her pan-pipe horn, and—

Down came the hoof again. Those memories should be expunged! Fleta had done the unpardonable.

Yet, glancing sidelong at Flach grazing beside her, she wished again that it was otherwise.

They grazed on into the night, and it was very satisfying. The creatures of the night came out, the mice and owls and goblins, and spied the unicorns and remained moderately clear. Goblins could be bad when roused and organized, but these were merely foraging individually, avoiding trouble. Just the same, she kept an ear on them; one could never be quite sure about goblins.

They slept on their feet, still grazing. In the morning they were rested and fed; it had been a good night.

Flach assumed human form. "Let me take a turn, Granddam! Let me carry thee!"

She assumed her woman form. "Thou be not yet grown, Flach," she said. "Thou must not carry a load; it would warp thy limbs."

"Not if thou wast in thy firefly form," he countered.

She hoped she would not regret this, but she did want him to get experience. She could resume her natural form if any threat manifested. Actually, the Adepts were watching; they would act if they thought it necessary. She wanted to keep them out of this, but it was a kind of reassurance.

She assumed firefly form, hovering in the air. He became a unicorn again. She flew to his head and perched between his ears, near his horn, clinging to his forelock.

He started off, going west, toward the Herd. At first his gait was irregular, but gradually he got it into shape and his stride became steadier. Practice would improve this, too.

But soon a dragon appeared, flying up from the south. It spied what it took to be a young, inexperienced unicorn, and came in for some fun and perhaps a meal. It was not large, and would have been no threat to Neysa herself, but she wasn't sure about Flach. She moved, getting ready to take off, so she could get clear of him and assume her natural form.

"Nay, Granddam!" he protested in passable horn talk. "Let me handle it."

He had big ambitions! If he was no better using his horn for combat than he had been using it for music at first, that dragon would make short work of him. Still, she could act at the last moment if she had to. She remained in place.

The dragon circled once, making sure that this young unicorn was as isolated as he looked. Then it lined up for a strafing run, its fire building.

Flach played a strange melody on his horn, fouling it up with attempted horn talk. Then she realized that he was trying to make magic. As a human being, he could do magic, and he had been learning spells four years before. Surely he had continued to think about them during his long hiatus as a werewolf. Now he had a chance to use what he had devised. But to attempt it in 'corn form—that was odd indeed! Could it possibly work?

A cloud formed above them. It expanded rapidly, pulsing with sickly colors. From this angle it was hard to tell exactly what its whole shape was, but it seemed rather like—yes, a floating human head! It had a wild tangle of yellow hair that fuzzed into invisible vapor, and two great red eyes, a bulbous nose, and a huge purple mouth-orifice with enormous buck teeth.

The dragon saw this apparition, and veered aside. Had something come to help the unicorn? But it circled back, realizing that there was no solidity to the thing. What was not solid could not hurt, and could be ignored.

The dragon came in again, and this time there was no doubt it meant business. The fire was starting to come; in a moment things would be very hot here! Neysa spread her wings.

"Nay, Granddam!" Flach protested. "I be ready!"

Quite nervous now, she nevertheless remained clinging to his forelock. What did this foolish child have in mind?

Flach blew another horn-talk melody. The apparition's grotesque mouth pursed. From it spurted a gush of green liquid. The stuff hurtled toward the dragon. Before the creature could react, the jet splashed into its snoot.

The dragon let out a growl of surprise and dismay. It wavered crazily in the air, abruptly clawing at its head. The green stuff was not splattering free; it was clinging gelatinously, cutting off the dragon's breath. Its fire, stifled, whooshed out without direction.

And the liquid clung even to the fire, forming huge bubbles. The dragon inhaled—and the green goo was sucked in too, causing it to choke.

Neysa could wait no longer. She spread her wings, took off, flew to the side, and resumed unicorn form. "What be that green?" she demanded in horn talk.

"Lime gelatin," Flach replied. "Nepe told me o' it. It be used in Proton to wrestle in, or to mate in, or as a Consequence when someone loses a wager."

"Gelatin?" It was not possible to be as specific in horn talk as in human talk; she did not know of this substance.

"Well, it be not exactly that, but an imitation that be yet gunkier," he honked with childish relish. "It clings awfully, and makes bubbles, and just gets worse as it dries. She says it be water-soluble, so washes off readily, but methinks the dragon will think not to wash."

Indeed, the dragon was not thinking of water at all. It veered almost into a tree, barely dodged it, and flew up, still scratching at its nose. Bubbles of gelatin were all around it, making it look even more grotesque than the fog-face.

Neysa was not much for practical jokes, but she had to admit that this was a rare prank to play on a dragon. The boy was a child; he had done a childish thing. But it had been effective, and that was what counted.

All the same, she decided to resume the regular mode of travel. Flach returned to human form, and she carried him on to the Herd.

Flach grew pensive again as they approached the Blue Demesnes. He had been joyful only when squelching the dragon, Neysa realized in retrospect; at other times he had seemed subdued or preoccupied. She had assumed this was because of his loss of freedom. He had, she judged, really liked being among the werewolves, and was more than somewhat smitten with the dark-furred bitch whom he had Promised. Naturally it was depressing to leave those friends who had supported him so loyally. But he liked Neysa and his human grandparents too;

that was obvious. Why, then, did he seem reluctant to join Stile and the Lady Blue?

Well, perhaps he felt guilty for hiding, these four years. It had been a joint conspiracy, but he had kept his location secret from Stile as well as the Adverse Adepts. Yet he had had to do that; they all knew that. Any contact with Stile would have been intercepted by the Adepts, and led them to him. So that could not be it.

They arrived, and Flach greeted his grandparents with genuine enthusiasm. Neysa, assuming human form to enter the castle, thought she had been mistaken; Flach was after all glad to be here, despite his changed status.

The first evening all seemed well. The boy told of his experience among the wolves, and of the adventure with the dragon. Stile laughed aloud, remembering the way of the frame of Proton, and the Lady smiled. Then they had a good meal, and Flach confessed to being tired, and he went early to bed, attended by the Lady.

Now Stile looked grim. "He's changed," he said.

"Aye." Neysa had never been much for human speech, but this much had to be said.

"But in four years, that is to be expected. He has grown, and learned much, and recently been separated from those he has come to know and love as well as he loves us."

"Aye."

"I checked him for enchantments. There are none on him. The Adepts appear to be abiding by the rules."

Neysa nodded. She was perversely glad that he had noted it too; it meant she hadn't imagined the problem. Indeed, perhaps it was as he supposed, merely the effect of separation and aging.

The Lady returned. "There be a geis on him," she said.

"Nay," Stile said. "No magic."

"There be a geis," she repeated.

It made sense to Neysa. A geis was a kind of obligation, imposed either magically or by honor. It restricted a person in some way, so that he could not perform with his normal freedom.

"He be prisoner now," Stile said. "We all be glad to have him, and will treat him well, but this be not o' his choice or ours. Also, the Adepts have access to the Book o' Magic while he be here, so be gaining power after the years o' impasse. That could depress him."

"Mayhap," the Lady agreed noncommittally.

They retired, and Neysa went out to graze; that was always her preference for the night. But her thoughts continued to turn on the boy. The Lady was right: something was wrong. Perhaps it was only his abrupt change of situation. Perhaps it was more.

In the morning Stile talked with Flach privately. Later he turned the boy over to Neysa for a ride around the premises. This was of course worthwhile, but Neysa knew that Stile wished to talk privately with the Lady. Something was certainly wrong.

Later, the Lady told Neysa the problem: "Stile meant to have Flach commune with his other self in Proton, to establish a dialogue and initiate an exchange o' information. In this manner may we keep pace with the Adepts and Citizens, that we maintain our position. But Flach says he can not. It seems the girl be not available."

Neysa considered that. She had understood that Flach and Nepe could communicate with each other across the frames regardless of their geographic positions. They had demonstrated this, when trying to escape the Adept cordon around the Pack. How could they be unable to do this now?

She mulled it over the following night, consciously or unconsciously, but came to no reasonable conclusion. She was sure that Nepe in the other frame would be treated well, as Flach was in this one, because the agreement was the same there: while she visited her grandparents, the Citizens had access to the Oracle. The Adepts and Citizens had waited for four years to restore this arrangement; they would not do anything to interrupt it again.

Unless Nepe had somehow managed to hide again—even from Flach? How could she do that?

As dawn brightened, she had an answer. by going to another scientific planet! Flach could reach her anywhere on Proton, but surely not away from there. She could have somehow sneaked away on one of their ships of space! That would mean that the enemy was not making progress after all, because Citizen Blue would not let them near the Oracle unless they produced Nepe. And Flach, if he knew where she was, would not tell, for that would give her away. If he *could* contact her where she hid, he would not, because the Adepts would be watching for that magic, and find her as they had before, through him.

She was so excited that she galloped into the castle, and changed to woman form, panting. "Stile! Stile!"

But it was the boy who was already up. "They be late from their chamber," he said. "Do folk their age still mate?"

"Human folk, aye, an they wish," she agreed. "They oft regard it as entertainment." How well she remembered! She did not want to speak of her revelation directly to the boy; he might have to deny it, and that would be very awkward. She would have to wait until Stile was alone.

She offered Flach another ride outside, instead. He countered with the suggestion that they run together. They did so, trotting across the meadows. Then they changed to their winged forms, she a firefly, he a bat, and flew. Then he became a harpy, astonishing her; she had heard he could do it, but was amazed at the reality. *It was a female form.*

"Aye," he screeched in harpy fashion. "There be not those barriers we thought 'tween us. I can be female an I choose, and Nepe can exchange and be male. But we do it not 'cept at need; it be not comfortable."

He had mentioned Nepe. Could she follow up on this, and verify her conjecture? She assumed woman form. "Then had thou left her in Phaze, she could have been the female harpy, and been comfortable."

"Nay. She knows not how to change form."

"Mayhap thou could exchange again, and we could teach her."

"Mayhap!" he agreed brightly. Then abruptly he sobered, and said no more on the subject.

Now she was sure: it was because he could not exchange without giving away Nepe's hiding place. She did not pursue the subject. She resumed her natural form, and he became a wolf, and they romped on back to the castle.

Later in the day, when the Lady was showing Flach how she made cookies, in timeless grandmotherly fashion, and he was showing her how he could lick the bowl clean, in equally timeless grandchild fashion, Neysa had a chance to talk with Stile.

"So he dare not," she concluded.

Stile nodded. "I think thou hast figured it, mare! That be a relief to me, for it means the impasse remains."

The rest of the visiting period passed amicably enough. Every day the boy did new things with his grandparents, learning spells and new games, and romped in the meadows with Neysa in one form or another. Flach brightened somewhat, discovering that they were not pushing him to contact Nepe, and it was almost as it had been in the old days.

Stile and Flach spent many hours playing chess. It seemed the boy had good aptitude, which was perhaps not surprising, considering that Stile remained the Phaze champion, and Fleta was now a ranking

player; it was in Flach's ancestry. They even played through some of
the games Stile had had with Icebeard. Stile had played the snow demon to twenty-three consecutive draws, then won one, ending their
private tournament. But the following year they had played again, and
after fifteen draws the demon had won one. It had become a regular
thing; they were delightfully evenly matched. Flach was evidently able
to appreciate the pretty nuances of the moves in a way that Neysa
could not.

Then, toward the end of the stay, Bane visited. Neysa was grazing
nearby as Stile came out to meet him. Because Bane served the other
side, by common consent they met beyond the castle, in nominally
neutral territory. "How be the boy?" he inquired.

"Somewhat subdued," Stile replied.

"To be expected, so soon after being taken from the Pack. His oath-
friends there be similarly subdued, I understand."

"How goes thy life in Proton?"

"Well enough, between bouts with the Book and Oracle."

Neysa kept her ears unperked, so as not to give away her interest.
How could they be working with the Book and Oracle?

"And how be little Nepe?" Stile inquired smoothly.

"Subdued. Thou knowest that they wished to serve thee, not the
others."

"Aye. But an she be well, as be Flach, thou needst have no concern."

"She be well, far as we can tell. She be with Blue now, o' course.
But one thing be odd: we understand that she contacts not Flach.
Methought thou wouldst be using them as Mach and I be used, to
keep the pace."

"All in good time," Stile said. "They be young, and have four years
to forget."

Bane nodded. "Surely so." Yet he seemed surprised. "I came to ask
thee to send Flach directly to Translucent's isle, since I lack Mach's
facility in transport."

"Readily done, an Neysa be granted entry."

"She be." Bane gave him a token, glanced across at Neysa, and
waved. She nodded, and continued grazing as if not really interested.

Bane departed. Immediately Neysa approached Stile. "Oath-friend,
let us travel a bit," Stile said, mounting her. She was glad to accede.

"Methinks our conjecture was mistaken," Stile said when they were
far enough away from the castle to avoid any risk of being overheard.
It was Stile's belief that it was the castle the Adepts snooped on, rather

than himself, now that things were quiet. "I wish not to alarm the Lady, but must know. Canst discover it for me?"

Neysa made an affirmative honk. She would certainly try!

She started early, so as to have time to talk to Flach if the occasion seemed propitious. This time she bore due west, toward the West Pole and the Translucent Demesnes. Flach was quiet, seeming not enthusiastic about returning to his dam.

They had thought that Nepe had escaped, so that Flach could not communicate with her without giving away her hiding place. Now they knew this was not the case. Why, then, was he reticent? It almost seemed as if he did not want to help his grandfather, and she knew that wasn't it. Yet she couldn't just ask; he would have told Stile if he intended to, and had to have reason for his silence. Also, the Adepts would be watching them now, making sure the boy was delivered; they would overhear anything said.

They came to the Lattice: the great pattern of cracks in the ground. She resented the founder spell the lattice demons had hit her with the last time she was here, but she could not do much about it unless the demons came to the surface.

And there was a demon head poking up! With a half-glad snort of challenge she lowered her horn and charged. The demon disappeared, hiding in the crevice, and she passed over without contact. She had expected this; still, it was satisfying.

"Slay them!" Flach cried, taking an interest.

More heads appeared. She still had the worst of the Lattice to traverse; were they going to try for her? She knew that her enemies the Adverse Adepts would never allow them to capture her, because she was on their business; still, she preferred to handle this nuisance herself. She picked up speed.

"Let me, Granddam!" Flach begged.

He had done well enough against the dragon, and perhaps this would make him say something. There was nothing like shared adventure to make folk talk. She made a honk of affirmation, coming to a halt on one of the Lattice plateaus.

He singsonged something. Another cloud appeared, with a grotesque face; he seemed to be partial to those, or perhaps it was the shape his magic was assuming. The demons gazed up at the cloud, distrusting it, but it seemed harmless, and after a moment they resumed their closure about Neysa.

Flach sang again. The cloud developed a nether aperture, from which a blob dropped.

"Get out, Granddam!" he cried.

Neysa bolted. The demons in front of her ducked down, but those at the sides closed in, trying to grab at her as she passed.

There was a sickly-sounding whoosh! Then the sound of coughing and choking from the bowels of the Lattice. Then the demons clambered out, not to attack Neysa, but to flee. What was this?

She slowed, curious about this inexplicable turnabout. "Don't stop, Granddam!" Flach exclaimed.

"Why?" she asked in horn talk.

"Because I dropped a stink bomb on them!"

Then the spreading vapor caught up with them. Neysa choked; it was the most putrid stench she had ever whiffed—and this was just the edge of it.

She leaped forward, escaping the miasma. No wonder the demons were fleeing; it must be intense down in the crevices! Trust the child to come up with another childish—but effective!—ploy.

Well, she really could not blame him. She had given him leave, and certainly the demons deserved it. In fact, it seemed a fitting retribution for that founder spell!

They readily won clear of the Lattice; the demons paid no further attention to them. She came to the regular field and forest, and resumed her normal trot.

"Thou hast become quite a little Adept," she remarked in horn talk.

"I had time to think of good spells," he said. "It was great, being with the Pack, but time there was." His mood had evidently lightened.

"Be it similar with Nepe?"

"Aye. She be one clever girl."

She hoped he would amplify, but he did not. Once again, she had been unable to discover his secret.

They stopped for the night at the foot of rolling hills. Flach assumed unicorn form again, and grazed with her as before.

So it went, on the long trip to the coast. Everything seemed normal with the boy, except his connection with Nepe. The secret remained undivulged. It was enough to make her horn go sour.

They reached the west coast. Flach held the token Bane had brought them, and Neysa strode into the sea. She had never been here before, and would not be very much disappointed if the charm did not work, so that they could not proceed farther. After all, this was not the neutral territory of the Red Demesnes; this was the enemy Translucent

Demesnes. Also, this was where Fleta was, and Neysa wasn't speaking to her filly. The encounter was bound to be awkward.

But the charm worked perfectly. The water closed over their heads, and seemed almost like air; they could breathe normally. Neysa picked her way through the seaweed and shells, and found a path. She followed this on down, and it broadened, becoming a satisfactory trail from which obstacles had been cleared. This gave her the chance to look around as she progressed.

It was impressive. Fish swam nearby, seeming from this vantage to be flying without wings. Seaweed sprouted profusely, reaching for the surface, forming brushlike patches. They passed a coral reef, where the growths were intricate and flowerlike, the blooms opening and closing in the slight current.

A big fish approached, swimming with beautiful ease. Neysa recognized its type by the fin on the back: a shark! She honked warning and readied her horn, uncertain how well she could do in this strange environment. But the fish shied away from the path; evidently it was not allowed to molest legitimate travelers.

The terrain changed, becoming somehow archaic. The vegetation and swimming forms in this region were strange. Neysa made a mild honk of surprise.

"Oh, sure," Flach said nonchalantly. "It's the Ordovician period, three or four hundred million years ago, I forget which, with some neat creatures. See, there be a trilobite—and there be a giant nautiloid! The one with the shell like a 'corn's horn!"

Neysa saw the trilobite. Its shell was indeed like a unicorn's horn, and she liked it better for that. The shell made its tentacled forepart seem less alien.

They came to a rise in the strange realm. "This be the isle!" Flach exclaimed joyfully. He slid off her back and charged ahead, plunging through a kind of curtain in the water. Neysa followed, and found herself indeed on an isle—a dry region within a giant bubble under the sea.

Flach flung herself into the arms of a young woman. That would be Fleta, his dam, Neysa's filly; Neysa had not seen her in eight years, and really did not care to look now. Instead she gazed around the rest of the isle.

Another young woman stood there. She was in a tan cloak, and her hair and eyes were tan. Tania, sister of the new Tan Adept. What was she doing here?

Tania did not wait to be introduced. "I like thee no better than thou likest me, old mare," she snapped. "Look not down thy nose at me, lest thou see what pleases thee not."

Neysa felt the old heat rising. She was not about to take any sneer from this arrogant woman! She brought down her horn.

"Nay, Granddam!" Flach called, spotting this developing quarrel. "Condemn her not; she let me escape!"

What? Neysa assumed woman form. "She tried to capture thee!" she said.

"But they think I tried not hard enough," Tania said. "So I be on duty here, to see that Fleta escapes not."

"But I be not prisoner!" Fleta protested. "And Neysa, my dam hast come at last to make amend?"

Neysa turned away from her.

"Thou hypocrite!" Tania screamed at her, her sinister eyes seeming to glow. "Comest all the way here to slight thy foal again?"

That did it. Neysa turned slowly to face Tania.

"Nay!" Flach cried. "This be an isle o' peace! No fighting!"

"It be beyond such caution," Neysa said grimly.

"Then make it words only!" he said. "No Eye, no horn!"

Neysa was not pleased with this notion, and Tania seemed no better satisfied. But the child was insistent. "An there be bloodshed here, Translucent will come, and we know not what will happen then! Let me make a spell o' containment, that thy words spread not beyond thyselves, and ye two settle thus."

There was something about his urgency, which bordered on desperation, that made Neysa pause. The boy was bright, and talented, and had some secret she had to fathom. That caused her to go along with his foolish wish. "No horn," she agreed.

"No Eye," Tania agreed, as grudgingly.

Flach singsonged something. Another cloud formed, but this one had no face. It expanded to take in Tania and herself, a bubble within the larger bubble of the isle.

Neysa wasted no time in pressing the attack. Words were not her preferred medium, but she could use them when she had to. "Thou, who didst think to capture Flach, and now be here to keep his dam here, dost accuse *me* o' hypocrisy? Thou, who didst spend four years pursuing him—and Bane?"

Tania gestured wildly, as if reacting in fury. But her words were oddly quiet. "Aye, mare. Listen to me now, for we have but little time, and there be danger. I sought the child that my side might gain the balance o' power. I sought Bane that I might bind him more firmly to our side, an he think to drift. But I lost the ploy; he loves me not, yet I love him."

"Thou—?" Neysa began, amazed.

"When I knew we had cornered the lad at last, and it came upon me to intercept him, I tried to let him go. I looked him in the eye, and knew him though he was cleverly masked as female. I stunned the figure made up to be male, thinking it were reasonable to fall for this ruse, that none could blame me. I let Flach go. But the Adepts saw through the ruse, both his and mine, and now I be confined here, nominally a guard. Canst believe that, mare?"

This was so completely different from her expectation that Neysa could hardly speak. "Why shouldst thou—?"

"Let him go?" Tania smiled ruefully. "Because it were the only way I could continue to be with Bane, an the search went on. I am descended to that level, I would be with him on any pretext, though I know he will ne'er love me."

Neysa gazed at her unbelievingly. Why should this woman make such a demeaning confession?

Tania held out her hand. "Touch me with thy horn, and verify."

Neysa bowed her forehead, touching the horn-button to the hand. The touch was true; the woman was speaking truth.

"Now believe this too," Tania continued, drawing back and waggling her finger as if making a savage point. "There be a geis o' silence on Flach, imposed by Purple. Translucent liked it not, but came so close to losing the lad that Purple gained leverage and imposed this. Flach dare not commune with Nepe in the other frame, lest his dam and her alien mother be killed. In this way our side gains power and thy side does not."

"The geis!" Neysa exclaimed.

"Now have I told thee. Now have I truly betrayed my side. An thou wishest to see me die, thou has but to tell o' this, mare."

"But why? Why dost thou do this thing?"

"When I came to love Bane, I came also to assume some o' his values, strange though they be. Now I be friend to Fleta. I would not see her die, or Agape in Proton. Or kept prisoner till my side wins, and then needed not more, and die anyway."

"But an that happened, thou wouldst have clear access to Bane!"

"Aye. But now I would take him not that way. This be the measure o' my fall."

"But—"

"Enough, mare; the spell dissipates. Now it be in thy hands. Fleta knows not."

Indeed, the little bubble was fading out; their privacy of vituperation was gone. Tania turned away as if smoldering; Neysa stood amazed.

Fleta and Flach were looking at her, as if trying to judge the outcome of the encounter. What was she to do?

She had to get away from here! Now she knew what was wrong with the boy—and knew why he had pushed her into the encounter with Tania. He had known Tania would tell what he could not, for he was watched as she was not. The watching Adepts would not have been concerned about the quarrel between Neysa and Tania; that was peripheral. She must not give away its true nature.

She had to hide what had happened. But how? She knew her life would not last long, if the Adepts realized what she had learned. She would have an accident on the way back, or she would die, seemingly of age. The Adepts were not bound by scruples—not the Purple Adept.

Then she realized what she had to do. But she had to hide it from whoever observed, by making a diversion. She had to provide some other seeming effect of her encounter with Tania.

She walked toward Fleta. "An the wicked Adept woman be friend to thee, can I be less?" She opened her arms.

"O my dam!" Fleta cried, and flung herself forward. They met in a solid embrace, Fleta's tears flowing. "O my Dam! Thou hast forgiven me at last!"

"There be naught to forgive," Neysa said, and realized it was true as her own tears flowed. By this unexpected device she had been brought to do what she should have done eight years before, and accepted her foal's decision. The barriers between species were breaking down, with Fleta's union with Mach, and Bane's with the alien female, and Suchevane's with Trool the Troll. Neysa knew she should have been the first, not the last, to accept this new reality.

Then, not daring to dally here, she bid farewell to Flach, resumed her natural form, and set off for the realm of the land. Tania still faced defiantly away. Neysa ignored her, as was proper in the circumstance.

Would she make it safely back? At this stage she didn't know. The Adepts would not dispatch her without reason, because it would be a pointless act of provocation at a time when they wanted things quiet. But if they suspected . . .

Then, just as she was about to pass through the bubble wall, she realized that she shouldn't risk it. She had to act now, to ensure that the situation changed. Going back and telling Stile would take too long and was too risky. There was a much faster and more certain way—one that Flach should have thought of himself, had he not been cowed by the pressure of the situation.

She changed back to woman form. "I forgot the charm!" she exclaimed. Indeed she had; she would need it to pass through the water without drowning.

"I have it!" Flach cried, running up to her.

She accepted the charm, and embraced him. "I be old and forgetful," she murmured. Then, directly in his ear, she whispered: "Tell Bane as he exchanges. Then wait." She kissed his ear and drew back, changing back to mare form.

Flach stood, apparently stunned by the simplicity of this solution. He could not commune with Nepe directly, because the Adepts were alert to that, but they would hardly expect him to commune with the man he had so recently seen in person. Bane would tell Mach, and then the two most concerned would know the threat against those they loved. They would know what to do.

Neysa walked on. Even if the Adepts suspected, now, it would do them no good to act against her. The moment Bane and Mach learned of the threats against their wives, hell would begin fermenting in the Adverse ranks!

8: *Bane*

Uncle Bane! An I commune with Nepe, my dam be killed!

Bane, in the process of exchanging with Mach, felt as if he had been knocked out of the connection. He stood in Proton, tuning in, but there was nothing more.

Mach! he thought after a moment. *Didst thou hear?*

Yes. That was Flach.

Ne'er did he send to me before! Dost believe he tells truth?

Yes. I think we now know why the two have ceased contact.

Bane pondered momentarily, as things fell into place. *Wouldst call it a violation o' the covenant?*

Yes. Our wives were not to be threatened.

Then thou hast aught to do in Phaze, and I in Proton.

Agreed. We must not commune again until it is done.

Thus quickly had their loyalties changed. They had known almost from the outset that they served the wrong side, but had been bound to it by honor. Now that the Adepts—and surely the Citizens—had violated the terms, the two of them were free to do what they wished. They would join Stile and Blue.

They communed no more, for any prolonged contact at this stage would become suspicious. The Adepts and Citizens could monitor the fact of their contact, but not its substance, just as they could monitor the children's contacts. For a long time the children had communed without being detected, because they did it only when Mach and Bane were communing, and made no separate signal. But after Flach and Nepe exchanged, and almost secured their freedom despite the net closing on Flach, their amazing ability was known, and the monitoring technique had quickly been refined to distinguish their contacts from those of Mach and Bane.

But this single communication was so surprising that Bane knew no provision had been made for it. Flach sending to Bane! And what a message! At one stroke this had solved the riddle of the children's recent attitude, and sundered the agreement that bound Mach and Bane to the forces opposing Stile and Blue. The parity of the impasse had supposedly been replaced by the parity of mutual connections between the frames. Now it was evident that one side was cheating, in an effort to make the critical breakthrough and assume power.

Bane kept his face straight as he pondered this. He had no trouble concealing his emotions, in this robot body! He had to act normal until he decided how to proceed. If Fleta was threatened in Phaze, Agape would be similarly threatened in Proton.

Yet how was this possible? Neither Mach nor Bane had set up anything like this in either frame—and they represented the only contact the Citizen and Adepts had between frames. Fleta might indeed be in danger in Phaze, but how could Agape be under a similar threat?

Bane knew the Citizens: they would have made it tight. Somehow they had done it; he could not afford to assume otherwise. Perhaps they had made Flach send to Nepe—

But Nepe would not have relayed such a message to the Citizens! A death threat against her mother? She was an amazingly clever girl, and even a stupid one would have realized that the threat could only be real if she told the Citizens. She would have kept it quiet, thus defusing it.

How, then? He came to no answer, yet he was sure there was one. Meanwhile he was proceeding to his rendezvous with Tania, to make his routine report.

He smiled internally, grimly. For the past four years, in Proton, Tania had been his liaison with the Citizens. She had tried to seduce Mach, suggesting that he had no woman in Proton and that she was appropriate. Mach had consistently put her off, but never with prejudice, because she could make a lot of mischief if she chose. Bane had made it clear that his love was in Proton, and he would consider nothing else. Still, it had been evident that she would take either of them if she could.

He had agreed with Mach to say nothing to her or anyone else in Proton of the situation with Tania in Phaze. Only to Agape, from whom he kept no secrets, and Troubot, who could be trusted. Troubot! Who had turned out to be Nepe! But still could be trusted.

In Phaze, Tania had used her blandishments openly, and despite the defensive spell Mach had given him, he had felt the impact. When it had become apparent that her ploy had reversed, and she had fallen in love with him, it had been hard not to yield to some degree. When she adopted what he considered to be decent ways, leaving her cynicism and cruelty behind, he was impressed despite his suspicion that this was artifice. When she befriended Fleta he had been more impressed, for Fleta was exceedingly choosey about her associations.

He wished he could discuss the matter with Agape. To what extent was there merit in the proposition that the two frames were separate, and that a man could have a woman in each? Stile and Blue, as alternate selves, had different women. But Mach and Bane, as alternate selves, already had different women. For each to have two—that seemed too much of a stretch of ethics. Yet the temptation existed.

Now he realized that Tania could be useful. He knew a lot about the one in Proton, because of his experience with the one in Phaze. He was sure he could get her help, if it could be done covertly. Perhaps she had been involved in Flach's action in sending the message; she was there with Fleta in Phaze, now, because the Adepts suspected her of trying to let Flach escape the net. The boy would not have known what to do about the threat against his mother, but Tania's more cynical mind could have handled it. Still, he could not see the boy confiding in her, so that matter remained in doubt. Could he trust her?

He reached Tan's office. Tania was there alone; the provocative serf secretary was absent.

He decided to gamble on her. "Tania," he said without preamble, "I need thy help." He knew that this was private; the office was always sealed off from unwanted intrusion.

She was surprised. "What, no sneer today, Bane?"

"Swear to me that thou willst betray my confidence not, and I will tell thee much that interests thee."

Her eyes assumed the look of those of her other self, though they lacked the magic power. "You want me to do something for you, and not tell, and you will tell me what I want to know? I believe I am safe in assuming that you are not thinking of asking me for sex."

"Aye. I promise naught more, but I think it be enough."

"I don't trust this, Bane. You never gave me the time of day before."

"I ne'er had need, before."

She walked around the room, considering. Bane, accustomed in youth to the clothing of Phaze, had never completely adjusted to the nudity of Proton serfs. She looked exactly like her other self, except for her lack of clothing, and he found that illicitly fascinating despite all the deliberate glimpses her other self had proffered. In Phaze he had a spell to ward off her seductions; here he did not.

"I won't kill anyone, or do anything against my side," she said.

"It be against thy side."

She laughed. "And why would you suppose I would do that?"

"Because, an thou didst, I might pursue thy case with Mach."

She halted abruptly. "You're serious!"

"Aye."

"Listen, Bane—if I go against my side, I can wind up dead!"

"An they learn o' it, aye. But things be changing, and mayhap the other side would protect thee."

She stared at him. "Are you changing sides? What of the covenant?"

"Swear, and we deal."

She paced again, and he watched her breasts and buttocks moving. She had been foolish to go after Mach, when she could have had any other man she chose. But perversity was evidently her basic component. She was fascinated with the notion of Phaze, and of magic, and with the notion of power; thus Mach became the object of her interest. Had there been any other available male with similar connections, she would have been as interested in that one. Indeed, her other self pursued Bane, because of his connection with Proton.

Then she nodded. "I'm a fool. I swear."

"In Phaze thine other self hast spent the past four years seeking to seduce me, just as thou hast done with Mach. Thine actions have been parallel. But with her the ploy turned; instead of corrupting me, she fell in love herself, and her nature changed. She be in bad grace with the Adverse Adepts, because she tried not hard enough to capture the lad Flach, Nepe's other self."

Tania nodded. "So you believe I am similarly vulnerable, and ready to help you."

"Aye."

"Aye," she echoed ironically. "Damn it, I know it's true; I felt her emotion. I echo it. I do want Mach—and Phaze, as she wants you and Proton. We are locked in this foolishness, letting a man rule us instead of the other way around. And you—you gave her no more satisfaction than Mach has me!"

"Aye."

Those eyes bore on him again. "But did you wish to?"

Bane was silent.

"You promised to tell, Bane! I need to know."

"Mach gave me a spell to ward her off. I ne'er touched her."

"You still haven't answered! Did you want to?"

"Aye," he said reluctantly. "When I returned here to Agape, at times she teased me, assuming her likeness."

"*My* likeness! And you had sex with her like that?"

"Aye," he said, even more reluctantly. "But I knew it was Agape, else ne'er would I—"

"You desire me now!" she exclaimed triumphantly.

"I love thee not!"

"Again you haven't answered! You desire me!"

"Thou knowest I may not answer that."

She nodded, satisfied. "And Mach would wish to—?"

"Aye." That much he could fairly answer.

She nodded again. "You were right. This interests me. If I help you, Mach may have reason to treat me more compatibly. And, judging by you, he would also have the desire."

It was his turn to nod.

Then she glanced at him sharply. "And what of you, if Mach is dealing similarly in Phaze?"

"I would have to talk with Agape."

"Who might not understand," she said, smiling.

"Who might understand too well."

She laughed. "What do you want me to do?"

The worst was over. "Make a reservation for departure from this planet."

"You could do that yourself!"

"And yield that berth to Agape."

She sobered. "Then you know."

There was his confirmation that Agape was similarly threatened. "Aye."

"But she can't just walk out, you know. The moment she steps beyond her suite—"

"Aye."

"And the child. She won't leave the child behind, after losing her for so long."

"That be a separate problem."

"And you. You had better be gone the same time."

"Aye."

"And me. They'll know as soon as it happens, and I'll be finished."

"Thou must go to Blue for asylum."

She faced him squarely. "If I do this, and Mach does not settle with me, *you* do."

"I can not!"

"I am not putting my life and career in jeopardy without that promise. I save Agape, one of you owes me, and you know how. In fact, Mach never settled for his prior debt to me, and this makes two. *Both* of you owe, now. No loophole."

He had not even come to terms with what Mach might commit him to in Phaze, and now he had to deal with it in Proton. But he knew her, and knew she would not yield. She wanted what she could get of Phaze, and she was used to hard dealing.

He thought of Agape, and knew he had to do it. "Aye."

She went to the desk and checked the screen. "Do you care where she goes?"

"Nay, I care only that she not be suspected. She will assume thy likeness. Once away, she may change her route."

"Of course. Then here's a ship to ConGlom; I go there on occasion for relaxation. It's fun to be able to wear clothes, offplanet; I have a trousseau there she may draw on."

"An they catch on, they will seek that planet. She dare not use thy trousseau."

She shrugged as she touched a button. "Reservation made; that ship leaves the port in two hours. I will go there, and if she doesn't board, I will, to cover my complicity. Tell her to meet me in a privacy stall— let's say number four hundred and one. Can she get there fifteen minutes before boarding?"

"She must."

She left the desk and approached him. She kissed him, and he had to accept it. He felt guilty for liking it. "Nice doing business with you, Bane. Now our time is up; go meet your love."

He left the office. The first step had been taken. Tania was a sharp, motivated woman; she had understood immediately, and driven her hard bargain. But this was a three-step project, being formulated on the spur. Step one: get Agape away. Step two: get Nepe away. Step three: get himself away. Each step had more than one substep, and any misstep could be disastrous. Had there been only one, he could have taken Agape to Citizen Blue for sanctuary. As it was, that sanctuary would have to be saved for the last resort.

He had to try something he had never tried before. If it failed, he would have to try something else, but he had no notion what. He had never thought this action was possible, until Flach had called to him mentally; that should mean that no one else had thought of it either. That was a critical advantage—if it worked.

Nepe! he called mentally, as if contacting his other self across the frame. *Nepe!*

Daddy! she responded immediately.

Contact! Just like that! But he couldn't pause to savor it. *I know the threat. I be changing sides. Help me get thy mother offplanet.*

She doesn't know! They are watching. Oh, Daddy, I didn't dare tell—

Aye. We needs must ship her to the spaceport, concealed. The flight to ConGlom within two hours. She must exchange with Tania in booth 401. Tell her that.

But they will not let her go! They are watching the apartment!

Yes. We must ship her out concealed. Order a monstrous vat o' ice cream mix—

Got it, Daddy! But they call in every hour—

Thou willst have to emulate her for the screen.

Can do! Tell Troubot to make the delivery; he'll know what to do.

But thou wert Troubot! There be no—

Trust me, Daddy! He exists. He's hiding, but go to this address and speak this code, and he will come. She rattled off the information, which Bane, with his computer brain, memorized instantly.

Once Agape be out, needs we must act quickly, he thought.

Sure!

That was it; they had no time for conversation. He went to the address, which fortunately was not far out of his route to the suite.

It turned out to be a storage region, where supplies of food, medicine and machine accessories were kept on a temporary basis, for immediate access by local service machines. The robots operating here were low grade, possessing no sentience; as long as he did not interfere with them, they had no awareness of his presence. There were no automatic recorders; such devices were expensive, and this was only a warehouse annex.

Nevertheless, he waited till no worker machines were in the immediate vicinity before acting. Then he spoke the code, quietly, not expecting any prompt response. Troubot was the name she had taken during her hiding; what could answer that call now?

A portage machine trundled by, carrying a load of packages of white powder. Bane stepped out of its way.

"Troubot," it murmured as it passed.

Well! "Make the delivery Nepe calls in," he said.

Troubot stacked the bags and maneuvered to turn around. "Of what nature?"

"Ten-gallon tub o' ice cream."

The machine trundled away toward the maintenance alcove, evidently to get an ice cream carrying body. Thus it would be ready to respond to the order, seemingly coincidentally.

Mach walked on out of the warehouse, unhurried. He merged with the traffic of the hall beyond: serfs, androids and lesser robots. There was always activity around warehouse areas, because the needs of Citizens and their serfs were constant. No sensors were tracking him at the moment; in the course of nine years he had come to know the capacities of this robot body well, and could now do things with it that Mach himself could not, because his living human mind was superior to the best that a machine mind could be. He could detect sensors, having modified this body some time back to do so. It was a great advantage! He had set things up, but he needed a pretext to dawdle while the ice cream was delivered. The Citizens would be least likely to suspect Agape of making her escape before Bane arrived to see her after two weeks' absence. But it would be suspicious if he delayed; he normally had one thing in mind at such times.

Well, he would not delay; he would be delayed by an outside party. It was time to exploit another hidden feature of this body.

He tuned in on a paging station. He sent a signal that mimicked its control sequence, as if a call were coming through. A call seeking Bane himself.

"Bane," the loudspeakers of the vicinity blared. "Incoming call. Please pick up at convenient unit."

"Damn!" Bane said, as if displeased. He walked to the nearest public phone station. "Bane here," he snapped. "Be this call important? I be on my way to—"

"It will take only a moment," a dulcet female voice cut in. He was generating it electronically in his own body, but it sounded authentic, and any recording would sound authentic also. It was almost impossible to trace the origin of local calls unless special procedures were invoked. "I am a visiting journalist, and I just wanted to—"

"I know thee not, nor any journalists," he said. "Look, I have been away for two weeks and have naught to—"

"Please, this will be very brief. I believe you are the only self-willed robot to have a—"

"I be not a rovot! I be a living man!"

"Beg pardon? I understood that—"

So it continued: his irate explanation that he was actually a man in a robot's body, for an interviewer who had difficulty getting that straight. He played both parts with a certain vigor, pleased with his imagination. By the time he finally won free of the persistent caller, almost half an hour had passed, and he appeared fit to explode.

He hurried on to his rendezvous with Agape. By this time, he trusted, Nepe should have explained, Troubot would have arrived with the ice cream, and Agape would have rejected such a ridiculous order—and melted and gone out with Troubot in lieu of it. There was still about an hour to the departure of the ship for ConGlom: sufficient time to trundle there without haste. All he had to do was make sure that the Citizens did not catch on before the ship took off.

He reached the suite, and touched the panel. His hand was coded for it; it opened and let him in.

He paused, checking the security. There were supposed to be no electronic spies operating within, but he never took that on faith. His own electronic mechanisms traced the circuits, verifying that all were accounted for. It was all right; nothing had changed. That meant that he could talk freely, here.

He entered the main chamber. Agape was there, standing behind a chair. He suffered a siege of alarm—then relaxed.

"Very good, Nepe," he said. "Thou dost resemble her exactly."

"Did I fool you for an instant, Daddy?" she demanded eagerly.

"For an instant," he agreed. "Longer, had I not known thou wouldst not fail me." He strode across the room and enfolded her, embracing her as if she were her mother.

"Easy, Daddy," she said. "I'm standing on the ice cream."

So she was. Her natural mass was less than half that of Agape, so she had perched on the top of the oblong container, and formed only that portion of the body from the narrowing of the waist up. She had done a superlative job; the breasts were full and perfect in their contours and heft, the arms were completely functional, and the neck and head so apt that it was hard to believe this was an emulation. Of course the original Agape was an emulation, which perhaps made it easier. Still, it was impressive.

"Thou hast done well, Nepe," he said. "Maintain this emulation while I call out; I want them to know Agape is here with me."

She remained as she was, while he crossed to the screen. She had positioned herself so that only her upper portion could be seen by the pickup. He activated it, knowing that the two-way connection would show his wife in the background. The Citizens would be monitoring this; their agents would be reassured, and no report would be made.

But the moment the line was opened, Bane extended his electronic expertise. He tuned in on a nearby line reserved for Citizens, and fixed a limited diversion that would allow him to monitor it without being detected unless this specific device was suspected. This technology was not generally known; in fact, he was practicing the Proton equivalent of magic. Mach had become the Robot Adept, now far more talented in that respect than Bane. But Bane, unadvertised, had become the equivalent in Proton, and now he was drawing on these unique skills.

"Hold all calls, this hour," he said. "Except from Citizens, of course." Then he disconnected, not waiting for confirmation. This was his normal procedure; the nature of his first-hour activity was generally known.

But now he had his secret loop established. Outsiders could neither call in nor spy on what happened here, but he would know what was going on outside. Already there was a stream of routine communications, as one Citizen contacted the office of another about some trifle. Mach monitored these on what in his living brain would have been a subconscious level; if any key reference occurred, he would be alerted.

"Now thou mayest talk," he told Nepe.

"Are you really changing sides, Daddy?" she asked, delighted. "How come?"

"The threats against thy mother and Fleta in Phaze represent a violation o' our covenant. Mach and I agreed to serve the Adverse Adepts and Contrary Citizens in return for their protection and sanction o' our liaisons with our chosen females. Since Mach made the first deal much has changed; he won the contest that required me to join him. But Stile's opposition to Mach's union with Fleta ended, so the original cause was gone; only our agreements held us. We have served loyally; as thou knowest, we finally did locate Flach and capture him, and through him, thee. But all along, we would have preferred to be on the other side. Evidently the Citizens and Adepts, knowing this, and balked for four years, decided to make one swift sweep and gain a permanent advantage by unethical means. They tried to conceal this from us, believing that they could secure the power they required in both frames before we realized. But Flach told me, and now I be acting, and Mach be acting, to remove ourselves and our loved ones from the enemy camp."

"I'm glad, Daddy! I didn't like hiding from you, but—"

"Each must serve the side he serves. Now we be united in purpose as well as in person, and needs must we plan for action. As soon as Agape be offplanet, we must get thee to Blue."

"But what about you, Daddy? Once they find out, they will make you prisoner."

"I have means o' escape. Thou dost be the one we must free next. We can use not the ice cream ploy again. Mayhap we can send thee to a game while we—" He hesitated.

"Daddy, I know what you do with Mommy. I kept track of you, those years, and Flach told me about Mach and Fleta."

"How couldst thou keep track o' that?" he asked, bemused. "E'en as Troubot, thou didst ne'er see the act."

"Same way you keep track of the Citizens. In my metal aspect I learned some things about wiring."

"Which doubtless be why it was so hard to find thee."

"You never *would* have found me, if you hadn't traced me through Flach," she said smugly.

"But it be harder for thee to hide this time. An I send thee out, they will be watching."

"I think you could carry me out, if I become part of you, like maybe a leg. Then you could use your blankout circuit to—"

"My what?"

"You know, the way you short around the circuits of the spybeams on you, and make yourself invisible to them. Then you could take me to Grandpa Blue—"

Bane was amazed again. How many of his secrets did she know? But probably that would work. By the time the Citizens realized that something was up, and checked the suite, they would find nothing there except ten gallons of ice cream mix.

"Very well. As soon as we be certain your mother be safe, and have not to emulate her any more—"

He broke off, for his intercept had just sent up a signal. . . . *made the reservation while interviewing him, and now is heading for the spaceport. Better intercept her and find out whether this has anything to do with Bane.*

I'll send a pair of androids with her person-code; there will be time.

"They be going to intercept and question Tania!" he exclaimed. "Must needs I stop that! Agape will be able to exchange with her not if there be androids there!"

"Go now, Daddy!" Nepe exclaimed. "I'll cover!"

"What, for me?"

"I can do you too, with a few minutes to set up." Already she was starting to change, her features melting.

"Thou dost be a wonder!" he said, stepping toward the portal. "I will return for thee when I can."

"I'll be waiting, Daddy," she said bravely.

He used his intercept circuit to tune in on the spy devices beyond the portal. In a moment he had nulled them without alerting their malfunction alarms. Then he opened the portal and stepped out.

A human serf was passing in the hall. Bane ignored him; it was only the spy device that counted. Later they might round up and question all serfs in the vicinity, and learn that Bane had been seen leaving, but by then it would be far too late.

He had little time. Agape would be meeting Tania about half an hour before the flight, and the androids could be arriving shortly before that, being dispatched from some local depot. The spaceport was a fair distance from this region. A walking pace would require at least an hour, and all he had was perhaps twenty minutes. A Citizen could readily get there in time, by taking private transport, but he was a serf. He had to have transportation—but the fast belts and rail tubes were all monitored, and he wasn't sure he could remain invisible to them.

But he had an answer. He stepped into a service alcove. There was a hall-brushing machine, awaiting its call. It had a huge roller brush in front, and a large bin for refuse behind.

Bane addressed it electronically, tapping into its communication circuit. He had talked verbally to Troubot, but then he had been walking openly; now he was hidden from electronic observation, and needed to remain so.

Activate, he sent. *Stand ready to accept load of refuse. Take that load via expedite route to spaceport depot and release it.*

The sweeper did not question these orders. It hummed into its version of life and opened the lid to its refuse bin. Bane climbed up to stand in the bin. It was too small for him to hide in, being only half his height and too narrow to allow him to squat. He touched his body efficiently, and in a moment removed his right leg. He propped this in the front right corner, and then disconnected his left leg. He put his hands on the rim of the bin, hefted himself up, and let the left leg wobble into the front left corner. Then he lowered his torso down in a maneuver a living body would have found difficult, until it wedged against his standing legs at the bottom of the bin. He squeezed his arms down and into the scant remaining space.

The sweeper slid its lid back over. It clicked into place, making an airtight seal. Bane was glad that this body did not need to breathe; it did so only for appearances, and for verbal communication.

The sweeper trundled forward, heading for the expedite route. This was a network of tunnels used for the swift transport of supplies and equipment. The sweeper rolled onto a transport cart, was tied down, and gave its destination.

Abruptly the motion was savage. No human limitations of atmosphere or acceleration were considered; machines were tougher. It was like being launched by a swinging club; one moment the cart was stationary, the next it was rolling down the tube at a horrendous velocity. There was a violent jerk as it changed tracks, proceeding at an angle down a new tube, orienting on the spaceport. Bane's legs rattled against his torso. But high velocity was what he wanted!

In only ten minutes the sweeper rolled into the spaceport depot. Its lid slid open. Bane got his arms up, put his hands on the rim on either side, and somewhat clumsily hoisted his body up. This was harder to do than letting it down, and getting the first leg attached was harder yet. But he managed to use his torso to nudge his leg into the appropriate place, and to set himself on it so that it took some weight; that freed a hand so that he could complete the connection. The second leg was easy.

He climbed out. *Return to assigned depot,* he sent to it. *Use alternate route, unrush.*

The machine closed its hatch and trundled off. It would probably not be missed, and its excursion might never be noted. Meanwhile, it had gotten him to the vicinity of the spaceport in ample time.

Now he extended his electronic awareness to locate Troubot. Yes, he was on his way in, carrying Agape in dissolved form. He repeated the identification code Nepe had given him. *Troubot: provide projected route,* he sent.

The machine responded with the coding for his route.

If intercepted, notify me.

Troubot, a self-willed machine, understood. He would do his best to protect his cargo.

Now Bane oriented on Tania, whose identity he knew well. She was also on her way in, using her brother's Citizen transport. She would arrive before Agape, which was as it should be.

Finally he checked for the two androids. They were close; they would arrive before Tania, and be awaiting her at the spaceport. They were orienting on her boarding pass, which was keyed to her identity.

Now it got tricky. If he intercepted the androids before they interviewed Tania, the Citizen expecting the report would realize that something was wrong. Any hint of a problem would cause them to put a hold on the takeoff, and all would be lost.

On the other hand, if they interviewed Tania, they might not finish before Agape had to make the exchange. That, too, would be disaster.

But in a moment he had a way to thread through: Agape and Tania did not actually have to meet; they merely needed to exchange places and identities in a manner that aroused no suspicion. He could get the pass from Tania and give it to Agape; Agape could board while the androids interviewed Tania. True, it might seem that Tania was in two places at once—but no one should be checking for that. It seemed a reasonable risk.

He hurried to intercept Tania as she emerged from the transport. "Give me the pass," he said. "Androids be waiting for talk with thee."

She caught on immediately. "Someone is checking on me, because of my sudden departure. That will be routine. But if I don't have the pass, how will they find me? You don't want them tracking *her*."

Excellent point. "I will come with thee, and mock the pass. They will check it not further after they encounter thee."

"You have unheralded talents," she murmured, glancing at him sidelong. "Fortunately, I like your company."

They changed course to intercept Agape's route, and waited a moment. Probably the androids would not search for Tania beyond the spaceport; they would have been told to find her there, and they were stupid. So they would not see Agape in Tania's likeness.

Troubot came. *Give this pass to Agape,* Bane sent to it. *Tell her to assume Tania's likeness, and board as soon as the ship be ready. Once aboard, she may hide as pleases her, until we join her at Planet Moeba.* He gave the pass to the machine.

Troubot trundled on without pause. Agape would know how to get from Planet ConGlom to Planet Moeba. There was no chance for more detailed planning.

Then he walked with Tania on toward the spaceport, maintaining a circuit that emulated the recognition pattern of the pass, with more force than the original, so that any sensors would tune in on this one instead. "Once they be satisfied that it be thee, I will depart," he said. "Thou canst reassure them that thy journey be routine."

"Nuh-uh, metal man," she said, taking his arm possessively. "I am now without my pass. If they think to check, they will know something's up, and I'll be in as much trouble as you. Stay with me, and see that I get out of this."

"But—"

"The moment they realize that she is gone, and that I had a part in it, zap," she continued, slicing her free hand across her throat. "And I think that will happen about one minute after that ship takes off. *You* will be on hand to get me out of it."

"But I must return to see that Nepe—"

"If, on the other hand, all proceeds smoothly, you will be able to see to the child too. My help comes at a price, and saving my hide is part of it."

Bane had no alternative but to go along with her. He suspected that she enjoyed asserting her position.

They came to the spaceport and approached the privacy booth 401. The two androids appeared, intercepting Tania exactly as directed. Both had the nondescript look of their kind; they were completely humanoid, including genitals, but somewhat slack-faced. "Tania," one said. "We must ask why you make this trip."

Tania glanced at the nearest wall clock. Takeoff was in just under half an hour, and boarding would occur in fifteen minutes. She had either to satisfy these androids, or keep them occupied so that they could not check the people actually boarding.

"I do not have to answer to you," she snapped aloofly. "My excursions are my private business."

"Citizen Tan sent us," the android said. "We speak for him."

"My brother knows my pleasures," she said. "Now look, gunkheads: I have only about ten minutes before I have to board, and I have latched on to a man for some spot entertainment until then. Just tell my brother I am my usual willful self, and let me be."

"Entertainment?" the android asked.

"Yes. In here." She drew Bane in toward the booth. He tried to resist, wanting no part of this ploy, but could not do so openly. Dealing with this woman was like handling quicksilver!

"But you haven't answered," the android protested. "Why do you make this trip?"

Tania paused. Bane knew she was figuring out the best way to take advantage of this situation, knowing that he could not make any objection. "Well, I got bored with the local men," she said. "I mean, look at this one: would you make love to him?"

The android turned to look at Mach directly. His dull eyes widened. "This is—"

Bane cut him off with a blow to the throat, utilizing reflexes that no living man, let alone an android, could match. Then he whirled on the other, catching him by the side of the neck and rendering him unconscious by a nerve block. He caught him as he tottered, and hauled him into the booth. Tania meanwhile manhandled the other android to follow. In a moment the four were crammed inside a booth intended for one to primp in comfort. One android was slumped on the toilet, and the other on the table before the wall-sized mirror.

"Well, robot, I seem to have misplayed it," she said, not entirely displeased. "Now we shall have to keep them here, and stay out of sight ourselves, until that ship takes off, so that nobody sees anything suspicious. Whatever shall we do for twenty minutes, handsome?"

"We can leave them here," he said, bothered. "They will recover not consciousness soon enough to report in time."

"No. My brother may call in, and they must answer, or there will be mischief. See?" She pried at the closed hand of the android who had done the talking. Sure enough, there was a communication button set into the palm.

Bane gritted his teeth, figuratively. It was true; they could not gamble on the call coming in and receiving no answer, before the ship left. They had either to haul the unconscious android along with them, which would surely arouse suspicion, or wait with him here until the danger passed.

"That is what I thought," she said, reaching up to catch hold of him around the neck. "You know, Bane, I have confined my attentions to Mach, because he is the one with no woman in Proton, but I think now those concerns are blurring. Phaze fascinates me, and if you are going to do it with my other self there anyway—"

"Thou dost push thy luck," he muttered, not responding physically.

"We are the same, she and I. I feel her emotion—and that emotion is for you rather than Mach. I never quite figured out what was wrong, until you told me of the situation in Phaze. I see now that I was trying for Mach only nominally; it was you I really wanted. Now I am helping you to save your lover, and I believe—"

"Sork," the android's hand said. "What report?"

Bane used his ability to activate the return connection. "She says she just wants a change from Proton men, sir," he said in the android's voice. "She says it is routine."

"What else?"

"That it is none of my business, sir."

There was a dry laugh. "All right, let her talk to me."

Bane held up the android's limp hand. "He wishes to talk to thee," he said.

"All right, Tan sir," she said, grimacing. "And what does my Citizen twin brother require of me now, sir?"

"A straight answer," Tan's voice snapped. "Why are you leaving the planet without notifying me?"

"I forgot, Citizen sir," she said, not bothering to conceal the malice. She resented the fact that he had gotten the Citizenship instead of her. "Now are you going to let me board, sir?"

"I don't think so. There's something funny about—" He paused, evidently making a connection. "Thee? The android wouldn't have said that!"

Oops! Bane had given himself away!

"You must have misheard," Tania said. "Bane's in with the amoeba wench, plumbing her protoplasm with his metal rod."

"One moment," Tan snapped. Bane knew he was putting in a priority call to the suite, to see who answered. He also knew that Nepe, in his likeness, would answer and cover for him.

Sure enough, soon Tan spoke again. "He's there, all right, looking mad about being interrupted. But I distinctly heard a 'thee.' *Who are you with?*"

Tania covered for him again. "All right, if you must know: I managed to talk a man into going with me. I—you know, Phaze, the way I—I've got him made up like Bane, and told him to talk like—"

"I doubt it," Tan said coldly. "More likely you found a way to coerce Bane into coming with you so you could seduce him, and Agape is emulating him at their suite. How the hell you got *her* to cooperate I can't guess. I won't have it; we need him here. Permission to depart the planet is denied; return immediately to the office, and bring him with you. We shall get to the bottom of this."

Tania glanced at Bane. Her brother had leaped to an apt conclusion, with one key error!

"Damn!" she said. "I hear and obey, Citizen Tan sir! But this matter is not finished."

"Agreed," he said, with an inflection that made her wince.

They stepped out of the booth. "Methinks we need a distraction," Bane said. "There be a few minutes yet till the ship launch. An he rethink the ploy—"

"And it is time for me to make my move," Tania said. "This will quickly unravel. If I know my brother, he will not depend on my sense of sibling duty; he'll send a competent force to arrest me—and you. Pull out your stops, robot; this is the time."

"Aye, wench," he agreed. "Follow!"

They ran to the nearest service exit to the takeoff ramp. Bane used his ability to make the door open for him as it would for a machine servitor. Beyond was a chamber in which the service machines were parked: huge forklifts, dozers and ramp cleaners. Bane went to one of the last: a machine taller than a man, with a sealable cockpit, and nozzles and brushes all around. "Climb in!" he told her, as he made the cockpit dome lift open.

"How?" she asked, halting before the monstrous caterpillar tread of the thing. It offered little purchase for a human being. Normally these machines were remote-controlled; the cockpit was there only in case a man should be assigned.

"I'll boost thee!" He caught her by knee and upper thigh and lifted her up so that she could scramble onto the top of the tread.

"Goose me again, why don't you," she muttered as his hand fell away from her thigh. But she made it to the cockpit and climbed in.

Bane followed. He zeroed in on the machine's control circuitry, and locked off the remote input. Now he alone controlled it. He studied its mechanisms.

"Get going!" Tania cried, jammed into the tiny cockpit beside him. "They'll be here any minute!"

Bane knew that. But he wanted to be certain of the cleaner's potential. He had chosen this machine because it most resembled an old-fashioned tank. Properly directed, it could defend itself, and could travel beyond the dome.

A group of androids burst into the chamber. "Here they are!" Tania exclaimed. "They've got stunners!"

He had anticipated as much. "Get comfortable," he said grimly. "It may be a hard ride."

"I can't get comfortable here! There's a gearstick poking my bottom."

"Lucky gearshift," he murmured, as the machine lurched out to meet the androids.

One of them fired. The shot was invisible, and was evidently deflected by the metal and plastic framework of the machine, for there was no effect. Still, this luck would not hold; he had to eliminate the menace.

He aimed a nozzle and fired. Foam squirted out to blast the androids. The force of it was formidable; it knocked them off their feet. Bubbles enclosed them, and they gesticulated wildly as they fought for good air to breathe.

"What is that stuff?" Tania asked admiringly.

"Merely light detergent. But methinks it would sting if it got in the eyes."

Indeed, several androids were rubbing their eyes. None were trying to use their stunners. This group had been effectively defeated.

But more would come, this time better prepared. Not enough time had passed to allow for the ship taking off. "Methinks we had better give them aught to ponder," he said, guiding the vehicle to the service entrance.

"Robots!" she cried, pointing.

That was what he had feared. Detergent foam would not stop those! So he charged them as they passed through the door. They were machines, but they were no match for the mass of the vehicle; they dived aside as he smashed into the door, and broke it in, along with a large segment of wall. Human and android people screamed. Tania grunted as she was bounced against the cockpit dome and back into Bane. Her knees were now jammed against his belly, and she clung to his neck for support. Her hair was in wild disarray, but she was smiling. This was her kind of mayhem!

But already the robots were righting themselves and orienting their weapons. Bane touched a lever, and water blasted out in a circular sheet, horizontally, sweeping them all off their feet again. "Rinse cycle," he murmured to the top of Tania's head, which was jammed against his right shoulder. "May short out some of those weapons."

Then he maneuvered the vehicle around and away from the smashed wall, retreating. "Takeoff!" he said gladly.

"This thing flies?" she demanded, astonished.

"The ship be launched," he explained. "Now it be safe to pass its ramp. I wanted to interfere not, before."

"Figures," she agreed.

Some robots were coming after them. Bane tried his third weapon, the sander. Powdery sand blasted out, and the big brushes extended, whipping it into a dust-storm frenzy, intended to scour away the worst runway buildup of grime or old paint.

"Those robots won't like that," Tania remarked, grinning.

But just to be sure, he aimed his foam nozzle and sent out a prolonged rearward jet of liquid detergent. He was rewarded by the sight of robots sliding helplessly back on a spreading wave of bubbles. They had finally been defeated.

They passed the main launch ramp. The ships did not take off vertically; they lay at an angle, and were catapulted up before their engines cut in, so as not to befoul the interior of the dome. Incoming ships landed outside, and were then hauled in on flatcars. It was an efficient system, but did not do much to abate the exterior pollution.

They passed through the dome wall, which was just a force field that served as a barrier between the clean inner air and the bad outer atmosphere. Here the view was murky; here the dust storms were natural.

"They'll have aircraft after us," Tania said. "We can't dodge those long, or shoot them down with squirts of water."

"Aye. Now we call for help."

He set up a radio circuit on a special channel. *Blue! Blue! Willst take me in?*

Thought thou wouldst ne'er ask, the laconic reply came. Then, flying low on the horizon, came a winged craft, bright blue. It looped around them, then slowed and glided down for a landing.

"Don this," Bane said, drawing from the back of the cockpit a helmet and breathing tank.

Tania wedged her head into it and made sure the seal was snug about her neck. Then Bane opened the canopy and let the atmosphere in. They clambered out and ran across to the airplane.

In a moment they were inside, and the plane was taking off. It was a remote-controlled unit, made to hold two.

"That's Tania!" Citizen Blue's voice came. "What of Agape?"

"She be offplanet now," Bane explained. "Tania and I be defecting to thy side, and Mach likewise in Phaze."

"What about Nepe?"

Bane had known he could not rescue Nepe the moment Tan caught on to the ploy, but had been distracted by the need to act swiftly and effectively. Now the realization struck with full force. "She be captive o' the Citizens. She covered for me, to get her mother out."

Tania turned to him, shaking her head. "I'm sorry, Bane," she said with genuine regret.

"I think we shall have to negotiate," Citizen Blue said, as the airplane flew them to the safety of his power.

"Aye," Bane agreed, depressed.

9: *Forel*

Forel cut through the brush, heading for home. He had always been an explorer, and now with his oath-friend Barelmosi gone, he found surcease from his disquiet only by increasingly distant excursions. He claimed that he wanted to find and run down prey, so that he could make his first individual Kill and be eligible for adult status, and that was true, but it was mostly his foolish notion that if he only ranged far enough, he might find and bring back his lost friend. He knew that Barel had been captured by the Adepts, knew there was no chance they would let him go, and knew that if Barel somehow escaped, he would not dare come here, where they would first look for him. Yet Forel ranged, hoping on a level more fundamental than that of reason.

But now he had to return, as he had promised Sirel and Terel, who feared he would get himself killed by a hunting dragon, or by a goblin snare. If he stayed out too long, they would come looking for him, and so put themselves at similar risk. He wanted that not!

He scooted under an overhanging bush and picked up speed in the straightaway between several large trees. But there was a sinister trace of mist descending, forming a low cloud. He had seen what unnatural clouds could do! He slid to a halt, trying to avoid it, but it expanded to embrace him.

Suddenly he was lost in choking fog. He could not see his way clear, and indeed, had to put his nose down to the ground to breathe. This was certainly magical, and surely not the work of his friend Barel!

"Wolf pup," a human voice came. "Are you Flach's friend?"

Flach: the human name of Barelmosi! Had he escaped after all? Were they casting another net for him?

"Aye, spook," he growled. "And may thou catch him not!"

A manshape came out of the obscurity. "I helped catch him before, but now I am changing sides. Will you help me free my son—and my wife?''

Forel stared up at the figure. It was the Rovot Adept!

"There is little time, wolf," the rovot continued. "Flach and Fleta are captive on an isle under the sea, and I can not go there now without arousing suspicion. But I can conjure you there, where you can verify that I am speaking the truth. Will you cooperate to that extent?''

It was obvious that the dread rovot had him captive, so could either kill him or compel him to do his bidding. It was better to go along, at least until his chances improved.

"Aye," he growled. "But I trust thee not, rovot!''

"Nor should you, wolf. Hold on; I am conjuring us to a safer place. This concealing cloud is too obvious, here.''

A concealing cloud: of course! Barel had used clouds as a device to hide things they had to hide, but only when no others except the oath-friends were present. They alone had known his nature, that he was the man-'corn, no wolf at all, but a creature of far greater potential. But he had rewarded their support with the benefits of his growing power, and their friendship with his own. He was, at the root, a youngster like themselves, who had left his origin to come to this Pack as they had. He was one of them in the ways that counted, and it had been entirely fitting that he and Sirel had Promised when they made their first Kills together. Forel hoped to do the same with Terel, when the time came, and he would become Forelte, and she Terelfo, until they were granted their kill syllables.

So it was not surprising that Barel's rovot father knew the uses of clouds. As Forel felt himself wrenched to somewhere distant, he was already gaining confidence. Maybe the rovot spoke truly, and was now on the right side. It would be wonderful if Barel no longer had to hide from his family! Barel had not spoken much of this, but they knew, as oath-friends did, what he was feeling. He loved his sire and his dam, and hated being apart from them, but knew he could not serve the side they served. His grandsire Stile, patron of all the better animals, had made that clear to him.

And he would return when he could; they all knew that. By ancestry Barel was man and unicorn, but by association he was wolf, and that would never change.

The realm steadied. Forel gazed out into a white chamber, irregularly globular, resembling the shell of a hollowed-out gourd. The floor was spongy but firm enough for good purchase.

"Turn manform," the rovot said. "We must talk quickly."

Obligingly, Forel assumed his human form, complete with his fur jacket and breeches, and the fur slippers needed to protect his frail human feet. In so doing he sacrificed advantages of nose and tooth, but gained that of human speech, which was more versatile than growl-talk. "Thou claimest to be on our side now, rovot?" he demanded as challengingly as he could manage. It was obvious that he was in the power of the Adept, but appearances were important.

"So I claim," the rovot agreed, taking no offense. "This is the situation: Bane and I served the Adverse Adepts not because we had any liking for their policies or ambitions, but because they supported my liaison with Fleta. Once that commitment was made, it continued and increased, as a matter of honor rather than preference. But after we recovered Flach, the Adepts violated the covenant between us by threatening to kill his mother if Flach communicated again with Nepe in Proton. This was false in two ways. It prevented the Adept Stile from using Flach's power to his advantage while the Adverse Adepts were using mine to their advantage. And it undercut my union with Fleta, upon which the covenant is based; I could not remain married to her if they killed her."

He looked directly at Forel. "Suppose, wolf, that you achieved your first Kill, and Promised to the bitch who—" He paused.

"Terel," Forel supplied grudgingly.

"To Terel. But instead of granting you adult status, Kurrelgyre killed her. Where would you stand?"

"The Pack Leader would ne'er do that!"

"Agreed. But what of an Adverse Adept?"

Forel nodded. "Methinks I take thy point."

"I mean to conjure you to my son, where you can quickly verify what I have told you. I want you to enable Flach and Fleta to escape the power of the Adepts. If you discover that what I have told you is not true, no one will be able to make you do anything more, for I dare not go into the Adept stronghold now. Of course you will be trapped there yourself. You will be taking a serious risk no matter how it turns out."

The rovot seemed sincere. But how could he be sure? The Adepts were notorious for the manner they dealt with animals, as more than one grown bitch had discovered to her cost. He had to ponder.

"Where be we?" he asked, hoping to elicit further proof of the rovot's intentions.

Mach smiled. "In a cloud, floating above the forest of the Animal

Heads. It changes its location with the wind, but will not move far in the next hour. You must tell Fleta that, or Tania, so they can find it. You can guide Flach here yourself."

"A cloud," Forel repeated, unbelieving. True, it did look like the interior of a cloud, but he knew that clouds were not always the way they looked.

Mach made a gesture. Suddenly the walls became transparent. There was blue sky beyond, interspersed by the white masses of other clouds at this level.

Forel looked down. There below was spread the panorama of the land, its forests and rivers and fields. He had ranged across it enough to recognize its nature, though he had never viewed it from such a height before. This really *was* a cloud!

With that simple confirmation came his acceptance of the rest. "Tell me how," he said.

The rovot seemed unsurprised at his process of decision. "Here are two amulets. Each will enable its invoker to assume the likeness of his companion. One is for Tania, one is for you. When I conjure you to the prison isle, give one to Tania and keep the other, and then the four of you must change forms and flee the isle and make your way here as swiftly and quietly as you can."

"But the Adepts!" Forel protested. "They will let us go not! And Tania—she be worst o' the Adepts; canst trust her?"

"Tania too has changed sides; she can be trusted now," the rovot said. "Here is one more amulet. Invoke this after Flach and Fleta change forms, and before you do. Do you understand?"

"Aye. I invoke my amulet last, and the other next to last. But what does it do?"

"It generates decoys."

Forel did not see how that related, but did not care to show his ignorance, so did not question it. The rovot gave him the three amulets and made sure he knew them apart. "Remember," the rovot concluded, "act immediately. The Adepts will realize that something is happening the moment you appear; you must act before they do, or all is lost."

"Aye." He certainly knew the importance of fleeing enemy territory quickly!

"Take a moment to rehearse in your mind what you will say and do," Mach told him. "I do not know precisely where you will land, but it must be in your human form, and you must waste no time deciding. Let me know when you are ready."

"Wait, rovot!" Forel cried. "I can not guide Barel out if I know not where we be! Where be this isle?"

"Near the West Pole, under the sea."

"But Barel's dam—he said she has but one foreign form, and that be a little bird. How can she run or fly under the sea?"

"Excellent question. The Adepts will not expect her to flee without using their spell to make the water like air. But these amulets provide for that; the vicinity of those invoking them will be all right. This is one reason why Tania and Fleta must travel together, and you and Flach. Together you can make it; apart you will be in trouble."

"This be great magic!" he exclaimed.

"Thank you."

He realized that the rovot was mocking him, lightly. Of course this was the greatest of the Adepts, able to do such things as others could only dream of.

"I be ready," he said.

The rovot gestured—and there was the wrench.

Forel was standing on a strange isle girt about by shimmering light, and beyond it the dark water in which strange creatures crawled or swam.

But he had no time to gawk. The wicked Adept Tania was sitting against a tree, nearest to him, her eyes widening in surprise. "Eye me not, Tan!" he cried. "I bring this amulet from the rovot! Use it to change forms with the mare, and stay with her that ye two may breathe. Flee to the cloud above the Animal-Head Demesnes!" He almost hurled the amulet at her, and ran on past her to find Barel.

The boy was playing with a wickerwork basket on the little beach. "Forel!" he exclaimed.

"I come from thy sire. Wait for the others to change, then assume a form for escape, and I will match thee; I have magic. Fast, fast; needs must we go before the Adepts act!"

Meanwhile Tania was running to Fleta, who turned toward the boys in surprise. She was in her natural form, grazing on the verdant patch of grass nearby; a forgotten mouthful of grass hung unchewed.

"Aye, dam!" Barel cried. "Do it! There be danger thou knowest not of!"

Fleta did not question her son. She became a hummingbird. Right after her, so did Tania.

"I shall be a fish," Flach cried, running toward the shimmering margin of the isle. "Follow me!" He dived through the curtain, and on the other side a catfish appeared.

Forel paused only to use the decoy spell. "Amulet, I invoke thee!" he cried, holding it up.

The amulet exploded. From it flew perhaps a thousand specks of dust, but each expanded as it moved, becoming larger. Those that went up formed into tiny birds that quickly grew into hummingbirds just like the two on the isle. Those that went down formed into tiny fish that grew into catfish. Some passed through the curtain and swam in the water; others landed on the sand and flopped their way toward the water, still growing.

Forel gaped. He had never seen such magic! This amulet had somehow tuned in to the forms the others assumed, and reproduced them by the hundreds, and every one of them seemed alive! Decoys indeed! How would the Adepts ever tell them from the originals?

Then a shadow loomed over the isle. Something awful was coming! Forel leaped for the water. "And thee!" he cried to the remaining amulet.

He passed through the curtain—and felt the water against his whiskers. He flexed his tail, and moved forward. He was a catfish!

He looked for Barel—but saw a dozen similar catfish, and more crawling on their fins from the beach. Which one was his friend?

Then one swam close. "Come, wolf," it said in fish-talk. "We must away!"

All too true! The shadow over the isle was intensifying, and he felt the tingle of terrible magic. He flexed his tail and used his fins vigorously, zooming away from the curtain. Barel-fish paced him. Swimming was easy, once he caught on to its mechanism. Maybe the amulet was helping, because he had no prior experience.

"Where be we going?" Barel asked as they plunged through seaweed. The other catfish were plunging similarly.

"A cloud o'er Animal Demesnes!" Forel replied. His expression in fish-talk was not apt, but Barel seemed to understand. Evidently Barel had had more practice in the form, though Forel had never seen him assume it before, and indeed, had not known that he knew any forms beyond man, 'corn, bat and wolf. Maybe he had worked it out after being captured.

As they progressed south, away from the isle, the decoy catfish thinned. Some had probably been caught by the strange predators, such as the tentacled creatures with great long pointed shells. But most of the thinning was merely because they were getting farther from the isle; the catfish were spreading out into wider territory.

Then there came a predator Forel recognized by description: a shark! Wolves stayed clear of deep water when they could, but they did know how to swim, so were versed in the dangers of the sea. The rule for sharks was simple: get out of the water!

But as fish, they could not get out. Could they hide from this monster?

Barel swam close. "Fear naught. We be electric catfish. An the shark be fool enough to bite, he'll get a shock."

The shark loomed near, then evidently recognized them and veered away. So it was true; Barel had chosen a form that could defend itself by the magic of electricity!

They swam on, until no other catfish were in sight. They had made it safely away! Barel angled upward, approaching the surface. Then he accelerated and leaped from the water, becoming a bat.

Forel followed, but feared this would not work for him. He would have to swim to shore instead, and resume wolf form, and pace Barel on the ground. But as he leaped, he changed—and suddenly he had wings! He too was a bat!

Flying was another new experience, and he hardly had time to wonder at the continuing potency of the amulet he had invoked; he had to concentrate on keeping his balance in the air. He wobbled, pumping his leathery wings as hard as he could, and barely managed to stay clear of the waves. Then he got a better grasp of the mechanism, and began to rise.

There was a globe above him. It looked like a ball of water, but there was a man inside it, looking out. Forel tried to veer away, but something held him; he could no longer move.

"So we have caught the errant fish," the man said. "And which of ye be 'corn?"

Then something hauled Forel into the floating ball. His magic was canceled, and he reverted to the form he had assumed before invoking the amulet. As a boy he stood within the globe, realizing that he faced the Translucent Adept.

Barel was beside him, also in boy form. "Damn thee!" Barel cried angrily at the Adept. "Methought us free!"

"Almost, you were," the Adept agreed. "But I had the wit to search out pairs o' fish, for they travel not normally that way, and when this pair turned bat, I knew. Now tell me: why and how didst thou make this break? I know there be more to it than simply pique."

"I have to answer not!" Barel said defiantly.

"I have treated thee well, and mean to continue so," the Adept said. "But I will have mine answer." He turned to Forel. "I ask it thee: answer!"

Forel felt magic impinging on him. He tried to resist, but could not. His mouth opened, and he spewed out all that he knew of this event.

The Adept sighed. "It be as I feared. I sponsored this aspect not, but the seeming failure to recover the lad for so long vitiated mine authority, and the others acceded to Purple's urgings and used the ploy o' threatening the mare. Now has that ploy borne its bitter fruit by alienating the rovot and setting us back. At least have I salvaged this bit o' it.''

The magic compulsion eased, and Forel was able to control his speech again. "Thou dost sound as if thou dost not like this business," he said boldly.

"Aye, wolf-boy. I second my side, o' course, but it was in my mind to forward our cause by dealing fairly. I blame the rovot not for changing sides; he had cause. It be an irony, for we were close to winning, legitimately; we needed only a fraction what Blue needed. Had the lad just been allowed to work for Blue, we had been fair and with the victory anyway. Now we be foul, and victory be problematical.''

Forel looked at Barel. "Aye," Barel said. "Translucent be e'er fair; it were Purple put the geis on me.''

"We gain one smidgeon o' this mess," Translucent said. "I be the one to salvage some, and the bad ploy failed, so my word regains its power. Be thankful it were not Purple caught ye two.''

Forel realized that they were indeed relatively well off. It would have been better to escape, but evidently they would not be mistreated.

"So my dam escaped?" Barel inquired.

"Aye, lad. She and Tania. The water be my domain. The search o' air was done by others, who mayhap lacked the wit to trace the pairs.''

The globe was now traveling briskly north, returning to the Translucent Demesnes. Forel saw the sea and shore passing below, much as he had seen the land from the rovot's cloud. He realized that the cloud would not be there any longer; now that Translucent had wrested its secret from him, the rovot would have to make his camp elsewhere. At least part of the mission had been accomplished!

They returned to the isle. "This be secure now," the Adept said. "All effort to escape be futile.''

"Aye," Barel said with resignation.

The Adept deposited them, then floated away in his watery globe. The two boys hugged each other, glad for this reunion despite the circumstances. "I thank thee for coming, oath-friend," Barel said. "At least it freed my dam.''

"What happens now?" Forel asked.

"Much depends on how it turns out in Proton. An all escape there, they will have no use for me, and mayhap we will be freed. But I fear it be not so."

"Why?"

"Because o' the parallel o' the frames. What happens in the one, happens in the other, by seeming coincidence. Mayhap our failure to escape will lead to Nepe being captive, or mayhap her failure led to ours. I know not exactly the means o' it, but it be nigh impossible to do a thing in one frame that be not parallel in the other."

"Nepe has a wolf-friend?"

Barel laughed. "Nay, but she has a rovot-friend. Same thing, mayhap. Not to diminish thee, but the parallels be strongest among the strongest; the Adepts have more impact than the little folk."

"I be little enough," Forel agreed ruefully.

"But now we can do naught. Let's revert to wolves and see what we can hunt."

"There be hunting here on this small isle?" Forel asked, surprised.

"Aye. It be a nice isle. Translucent be a kind captor."

Barel changed, and Forel followed. Sure enough, there were rabbits, and before long Forel had caught and killed one.

"First Kill!" he growled, delighted. "My first Kill!"

"Aye," Barel agreed, seeming unsurprised. "Now canst watch for what Terel does!"

"But she be free, and I be captive!"

"Mayhap not fore'er," Barel said optimistically.

They shared the rabbit, as there was no chance to drag it back to the Pack from here. Forel knew that Barel would give witness to the kill, at such time as this was possible. He was right: this was a nice isle.

Three days later the water globe returned. "It be like this," Translucent said. "Thy girl-self in Proton be captive too, but not the alien female. Bane changed sides, same's Mach did here. Dost know this?"

"Aye," Barel said. "Nepe told me."

Forel was surprised; he hadn't realized that the situation had been confirmed. But of course Barel could commune with his other self without showing it to others.

"It be in our minds to use thee and the girl-child in lieu o' thy sires, as thy powers be similar—or, methinks, moreso."

"We will work not for thy side!" Barel protested.

"That be not the question; an it come to that, Tan will make thee perform. Nay, the question be how to do it when the other side still controls Book and Oracle. We can send thee no longer to visit thy grandsire in return for that access.''

Barel nodded. "So it be impasse, again."

"Impasse," the Adept agreed. "Yet we wish still to gain power, and thy sire and grandsire wish to be united with thee. So we be dealing: double or nothing, here and in Proton-frame. An my side win, we gain Book and Oracle and the service o' your sires to exploit them. An the other side win, we turn over our hostages and our drive for power be finished."

Forel, listening, was amazed at the scale of the dealings. The ultimate power in the frames was about to be decided—all because he had not quite succeeded in freeing Barel!

"Why be ye telling us?" Barel asked.

"Commune with thine other self, and tell me what thou dost learn."

Barel was silent, evidently concentrating. After a bit he said: "Nepe says thou dost mean to set up six big contests, three in each frame, to determine who wins. Dost need us to verify the decisions o' the other frame."

"That be so, lad. Thou knowst we can allow all communications to be in the hands o' the enemy not. Thou hast now demonstrated thy proficiency at this; certainly it will do for the contests."

Forel saw that it would work; Barel would have to tell the truth, because only that would match what the other side presented. The Citizens of Proton-frame would not tell her anything they knew to be false, knowing it had to match the Phaze information.

"Why be ye taking all this trouble to explain to me?" Barel asked. "Surely must needs I go along, whate'er mine own preference."

"It be easier on all o' us an thou hast motivation," the Adept said. "Must needs I take thee to the negotiations, but also must needs I keep thee closely guarded, that thou be not taken from me."

"An I give mine oath, I will not flee thee," Barel said stiffly. "Nor would those o' my grandsire's side take me thus."

Translucent smiled grimly. "Not them. Ours."

Both boys looked at him, perplexed.

"Purple would take thee, and deal his way," Translucent clarified.

Suddenly it was clear. Translucent had to watch out for his side as much as for the other, because his allies lacked honor.

"Then be I satisfied to be under thy guard," Barel said.

"I thought thou mightest feel thus. Now will I make thee a small side deal: cooperate in what we ask, and provide me with aught I needs must know, and I will provide thee a modest reward."

"I need no reward from thee!" Barel said, affronted. "I do what needs I must."

"E'en so. Now board my bubble, the two of ye, and we go to deal."

They stepped into his water globe. It floated up, through the top of the curtain that contained the air of the isle, and on through the water. It lifted into the air above, gained elevation, then coursed west.

Their speed did not seem great, but it must have been, because soon Forel saw them coming down at the old Oracle's palace, halfway across the main continent of Phaze. Adepts really knew how to travel when they wanted to!

"Now here there be truce," the Adept said. "We be here to negotiate. Only the leaders o' each Demesne be here, and all be on honor to provoke naught. Ne'ertheless Flach must needs be confined; Forel be messenger."

"Me?" Forel asked, astonished. He had not thought the Adept even knew his name!

"I will be within," Translucent explained. "My bubble will be without, as will be the conveyances o' the others. Flach will verify for our side, and thou, pup, willst carry the news. Understand?"

"Aye," Forel said, awed.

"Then comest thou with me now, and mark the spot o' this bubble. Naught can pass in or out o' it other than we two, and none will interfere with thee."

The Adept stepped out as if the wall of the globe had no substance, and Forel followed. They were on the green turf surrounding the palace, and other conveyances or creatures formed a wide circle around it. There were carts and sledges and even a sailing boat anchored in air, and horses and huge birds and a massive wooden golem, and next to the globe was a formidable flying dragon.

Translucent swept toward the palace entrance without regard for the sights, but Forel, following, was dazed. He had never imagined such a setting, and never thought he would ever be a part of such magical dealings. He was nervous, too, despite the Adept's reassurance; the dragon's head did not turn, but its eyes were tracking him.

The palace had not seemed large from a distance, but it loomed impressively as they approached the main entrance. Inside, it seemed larger yet: towering ceilings for each huge chamber, and elaborate arches between the halls. There were carpets on the walls that showed murals of great events of the past, exciting an intense curiosity in him. He, as a young wolf from a distant Pack, knew little of such history; until now he had not missed it, but he knew that he could never rest again until he fathomed the events of the murals.

They came to a tremendous cathedral-like chamber, and here were the assorted parties assembled. Forel recognized the several Adepts immediately, though he had never before seen them: Blue, who was Barel's grandsire, in his blue cloak, looking no bigger than a child, and who used singsong rhymes to work his enchantments. Red, who was actually a troll, grotesque, but perhaps the most powerful of all, because he possessed the Book of Magic; he made amulets of singular potency. Brown, a woman with brown hair, of indeterminate age, mistress of the wooden golems. These three had held off the force of the Adverse Adepts for a score years, because of the strength and versatility of their magic. Now they were joined by Barel's sire, the rovot, who had become the strongest of all because of his studies in the Book of Magic.

On the other side of the chamber were gathered the eight Adverse Adepts, in their color-coded robes. White, also called the Snow Queen, with her glyphs. Yellow, the bane of animals. Black the line. Orange, of the plants. Green fire. Sinister young Tan, with the Evil Eye. Purple, who lived in the Purple Mountains and controlled the forces of geology. And Translucent, of course, in his watery robe, controlling the forces of water.

Yet, for all their horrible power, they looked mostly like ordinary human folk, a number of them getting old and fat. How deceptive appearances could be!

Between the two groups of Adepts were the animals: a unicorn, bat and wolf—it was Kurrelgyre, his own Pack leader!—near Stile's group, and an assortment of monsters closer to the Adverse group. There was a hulking ogre, a dragon, a monstrous roc bird, a goblin, a troll, a harpy, a human form with the head of a snake, and a giant man. The assorted Little Folk were with Stile, while the assorted demons were with the other side. Perhaps there were others, but he couldn't look; he was being summoned.

"The wolf-boy be our runner to Flach," the Translucent Adept was saying. "Pup, tell where Flach be."

"He—he be in thy water globe," Forel stammered.

"Ill-treated?"

"Nay."

Kurrelgyre shifted to wolf form. "Change, Forel," he said in growl-talk.

Forel looked at Translucent. "He tells me to—"

"Aye, change," the Adept said.

Forel assumed wolf form. "It be true," he told the Pack Leader. "We be on the isle where the mare was."

"Come here," Kurrelgyre growled.

Forel looked at Translucent, but the man made no objection. He walked slowly to the grown wolf.

They sniffed noses. Then Kurrelgyre turned away, dismissing him. The old wolf resumed man form. "There be no geis on him," he said. "He tells truth."

The Blue Adept nodded. "We accept him as runner." He glanced at the rovot. "Now if thou willst tell o' the decision in Proton—"

"Pup!" Translucent cut in. "Go get it from Flach: the decision in Proton-frame."

Forel hurried out, remaining in wolf form. He understood what was wanted: what he learned from Barel should match what the rovot reported. That way both sides knew there was no deception.

Outside, he broke into a lope, heading straight for the water globe. But now the dragon moved to intercept him. He swerved to avoid it, but it moved to cut him off again. It knew his destination, having watched before; it knew he was the same creature it had eyed.

Forel stopped, uncertain what to do. He had to get to the globe, to talk with Forel, but the dragon intended to eat him instead. He saw no way to pass; those huge teeth would snap him up immediately. His only defense was to stay beyond range; he could avoid the dragon by remaining close to the palace, because the dragon knew it would get in trouble if it were there. But how could he carry out his mission?

Then someone emerged from the palace; Forel almost bumped into him. It was the Black Adept! Immediately the dragon lay down, pretending to sleep. Could Forel take advantage of this respite to get through? But how would he get back, if the Adept were no longer there to make the dragon behave?

But while he hesitated, the Adept did not. "Dost not grasp the meaning o' truce, creature?" he exclaimed.

Forel cowered, expecting yet more trouble. But the Adept's words were directed at the dragon. He raised his arm, his finger pointing, and suddenly a black line shot from it. The line flew to the dragon, and whipped around the reptile's form. Now the dragon struggled, discarding the pretense of sleep, but it was no use. The line wrapped around and around, until the dragon was confined so closely that it could barely breathe.

The Adept turned and re-entered the palace. Now Forel saw that the line remained attached to him; it trailed wherever he went. Strange man!

But his power was not to be doubted. The dragon lay trussed and whimpering; he was no longer any threat. Evidently it was the Black Adept's steed; its misbehavior had been an embarrassment, so the Adept had disciplined it most effectively. No creature of any sense ever crossed any Adept!

Forel ran to the globe and plunged in, changing to boy form. Barel was there, smiling. "I could come out not," he said. "The globe be impervious to me. So I told Nepe, and she told Bane, and he told Mach."

"And the rovot told the Black Adept!" Forel cried, understanding. "Methought it coincidence he came out!"

"Ne'er so, here," Barel said, satisfied. "Black cared naught for thee, but aught for his pride. E'en those without honor have pride."

"I came to ask thee the nature o' the decision in Proton-frame, that they may verify what thy sire tells."

"Aye, I know it already: they be set to have three Games, and who wins two, wins all. An Citizen Blue wins, Nepe be returned and the Contrary Citizens give up. An the Citizens win, they get the Oracle, and my sire and Bane returned to work for them. It be all or nothing, decided by the Games."

"They play mere games?" Forel asked, amazed.

"They be important Games," Barel said, smiling. "Tell the Adepts; they will understand."

Dubiously, Forel changed back to wolf form and left the globe. He was sure that Barel was not teasing him—but was someone else? Would he be laughed out of the palace when he reported that they were playing games in Proton-frame?

By the time he re-entered the main chamber, the rovot's report was done. The Adepts were waiting for him. Abashed, Forel slunk forward, tail held low.

"Report, pup," Translucent snapped.

Forel changed to boy form. "They—they be playing games," he said, and braced himself for the laughter. But none came. "Two o' three, for Nepe or the Oracle."

"How can they use the Oracle?" Translucent demanded.

"That be the stake too. The rovot and Bane to work as before, for the Adepts."

Translucent nodded. "Let's get on with it, then."

Evidently his answer *did* accord with the one the rovot had given! They took games seriously in Proton-frame!

Forel was forgotten as the Adepts got down to negotiations. It was mainly between Blue and Translucent, but others put in words on occasion.

The essence was that all were agreed that this matter should be settled, and that the stakes in Phaze were the Book of Magic and the boy Flach, who was Barel. The rovot and Bane would serve the winner. Where they differed was in how to settle it.

"Let's make it a contest o' single champions," Stile said. "I will stand for our side; who will stand for thine?" But none came forth from the Adverse Adepts; they knew that none of them could be sure of prevailing either physically or magically against Stile. This was a seeming oddity, because Stile was the smallest among them, and old, and lived simply, as if he had little magic. How deceiving appearances could be!

"Let's make it a war of animals," Purple said. "Ours 'gainst thine." But Blue demurred, for there were more vicious animals supporting the Adverse Adepts than there were supporting Stile, and some of them were dragons and rocs: it would not be a fair contest.

"But my golems will meet thy animals," Brown offered.

"Thy golems be impervious to pain!" Purple retorted.

"We be going round and round," Translucent said impatiently. "Let's hear a suggestion from the animals, then!" He glared around, but there was no peep from the animals. "What stuff be ye made o'?" he demanded. "Here we have a simple matter o' dominance to settle; must it come to total internecine warfare? Why, this pup could do better than that!"

"Ask the pup, then," Purple snapped.

Oops! Forel tried to hide under a chair, but he was in boy form and could not do it before all eyes found him out. "Aye," Translucent said, his gaze fixing on him. "How wouldst thou settle this?"

Forel knew he was stuck for it. He could not try to avoid answering, however foolish he made himself, because he was bound to do what Translucent asked. Well, all he could do was say something, and let it be rejected with disgust, and then he would be off the tooth.

"I—methinks I—I would have a siege," he said, remembering a game of battle he had played with other pups. "Two sides, each laying siege to the other's flag, and the one who captures the other flag without losing its own—" He stalled, cowed by their silence.

"A siege," Translucent said, nodding. He glanced at Kurrelgyre. "Would thy Pack meet similar o' ours in such a game?"

"Aye," the Pack Leader said immediately. "An it be limited to an equivalent force, and no Adept magic."

Translucent gazed at the remaining animal leaders. "Any o' ours to meet this Pack?"

There was a clamor of response. They were all ready! Forel was amazed; had not expected to be taken seriously.

"I see the dragons be ready," Translucent said. "Now—"

"Nay!" Stile cut in. "Werewolves be brave, but that be foolish. Match them 'gainst landbound creatures, near their size."

"Nay, size be no issue," Kurrelgyre protested. "Make the group o' similar strength, be all. Few large, or many small, and we'll accommodate."

"Few large," Translucent said. "Such as ogres—" Here the ogre chief raised a huge calloused fist. "Or many small, such as goblins." And the goblin chief jumped up, eager to oblige.

"Put up sample tribes, and let us choose one," Stile suggested.

"My tribe will do it!" the goblin said.

Stile turned to Kurrelgyre. "Wouldst meet that one?"

"Aye," the werewolf said. "They be a long-time nuisance; my wolves would be glad to deal with them."

"Then I think we have a match," Stile said.

But there was another clamor from the other representatives; they all wanted to participate. "Make it three sieges," Translucent suggested. "Each a different set."

"But without blood," Stile said.

"Without blood!" Purple exclaimed. "Mayhem be the point!"

"Nay. The point be thy style or mine. I will not shed blood unnecessarily to establish a bloodless settlement. Blunt the weapons."

Purple was disgusted, but in the end the compromise was forged: Adept magic on both sides would be used to make any wounds nonlethal. A wolf's bite might seem to tear out a goblin's throat, and blood would flow, but that part would be illusion; the goblin would be unconscious for the duration, but unhurt. A goblin's club might knock a wolf senseless, but the wolf would wake after the siege unharmed.

They also set up three sieges: first a vampire Flock would engage a harpy Flock, then a unicorn Herd would meet an ogre Clan, and finally the wolf Pack would settle with the goblin Tribe. Two victories would settle the issue, and that side would gain the Book of Magic and the services of Rovot and Bane, or would recover Flach and keep the rest. In short, the future dominance of the frame would be decided by these contests, just as would be the case in Proton.

"But what if one side wins Proton, and the other Phaze?" Brown asked.

Translucent laughed. "Then we play more games, and yet more, till the sides agree."

Stile nodded. He wanted the issue settled as much as Translucent did.

So it was agreed. A committee was appointed to work out the details, and the others dispersed. Forel reported to Barel in the globe, who relayed the news to Nepe, verifying what the rovot was sending to the other side.

"Before I go," Translucent said, approaching Kurrelgyre. "I promised a small reward, and my hostages behaved well, and I keep my word. Wolf, I would exchange this one," he indicated Forel, "for another." He glanced at Forel. "Who be Flach's bitch?"

"He has no bitch, only his Promised," Forel said.

"Whate'er. Who be she?"

"Sirelmoba."

Translucent returned to Kurrelgyre. "Forel for Sirelmoba. She would keep him better company on the isle."

"Agreed," Kurrelgyre said.

"One thing more. This one be blooded. He made his first Kill on the isle."

"Agreed," the Pack Leader said again.

So it was done, to Forel's amazement and delight. He would return to the Pack and receive his new syllable, and Barel would have the company of the one closest to him. The Adept had indeed been more than fair. Now he understood why even his enemies treated Translucent with respect; he deserved it.

10: *Sheen*

Sheen walked beside Citizen Blue to the Game Annex. The Annex had been closed for all residents except for this single event. "I fear you are making an error," she said.

"It is a gamble we must take," he countered. "You are an excellent player, and you have a consistency that fleshy creatures lack. Our chances are best with consistency."

"But Citizen Purple is an unscrupulous man, and a veteran gamesman. You need to put up your best against him, and you are the best."

"But he knows me well. He will have traps for me. You were a surprise; he is relatively unprepared for you. Therefore you are the better match, though you may not be the better player."

The process of the selection of players had been the subject of intense negotiation and compromise. Each side wanted the other to designate its player first, so that the best prospect against that player could be chosen. Finally they had settled on one first-designation by the Contrary Citizens, and one by Blue's side. One match would be different: each side would get to choose its opponent from the ranks of the other. Thus the selection would be for the weakest players instead of the strongest. The selection would be done for the second game, immediately before it, so that there could be no preparation.

The Citizens had put up Purple. Blue had had twelve hours to put up his champion. When the third game came, the situation would be reversed, and the Citizens would have the advantage. But perhaps, if things went well, there would be no third game.

Sheen did not worry unduly, because as a self-willed machine she could control her emotions. But she knew that victory was by no means certain, and that Purple, even caught by surprise, remained a better player than she. The odds favored her loss to him, and that would prejudice Blue's case. Yet of course he had to save himself for the final game, to bring the victory if the first two games were not sufficient.

They came to the game chamber. Here Blue kissed her and turned away; he would watch with others in an audience chamber. For the manipulation of the grid, only the two direct players would be there. There would be no advice from the sidelines.

She stepped up to the console and stood waiting. In a moment Citizen Purple entered, like an ancient king in his elaborate purple robe. He even wore a purple diadem set with precious amethyst stones. Huge, bearded, confident, he was a daunting presence.

But she, a robot, was not daunted. She simply recognized and catalogued the effects, in case any of them indicated any aspect of his nature that might be exploited for her advantage in the game. She cared nothing for kings or Citizens, only for the factors of the moment.

Purple stared at her over the console, his gaze commencing at her forehead, inspecting her brown tresses, crossing her own gaze without taking note of it, and coursing down to linger on her bare breasts. But again his effort was wasted; her body was naked, in the fashion of all serfs, and her breasts were pseudoflesh coverings over utility cabinets. Humanoid males tended to ignore the inner reality and focus on the outer form, so that they found a breast interesting regardless whether it was fashioned of living flesh, amoebic mass or plastic, but that was their foible; Sheen was indifferent to his stare. When Blue looked at her body, she took notice, not otherwise.

"If you are ready, sir," she said after a moment.

His hand crashed down on his side of the console. Her side lighted, showing the primary grid.

PRIMARY GRID

	NAKED	TOOL	MACHINE	ANIMAL
1. PHYSICAL				
2. MENTAL				
3. CHANCE				
4. ARTS				

She saw by the highlighting that she had the numbers. For a moment she was tempted to select CHANCE and be done with it. But that was probably not rational, because Blue believed she had a better than even chance to win in a game of skill. Her long association with living human beings, and her female programming, did account for some irrationality, but she was capable of overruling it.

What would he choose? She glanced up, and saw his porcine eyes fastened again on her breasts. Suddenly she knew: he had chosen NAKED, because he could not look upon an unavailable woman without desiring her. It was his way; he had lusted after Tania's voluptuous secretary Tsetse, and connived without Tania's knowledge to have access to her. Now that Tania had defected, Tsetse had wasted no time in denouncing her and becoming Purple's secretary, confessing what she had done in the past. That had had two effects: Tania's fury, and Purple's loss of interest. He had little taste for what was no longer forbidden. But Sheen herself was perhaps the most forbidden female: the wife of Purple's major enemy. Oh, yes, he desired her now, and so great was his compulsion that he had to grasp at any straw to get closer to her. With luck, he might get her into a gelatin wrestling match, and possess her as he pinned her. Her detestation of both him and his act would only increase his passion.

Now it was clearer why Blue had chosen her to play against this man. Purple's nature distorted his judgment, making him vulnerable to manipulation. He had to know she would never let him close to a gelatin chamber, or any other body-to-body sport, yet he had to play for it.

She almost smiled. Too bad her robot strength was governed, so that she could exert no more force than a healthy living woman might, unless threatened with destruction. Otherwise, she could lead him into that gelatin, and pin him down, and win. He might even go knowingly into the loss, just to have that bodily contact in such an environment. But fair was fair; she had to be the woman she seemed, and he knew that.

Well, she would tempt him a bit. She touched 1. PHYSICAL.

Immediately the secondary grid formed: 1D. PHYSICAL ANIMAL. Just as she had known!

Then she did a doubletake, a programmed mannerism not often invoked. Animal? He had fooled her!

She glanced up. There were his eyes, still fixed on her breasts. He was having his fun with her in two ways: ogling her body, and deceiving her about his intentions. He was of course a master player, and this was effective strategy. Would she have chosen PHYSICAL if she had guessed?

She had the numbers again: 5. SEPARATE. 6. INTERACTIVE. 7. COMBAT. 8. COOPERATIVE. She tried again to guess what he might choose. His options were E EARTH F FIRE G GAS H H$_2$O, translating respectively to the various surfaces: Flat, Variable, Discontinuous and Liquid.

He was an old man, tough, but surely not as much so, physically, as he once had been. He should prefer to remain on his stout feet, on a flat plain or a mountainous slope. He would not like to get into the water, riding dolphins or sharks, and discontinuous would be beyond him.

That being the case, she should make it as hard for him as she could. She was nominally old and female, but actually her robot body remained as strong as ever. Strength counted in other ways than direct force of limb; she might not be able to overcome him in a wrestling match, but she could surely outlast him in a match requiring repetition or endurance. More of that was often needed in animal contests—that was generally recognized. Riding a horse, for example, was not a state of rest—not if the animal was frisky, as it would be in a racing or combat situation.

Combat. Well, why not? That could be jousting on horseback, and she had learned to ride, because Blue was the top rider on the planet. It had taken special modification of her programming, but she had done it for him, and had become capable of riding almost any animal, tame or wild. She knew that the Lady Blue (now the Lady Stile) in Phaze was expert, and as the years had passed she had felt steadily closer to the Lady. The mechanism of parallelism between the frames had never been well understood, and with the separation of the past decades there had been little chance to study it, but it seemed that it was a gradual thing. That individuals were not necessarily fixed from birth as parallels; some were, like the two Tanias, but some became parallel over the course of their lives. She liked to think that she was approaching other-selfism with the Lady Blue. Certainly a number of Citizens, by position and inclination, had become increasingly like their Adept counterparts, by Mach and Bane's accounts. So Sheen had learned to ride, deliberately fostering her emulation of the Lady. It had been no more than an exercise of a foolish dream—until Mach had exchanged with Bane, proving that a robot could be the other self of a living person.

These thoughts took little time; they were a rehash of familiar ground. She was already in the process of touching COMBAT.

The tertiary grid appeared—and she had another surprise. Purple had chosen Discontinuity! That meant they would be doing physical battle in the air, or on broken surfaces. She was not well rehearsed in that. The cunning Citizen had outmaneuvered her again.

Sheen knew she was in trouble. Purple would not have chosen GAS unless he felt competent in that medium. He must have practiced in some aspect of this, so that he could have an advantage when he needed it. She had practiced none but the flying horse, for private pleasure.

Still, there were ways and ways. She remembered a little-used option that Blue had discovered, that might be used to turn this grid to her advantage. She needed a way to be sure that she was not playing Purple's game, and she no longer trusted her judgment in this respect. He had fooled her twice, and might maneuver her into accepting the very option he desired. But not if she invoked her ploy.

The tertiary grid was empty, like the others, but unlike the others, it would be filled. A list of options was at the side: specific games they could choose to fill the grid. This was often the most dramatic part of a Game: the maneuvering in the final grid. When players of known skills competed, the actual playoff could be mainly a matter of form; the outcome was known, because of the unequal skills of the contestants. In the two early grids it was too indefinite; it could go either way. But here in the small grid, the one with only nine squares, the real nature and odds of the encounter were determined.

All of the choices related to physical combat involving animals. The definition of "animal" was broad; androids and even some cyborgs counted in particular cases, as well as true animals. Most of them involved birds, whether natural or artificial.

There was an advantage in placing the first choice, because the one who did would get five choices to the other's four, weighting the grid in his favor. But this was offset by a corresponding advantage given to the other in the play: choice of color in chess, of offense or defense in football, or initial serve in tennis, and so on. Where this was not applicable, the other player would get the choice of numbers or letters, which could make a critical difference if placements were careless. Experienced players tended to go for the play advantage, being competent in most games; beginners preferred stacking the choices.

"Take it, wench," Purple said, his eyes stroking her torso again. By this time a normal woman would be flustered by the direct and pointed attention, knowing that the Citizen had a far better than even chance to realize whatever ambition he had for interaction with her, regardless of the outcome of the Game. But Sheen was hardly normal; even had she been of fleshly nature, she remained Citizen Blue's wife. Not even his compatriots would support him if he waylaid her. Thus he confined his aggression to his eyes and his voice, doing what he could to unnerve her. It was usually a good ploy; the slightest shakiness in either the choices or the actual play could make the difference in the outcome.

So she had the first choice, as though Purple had no concern for any trifling advantage she might gain. Again, the psychological ploy was wasted on her; as a machine, she simply was not subject to irrational nuances of doubt, only rational ones. Her concern was to play correctly—and he had just given her the break she needed. Now she would have two chances in three to get a playoff she liked.

She touched the choice of Sparrow Sparring, and the center square of her grid. Immediately the words transferred. She had the best location, some thought, though in practice it made little difference. She had worked with animals, including birds, in her effort to emulate the Lady Blue, because the Lady had worked to heal many sick or injured creatures who came to the Blue Demesnes in Phaze. Sparrow Sparring involved the projection of the player's commands to living birds, who flew up and attacked each other with beak and claw. The birds, not naturally vicious, were trained for this, and both beaks and claws were capped by soft material that left a smear of color on the target rather than causing injury. The one who inflicted a severe enough "injury" on the other received the reward of especially tasty seed, and that bird's manager won the game. Sheen had developed a certain empathy with the small birds, and now had what she thought of as "sparrow circuits" so that she could direct them effectively. It was not just a matter of giving specific commands; it was a matter of proper motivation and superior strategy. She believed she could win this one, because Purple was liable to be too callous in his treatment of small, weak creatures.

His turn: he set Cock Fighting into the upper left square, 9J. The numbers carried on from the prior sequence, and the letters skipped "I" in the standard manner to avoid confusion with the number "1." These would be fierce flying roosters who could strike on the ground or in the air; the cock pit was a cage with assorted perches and baffles so that each combatant could choose his turf and dodge about tactically. As with the sparrows, the birds' weapons were mock; the little blades affixed to their legs—the spurs—delivered color smears instead of lethal cuts. Once the fights had been real, but Citizen Blue had decreed that they be moderated: no real blood was shed in the name of entertainment any more. A number of die-hard players were disgusted, but Blue held the dominant hand. Sheen hoped to do her part to ensure that he continued to govern; if the Contrary Citizens prevailed, blood would flow again in more than the figurative sense.

Her turn: she put Hawk Lasso in 11L, the bottom right corner. In this one the hawks carried loops of fine cord, and tried to snare each other. The first to get a tight loop around the other's neck, tail or feet was the victor. There were safeguards, and the birds were apt flyers; they seemed to enjoy it, though the command-impulses sent by the players prevented them from playing it their way.

He filled in Dog Fight in 10J, right below his prior entry. This was the zero-gee variant, with a spherical cage; the dogs used the wall only as a launching surface to attack each other. It was difficult to get in a good bite, without the anchorage of gravity, and the dogs required special training before they became competent. The trained dogs were evenly matched, as were all the contest animals; it was the skill of the players who directed strategy and tactics that made the difference. The teeth were blunted, to prevent harm, but Sheen did not want to tackle the Citizen in this arena; he was too bloodthirsty, and probably had practiced secretly with dogs whose teeth were sharp.

Now it was her turn, and she had only one spot to fill this time: 11J. That was because she could not afford to let Purple fill in a complete column of his choices, for that would represent his victory in the grid. He would simply select that column, and she would be stuck with one of his choices, having no chance at any of her own. In this sense the grid was like its primitive progenitor, tic-tac-toe: three in a row spelled victory. So she filled in Jet Birds, giving herself one option in that column.

He put Owl Bomb in the top center box. In this contest trained owls would be directed to drop bombs of colored water on each other. The liquid was harmless, but was scented in a manner the birds did not like. The cage was large, so that they had ample flying room. Each tried to get above the other so as to be able to score with the bomb, but of course the ceiling was the limit. The owls knew how to launch their bombs upward against an opponent pinned against the ceiling, so "upsmanship" was not the only strategy.

Now she had to fill in 9L, to prevent him from getting a full row of choices. That was the thing about his "generous" yielding of the first placement to her: because he could go with either the numbers or the letters, nothing was safe for her. She put in Pigeon Kites: a contest in which pigeons actually flew little kites in the stiff air currents provided by nozzles. The strings were triangular in cross-section, each edge sharp and serrated. The trick was to down the opponent's kite, either by cutting its string or pre-empting its wind so that it dropped out of control. The pigeons, though trained, were not smart; most of the skill had to be that of the players, sending repeated and specific directives. *Move left, fly up, turn, drop down,* and so on. The maneuvers could get quite intricate.

Now she had chances to complete either the L column or the 11 row. But this represented no victory for her, because he had the option. He would simply block out one, and choose the other. For example, he could fill 10L, then play the grid from the numbers, so as to prevent her from choosing the 11 row that would have her three choices. Only a duffer would play it otherwise.

He filled Laser Duel: Eagle in the L column. In this, the eagles were artificial, being cyborgs in eagle form. Their living brains qualified them as animals. Each carried a laser pistol that it could fire straight ahead. If a score was made, the victim's system shorted out and the bird fell to the net below. This one was a favorite with the younger players, especially the males; they loved to fire lasers, even vicariously, and chortled when an eagle spun out of control.

Now there was one box left to fill, 11K. She would have her row, but since she would have to work from the letters, she had no chance to benefit from it. She had a better ploy, and this was the time for it.

"Dragon Duel," she said.

A word lighted below her grid: ERROR—NO SUCH GAME EXISTS.

"But it fits the category," she said. "The listed choices are only suggestions; the players can choose what they wish, as long as they remain within the definitions of the encounter." She glanced up at Purple. "Isn't that correct, sir?"

The Citizen hefted his gaze from her bosom. "True, doxie. You want it, you can have it."

"I want it."

Now the voice of the Game Computer sounded. "An extension of the game options has been proposed. Judgment Committee number 452 report immediately to Game Console 23."

Purple licked his lips. "You really want to do this, peaches?" he inquired with relish. He, as a Phaze fan, had long experience with mocked-up dragons.

"I do."

"I'll make you a side deal, sweetbuns. I'll give you that arena—"

"No deal," she snapped. She might win or she might lose, but she had no intention of committing her body to his lechery in addition. Her ploy was that he would be so intrigued by the new contest that he would elect to play it anyway.

There was a stir in the audience chamber as the members of the Judgment Committee arrived. A number of the watchers evidently had not known that specific games or even categories could be added in this manner. To have it happen during a contest as important as this was rare excitement.

The committee consisted of one female Citizen, one male Citizen, one female serf, one male serf, and the Game Computer, represented by a humanoid robot whose outer surface was transparent so that its wires, hydraulics and electronic components showed. It took charge at once.

"The serf Sheen will explain the nature of the proposed game."

Sheen was ready. "The Dragon Duel would consist of each player guiding an android or cyborg flying dragon whose weapons would be those of the genuine dragons of Phaze: fiery breath and metallic talons. The technology of such creations is available, and the nature of dragons is known. The players will control their dragons in the same manner they control other animals: by projecting commands to them. The dragon that downs its opponent will be the winner."

"Modification," Citizen Purple said. "Instead of sending commands, the players will actually ride their dragons. This will make the game far more personal and dramatic."

That caught Sheen by surprise. She had expected him to be silent, letting her make or break her case. If the committee concluded that the proposed game was impractical, then the square on which she had asked to enter it was forfeit, and her opponent would get to place a choice of his own there. Thus Purple stood a reasonable chance of gaining an advantage merely by keeping his mouth shut. But as it was, he had become a co-proponent of the notion, and so would gain no advantage if it were turned down. This was something he was entitled to do, just as she was entitled to ask for the new game.

The male Citizen on the committee had a question. "Large creature constructs are valuable. How would you justify the waste of resources entailed in shooting down expensive dragons?"

"By making the weapons token, sir," she replied. "The dragon fire could be a beam of light that would trigger the short-circuiting of key circuits in the victim where it struck. There would be no loss of equipment, and the dragons could be used repeatedly without suffering actual damage."

The female serf had a question for Purple. "Sir, you say the players will ride the dragons. What if they fall off?"

Citizen Purple eyed her. She was reasonably young and pretty, and flushed becomingly under her gaze. "Harnesses," he said. "Saddles. No one will fall unless the dragon does, and it will be protected from crashing."

"The Game facilities are limited," the female Citizen said. "Where would such a game be played?"

Sheen knew she was in trouble. "I had thought of small dragons, sir. In Phaze there are dragons of all sizes, and some are hardly bigger than birds, and could compete in an existing arena, controlled by sent directives."

"As it happens," Purple said, "I have larger models of dragons on my estate at the Purple Mountain Range, that can be ridden. I will make my estate and equipment available to the Game Annex for this limited purpose. There will be no cost to the city."

Sheen was amazed. Purple was actively pursuing her ploy! She had known he had mock fantasy creatures on his monstrous estate, but had never thought he would offer these for public use. Her notion had been intended to catch his fancy; it had succeeded beyond her expectation.

"How long would it take to set up?" the male citizen inquired.

"No time," Purple replied grandly "The dragons and facilities are available now."

The committee consulted, then voted. The game was judged on feasibility and interest; Citizen Purple's offer made it feasible, his way, and it was obvious that everyone was interested. The game was accepted.

TERTIARY GRID: 1D7G
Physical Animal–Assisted Combat, Discontinuous Surface

	J	K	L
9	Cock Fight	Owl Bomb	Pigeon Kite
10	Dog Fight	Sparrow Spar	Eagle Duel
11	Jet Birds	Dragon Duel	Hawk Lasso

Sheen realized that she had misplayed her ploy. She had not allowed for the Citizen's modification, and now the new game was far more to his specification than to hers. Still, the dynamics of managing a flying dragon should be similar, whether done by remote suggestion or direct personal contact.

But they still had the grid to play. Purple had the choice of numbers or letters—and he amazed her again by taking the letters. That gave her the chance to choose row 11 and be guaranteed a game of her choice.

"Take it, luscious," the Citizen said grandly. "You asked for it, you got it; now put your body where your mouth is."

He really wanted to play that game! Sheen realized that she was committed; she had asked for it, and had gotten it, and now would look like a bad sport if she didn't follow through. Of course she should not let appearances interfere with sensible choosing—yet it did seem sensible to her. She had rehearsed the dynamics of flying in the past; she should be able to manage a properly designed dragon.

She touched 11. Immediately the box lighted. They had selected Dragon Duel.

The Citizen's estate turned out to be capacious indeed. It covered a region of the Purple Mountain Range hundreds of kilometers square. Citizen Blue had the greatest financial leverage, therefore the most power, but he had never gone in for luxurious surroundings. Purple obviously believed in catering to his selfish interests. But it was impressive not only for scale; the detail was intricate. This was a replica of Phaze, so realistic as to be deceptive. Sheen had been there, decades ago when she was new, and her memory banks were untarnished by time; she could appreciate the accuracy of this replication. Purple's devotion to the image of Phaze was obviously genuine.

Citizen Blue brought in his own crew to check the mechanism of the dragons. They were in perfect working order: giant metal and plastic bodies governed by living animal brains crafted in the laboratory for this purpose. When they were put through test flight, they seemed indeed alive, glaring balefully around as if wishing to chomp the spectators. Probably those living minds hated this servitude, and would indeed attack if not bound by effective strictures.

The dragons were ready. Sheen mounted hers and was given instructions: the creature was responsive to the pressures of the rider's legs, as with a horse, with additional leg-commands for ascending and descending. It would not react to the human voice, as this was unreliable during wind-sheering maneuvers. It would obey immediately, so that very soon it would seem like an extension of herself. She was also permitted to take off first, so as to gain the feel of it before the combat started.

She was in a saddle, and in a harness that she could not have escaped had she wanted to. She would not fall from the dragon, and it could not crash, because there were repulsive magnetic fields at the ground that would buoy it. She wore goggles to protect her eyes from wind, flying dust, or the bright flashes of the "fire" jets. She, as a robot, had less need of these than a living woman might, but was satisfied to accept any protection offered.

She knew she was outclassed; the Citizen had had decades to perfect his technique on artificial dragons, and would be far superior in the air. But she did have some small assets. She weighed less, for Purple was portly, and since the two dragons were even, hers should have a slight edge in velocity and maneuverability. She also had the ability to catalogue the precise nature of the commands she gave the dragon, and their effects, and repeat these exactly. The living human brain was more sophisticated than hers in most respects, but when it came to rote learning, hers was better. Thus she could quickly calibrate her maneuvers to an extent the arrogant Citizen might not appreciate, and so he could underestimate her. That could be critical!

They launched. The repulsor field came on, and the dragon flapped its great wings, but that was not all. It had downward-pointing nozzles along the underside of its body and wings that jetted air; this provided extra lift. In Phaze the flight of dragons was augmented by magic; the wings alone were not sufficient. Here science did the job. If one dragon flew under another, here, it would be pushed down by the jets; but these were set to splay out so that the effect was not dangerous except at close range. Still, it was a strategy to remain aware of; if she saw Purple's dragon trying to come down on hers from above, she would get out of the way. In this respect the jets substituted for an attack by the feet; these dragons had no feet.

She had been pondering strategies for the combat from the moment the game had been set. She had to surprise the Citizen in some way, and that was her greatest challenge, because her mind was bound to be both less experienced and less original than his. What could she come up with that he would not anticipate? She could think of only one thing—and, like her ploy of choosing a game not on the list, it had to be done only at the end. Only if she was bound to lose anyway would it become worthwhile.

The ride was uneven. The dragon lurched forward and up with each wingstroke; it would have been almost impossible to remain mounted bareback! She had seen pictures of maidens riding dragons without harness, saddle or reins; indeed, she had read such stories to Mach, bringing him up just like the boy he emulated. But she had felt obliged to explain to him that this was sheer fantasy; only with magic could such riding be done. He had looked and nodded. "Or a spot floating force field" he had suggested. He had been literal as a robot—but later it had turned out that the seed of magic had indeed taken hold of his soul, and he had found a way to go to Phaze.

Now here she was, a naked woman on a dragon—but the saddle and harness enclosed her to such an extent that she might as well have been clothed. Her arms and legs were mobile, but her body was locked in place. The harness straps were padded, but she knew that a real woman would soon have chafed flesh, because of the violence of the motion.

She pressed with her knees, and the dragon veered immediately. It was responsive, all right! She squeezed in the "down" configuration, and the dragon leveled out, then nosed down. She reversed signals immediately, and it wobbled, then resumed its climb into the bright sky. Already the trees were well below, and the landscape was opening out. Ahead was the impressive slope of the Purple Mountain Range, but behind was a lot of open air.

She decided to experiment. She made the dragon level out, and fly directly toward the mountains, which rose higher than her present elevation. Would it veer clear on its own, or would it obey her?

The dragon turned its head, glancing back at her. Its neck was not limber enough to enable it to aim its head fully back, and as she looked into its baleful red eye, she understood why. The living brain that animated this body hated her, because she was directing it; it would gladly destroy her if it could. It knew it could not—not intentionally. But by accident—perhaps.

The head faced forward again, and the dragon stroked more vigorously forward. It *wanted* to crash into the slope of the mountain! Since it could not do so literally, what did it think would happen? She tried to analyze the dynamics, and thought she knew.

Sure enough, the dragon plowed into the invisible repulsor field at full speed and glanced off. It did a vertical loop, so that she was upside down. She gave it the roll-over command with her feet, and, reluctantly, it turned over and flew level. It had obviously hoped that the surprise would shake her, perhaps causing her to vomit; it did not know that it had done exactly what she wanted. She had gained a vital bit of information.

Meanwhile, Purple's dragon had launched. She was required to give him time to assume an elevation similar to her own; thereafter there were no conventions. The better dragon-flyer would win—or the more cunning one. She was neither, unless her concluding ploy worked.

All too soon, the Citizen was with her. The duel was on!

She knew she could not flee or hide. Her only chance at the outset was attack, to keep the Citizen occupied, and hope she made a lucky score. She guided her steed toward the other.

Purple was not fazed. He oriented his own dragon to come straight at her. A direct collision was impossible; the cyborg dragons would not allow it, tempted though they might be. They would take turns passing above and below each other.

She gave her beast the toe-stab that was the fire command. The dragon dutifully aimed its snout and fired its laser. But this was not an instant thing; the seeming fire curled out visibly. That gave the Citizen time to dodge, and the fire passed below. Then Sheen's steed was struck by the downblast of the other's elevation jets, and she had to guide her mount to stability.

She heard something. She craned her neck to look backward—and saw the Citizen's dragon looping straight up. Then, as it hit the top of its loop, it rolled over and oriented on her. The fire started.

She made her dragon veer to the side, and the jet missed. That was a maneuver she hadn't thought of! The vertical loop was faster than a horizontal turn would have been; she had almost been caught as a sitting duck, as it were.

She made a horizontal circle. Could she catch him from the side, so that he could not fire back immediately? She tried, but found it to be impractical; the slowness of the fire meant that it would either miss far behind the other dragon or, if aimed sufficiently ahead, be readily avoidable. That slowness—how was that possible, with lasers? It had to be a timed sequence, twin beams invisible until they intersected, then "catching fire" at a distance from the snout. That region of intersection was moved outward as the beams shone, so that the fire progressed forward in the manner of a real flame. Clever—and frustrating for her, because the Citizen was better at these maneuvers than she was.

She would have to get very close to be sure of her shot—and that would make her vulnerable to Purple's shot. Unless she could close from behind.

She turned to follow the other dragon, and urged her steed forward. Yes—her lighter weight made a difference, and they were gaining! She could close slowly, and toast the other's tail!

But when the Citizen saw what she was doing, he dived. Now his extra weight helped his steed, and he gained. As they swooped low, he looped up again, and she had to dodge to avoid his shot. But she tried a ploy of her own: after she moved aside, she moved back, orienting on him as he slowed at the top of his loop. If she could catch him now—

But he fired first. She had forgotten that the dragons could move their heads as they fired; they did not have to be straight forward. She had to bank desperately to avoid getting tagged, and did not quite succeed; there was a flare of light at her dragon's right wingtip, and her ride became ragged. Some of the control circuits had been shorted out, and the wing was crippled.

She was losing in rapid order. It was time to use her final ploy. She guided the dragon upward, and it made erratic progress while the Citizen made a smooth horizontal turn. As his dragon set up for another shot, Sheen gave her mount conflicting commands: climb and dive. It was the kind of error a novice or a flustered combatant would make. A steed who liked its rider and was used to the rider's ways might have paused, waiting for the correction. This one did not like its rider, so took the pretext to go out of control. It lifted its forepart, let its rearpart drop, blasted with its elevation jets, and spun out of control.

Which was exactly what Sheen wanted.

They plummeted toward the ground, while the Citizen cruised down, orienting for a shot when the repulsor field halted the fall and left the dragon spinning in place. But Sheen started a series of commands just before then, and recovered control. Her dragon had to obey. Instead of crashing in air, the dragon bounced back up, in yo-yo fashion—and as it did, she fired, causing its jet to swing in an arc toward the Citizen's steed. This was her ploy: to catch the Citizen just when he thought he had a helpless target.

But Purple's dragon was not hovering, it was circling. Sheen's shot missed by a wide margin.

Then Purple's dragon fired from behind her, and she was unable to get up speed to avoid it. She knew before it struck that she was lost. The Citizen had anticipated her, and the victory was his.

The mock fire did not hurt her physically, of course. But she knew she had failed her husband in this most important contest. She had indeed been overmatched, and Citizen Blue would pay the price. Her emotional circuitry took over, and she wept.

11: *Phoebe*

Phoebe perched in her den, desolate. She had done wrong; she knew it. She had let an unharpylike compassion lead her into helping the 'corn-boy Flach escape—and Translucent had caught her at it. Yet the boy was the foal of the unicorn Fleta, who had befriended her and cured her tailfeather itch, and of the Rovot Adept, who had given her a hairdo that had made her the Flock Leader. How could she turn Flach away? She knew that a true harpy would have pounced on the boy and offered him up to the Adepts, gleefully reneging on any debt owed his family. By her action she had proved that she lacked the proper harpy attitude. So now she was barred again from the Flock, and there was to be a scratch-off to select a new leader, and she was in the dumps.

Yet such was her depravity, she knew she would do it again. The rovot and unicorn had given her an illicit taste of something virtually unknown in harpydom: friendship. Now she cravenly clung to the notion. She wanted to be among folk who cared for those they were with, instead of perpetually cursing them. So here she was, deprived of the kind of company she no longer desired anyway. She was sorry the lad had been recaptured. It was an irony that he had been hiding from those same folk who had befriended her. But she knew that they did not really want to be on the side of the Adverse Adepts, any more than she did. They too were stuck in a nasty situation.

She went down to her spring and peered at her reflection. Her fright wig was sagging; the rovot's spell was slowly wearing off. But it had become the mark of her leadership among the harpies of her Flock, and its appeal to her was fading with the appeal of association with the Flock. She was ready to let it dissolve away. But because it was the gift of the rovot, she would not hurry it.

She was hungry, so she hunted. Fortunately for her, this region was rich with small prey, because an Adept enchantment prevented her from leaving it. They were still mulling over her fate; they might kill her, or they might merely maim her, depending on their judgment. If she had any way, she would flee to the other side for sanctuary, but she knew she could not. She was in the same situation as the near-Adept Tania, who it seemed had now helped or tried to help the enemy twice. Had Tania not been the sister of an Adept, and a rather pretty young woman, too, she might have suffered grievously, the first time. Had she not managed to defect, she would certainly have suffered the second time. Phoebe knew the cause of her problem; it was common gossip in the Flock. She had been so foolish as to fall in love with Bane, the son of the Adept Stile. They were working on the same side, so she had not been able to use her Eye on him and bend him to her cruel will; instead he had bent her to his kind will, and thereby destroyed her nature. Even as Phoebe's nature had been destroyed. Ah, the corruption wrought by exposure to decency!

She flew low through the forest, and spied a foolish fat rat gnawing on a gourd by day. She gave a rat-terrorizing screech and pounced. The rat jumped away, but she snatched it in mid-leap. Harpies were the champions of snatch! The Harpilympics featured the two-claw snatch and the one-claw snatch and the single, double and triple snatches, and the winners were so fast that the motion of their claws could not be seen; the prey went from ground to mouth seemingly of its own volition. She had seen one prize-winning demonstration in which a mouse, rat and rabbit had been snatched, with the first finishing in the mouth of the second, and the second in the mouth of the third, and the third in the mouth of the harpy, all seemingly in a single blurred motion. Triple snatch galore!

There was a rumble behind her. She flew up, startled, and turned in air to look back, the rat still struggling in her claws. A cleft opened in the ground, and from it rose a fat man in a purple robe. "Purple Adept!" she screeched, astonished and hardly pleased. "Hast come to dispatch me at last, thou bulging sausage?"

The ground closed, leaving him standing, unperturbed. "Merely to make thee choose, bird brain," he said equably.

"An I had a choice, would I choose to snatch thine eyeballs from thy foul face, and thy tongue too, and wrap them that they squirt not too much when I chomp them," she screeched.

"An thou not be quiet, hen, willst thou hear not mine offer."

"This for thine offer, offal!" she screeched, letting go the very foulest of droppings. "An thou meanest not to torture me to death, get thy presence gone from here ere I suffocate from the mere smell o' thee!''

"The offer be this: resume the leadership o' thy Flock, or be afflicted with the return of thy tailfeather itch, ten times as bad as before.''

He had certainly pinpointed the opposite extremes of her preference! But she knew better than to trust this. "Where be the catch, flatus?''

"There be a task for thy Flock to perform.''

"Harpies perform tasks not!'' she screeched. "We be dirty birds o' prey, not beasts o' burden!''

"This be a mock combat situation,'' he explained. "Thou must engage in a siege 'gainst a vampire Flock, the one to capture the flag o' the other and lose not its own.''

"Mock?'' she screeched, still looking for the catch she knew was there. "The only one I wish to mock is thee, thou miserable excuse for feculence!''

"Teeth and claws be nulled; their action seems real, but the victim suffers mere loss o' function, not o' limb or life, and after the siege be done, all victims recover without further effect.''

"What kind o' combat be that?'' she screeched. "Action without the splatter o' blood be no action at all!''

"I agree with thee, stinkfeather, but such be the rule. It be part o' the compromise hammered out with Stile.''

"With Stile! Thou hast no dealings with the Blue Demesnes!'' But this interested her more than she could afford to let on. If some way offered to defect to Stile . . .

"This siege be 'gainst a Flock o' bats supporting Stile. It be one o' three, and two o' three gives the final victory. Canst snatch a flag from bats, dangledugs?''

Now the catch was coming clear. She wanted to defect to the side of the Adept Stile—and here she had to oppose it. The Purple Adept, suspecting this, had devised an exquisite torment: she would have to labor to deny Blue the ultimate power. Was she to do this, as she knew she could, or suffer the torment of the tenfold tailfeather itch? She knew the Adept was making no bluff; his threat was well within his power of implementation.

She was a coward; she knew it. She could face dismemberment or death, but not the tailfeather itch. It would tear her up to do this to Stile or his minions, but she could not face the alternative. "Aye,'' she murmured.

"Methinks I did not hear thee, frightface,'' he said. "Dost agree to serve?''

"Aye,'' she said reluctantly.

"I saw no ripple."

"Aye!" she screeched, and now the ripple radiated out, committing her to her ultimate. She would do her very best to accomplish the thing she hated to accomplish.

"Aye," he agreed, smiling smugly, and his cleft in the ground opened and took him in.

Phoebe surveyed the grounds of the siege personally. She well understood the importance of terrain, having had to hunt alone for the years of her tailfeather itch; a hunter who knew her ground had a significant, often critical advantage over one who did not. The key to success was to drive the prey into terrain unfamiliar to it; then it could readily be trapped and snatched.

In this case the prey was a flag; it could not be driven or spooked. But the importance of knowing the ground remained, for creatures would be carrying that flag. Bats would be guarding it, thus they were prey. Also, bats would be seeking to steal her own flag, and any who got hold of that flag had to be caught immediately. The parallels to genuine hunting were close enough.

Her flag was mounted at the top of a towering pine tree. She had no choice about that; the Adepts had determined the regions and placements beforehand. The bats would fly low, using the concealment of the mixed forest, perhaps even crawling up the trunk of the pine tree to reach the flag. Once one of them got it—the thing was of very light fabric, so that it weighed almost nothing—that bat would head for the sky, using its superior speed to outdistance the pursuit of the harpies. The moment the two flags were put together by one creature, the siege would be over, and the victor the team of the one who held the flags.

She would have to assign hens to guard that tree, to nab any bat who tried to climb it. That was simple enough. Prevention was obviously the best defense; she had to see that no bat got close to that flag.

She flew across to the enemy flag. This was mounted on a pole atop a small mountain peak. It would be easy to access it by air, but the hens would be readily spotted. Bats in manform would be able to pick off the harpies, using bows and arrows. That was the problem: while a harpy was more than a match for a bat or several bats, a manform vamp with a good weapon was a match for several harpies. The hens could fly high, out of range of the arrows, but would have to descend to within range to snatch the flag. That was no good; they would be riddled in short order. The arrows, like other weapons, might have only a temporary effect, but the siege could be lost if they made a careless approach.

She flew in increasing spirals around the full region, peering at everything. Here there was a chaparral, a thick tangle of small evergreen oak trees, a fairly effective barrier to the manform but not to batform. There was an inlet of the eastern sea, tapering from broad to narrow and finally ending at the mouth of a small river. That would be easy for either form to fly over, but the manforms would have to swim, where they would be vulnerable to harpy attack. There was a ridge of hills angling roughly between the two flags, that would serve as excellent cover for manforms with weapons. There were fire-cleared glades, and patches of thin forest; the cleared regions formed a random and fairly intricate pattern that could offer both promise and danger for infiltrators.

The east part of the siege area was limited by the Eastern Sea that surrounded the East Pole. This was infested by salt-water predators and was unsafe for any land or air creatures not protected by magic. But the inlet was fresh water, from the river, and she spied no dangerous marine creatures there. Interesting. This region was as new to the bats as to the harpies, being neutral ground; the bats might not realize the significance of the fresh water here.

She completed her survey. Bats were doing a similar job; this was a time of truce before the siege. She ignored them, and returned to her headquarters. She had learned what she wanted, and was now working out a strategy for victory.

For she had decided: she might wish that the Adept Stile's side could win, but she had made a deal, and she would give it her best. The bats would only beat the hens by out-sieging them and she doubted they could do it. Strategy had always been her forte, as the Purple Adept had obviously known; some other hen might have botched the siege, but Phoebe would not.

Part of her wished that the bats had a superior strategist who could defeat her, so that Stile could win. But the rest of her knew that would be terrible for her, and not just because a loss would beget the tenfold tailfeather itch. She had pride, after all; she had to prove she was the best, no matter what the cost. Prove that she had not really been corrupted by decency. She hated this, but it was the way it was.

Now she faced her Flock. "There be our flag," she screeched. "Across the valley there, be the bats' flag, mounted on a hill. The game be this: we must snatch the enemy flag and bring it back to join ours, and that be the victory. But we may not touch our own flag, only the enemy. An they take it, we must destroy who carries it, and leave it lie, and guard it till we bring theirs to it. Questions?"

"Can we kill them?" a horrendous old harpy screeched.

"Nay, Sabreclaw. But we may try. Our claws be enchanted so they poison not, only stun, and the same for the bats' weapons. This be a play-siege, but do thy worst, for it will seem real, and only when it ends will the wounded and dead recover."

"Those bats be under the tutelage o' Vodlevile and his cub Vidselud," a grizzled old harpy screeched. "They be friends to Stile, and be no fools. What be our strategy?"

"Right dost thou be, Hawktooth," Phoebe screeched. "They be no mean adversaries. They have both speed and power o'er us, in one form or t'other. But our strategies be two. For the defense thou willst govern, taking thy place in the tree below and snatching and dispatching any bats who come near. But beware, for thou willst have too few hens to do it well; thou must be cunning and waste no effort on trifles, lest they overwhelm thee and take the flag and fly it high and fast beyond thy means to reco'er."

"Too few hens?" Hawktooth screeched. "Why?"

"Because we need the rest on offense. As we do our job, thou willst not be hard-pressed long."

At the word "offense," the members of the Flock pressed in more closely. That was what they liked.

"Thou, Sabreclaw, willst lead the attack on the enemy flag, with six tough birds o' thine own choosing," Phoebe continued. "But this be no easy thing."

"Give me six foul hens and false, and there be naught to stand in our way!" Sabreclaw screeched boldly. "We'll smear those bats into spatters o' blood!" There was a raucous chorus of agreement. How these birds loved blood! This was of course the root of the traditional enmity between harpies and vampires: competition for blood.

"Nay," Phoebe screeched, quelling the commotion. "This be a secret attack, avoiding mayhem."

There was disgust, horror and outrage. "What kind o' attack be that?" Sabreclaw demanded righteously. "An attack without blood be no mission for a harpy!"

"Blood with no victory be no mission for us," Phoebe countered. "Dost want to hangfeather in shame for losing the siege to mere bats?"

They had to admit, grudgingly, that she had a point, albeit a technicality. They wanted blood *and* victory, not one or the other.

A nasty thought pushed into Phoebe's consciousness, like a tapeworm in the gut of an otherwise edible morsel. Was she assigning the most ferocious hen of the Flock to this mission in the hope that Sabreclaw would be unable to control her lust for bloodshed, and would go on a rampage and mess up her mission, so that they would lose the siege? That would bring no direct shame to Phoebe, if it was clear that her strategy would have been effective. Yet if it were also clear that she could have assigned a hen who would have obeyed orders . . .

She had to do this right. "Thou willst commit to doing this right, or needs I must appoint an other squad leader," Phoebe told Sabreclaw firmly. "The success o' the siege depends on this, and the shame be mine if there be not discipline in the ranks."

Sabreclaw had to commit to doing it right, lest she be summarily removed from the action. "But an there be no other way, then—"

"Then blood," Phoebe agreed. "Likely once thou dost put thy claw on the flag, and before thou canst rise beyond the range o' their weapons, there be action. But before then, thou and thine be the meekest o' sparrows."

"Aye, and dragons after!" They were coming to terms with it, realizing that the blood would likely be only delayed, not aborted. "But how do we get close? That flag be in plain view, and the bats be not batty enough to leave it unguarded!"

"Precisely," Phoebe agreed. "That be exactly why the sneak-snatch be necessary. Another squad will mount the overt attack, distracting the bats, whilst thou dost lead thy squad down under cover o' the trees and through the chaparral—" Here she paused to scratch a diagram in the dirt below her perch. "Needs must scurry like rats, wings furled, to pass this thicket, but the bats, assured we will not be there, will leave it unguarded or lightly guarded. Take out the guard silently and ferry through single file. Here there be water, an inlet o' the Eastern Sea. Find the old tree fallen into it, and grasp the trunk o' it and climb down into the water—"

"What?!"

"And under the water," Phoebe continued relentlessly. "It be a well-known fact that most creatures believe that harpies hate water—"

"We do hate water!" Sabreclaw screeched.

"And lack the gumption to go near it. But the truth be that though harpies may have a strong and justified aversion to water, they be not afraid o' it, and can handle it when the dictates o' courage demand. Dost disagree?"

There were evidently a number in the Flock who wanted to disagree, but none did, oddly.

"By going under the water, canst pass where no bat expects," Phoebe explained. "The inlet be narrow here, and the water fresh, so no saltsea predators be there. Hold breath, set claws in sunken tree, pull along, and the farthest branch be at a clutch o' reeds the other

side, concealment for emergence. Crawl out unobserved, seek cover o'
nearby forest arm, and continue on toward the mountain bearing their
flag. Take ne'er to the air, and hide whene'er a bat shows, making no
disturbance. Then, when there be no chance to get closer unobserved,
make a mass rush for the flag, taking out all bats in range, and snatch
it and wing for the sky and bring it back to join ours." Phoebe fixed
Sabreclaw with a steely gaze. "Canst do?"

Sabreclaw hesitated, but realized that this was the way it had to be.
"Can do," she agreed. It was obvious that she dreaded the crawl under
water, but saw the merit of the plan, and knew she had to prove that
harpies weren't afraid of anything.

"Then pick thy squad," Phoebe said. "When the siege starts, take
thy time, go down out o' sight when none be watching, and let none
see thee advance. The success o' this siege be in thy claws, and the
glory be thine an ye succeed."

Sabreclaw set about selecting her squad of tough hens, and Phoebe
went on to more routine matters. The remaining hens were assigned
to offense and defense, and there was one suicide squad who would
make a determined raid on the enemy flag at about the time Sabreclaw's squad was passing under the water, to draw the attention of the
bats. It was all intended to seem conventional enough, as if harpies
lacked the wit for innovation or subtlety, and with luck the bats would
underestimate the opposition.

The siege began at noon, and would continue until settlement. The
harpies knew they had to win it by day, because the bats were supreme
by night. But Phoebe figured to do it in the first hour; if her sneak
ploy failed, they would be in deep droppings. She had rehearsed all
the squads in their tasks; in addition to the flag defense and the flag
offense, there were the mock offense and the general defense to be seen
to. Phoebe herself would hover above and go where needed to buttress
a problem area.

She went forward with her lieutenants Hawktooth and Sabreclaw,
to meet the bat leader Vodlevile, his son Vidselud, and a female bat.
When the bats assumed their manforms, Phoebe was amazed. "Suchevane!" she screeched, recognizing the loveliest of all the vamps. "How
camest thou to be here? Methought thou wedded to the Red Adept!"
For the alien from Proton-frame, Agape, had exchanged bodies with
the unicorn Fleta eight years prior, and come to Phoebe for help, then
gone on to the Red Adept, who had finally solved her problem. In
the process Suchevane had gotten to know the Adept; she was beautiful and lonely, and he was powerful and lonely, and one thing had

led to another, and now they had their mixedbreed son, Al. In the old days such a union would have been impossible, but the rovot and the 'corn had shown the way.

"The Flock be short a member, so I returned," Suchevane replied.

"But this be a siege!" Phoebe protested. "It be very like war. We dirty birds thrive on it, but thou dost be too delicate for aught like this."

"Delicate? I raised the child o' a troll!"

She had a point. "Well, the mayhem be but mock," Phoebe said. " 'Twere else a shame to mangle thy pretty features."

"Aye," Suchevane agreed, smiling. Such was her beauty, despite her advancing age and state of motherhood, that the harpy minions were nauseated.

"Thou knowest the Adepts, human folk, and animals be watching," Vodlevile said. "E'en as their magic nulls our weapons, it sends the image o' this activity out. This be why none o' us may contact other beyond the demarked region, lest they learn things illicitly."

"Aye," Phoebe screeched moderately. "We mean to win, an all will see how we do it. There be no rules o' conduct here."

"Save touching not thine own flag," he said. "Then let us part now, and next we meet as combatants."

"Aye," she repeated. Then she and her minions flew back toward their flag, and he and his minions turned bat and returned to theirs.

"Easy pickings!" Sabreclaw screeched.

"Nay, that Vodlevile be a cunning one," Hawktooth warned. "And that hussy, the bride o' the troll—no good can come o' the like o' that."

Phoebe was inclined to agree. Suchevane had not spent eight years with the Troll Adept without learning something about the applications of power. It would be best to take her out early, as well as Vodlevile and Vidselud, so as to render the enemy leaderless. Of course, the bats would be trying to do the same to them. "Watch thy tails," she warned the other two. "We three be marked hens, now."

"Aye," they screeched in chorus.

"Ho'er through the fog and filthy air!" she screeched at the Flock as they rejoined it. It was the code for the start of hostilities. Immediately the hens launched up and out, screeching a splendid cacophony. Simultaneously the bats fountained up from their starting point; Phoebe saw the cloud of them, before it dissolved into its business formation and was hidden behind the trees.

Her squads went out as assigned. The Mock Attack Squad made a hullabaloo and flew forward toward the enemy. Behind this noisy cover, the Flag Defense Squad went back and disappeared into the foliage of the big pine tree. The General Defense Squad faded into the brush between the other two. The Sneak Attack Squad simply disappeared.

The bats came on without hesitation. Phoebe climbed high, out of range of arrows, and watched the unfolding engagement. She saw the Mock Attack hens charging up and taking cover behind trees as they spied manforms; that way the spears and arrows could not catch them. The manform bats paused, naturally enough; they knew better than to charge past harpy-infested trees, for the hens would spring out suddenly and claw their heads, blinding or killing them.

However, a number of bats were flying above the trees, getting beyond the first line of harpies. They were not landing near, to tackle the hens from the rear; they were going on toward the harpy flag. That didn't worry Phoebe; the moment the bats approached it, the defensive harpies would fly up and snatch them. The bats could not get through in batform while there were defenders. They would have to eliminate the defenders first.

The bats dropped to the ground part way there. Some of them became manforms, while others remained bats. What were they doing?

Soon enough, she saw. The manforms were using their weapons to cover the advancing batforms. A bat would fly forward; when a harpy flapped up to snatch it, a manform would loose an arrow at the bird. That was dangerous!

"Messenger!" Phoebe screeched, and a hen assigned to this duty flapped up to join her. "Go tell the Defense Squad to go for the manforms instead. Three birds to a man; pounce from cover and destroy. Do not fly up into their arrows!"

The messenger-hen flew down, and shortly was screeching the new orders. Phoebe watched as three charged one manform. He put an arrow through the first, but the other two came down on him and scratched his eyes out. Then they picked up a new third companion and went after the next manform. This one tried to change to batform and escape, but a hen snatched him out of the air and bit off his head. Of course these effects were more apparent than real, thanks to the magic of the Adepts, but it was evident that most of the dirty birds had forgotten that. The new defense was working!

Meanwhile the forward line of hens was making progress. They were flitting from tree to tree, forcing the manforms to stay well clear of the trees, because within the region enclosed by branches the smaller henforms were more deadly. But then they came to a wide clearing, and here the weapons of the manforms dominated.

Phoebe realized that someone was liable to do something brave and stupid at this stage, so she sent another message: "Cross that clearing not! Go round it! Worry not about the time it takes, just protect your tailfeathers!" For time was hardly of the essence; this was a mock attack, and the longer it distracted the enemy, the better. The detour around the clearing was actually an advantage.

She hoped that Sabreclaw's genuine attack squad was making progress. If it proceeded too slowly, it might be successful—after the bats had won the siege. But she could not check on them; they did not exist, as far as the others were concerned, until they struck by surprise.

The bats, having taken some losses, had regrouped, and now were advancing in a leapfrogging wedge formation. Several bats would fly forward together, covered by several manforms with bows, and several other manforms protected the bowmen with spears. When the hens attacked, the bowmen got some at a distance, and the spearmen got some close, so the hens were taking heavy losses.

The Mock Offense was working its way around the clearing, as directed. But Phoebe realized that this was now working to the advantage of the bats, because their flag was not really threatened yet. They could deploy relatively few manforms to keep the hens in check, and that freed more bats for the active front nearer the harpy flag. No wonder the tide was turning!

But if she recalled the Mock Attack Squad, that would only free the remaining defensive bats, and they could fly forward faster than the harpies. That was no good. There were problems all around because they were short of personnel; the seven secret birds were sorely needed now! Soon the bats would be at the flag tree, and that was too close.

Phoebe realized that it was time for her to join the fray. They had to hold off the bat attack until the Secret Squad could strike. If they could hold out long enough, they would win. If not—

She flew down toward the point of the bat wedge. It was a virtual phalanx; indeed, the spearmen carried small shields. No wonder the hens were having the worst of it! How could she break this up? A direct charge would be ruinously costly; three or four or five hens would be dispatched for every manform they took out. But if they did not interfere with the phalanx, it would reach the tree, and then there would be overwhelming bat force surrounding the harpy flag.

She scratched the ground of her mind, searching for an answer—and turned up a risky but promising ploy. If the hens could hide, and let the phalanx march right into the ambush, then they could attack from within the cover of the shields, too close for arrows or spears to have effect. They could wreak horrible havoc before the bats reorganized.

She came to ground well ahead of the phalanx, out of its sight. Her beady eye had spied a small gully that would do for her purpose. "Hens!" she screeched with minimal volume, so that her voice would not carry to the sharp-eared bats. "Here to me!"

Soon she had half a dozen harpies clustered around her. "That batty phalanx be destroying us," she whisper-screeched. "Needs must we get inside it. Its path be by here; this be the clearest approach to our flag-tree. Hunch down, within this gully, fill it with your bodies, and I will scratch dirt o'er you, and leaves. They will take it to be a level approach. When you feel the weight o' their passage, burst up within their formation and scratch them to pieces fast as e'er you can! They will turn and finally wipe you out; this be a suicide mission. But remember that it be only till siege-end; then all be undone, and all be heroes. Meanwhile see how many each can take out. An it be enough, it will preserve our flag and our victory."

She was an effective screecher, because of her fright-wig; they quickly agreed and huddled down into the gully, their gross bodies filling it from side to side. Each hen spread her wings enough to hold up some dirt. Phoebe scratched earth and leaves and twigs over them desperately, cursing every root that inhibited her, trying to get them covered before the bats arrived and saw what was going on. Then she saw that she had a scraped area of ground that could be a giveaway, so she had to go farther afield and scratch a shower of dry leaves across that. The whole thing seemed too obvious; they would catch on, and poke their spears into the ground ahead, and wipe out the lurking hens before they could get started!

What could she do? She couldn't call on the hens hidden in the tree; they were the last-ditch defense of the flag. All her other hens were occupied elsewhere. She needed some kind of distraction, so the batmen wouldn't notice the scuffled ground until too late.

She heard their approach. They were marching in step, no longer bothering to fly ahead in their batforms. The phalanx was all they needed to crush the opposition. Phoebe wished she had anticipated this ploy, so that she could have better prepared her hens for it.

She had to do it herself. She flew low across the ground to the nearest tree-cover. Then she flew up into the sky, toward the approaching phalanx, as if unaware of it. "I hear a bat!" she screeched at top volume. "I'll mash it!"

Then she hove into sight of the phalanx, and did a dramatic doubletake. "Awk! It be a squintillion bats! Retreat, cohorts!" She spun in air, and did a tripletake. "Where be my cohorts?"

An arrow sailed toward her. She was alert for it, and took such little evasive action that it actually brushed her tail feathers. As it passed, she made a fortissimo screech and did a flip in the air. "Ouch; that scorched my tail!"

Now she tumbled down as though injured, going into the scuffled region. She flapped furiously just above the ground, stirring up dust and leaves, and barely managed to avoid a crash. Now the ground had an excuse to be scuffed!

She swooped into the lowest region of the flag tree, hiding from the phalanx. She had, she hoped, done her job of distraction. She had heard a laugh during her acrobatics; the batmen had enjoyed seeing her supposed distress. Now they were confident that there would be little further resistance, and they knew that would be at the flag tree. If they paid no attention to the ground—

The phalanx marched on, taking the most open course, avoiding cover where harpies might lurk. The gully was evident to the sides; the filled center of it seemed to be the obvious place to cross without messing up their formation. Had the bats not been so confident, they might have wondered at this convenient filling of a natural formation. But they stepped right up to it, and on it.

There was a shriek from the ground. Sand and leaves burst up, as if an explosion had occurred. The harpies emerged at the batmen's feet and commenced scratching. They were too low for the shields, and scooted under them before the bats realized.

For a moment the phalanx held its form. But the sounds of combat sounded within it: exultant screeching and mortified cursing. The formation broke apart as the batmen tried to use their weapons against the attackers underfoot, and succeeded mainly in stabbing each other. Beautiful!

There had been about twenty manforms in the phalanx. By the time they broke far enough apart to use their weapons to destroy the six harpies, a dozen of them had been scratched too badly to continue. The hens had taken out two for one—an excellent score, though not as good as Phoebe had hoped. There were still more batmen advancing than harpies hidden in the tree. This was going to be tight.

How much time had passed? It seemed but a moment, and it also seemed an hour. How close was the Sneak Squad to the enemy flag? Phoebe could not know.

The eight remaining batmen reformed their phalanx, and marched more carefully toward the tree. They knew there would be trouble here, and that it would be unsafe to change form until they were sure every defender was out of it. This would be hand-to-claw, arm-to-wing combat until one force or the other was wiped out, no quarter given.

The phalanx moved right up to the tree. Then, abruptly, it broke apart, and all the manforms leaped for the tree. The defending harpies had been expecting action, but this was deceptively fast; the manforms were in among them before they realized, just as the buried birds had caught the phalanx by surprise. There was immediate turmoil in the tree, as spear poked at body, and claw struck at flesh. Phoebe scuttled aside as a spear came for her; fortunately the thick pine foliage masked her position, so the shaft was not well aimed. She found a leg and gave it one good slash; blood welled out as the poison went in, and the manform stiffened and fell back.

She looked around, but though she heard action everywhere, she could not see it, and was afraid to move lest she interfere with one of her own. She heard an agonized screech, and knew that a hen had received a mortal stab. Then she heard the heavy crash of another manform falling. It seemed about even—but there were two more bats than harpies, so even wasn't good enough. If one bat was left over—

Then, peering worriedly up, she saw one bat appear from the distance, flying directly toward the flag. The bats had kept one in reserve! Now that all the harpies were locked in battle with the attacking batmen, no one was guarding the top spire. It could be a clean pickup, with no one even realizing that the flag was gone until too late.

All harpies were locked in battle except one. By the mischance of the obscurity of the action within the cover of the tree, Phoebe herself was free. She launched herself up, flying desperately around behind the tree so that the lone bat would not see her. It was a faster flyer than she, and it had the advantage of flying high and level, but she was closer. She could get there by the time it did, and that was all she needed.

But she had been aloft during much of the action, and she had expended her strength recklessly scratching soil over the hens in the gully. Her ascent slowed as her wing muscles tired. Was she to be too late? It seemed she would. But she kept struggling upward, determined to do her utmost, lest she be accused of holding back intentionally. How could anyone know, if she missed that bat and let the flag get away, whether she had really been tired, or had really wanted Stile's side to win? How could *she* know?

The bat got there first, but not by much. Phoebe saw it clutch the red flag and try to fly. But the flag was firmly tied to the tree, so that no stray gust of wind would dislodge it. The bat had to cling to the slender branch of the tree and tug repeatedly at the cloth, working it loose—and in that time, Phoebe completed her climb and reached the spot herself.

The bat got the flag loose just as Phoebe arrived. It spread its wings—and Phoebe's slash severed one wing and sent it tumbling toward the ground, still clutching the flag.

Then Phoebe suffered a shock of horror. She wasn't good at recognizing bats in their batforms, but up close she could do it by smell. That bat was female—and it was Suchevane. Of course they would have saved the lovely vamp for noncombat duty! Phoebe had just struck down a friend, one who had helped the alien Agape as Phoebe herself had, years ago.

She saw the bat strike the ground. It was so small and light that the fall really would not hurt it much, and the wing would be instantly repaired when the siege was over. Still, it had seemed so real, and in any other circumstance could have been real. Of all the folk Phoebe did not want to hurt, Suchevane was near the top of the list. At what cost had she won her victory?

Then she saw a manbat emerge from the tree, evidently having dispatched his opposite number. He ran for the flag. The siege was not yet over!

Phoebe, hovering tiredly, did what she had to. She dive-bombed the manform. It was much faster going down than going up, especially this way. As the manform bent to pick up the flag, she swooped across and caught his head in her talons. The bladelike edges sliced into his neck, finishing him instantly. A standing manform might have fended her off with his arms, but this one was in a vulnerable position at the moment.

The manform dropped, unconscious, and rolled over, the flag in his hand. She looped back—and saw that it was Vidselud, the Bat Chief's son. She felt another surge of anguish. He was about third on her list of bats not to hurt. Had she known—could she have done otherwise?

A third enemy emerged from the tree. This was Vodlevile, the Chief himself, holding a spear. He hurled it at Phoebe. She scrambled aside, but it caught the tip of her right wing. She felt the pain of the wound exactly as if it were real—could the Adepts be playing a macabre joke, making them believe that real injuries and deaths were mock?—but not mortal. She would be unable to fly well, if at all, but she could still get around on the ground. She took up a position between the batman and the flag.

Now Vodlevile was without his weapon, but that hardly slowed him. He charged her. Phoebe knew that if she got out of the way, he would pick up the flag and run, and she would be unable to catch him. But if she did not, he would crush her. Worse yet, he was about number two on her list of those she wished not to hurt. The others she had struck down before she realized their identities, but this time she knew. What was she to do?

She jumped up as he reached her, flapping her wings for stability despite the pain, lashing out with her talons. She hoped he was smart enough to dodge aside.

He was. Her strike missed, but he lost his balance and rolled on the ground. She struck the ground herself, and ran toward him, knowing she had to scratch him before he got back to his feet. Wishing she didn't have to. But she was too late; he was up and moving.

She scrambled to the side, keeping herself between him and the fallen flag. It was her only chance. He had to get by her to take it up, and if he could not—

He paused. "Good show, Phoebe!" he gasped. "But thou canst not balk me fore'er. Already dost thou be tiring from loss o' blood."

It was true. Her wings felt leaden, and her legs were tiring. She could not fight much longer.

He charged, trying to pass her. She jumped at his feet, entangling them. He tripped and fell—but his hand flung out and got hold of the spear. He rolled on his back, brought the haft about, and clubbed her with it, knocking her down on her back. Yet the blow was not as hard as it might have been; he didn't want to hurt her either. The spear twisted from his hand and fell to the ground again, but it had done its job.

Phoebe knew at that moment that she was done for. The frame seemed to be spinning, and she could not summon strength to get back to her feet. Vodlevile, in contrast, was getting up. She could no longer block him from the flag.

Then she heard a heavy flapping. "Fie, batface!" Sabreclaw screeched. "Defend thyself, an thou hast the nerve!"

They had made it! Phoebe saw Vodlevile dive for his spear, but Sabreclaw only feinted at him. Instead she dived for the ground—and the red flag. She clapped the bat's blue flag down on it. There was the sound of a gong. That suddenly the siege was over. The harpies had won!

Then Phoebe gave herself over to unconsciousness. She had done her best, strategically and physically, and it had been enough. She had vindicated herself. If only it could have been otherwise!

But she was not after all permitted to sleep. Abruptly the pain and fatigue were gone, and she was whole again. Nearby, Vidselud and Suchevane were getting up, and other bodies were stirring. The siege was over, and the bloodshed was undone. It never had been real; the Adepts had spoken truly after all. Only the victory was real—the one she wished she had not had to win.

12 : *Troubot*

Merle looked at the six hens, puzzled. "I have not been paying enough attention to you," she remarked with concern. "You have become strangers to me." Indeed, the birds seemed wary of her, huddling at the far side of the coop. "Come, Henrietta, come, Henbane," she cooed, squatting and extending a hand. Her short skirt slid up her thighs; she wore nothing beneath. "Here. Henna—I have treat grain. Come and take it; I want to be friends again."

Slowly the hens approached, wary of her. She did not make any sudden motion, and eventually one essayed a peck at what she held in her hand. "That's it, Henpeck; I certainly won't hurt you. A man I might usher into Heaven or Hell, but not my pets. I'm sorry I neglected you. I've been so busy recently, but I won't bore you with the details."

The hens formed a semicircle before her, looking at her quizzically. "You mean you are interested?" she inquired, smiling. She was a lovely woman, slender overall yet possessed of truly shapely anatomy that showed in somewhat indecorous manner as she squatted and leaned forward. Her hair was dark, with a blue tint; it changed color slightly every day, so that she never became stale. Similarly her clothing shifted color and style subtly but steadily. Merle was always fresh without being brash.

"Well, that's very nice of you, Heningway," she remarked, spreading some treat grain on the ground before them. "Trust you to have a literary bent! And you, Henline—always on the edge. Listen and I will tell you."

The hens settled, attentively. Merle leaned back and sat on the floor, carefully, so that her legs would not cramp. "You see, I am a friend of Citizen Blue," she said conversationally. "It all started some years back when the serf Stile won the Tourney and became a Citizen. Now your average new Citizen quickly gets lost in the marvels of power and wealth to which he is vastly unaccustomed, but Stile was of different mesh. He was ambitious—oh, my, was he ambitious!—and he went right after the big money, which is the same as the big power. That was when I encountered him: in his preliminary gambles and games, when he was getting the hang of it. He took me for a hundred grams of Protonite in a poker game—a nice little haul for him, at the time. That won my interest, and thereafter I followed his career. In fact, in due course I became a bit smitten with him, though he was a young-ster only a fraction my age."

She paused, her gaze passing fondly across the hens. She reached out and stroked Heningway, who ducked her head nervously but did not retreat. "You make such a good audience, my pretties," she remarked. "Never any backtalk, never any danger of my secrets being gossiped out. Not even a cackle when I confess something stupid. Ah, what a story you could tell of my indiscretions, if you were in the business!"

She smiled reminiscently, enjoying the indiscretions, then resumed her narrative. "In the end I made him a deal: my help in his endeavor in exchange for his single tryst with me. I called him my bantam—you may have noted my affinity for chickens—and I confess I was hot for him, both personally and as a matter of pride. You see, I have had an undisclosed number of rejuvenations; I am of great-grandmotherly age, not the maiden I appear. I knew my body interested him, as indeed it should; I crafted it to appeal to the masculine taste in subdued but potent manner. Some women believe that mass is everything, and have their breasts and buttocks expanded enormously; it is true that men notice these attributes, but they also convey a suggestion of cheapness. Proportion is the secret; modest projections whose contours are es-thetic attract the male interest on a more subtle level, and the resultant desire can be more pervasive and lasting. It is the difference between fish eggs and caviar. So Stile wanted me, but could not admit it; I had to trap him into a commitment. He found my age to be more of a barrier than my nature; indeed, he was having relations with a machine at the time. Men are like that."

She paused, eying the hens speculatively. "I don't suppose you'd like to have a rooster here?"

The hens looked dismayed.

Merle laughed. "Yes, it is true that a rooster's notion of love is what my kind would call rape. Not a really significant difference between the species, but we females can live without it. That, perhaps, is an aspect of the attraction Stile had for me: not only was he small, being shorter than I, but he was a gentleman in the old sense. It was an unconscious chivalry I found most charming. He was more of a man in every respect than most, but small, and shy, and charming in his naïveté. But what a change he wrought in Proton society! He assumed power, and brought the frames together, then separated them after alleviating the imbalance which had developed because of the export of Protonite. You see, the parallelism between Proton and Phaze is such that what is not equivalent tends to become so, but the Phazite had remained while the Protonite was diminishing, and that struck at the very root of the nature of the frames, and would have led to mutual destruction had he not acted. So he did what had to be done, and separated the frames so that no more mischief could occur, and settled in Phaze."

She paused again, as if interrupted, but the hens were rapt. "What's that, you say? How could he meet his commitment to me, if he was gone? Well he did, in his fashion. He left his beautiful bantam body here, taken over by his other self, the Blue Adept of Phaze. The Citizens had to accept this exchange, because many of them had other selves in Phaze and had agreed that in the event of the death of one of them, the Phaze alternate would be accepted in lieu. It was a device for ensuring proper succession, you see. So Citizen Blue appeared, wielding the power of Stile, and the battle between them has continued ever since. The Contrary Citizens wish to recover control so that they can exploit the planet without regard for tomorrow, while Blue fights to maintain a proper balance, and also to liberalize Proton society. Philosophy is no concern of mine, but I do like Blue as I liked Stile, so I support him. And it was Blue who discharged Stile's commitment to me." She rolled her eyes. "Oh, what a night we had! The man was between loves at the time, having lost his wife to his other self, and not yet committed to the robot woman; he had a lot to give. He really made me feel the age I looked. But that was it; thereafter he married the machine, and has been faithful to her since. Still, I am minded to play a little game with him, if you do not object. After all, I like to think that I am approaching parallelism with the Yellow Adept, who can use an elixir to make herself as blushingly beautiful as she once may have been, and who was once rather taken with Stile herself. We do have our little ways with those of the masculine persuasion."

The hens looked at her quizzically. They now had an excellent view of what she offered men, as they squatted almost within the area enclosed by her spread legs, but did not seem to understand.

"You see, things have heated up recently," she explained. "Blue's robot son Mach managed to exchange with Stile's human son Bane in Phaze, establishing the first contact between the frames in twenty years. What a can of worms that opened! We humans don't appreciate worms the way you chickens do. The robot boy, delighted to have a living body, fell in love with a unicorn there, while the human boy loved an alien creature here. Didn't that make conventional folk sweat! Now both those couples have offspring, who have become pawns in the larger power play. Little Nepe is captive of the Citizens, and little Flach captive of the Adepts in Phaze. So they have scheduled a big double tourney to settle it, and the winner will have the ultimate power. Am I boring you?"

The hens gazed at her. They did not seem bored.

"Well, then, I shall tell you the rest of it. I have been busy helping Citizen Blue with the negotiations. The details of the Proton Tourney had to be worked out to satisfy the disparate interests of both sides, and this was most difficult to do, because of course each wanted the advantage. My mind has not been so pleasantly exerted in decades! We finally hammered out a compromise. For the first contest, each side would choose a player from the elder generation—the ones who fought each other when Stile was on the scene in Proton. Thus Citizen Purple met the robot Sheen, Blue's wife, in a dragon duel, and I regret to say defeated her in fair play. For the third contest, each side will choose a representative from the middle generation, those who came on the scene when Mach and Bane exchanged places. And for the second contest, players have been chosen from the young generation, or those who entered the picture more recently. That completes the span of generations. But because this contest may be crucial—there may be no third contest, if the Citizens win this one—they arranged another device. Each side got to choose the opponent the other side would put up."

She laughed. "Yes, I see how that amazes you! How could such a thing be workable? Wouldn't the choices be designed to be the worst possible players, to guarantee the loss? And the answer is, of course— but the array of choices is sharply limited. Only those who actually have participated in significant events were eligible. The Oracle passed judgment, rejecting ineligible nominations. Thus the Citizens came to be represented by a young woman named Tsetse—some time I really must explore the derivation of that name!—who has no Game training but who, being the secretary of Citizen Tan's sister and the mistress of Citizen Purple, qualifies despite the defection to Tania. Her assets are said to be almost entirely in her body, not her brain. The Citizens are not pleased, but are stuck for it. And Blue's side is to be represented by a robot friend of little Nepe's called Troubot, former information expediter for the Citizens. Now you might think such a robot would be ineligible to represent Blue, but the Citizens pointed out that he in effect defected when he helped Nepe's alien mother to escape the planet, and to that logic the Oracle acceded. So Troubot it is; he will play against Tsetse for extraordinarily high stakes. But there is just one little problem."

She paused again, artfully, and sure enough, the hens peered at her attentively, enraptured by her narration. Merle was good at making an effect, and she enjoyed it now. "But I doubt that you would be interested in such a detail. Perhaps it is time for me to go tease Blue."

Heningway actually stood and came closer, as if to plead for the finale. Merle stroked her again and relented. "Very well, it is this: Troubot can not be found. He is hiding, surely fearing the vengeance of the Citizens, and though the call has been spread across the networks, he has not responded. I am not a robot, but I believe I can guess his concern: how can he be sure the call is legitimate? It could have been put out by the Citizens, to lure him in, so that they can capture and destroy him. Naturally he is cautious. But as it happens, the call is legitimate, and if Blue does not succeed in presenting Troubot for the contest by tomorrow, Blue will have to forfeit the game and the planet to the Contrary Citizens. So you can see the matter is critical. Blue is desperate—exactly as the Citizens hoped. They have found a ploy that may defeat him by default, and Tsetse will never have to play. It's a beautiful tactic, I must confess; I could hardly have thought of one better."

She stood. "Well, you have been an excellent audience, but I think I shall go call Blue and tease him a bit. I'll make him come here, so you can see him sweat. Enjoy yourselves!"

Merle departed, closing the chamber door behind her. The hens remained where they were for a time, listening; only when they heard the second door close, signaling the woman's entry into her house proper, did they rise. Then Heningway went to the door to peek out, while the others milled about aimlessly, pecking at stray grains.

Heningway, reassured that the woman really was gone, returned to the center of the little flock. She gave a coded series of clucks. Immediately the others clustered close. They huddled, stretching their necks, touching their beaks together. With that contact, their nature changed. A person watching would have seen only their peculiar formation, but one who tuned in their electrical activity would have discovered the reality.

For the six individuals represented the components of a larger apparatus. The little flock was not a flock, but the parts of a self-willed robot. Each part was equipped with chicken legs and chicken head and feathers, but was not alive. Each was set up to emulate the simple acts of a hen: walking, pecking, defecating. The droppings were of pseudo-organic matter, because these hens had no digestive systems. The main brain unit was in the part labeled Heningway, with supplementary parts distributed among the others so that they could react to events in a reasonable manner. Fortunately, hens were not expected to be overly ambitious, and this was an extremely protected environment.

The whole entity was Troubot, the machine for which everyone was searching. He had delivered Agape to the spaceport, then gone into hiding, knowing that he was now a marked machine. From his years of association with Nepe he had learned much, and knew how to hide so that he could not be found. The principle, she had explained, was surprise: to do the unexpected. Thus she had become a machine, the one form others thought impossible for her. Of course she had never been a true machine, but rather a cyborg, but she had so masked her living portion that it was virtually indistinguishable from inanimate substance. This was, she had explained, merely an extension of her natural ability to harden her substance into bonelike or hornlike rigidity. It was normally done only to part of the body, for the sake of stability, or to emulate the body of some other form, such as the human form. But with effort and practice she had extended it to almost the whole of her body, and had made her flesh harder than bone or hoof, so that it most resembled metal. Thus she had remained safely hidden despite a thorough search for her, because they were not searching for a robot.

Troubot had learned the principle, and applied it well. First he had considered what would be the least likely form for him to assume, and concluded that it would be that of a living creature. But he realized that this would be a creature of at least his present size, and if others reasoned that he might assume such a form, they had but to check for all new creatures at or above that size; that of a large dog. There were not many, and virtually all were on the estates of Citizens, and duly registered; verification could be very quick, and he would soon be isolated. That was too much of a chance to take. So he worked out a second ploy, reducing the size by breaking himself into components. He had learned how to do this by studying the manuals available in the information service that he used; it took some special engineering, but he had had years to work it out, and had done so. Now he had used it, becoming a flock of six hens, concealing himself by flesh, size, number and sex. He had replaced the flock of this Citizen, having ascertained that though she maintained her birds well, she had grown out of the habit of visiting them, so that for weeks at a time they were fed only by the automatic servitors.

He had come to her estate, bridged the security measures—she really was not security conscious, being a socialite who lived mainly for the challenge of social relations—and taken her birds to a holding area for quarantine. He had set it up so that they would be fed just as before, in a chamber much as before, and no notice of this detention was fed into the planetary records. As a trouble-shooting robot, he was good at this sort of thing; he had taught Nepe how, just as she had taught him her skills, during the years of their friendship. Thus the hens were safe, and could be replaced in Merle's coop at any time, no one the wiser. In this manner he had disappeared, and the searchers had had no better luck locating him than they had had with Nepe. Only the capture of her other self in Phaze had led to her exposure. Then he had resumed the job she had done for him, and when it appeared there would be suspicion because of his association with her, he had moved into other employment, remaining free.

But after he helped Agape the search became far more intense. It seemed everybody wanted him, and he wasn't sure for what reason. Nepe had put it succinctly: "Hide, Troubot, and don't get caught!" That he had done.

Now Merle had resumed paying attention to her hens. Did she know? If so, what did it mean? She was aligned with Blue, but was of an independent nature; no one ever knew what was in her heart. As a general rule, she did what was best for Merle, and never let an opportunity pass for some private advancement.

He could try to move out, bringing back the regular hens. But if she had caught on to him, she would have set new monitors, and the attempt would be foiled. Perhaps she only suspected—and was waiting for something that would confirm her idea, without making an issue. This was her kind of subtlety. Troubot had decided to stand pat; Merle would either expose him, or she would not, as her whim dictated.

This last session had been the worst. Before, she had merely looked in on the flock; this time she had joined it. He had fashioned each part to resemble a specific hen, but could not pass more than a cursory inspection. His hope had been based on the assumption that the Citizen would pay no more attention to her hens than she had in the past. This change in her attitude was alarming. And for her to speak so openly and clearly of her history with Stile and Blue, and of his own disappearance . . .

There was little doubt now: she knew. He was surely at her mercy—which was perhaps where she wanted him to be. Why had she taken so much trouble to explain things to him?

He had known of the intensity of the search, but had not known of this extra element. He had been chosen to represent Citizen Blue in a key Game-match? That was an amazing development. If it was true, he should certainly come forth and do what he could, because his association with Nepe had also put him firmly on her side, and therefore Blue's side. But *was* it true? How could he be sure that Merle, for reasons of her own, was not teasing him, so that he might expose himself and fall into the wrong hands? If she did not want to betray Blue openly—because, as she so candidly put it, she hoped to arrange another sexual liaison with him—but actually sympathized with the other side, this could be a way. If that were her plan, the best thing he could do would be to sit tight, refusing to reveal himself. That would force her to do her own dirty work, and pay the penalty. Troubot was sure that Merle had no concern at all for his welfare, but only hoped to use him in some fashion to her advantage.

But if what she said was true, and he did not come forth, Citizen Blue could lose his match by default. Probably the Citizens had selected Troubot in part because of this. They hoped that Troubot would not trust the summons, and so would serve their objective.

Troubot did not have feelings in the living sense, but he was a sophisticated self-willed machine who could react emotionally when applicable circuits were set up and invoked. In the course of his association with Nepe, he had set up such circuits, and felt a reasonable facsimile of friendship for her, and loyalty to the principles she had adopted. Thus there was an emotional component involved, which he could cut out, but only at the cost of his feeling for Nepe. He did not like to do that, because his feeling toward Nepe was the only thing that really distinguished him from an ordinary self-willed machine. He knew that if he voided that circuit, he would be unlikely to re-invoke it later, because his nature would be changed; he simply would not care any more. It would be like death in a living creature. So he retained the circuit—and so he suffered now this agony of indecision. He knew he wanted to help Nepe and her grandfather Blue; he did not know in what way he best could do that. Should he believe Merle, or doubt her?

He lacked the circuitry to resolve such a conflict. He was not, after all, the Oracle, whose nature was more sophisticated than that of any other machine. He was not even similar to Sheen, or Mach; he was just an ordinary self-willed robot who had been influenced by long and close association with a living alien child who understood robots because her father was one. Perhaps that had made him unusual among machines, but it did not provide him with superior intellectual competence. He had modified his body and his emotion, but his intellect was locked in to what it had been at the start. He had been smart at the start—too smart, for a machine, and therefore out of tolerance— but he had never been able to approach Nepe's level.

So he waited, doing nothing. He let his components separate, and reverted to the lesser state that was not the sum of his parts. As six units he was conscious, but unable to utilize his full mental capacity; too much of it had been distributed to the others, to make them separately functional. As Heningway, he possessed the main awareness, and could make decisions, but was hesitant to without being able to draw on his full complement. He pecked up a seed, which he could not digest, biding his time.

Soon Merle returned. "Well, chickens," she said brightly. "I have just called Blue, and prevailed on him to appear here within the hour, alone. Would you like me to enable you to witness my bit of sport with him?"

Troubot tried to reason whether he should make a response. If she did not know his nature, he did not want to give it away, but his brief mergence with his other parts had enabled him to think more comprehensively, and he had concluded that she did know; therefore there was no point in hiding from her. He did want to see Citizen Blue, because he understood that that was a man he could trust and possibly find sanctuary with. So he should make a positive response; that seemed clear enough.

He stepped forward, making one cluck.

"Well, now, Heningway! You are becoming positively literary!" she exclaimed, pleased. In the course of his researches he had encountered a name that resembled the one she had bestowed on this hen; perhaps she was making a pun. "Very well, I shall do it. He will be here within the half hour; I shall go change, and a servitor will install appropriate furniture here." She looked sternly at the hens. "Do not drop anything untoward on it!"

She exited. In a moment a rolling transport brought in a couch that looked much like a bed. Then the machine set up a baffle that consisted of a curtain, so that the couch was concealed from the view of the main coop.

Troubot reassembled his units, touching beaks, so he could ponder this development. It seemed obvious that Merle intended to seduce Citizen Blue in exchange for the information about Troubot's location. Was this proper? He doubted it, but was not certain of his proper response. He knew that if he were alive, he would resent being used this way; as it was, he merely noted it, and disbanded, making no decision.

As scheduled, Merle returned, wearing a voluminous mock-fur coat, escorting Citizen Blue, who was in his usual blue cloak. She turned to close and secure the door behind them. "There—now we are secure," she said. "This is the only chamber where I am assured that no monitors are active; no one can eavesdrop on us here except my flock of chickens, and they really do not pass judgments."

Blue ignored the hens. "Merle, thou didst say thou hadst something important for me."

"Indeed I do," she said. "You may remember our tryst of some years back. I have a hunger for something similar."

He frowned. "I be married now."

"To a machine."

"Aye. But still married. Thou knowest how I feel about this matter. I have problems enough without—"

"I love it when you talk Phazish!"

Blue paused. "I revert to it unconsciously when under stress. I apologize. Now I assume you did not call me here to waste my time and yours. What do you really have on your mind?"

Merle opened her coat, then slid out of it. She was nude beneath, of course. "I just told you, Blue."

"Impossible!" he snapped.

"By no means, my bantam lover. See, I have prepared." She drew the curtain, revealing the couch.

"What makes you think I would indulge you at this time?" he asked, openly irritated.

"Suppose I were to say that I had information you very much wanted, for a price?"

"The only information I want is—" He paused. "You know—?"

"Where Troubot is. Yes, I believe I do, bantam. And I might even tell you. Would that information be worth the price?"

Now he hesitated. "I would have to ask my wife."

"I shall be happy to query her for you, Blue. I am sure she will understand. She did before."

He reconsidered. "That will not be necessary. Merle, are you saying you have this information, or are you teasing me?"

"I am doing both, dear boy. Join me on the couch, and in due course I will tell you."

"Damn thee!" he swore. "To put such a price on such a need!"

Merle sighed. "Now I have made him angry, and that spoils the mood. Very well, I will postpone my satisfaction. I will give you Troubot, and you will be the judge of the nature and the timing of my reward. I believe that is more than fair; don't you agree?"

"Damn thee!" he repeated.

Merle turned to face the hens. "As you can see, this is definitely Citizen Blue. Any lesser man would have taken my offering and damned with the price. Show yourself."

Troubot, as Heningway, stepped forward. He clucked to the others, and they joined him.

Citizen Blue stared. "The chickens?"

"A most effective ruse, wouldn't you say?"

"I'm not sure I believe this! How could he be in six living parts?"

"Six parts yes, living no. That is pseudoflesh. Take him and verify him; you will discover him to be a single self-willed robot."

Blue began to believe. "I never thought to check for something like this, and neither did the Citizens. It just could be! But I'm not sure I can distinguish one self-willed machine from another; this could be a plant by the Citizens."

"That had occurred to me," she said. "Therefore we must take the next step with suitable dispatch. We must bring in the one person who can identify Troubot without doubt."

"That can only be Nepe! But she be captive o' the enemy!"

"So we deal with the enemy. They have a similar interest, after all; what is to stop us from planting our own imitation, a machine designed to be a likely winner in a Game?"

"Mine honor!" he flared.

"But the Contrary Citizens hardly believe in honor. They will distrust yours, without reason, and mine, with reason. They must be assured of Troubot's identity too. So call them; they will bring her here."

Citizen Blue considered, and nodded. "Thou be earning thy keep," he said.

"I always do. I only regret that it requires such a situation to entice you to do what any other man would do without price."

Now he laughed. "It were a good night, that one! Methought the dawn would ne'er come!"

"I delayed it by retiming the lights."

He stared at her, then shook his head. "Mind thee, my wife will have thy head for this!"

"Make the call; time is short."

"Aye." He opened the door and stepped out, while she picked up her coat and put it on. Then she sat in the couch and waited.

"You see, chickens, there is more than just coming forward," she said. "You have to be verified. This is the only way to do it. I do have your best interest at heart, and I trust you will do what needs to be done. If you fail to convince Nepe, all is lost. Make sure you appreciate that."

Troubot appreciated it. Merle was more of a person than he had credited. Again he understood that the intricacies of human logic and action went beyond his own capacities.

Later that afternoon a second party arrived: Merle, Blue, Citizen Translucent and Nepe. The contrast between the two men was sharp. Translucent was large and stout in his almost transparent robe, while Blue was so small in his blue robe as to seem childlike; Nepe looked more like his sister than his granddaughter. This was a parlay under truce between those who could be trusted; Translucent was the only one of the Contrary Citizens with a sufficient sense of honor.

Translucent and Blue sat on the couch, and Nepe sat on her grandfather's lap and hugged him. She knew she would have to return to captivity with Translucent; this was her only chance to visit with the one who by appearances meant more to her than her father. Troubot knew that Blue had not expected issue from a man in the body of a robot with an alien creature, yet it had happened, and Blue had taken the child to his heart at the outset. He had also used her as a tool against the Contrary Citizens, but with her full consent. Nepe had told Troubot everything, needing a confidant in her isolation, and in the process he had become more human than could otherwise have been the case.

"Now that we are private, here is the situation," Merle said. "The Contrary Citizens have chosen the self-willed robot servitor identified as Troubot to represent Citizen Blue in the second contest of three, to decide who shall have ultimate power in the frame. But Troubot is in hiding, and Blue will have to default if Troubot is not found in time. Only one person can identify this machine, and that person is Nepe, who is his friend." Merle looked at the child. "Nepe, do you understand that you must speak the truth and only the truth in this matter?"

"I do," Nepe said.

Merle glanced at the two men. "Do each of you accept her veracity in this?"

Each man nodded.

Merle spoke to Nepe again. "Then I ask you, Nepe: do you see your friend Troubot here?"

"Here?" Nepe asked, startled. "I thought we were going to go find him!"

"We may be. Please answer the question."

"But there's no one here but—" Her eyes fell on the hens, and went abruptly round. "Gosh! It *is*!" She jumped down and ran to the little flock. She plumped down on the ground and opened her arms, trying to hug all the hens at once. "How clever of you, Troubot! You even had *me* fooled!"

"But how can you be sure?" Merle asked.

"He's my friend! I'd know him anywhere, if I looked."

Merle smiled. "You must pardon those of us who lack your ability. How can *we* be sure?"

Nepe considered. "We have a secret code that only the two of us know. Let me tell it to you, and he will respond to you only when you use it."

"Fair enough," Merle said.

Nepe got up, went to the woman, and whispered something. Then Merle spoke to the two men, who had remained passive. "Agree among yourselves when I should give the code, and see whether the response is there."

Translucent shrugged, and brought out a stylus and pad. He wrote something, then tore off the sheet and passed it to Merle. Blue brought out a similar pad and made a note, also passing it to Merle. She looked at each, then folded them, smiling. "Each of you has written a number, and the one modifies the other. I shall use the result, which neither of you know."

She faced the hens. "Troubot, here is the code: three, fifteen, one."

Troubot did not respond. The code was numeric, but she had the wrong numbers.

"Troubot," she said again, "here is the code: nine, twenty-nine, ninety-nine."

Again he did not respond.

"Troubot, here is the code: four, four, four to the fourth power, forever four."

That was it: Nepe's age when they had met, formed into a cherished memory. Heningway clucked, and the others came together to huddle. They formed their pattern in front of Merle, all beaks touching.

"We seem to have a response," Merle said. "Is it the right time?"

"I wrote the number six," Translucent said.

"I divided by two," Blue said.

"Indeed you did," Merle agreed. "And six divided by two is three; I gave the code the third time. This test may have been crude, but seems indicative. Are we satisfied?"

They looked at the flock, which was clustered around Nepe again. They were satisfied.

Troubot assembled himself, removing the fleshly vestments and becoming a single entity again. Now he could function fully. They took down his stats: the part numbers of his components and the electrical pattern of his brain circuitry, so there could be no subsequent confusion about his identity. Then Translucent and Nepe left, and Citizen Blue took Troubot with him. Merle was left to recover her hens from the quarantine chamber.

It was good being legitimate again, the doubt gone. But now he had a new responsibility: to represent Citizen Blue in a contest that was already partly lost. If he lost the game, Blue was done for. Troubot had never before played a Game, though he was familiar with its rules. He understood that his opponent Tsetse had not played either, but still it seemed doubtful. The matchup was too odd, for stakes too high.

Citizen Blue gave him access to the information net, and he spent the night reviewing strategies of the grid, and checking the course of past games. He was as ready as he could be, considering that he had not been designed for this endeavor.

Tsetse entered the chamber after Troubot had taken his place at the console. He was a machine, but he had learned to catalogue living folk according to their physical esthetics by human definition, and she was what was best described as luscious. He had of course researched her stats, and learned that she was of average intelligence and creativity and personality, and below average in motivation; only her outstanding body displaced her from the ordinary. He would do well to engage her in a mental game, where he should have an advantage. But she would seek to avoid this, being properly coached. In fact, she might well seek to avoid all games of skill, and go for CHANCE, making the issue random. This might indeed be the Citizens' best strategy; if they won, they won everything, while if they lost, they would still be even.

He had the letters. That meant he could not put it into the MEN-
TAL arena. He was already a machine, so would have less advantage
than she by drawing on the powers of a machine; the same went for
tools. The animal category had potential complications he preferred to
avoid. This being the case, he went for the simplest: NAKED.

To his relief, she too selected the simplest: PHYSICAL. It would
be just the two of them, with their own unaugmented abilities.

For the secondary grid he had the numbers. Again he chose the
simplest: SEPARATE. That meant that they would do, essentially,
their own things, not being dependent on each other. A foot race was
separate, while a game of tag was interactive. Of course she could get
him in trouble by her choice of surface: if she chose a water contest,
he would have difficulty. He could modify his body to move in water,
but this might not be permitted. She, in contrast, had a body that
seemed designed by nature for swimming. However, he had found no
reference to swimming in her record, and hoped that she was of the
type who went to the water only for appearances.

She chose Variable Surface, again to his relief. He might have to
navigate a slope, but that was easier than dealing with water. He would
try to line up good options, and hope for the best on the tertiary grid.

She made the first placement, and Sand Dunes appeared in the center. Sand was another prospect he did not relish; his wheels would lose
traction in it.

He put Maze Path in the top row, center. That brought a mental
element into it, giving him the advantage.

She put Snow Bank in the upper left corner. There was another
problem for him: snow. She had been well enough rehearsed, and was
playing correctly.

He countered with Limestone Cliff in the lower right corner. He
could project points to grip the rock and climb well enough, while she
should have more trouble.

She put Glass Mountain in the upper right corner. That was mixed,
for him; the glass would be too hard for his points, but his wheels
could get traction when it was dry.

He put Tight Rope in the left column, down one. As a machine,
he could achieve almost perfect balance, and his wheels could remain
firm on the rope, while the woman might become highly unstable.

She put Greased Hills in the bottom left column. That was a mistake
on her part; he could handle grease by poking his points through to
the sand beneath.

He put Cross Country in the center of the third column, then realized that he should have put it in the bottom center column, giving him three good choices in the bottom row.

She filled in the last box with Dust Slide. He liked dust no better than snow; that spoiled that row for him.

Now the grid was complete.

TERTIARY GRID: 1A5F
Physical Naked Separate, Variable Surface

Snow Bank	Maze Path	Glass Mtn
Tight Rope	Sand Dunes	Cross Country
Greased Hills	Dust Slide	Limestone

He had the choice of rows or columns. He chose the rows. She would figure him to take the middle row, because two of his choices were there, so she should choose the center column, to stick him with Sand Dunes. Therefore he chose the top row.

But she, for what reason he might never understand, had selected the third column. The result was Glass Mountain: one of her choices, but really not bad for him.

They adjourned to the mountain. As true mountains went, this was small, but as inner-dome artifacts went, it was big. The mountain was indeed formed of glass, or at least had a glass exterior. It was broad at the base, and slanted up to a peak about ten meters high. It was ridged and channeled, with many facets and some almost vertical cliffs which represented impassable barriers to naked—i.e., bare-handed—folk. Its contours were changed for each game, so that there was no point in memorizing its outline. It was normally so constructed that a person could not simply pick a gentle slope and mount to the top; he had to ascertain, usually by trial and error, which route was feasible, and do it before his opponent did. The first one to the top was the winner.

This was "separate"; that meant that one player could not directly interfere with the other, such as by shoving him off the mountain. But the categories were seldom pristine; there was inevitably some interaction, as when one player got to the best route before the other and so forced the other either to follow behind or to choose another route. In this case there was an added fillip: water bombs. These were little balloons filled with water which, when burst against the glass, made it too slippery for progress. A player could take as many bombs as he could hold, and use them to reduce the friction of the path his opponent had chosen. The effect lasted only a few seconds, but could make the difference when both were racing toward the top on different paths.

Troubot feared that his wheels would be more susceptible to slipperiness than Tsetse's feet, because she could step over wet spots while he could not. But he had greater capacity to hold water bombs. He could fill his hopper with them, while she could carry only what she could hold in her arms. Still, he did not know how agile she was, or what the best route was. This was still anybody's game. The audience evidently thought so; the monitor lights indicated a massive viewing, which could not be accounted for solely by the importance of the contest.

Of course, Tsetse was a lovely young woman. That would account for a significant enhancement of the number of viewers. She would be bending over to scramble up tricky slants, and perhaps taking spread-legged tumbles. That sort of thing was always big with the serfs. They would be rooting for her, to win or tumble or both, but their reactions did not matter, because they would not be audible here.

They started. Tsetse ran to the mountain and clambered nimbly enough up the first channel that offered. Troubot went instead to the bomb dispensary and carefully set a dozen into his hopper. This might raise his center of gravity and make his climb more difficult, but the bombs should be more of an asset than a liability.

Tsetse's channel faded out, leaving her on a flat facet whose tilt was more to the vertical. She climbed this carefully, her toes just beginning to skid. She was about four meters up. Troubot waited below, watching carefully, analyzing the slope she navigated; it did not matter who tested it, for this purpose.

Then, just as she was about to reach the top of the facet so that she could step onto a more promising new channel above, Troubot flexed a metal arm and lofted a water bomb. His aim was good, of course; the bomb landed just above her, and the water coursed down across her feet. Friction diminished abruptly. She screamed as she lost her footing and slid down to the base of the mountain, in exactly the fashion the audience had hoped for.

Troubot did not wait to watch; he was not a living human male and would have had no gratification from the sight. He had merely taken the opportunity to test the efficacy of the water so that he could estimate the coefficient of friction before and after. He believed she was on the wrong path, but wasn't sure, so this would set her back while he tried an alternate route himself.

He found a facet that started steep, but curved to diminish the angle above. He started up this one, his wheels barely holding at the base. Yes, this seemed more promising; above the facet was a channel that cured upward around the mountain. He rolled up this.

Splat! A water bomb struck his body. It burst, and the water cascaded down around his wheels. Traction was gone; he slipped helplessly, and in a moment was at the bottom. The mountain had a soft curtain or buffer at the base, to absorb the shock of landings, so that players would not be hurt by their involuntary slides. But he had lost his progress. Tsetse had retaliated.

Troubot realized that neither of them would be able to make progress if things continued like this; one could always remain at the base and bring down the other. But they were hardly likely to cooperate. So he rolled around the mountain, looking for a third route of ascent; he would have to let the woman try her own at the same time. If she got ahead of him, near the top, he would throw another bomb and stop her, while she would be unable to carry bombs aloft and still use her hands effectively for climbing.

She did not follow; evidently she was satisfied to return to her first path and follow it farther up, while he tried his new one. He was certainly ready for that, because he believed the odds were against either of the others being the right one.

He found a new route, and moved up it. This was the best one yet; it slanted slightly to the side, but took him two thirds of the way up toward the peak. If it went all the way—

It did not, exactly. It abruptly became vertical, and he could not ascend farther. Would he have to go all the way back down, while Tsetse continued on up? No, he saw a gentle ledge to the right that sloped toward her original route. He maneuvered very carefully, and managed to get fairly on it. He rounded the curve of the mountain— and there was Tsetse coming up toward him.

He picked up a bomb from his hopper, but hesitated. If they met on this path, there was evidently no future in it for either of them. What was the point in washing her off it? Better to leave her here, where she could go nowhere.

But she seemed to have a similar notion. She clambered to the side, and down the mountain. Her feet skidded, but it didn't matter; she was going down anyway. Before he could do it himself, she was down and around, going for the first path he had tried.

He pondered. He could go down and around himself, and loft a bomb at her, stopping her progress. But she would do it back to him the moment he tried. Meanwhile, he was already well up on the mountain, now; if he could find a way to intercept that other path, and get on it ahead of her, he could win.

He tried, but the mountain was implacable: he could not get to the other path. He could only see her head come into sight as she reached the point he had before she bombed him. She seemed on the way to victory.

But he didn't have to be at ground level to stop her! He threw his bomb in a high arc over the curve of the mountain. It came down neatly on her head. "Oh!" she sputtered, but she did not lose her footing. His aim had been good, but she had moved, so that the bomb had hit her instead of the path before her.

He lofted another. This time she lifted her hand and caught it. It broke, but did not dislodge her. The water needed to strike her feet, or the path upslope, to be effective; her head or hand dissipated its effect too much.

If he threw another, she might manage to catch it unbroken, and hurl it back at him. He decided to wait for her to resume her climb, so that he could score on the path while her hands were occupied in climbing. But she waited, watching him. She might not be the smartest of women, but she was canny enough for this! It was a standoff.

But as he waited, another thought came to him. The first path had not gone anywhere, and neither had the third. It seemed likely that none of the paths that started at the base went all the way up. More likely, the final path would begin somewhere farther up. The player who figured this out first, and got to it, should be the winner.

But where could such a path be? He had been balked by the vertical tilt of the third path, and managed to cross to this one. The mountain was not large enough for many more sites.

He retraced his route. This time he saw it: another slight ledge piking up on the other side of the vertical path. It looked as if it did not go anywhere—but that could be deceptive.

He moved slowly and carefully, and managed to cross to that other ledge. Then he heard something: there was Tsetse, well up toward the peak, on the other side; all he saw was her right shoulder. Her path *did* go all the way up, and he had wasted time trying for this other one.

But he still had a chance. He brought out another water bomb. He threw it up, not at Tsetse, but at the peak of the mountain itself. The bomb came down on the point and broke; its water flowed down mostly on Tsetse's side.

She made an exclamation of horror; then she slid down. But the slope immediately below her was not steep, and the amount of water had been slight; she managed to recover after only a meter or two.

Meanwhile, Troubot found that his new path did move on up. It was a better path than it seemed from below; the curvature of the mountain tended to conceal it. He followed it up, and soon realized that it, too, reached the top.

Tsetse was climbing again. Troubot threw another bomb, and rendered her path slippery again. She had to wait for it to clear before proceeding, and meanwhile he continued his ascent. She apparently had no bombs of her own. His decision to load up on them seemed to spell a critical advantage for him.

Then, as he was almost close enough to touch the peak and win, she moved. She *did* have a bomb; now it was looping toward him.

Its aim was good; it was going to splatter on the path just above him. He could not reach it in time. He did not try. Instead, he hurled a bomb of his own, not at Tsetse, but at the other bomb.

The two bombs met in air, and exploded. But his had been thrown later and harder, and its force carried the spray of water away from the path. Some water fell, but not enough to dislodge him. He paused to be sure the path was not too wet, then proceeded on up.

Tsetse, peering around the slope, saw this, and scrambled toward the peak herself. Troubot lobbed another bomb at her, and washed her back down to the lesser slope again. Before she could recover, he made it the rest of the way and clapped his metal arm on the top of the peak.

A gong sounded. He had won!

Tsetse, below, looked so forlorn that he knew he would have felt terrible remorse, had he been a living man of her species. But as it was, what he felt was more like joy.

13: Clip

It was a long trek to the Ogre Demesnes, but Clip was glad for it, because it gave him time to think. He had to represent the Adept Stile against the ogres, and he was not at all sure his unicorns could win this siege. These days of travel with the Herd allowed him many hours to ponder strategies.

In the evenings and nights the Herd grazed, sleeping afoot. Clip intended to do the same, but this evening he summoned his sister and niece for a conference in human form.

"My mind be taut with doubt," he confessed. "It be easy for others to say a 'corn can beat an ogre, being faster, smarter and more versatile, but that be illusion. In single fair combat it be either's win."

"Aye," Neysa agreed. She had had experience with many kinds of creatures, and had long since lost the bravado of youth.

"But can a 'corn not run an ogre through belly or heart with horn, and be done with it?" Fleta asked.

Clip looked at her. In human form, as in her natural one, she was much like her mother. Each had the same black hide, and the socks on the hind feet: Neysa's white, Fleta's golden, in contrast to his own blue hide and red socks. In this human form that meant black hair and black clothing, and white or yellow socks. Neysa was old and Fleta young, but that seemed to be most of the difference between them. He was so glad they had reconciled at last!

"A 'corn can run an ogre through, aye," he said. "But an ogre can smash a 'corn dead with one blow o' his hamfist."

"But ogres change form not," she persisted. "A 'corn could assume an aerial form and fly in close—"

"And the ogre will throw a rock and knock that flyer out o' the air," Clip responded. "Their aim be deadly!"

"Then in manform, with weapons—good bows and arrows!" she persisted.

"An ogre can hardly be hurt by an arrow; it only tickles his hide. He can throw a rock as far as an arrow can fly, so the bowman needs must look to his own hide."

Fleta was silent; she now appreciated the problem. Unicorns normally ranged the fields, running and grazing; they seldom encountered ogres, who were more attuned to the jungle, and to canyons, where there was plenty to bash. In addition, she had been much occupied in recent years with her romance with the rovot, and the raising of their foal, and the loss of that foal. How would she know about ogres?

"How relate they to music?" Neysa asked.

"That be uncertain. I was traveling alone once, and was playing my horn, and came upon an ogre who seemed to be sleeping. I paused, wary o' him, and then he woke and growled. I was tired, and sought not a fight, so pretended to see him not. I resumed my playing and trotted on, and he just stood there listening. After, I marveled, and thought mayhap he had liked my playing; the Adept Stile has termed my horn a mellow saxophone. But I be not sure; mayhap the ogre was tired too."

"This accords with what I have noted," Neysa said. "Methinks the ogres like music, or at least be intrigued by it."

Clip was interested. "Thinkst thou that many would pause for a serenade?"

"Mayhap."

"We could do a rare show," Clip said, working it out. "Dancing in step, to our music, keeping a strong beat. An it distracted them, it be a fun way to fight."

"In a siege?" Fleta asked, growing excited. "But that were folly for them!"

"Ogres be magnificently stupid," Clip said. "Folly be well within their capability."

"But how can we be sure? If we set up to play, and it worked not—"

"Aye," Clip said. "Needs must we verify the effect, privately, lest we run great risk."

"I will go ahead and play for one!" Fleta said eagerly. She changed form, and pranced as she played her pan-pipe horn, two melodies in counterpoint.

Clip paused. It had been years since he had heard her play. He had forgotten her unusual talent: one horn, two tunes! It was a very pretty effect. She might have done well in the Unilympics, had she not been barred because of her miscegenation with the rovot.

Then he returned to the serious business at hoof. "Not thou, niece. Thou be too inexperienced to risk thyself thus. I will do it."

"But we seek to know the effect o' a chorus," she protested, returning to girlform. "At least let me go with thee, so we can play together. That be a fairer test."

How neatly she had diverted his decision! She had not opposed it, merely modified it. He could not have tolerated the former, for as Herd Stallion he had a position to maintain, but could accept the latter. "Aye, then. But stray thou not far from me, an we hit ogre country."

"Nary a hoofprint!" she promised.

"Cover for us," he told Neysa, who nodded. If anything occurred that required his attention, she would handle it without revealing his absence. The Herd could continue grazing undisturbed. Of course there were lookouts posted; nothing would come upon the Herd by surprise.

They started out, trotting side by side. He was fatigued from the days of constant travel, but the notion of finding a way to distract the ogres invigorated him, and he stepped right along. Fleta, younger, kept pace. He had had little to do with her, because she had been absent from the Herd most of the time, but unlike Neysa, he had not condemned her association with the rovot. In fact, he had been privately understanding. The rovot looked just like Bane, and she had always been Bane's friend, and more than a friend. Animals were not supposed to have sexual encounters with human beings, but there was always a certain amount of experimentation that occurred, particularly among the young.

He himself, in his youth, had encountered a human village girl who had required cheering; she had shied away from him at first, until he showed her that he was a unicorn. His problem had been that he was a stallion cast out of the Herd, a "lesser male" who was denied sex with mares of the Herd until such time as he became strong enough and bold enough to challenge a Herd Stallion for dominance. Her problem had been that she loved a village lad who did not love her; she had not wished to be unfaithful to him, lest he change his mind and return to her. But she did not regard a relationship with a unicorn to be significant in that manner. In addition, she was inexperienced, and wished to gain a better notion what it was all about, so that she could acquit herself well if the opportunity arose. So there had been an affair, and they had learned much together. Unicorn mares were interested in sex only when they came into heat, whereas human girls could do it anytime. It had been most interesting.

Then the man of her interest *had* returned, and Clip had departed speedily and quietly. It was understood that neither of them would ever tell others of this matter; it had been purely a private thing, of no larger significance. He had never had a relationship with another human girl, but he remembered that one with fondness. Of course it had not been as good with her as with any true mare, but it had been good enough, and he had liked her. So now he respected his niece for having the courage to do openly what was normally done secretly, and to fight for her right to her relationship despite the condemnation of her dam and most others.

Neysa, of course, had been far more straight-maned about it. It was not the fact of interspecies action that bothered her, for she herself had had an affair with the Adept Stile before he married the Lady Blue. It had been the openness of it, and the insistence that it be legitimized. Fleta had wanted to *marry* the rovot: a deed virtually unknown among unicorns, and certainly not appropriate miscegenously. That was the difference between Clip and his sister: she was more conservative, and held more closely to the old values, flawed as they might be. It was understood that a stallion would take whatever sexual experience he could get, but that a mare would indulge outside of heat only for extraordinary reason, and then would be discreet. Indeed Neysa had been discreet; among unicorns, only he, her brother, knew for certain how close she had been to Stile.

Fleta, with Stile's son, had been discreet. But then with the rovot she had been blatant, and that was the essence of her crime. Yet later she had proven that it could be done: that offspring was possible. That had been a shock to all of Phaze, and values were still quivering. Now with Neysa's change of heart, Fleta was accepted, and applauded for her courage and her achievement. Indeed, the exploits of the colt Flach had charmed them all, as he defied both parents and Adepts and remained hidden despite their worst efforts. There was true unicorn stubbornness.

Now, of course, they were fighting to recover Flach from captivity by the Adepts. Fleta might seem to be the bubbling, cheerful young creature of old, but she was not; the years of her separation from her foal had sobered her. She had wanted him to stay free, knowing how vitally that helped Stile's cause, but she had also wanted him with her. Such inner conflict was not kind to individuals, even tough unicorns.

They ran into the sunset, eyes on the ground, making what time they could while light remained. Unicorns could see well enough at night, but this was unfamiliar terrain, and when the darkness closed they would have to slow to a safe walk.

Fleta began to play a little duet on her horn, from the sheer exuberance of the sensation of freedom lent by the hour. Her hooves carried the beat. Oh, yes, it was nice music, her pan-pipes! Each note was simple, but the combination was special. When she played the two very similar notes there was a beat, not of the hooves but of the merging themes. Surely the rovot had been entranced by this, as by her other virtues.

They slowed, proceeding onward toward the west, finding the open regions by sight and sound and smell. The air gradually cooled, and the stars came out. It was surprisingly nice. Clip remembered his travels with Belle, the most beautiful of mares, with the iridescent mane and the sound of ringing bells. She had become his first true love, and remained so as he mastered his Herd. Of course now he had many mares to service, and she was busy with her fourth foal, but the bond between them had never been broken; she would always be his lead mare. In the early years they had had to avoid Herds and travel by night, but it had been no chore. They had played such lovely music together!

So it went, that night, a pleasure of reminiscences, as they approached the Ogre Demesnes. By dawn they were there—and by the smell, nearing an ogre family. They centered on it, tracking the odor, until they came upon it: a ponderous male, a horrendously ugly female, and a homely cub. The male was bashing a dead tree apart, while the female and cub were shaking out the big fragments and catching the vermin in them: roaches, mice, toads and snakes. A fine ogre meal was in the making.

But all three paused the moment the two unicorns came into sight. It took several seconds for the male to come to a conclusion, but it was the expected one. He roared, and lumbered toward this new prey.

Actually, two fit unicorns should have been a match for two grown ogres. But that was not Clip's purpose in coming here. He stood his ground and played his horn. The mellowness of it spread out almost visibly, touching the ogres. Would they listen?

They paused, cocking their gross ears. Their expressions shifted slowly from rage in the male and surprise in the female and curiosity in the cub to universal perplexity. Beauty of any nature was foreign to ogres; they did not know what to do with it. Perhaps somewhere in their dim ancestry there had been a trace of it, and a suggestion of that awareness remained, a useless vestige that had not yet been properly bred out of the species.

Then the male shook it off, and prepared to roar again, to properly renew his attack.

Fleta began to play, accompanying Clip's melody. Her pan-pipes augmented his saxophone timbre nicely, and the result was extraordinarily pretty.

The ogres paused again, their perplexity deepening to virtual wonder. This time the male did not shake it off; two musicians overwhelmed his single mind. It seemed that the tableau would remain as long as the music continued.

Clip decided to test this further. Still playing, he advanced on the male, ready to move quickly if the ogre snapped out of it. Fleta followed, maintaining her harmony.

Clip came right up to the male, and the male did not move. Slack-jawed, the ogre listened, immobile. This was better than anticipated!

Finally Clip essayed the ultimate: he actually nudged the male ogre with the tip of his horn. The creature did not react.

That sufficed. Music was the key to the control of ogres! If just two players were enough to entrance an ogre family, think what an entire Herd Orchestra could do!

Clip signaled Fleta with a twitch of his horn. They retreated, never breaking off their duet. Then, at a safe distance, they ended the music.

The ogres shook their heads as if coming out of a trance. The male blinked, spied the unicorns, and opened his mouth to roar.

Immediately Clip and Fleta resumed playing. The ogre paused in mid-gape, as before.

They moved away, continuing their playing, until they were well clear of the ogre family. This had been a most successful experiment!

They headed back east. They were tired, but did not want to rest in unfamiliar country, away from the Herd. But they did not hurry; a regular walk was good enough.

After a while, Fleta assumed her hummingbird form and perched on Clip's head, resting. Three hours later, they exchanged: she resumed 'corn form while he became a hawk and rode her head. Thus they were able to take turns resting and sleeping, without losing time.

In the afternoon they encountered the Herd. Neysa had kept it moving forward at a leisurely pace, so that any watching Adepts would not notice anything odd. There was even a small bird riding her head, that might be taken for a hummingbird from a distance, while a hawk rode another unicorn. Thus even the absence of the two was tacitly accounted for.

They changed to human form and walked while they told Neysa what had happened. They had a tool to use against the ogres!

Clip went out to meet the chief ogre at the start of the siege. "May the best team win," Clip said, assuming manform.

"Arrrgh!" the ogre roared, taking a swipe at him.

The formal amenities accomplished, they retreated to their groups. The siege was on.

Clip had divided his forces into three: Fleta was in charge of the defense of the blue flag, with a quarter of the unicorns in a number of guises. Clip was in charge of the attack on the red flag, with another quarter of the Herd. The rest of the 'corns were scattered between, on their own; they would track individual ogres and try to take them out as opportunity offered.

Clip hoped that there would be no real action. His attack force consisted not of the best fighters, but the best players. They would charm the ogres into stasis, so that they would not defend their flag. With sufficient luck, the siege would be won almost as it began.

His contingent trotted out, in step. From the distance ahead there was a horrendous roar as the ogre attack force commenced its charge.

The two groups came into sight of each other. The ogres hurled a barrage of rocks. The unicorns stepped aside, without breaking step, each one dodging the stone that came for him. The aim of the rocks was good, but the range was such that there was plenty of time to see them coming. They thudded into the ground all around the unicorns, hitting none. Then the formation closed up again. The beat had never faltered. The ogres hardly cared; they preferred smashing things with their hamfists anyway.

As ogres and unicorns closed, Clip sounded the signal. There was a pause of four hoofbeats. Then the music started: Clip's sax, joined by the other "brass" sounds: trombone, trumpet, bugle, French horn and tuba. The "wood" sounds: piccolo, violin, cello, lute, guitar and harp. The "percussions": cymbals, bells, xylophone, chimes, and assorted drums. A few stray types, such as organ, music-box and piano. All of these terms were necessarily crude, because the human tongue lacked proper descriptions, just as the human instruments lacked proper quality of tone. The unicorn variety was more or less infinite, with each individual possessing a sound not quite like any other. A group of 'corns playing together represented musical expertise unmatched elsewhere.

The ogres ground to a halt, their maws gaping in idiotic wonder. Their remaining rocks dropped from flaccid hamfingers. They listened to the serenade.

The unicorns marched in step, keeping perfect beat, playing their intricate melody. They guided around the standing ogres and went on toward the red flag, unchallenged.

Then Neysa changed to her firefly form and flew up and ahead, going straight for the high tree from which the flag fluttered. Clip had decided not to risk a larger flying form, lest it distract the ogres from the music. Indeed, once Neysa was safely aloft, her tiny body lost to view in the distance, he brought the party to a halt. They marched in place, serenading the ogres. The idea was to hold the ogres' attention until the flag was safely away.

Neysa reached the flag. It was of course too heavy for her to carry in that form. She lighted on the trunk of the tree below it and changed to human form. Then, clinging with one hand, she reached up with the other to grasp the flag.

It didn't come. Clip, watching while he stepped and played, realized what the problem was: an ogre had tied it in place, and the knot was too tight for a woman form to free one-handed. She would have to break off the top of the tree to get it loose.

She tried, but the trunk was too strong. That was understandable; not far below, it was supporting her human weight. She would just have to keep working at the knot; eventually it should come loose.

They continued playing, holding the ogres spellbound. The effect evidently included the ogres farther away, because there was no sound of crashing or roaring anywhere. There was only the serenade.

Neysa managed to climb up a bit farther, and to hold on with her legs. She got her teeth on the knot. Now, reluctantly, it was loosening. Soon she would have it!

Suddenly there was the roar of a dragon, horribly loud. For a moment it overrode the music.

The ogres recovered. Their leader roared. Then all of them were roaring, following his example—and the unicorns were drowned out.

Disaster! The ogres, finding the unicorns behind them, wheeled and charged, roaring continuously. The music was no longer effective, because it could not be heard. The unicorns had to get away—and they were almost surrounded.

Fortunately Clip had drilled them on a fallback procedure. They formed a compact group, their rears together, their horns pointing outward. The ogres could not readily attack this group without getting horned.

Meanwhile the members of the Herd who were farther back saw the problem. They assumed their manforms and brought out their bows. Soon arrows were annoying the ogres from behind them.

These ogres turned and charged the manforms. They picked their dropped rocks and hurled them, forcing the 'corns to take cover behind trees. Then, realizing that there was a flag to fetch, the ogres tramped onward, gathering in their forces as they went, becoming a seemingly invincible force.

Clip knew that this was no good. His grand ploy had failed and his 'corns were in danger. Neysa had disappeared; she must have changed back to firefly form when the ogres resumed action, because any who spied her in the tree could knock her out with a single hurled stone. It was time to look to their own flag!

He set the example. He changed to hawkform and flew quickly up and away. The others did the same; he had had the caution to include in this group only those who had flying forms. The ogres oriented and threw rocks, but the change was so quick that they were too late; few if any escaping 'corns were caught.

Now they were in for it. The ogres, freed of distraction, were forging toward the blue flag. Fleta had imaginatively set some traps, just in case; when the ogres tramped straight forward, they blundered into a giant pitfall. They promptly proceeded to bash their way out of it, but this brought down a great deal of dirt, halfway burying them, and served to slow them down. Thereafter the ogres made long poles and poked them at the ground ahead, feeling out a safe path. This also slowed them, but not enough.

Manform 'corns hid behind trees and emerged only to throw spears at the advancing horde. The ogres hurled rocks back, but took losses. Thereafter they kept their hairy arms cocked, ready to throw a rock at any living thing that showed, and the 'corns had to desist. The ogres advanced.

What were they to do? Clip's best play had failed, and it was clear that the ogres would in time reach the flag and take it down. Was there no stopping them?

It occurred to him, in this hour of desolation, that there had been something funny about that dragon roar that had ruined his ploy of music. There were supposed to be no dragons here! How could one have roared so loud and close as to drown out the massed unicorns? Where was that dragon? It had never shown up.

Clip ground his teeth. Was it possible that there had been no dragon? That the Adepts had made that sound to ruin his ploy? If so, they had cheated—but how could it be proven?

A hummingbird came to him. It became Fleta. "Uncle, I have a plan, a ruse—willst let me try?"

"An thou hast a way, mare, try it!" he agreed.

"But methinks I will need thy help. I will lead an ogre, and thou must dispatch it only when I say. Canst do that?"

Just like that: dispatch an ogre! But if the monster were distracted, it was possible. "Aye."

"Remember, only when I say, else all be lost. This be one odd ploy."

Clip became cautious. "Must needs I know more o' this."

"I mean to lead it to our flag—"

"That be no problem! They be going there anyway!"

"Ahead o' the others," she continued. "And let it take the flag—"

"*What?*"

"Shortly before thou dost dispatch it."

Oh. Now that he thought about it, he realized that this would make it easier to eliminate the ogre, because it would be thinking only of the flag. Still, it was chancy. "Better to dispatch it before it gets the flag," he said.

"Nay, Uncle! It must be after! Only after, when I tell thee!"

Why did she want it this way? He decided to do it her way. It wouldn't hurt, as long as he did stop the ogre. But he did not see how this would stop the overall thrust of the remaining ogres. There would not be time to lead each of them up alone, so soon the region of the flag would be swamped with the monsters. "Aye," he said.

She changed to 'corn form and trotted out and around until she spied an especially big and ugly ogre, poking his way along a bit to the side of the others. She changed to girlform, while Clip assumed hawk-form and perched in a tree, watching.

"Hey, lady-snout!" Fleta called to the ogre. "Dost put thy hair in curlers and paint thy face to make it so pretty?"

Irony was of course lost on the creature. It took her words literally—and was furious, because no ogre could afford to be considered pretty. It roared and stepped toward her, but hesitated, because of the fear for pitfalls and ambushes. Its beady eyes searched the forest, and it hefted a giant stone menacingly.

"Slow, too!" Fleta taunted. "Why, I could outrun thee in *this* form!"

That was another potent insult, for she was a mere slip of a creature compared to him. The ogre watched for ambushes, but was just barely smart enough to realize that if he pursued her along the exact route she took, there would be no pitfalls she did not fall into first. He took off after her.

Fleta ran, and now Clip saw reason for her name: she was buxom and pretty (for those who might like the human type), but also fleet of foot. Her black hair-mane flung out behind as she moved, and her buttocks twinkled in a manner that made the ogre's mouth water. Ogres loved to eat humanform flesh, and girlform flesh was acknowledged to be the tastiest. She was the best possible lure, to make the ogre forget what little caution it might possess and pursue blindly. It would be easy to trap or waylay this ogre!

Yet she had demanded that this wait until after the ogre got the flag. Clip flew after, flitting from tree to tree so as to minimize his exposure to thrown rocks, and hoped this was not as crazy as it seemed.

Fleta, remaining just ahead of the monster, led it safely to the flag. "See, there's our flag, and you can't get it because then you'd lose me!" Fleta called. "What a fool thou dost be!"

The ogre grinned, pleased at the compliment. But her words did serve to remind him of his original mission. Quickly he hauled himself hamfist over hamfist up the tree, until he grabbed the flag, then slid down. Fleta, in supposed astonishment, had not moved. "Thou didst take our flag," she exclaimed. "Be I not tasty enough?"

The ogre stuffed the flag in his ear for safekeeping and lurched after her. Fleta screamed as if in horror and ran again. She led the ogre to the side, some distance from the original flag site, then dived under a giant spruce tree. "I be safe here!" she cried.

But one of her dainty feet poked out. She had not gotten completely out of sight! The ogre grabbed—just as the foot was pulled out of the way. The ogre grabbed again, plunging under the tree, until it too was lost in the maze of branches.

"*Now, Uncle!*" Fleta called.

Clip, hovering nervously near, was more than ready. He flitted to the ground, converting to his natural form and landing squarely on four feet. He saw the hummingbird sail up out of harm's way; then he rammed horn-first into the bulk of the ogre tangled in the foliage.

His first strike caught the monster from behind. His horn sank in half its length before he jerked it out, but the brute had not received a mortal wound. The ogre wrenched around, a hamfist striking out. It smashed into a large branch, snapping it off—and Clip's second strike drove in under the ogre's massive arm, seeking the heart.

But the angle was wrong, and he only punctured a gross lung. He jerked back, and the ogre reached for him with both arms, catching at his head. Unable to get away, Clip launched forward, his horn driving up the ogre's flaring nose.

This time the stroke was true: the tip of the horn punctured the creature's small brain. The ogre made a gasp of irritation, and collapsed.

Clip backed out of the foliage, assuming manform. The ogre was entirely out of sight; only the broken branches and skuff-marks on the ground showed where he had gone. "Cover the traces so he can't be found," Fleta said. She drew from her pocket a bright blue flag.

Clip was appalled. "Thou hast our flag? We dare not touch it, lest we be disqualified!"

"Nay, this be not our flag," she said brightly. "See, it be brighter, and not quite the right shape; it were the best we could do on the spur."

"But—"

"I shall just put this fake flag up where ours was," she explained.

"But all they have to do is take the real one, which they can readily do—"

"An they see it, aye," she agreed. "Thou must make sure they do not." She ran back toward the original flag location.

Clip went back to look at the dead ogre. Sure enough, the original flag was still stuffed in its ear. He fetched a broken bough and used it to sweep the ground, masking the traces. Then he set it on the ogre, further concealing him. Only a person who knew where to look would find either ogre or flag.

Yet wasn't this merely delaying the inevitable? If the ogres were stupid enough to take the fake flag back, they would realize that it was fake when the authorities checked it. Then they would return to make a thorough search, and find the real one.

Unless—

Suddenly the full nature of Fleta's ploy came clear to him! Beautiful! He changed to hawkform and flew back toward the other end of the arena, where the red flag still flew.

He encountered other unicorns, in their several forms, harassing the advancing ogres. He stopped a moment with each, quickly explaining what was to occur, and how each should react. He found distressingly few; the ogres had been striking back with increasing effectiveness, and taken a heavy toll of the defenders.

He reached the vicinity of the red flag. A number of ogres were clustered at the base of its tree, ready to defend it against any enemy intrusion. At this stage, no such intrusion was likely; the ranks of the unicorns had been too drastically depleted. It was obvious that the ogres were going to win the siege.

But Clip went from 'corn to 'corn, explaining. Some were incredulous, but it was the only hope remaining, and they agreed to do what he asked. He knew that Fleta was doing the same, back near the blue flag.

There was a roar from the distance: the ogres had broken through to the flag! The ground shook as they charged back in a mass, and soon the lead ogre appeared, taking a swatch of blue.

A firefly flew up to Clip. He knew it was Neysa, giving up on the red flag; she was too small in this form, and too vulnerable in her woman form. "It be all right," he said to her, quietly so that no ogre would overhear. "Just follow my lead!"

She reverted to natural form, showing doubt in every mannerism. How could he stop the ogres now?

All around were unicorns, looking similarly dejected. Some few tried to balk the ogres, but these were quickly dispatched. It was obviously a lost cause.

The ogre with the blue flag charged up to the tree and climbed it. When he got high up on it, the thing bent and swayed, but he got far enough to reach the red flag. He jammed the two together. A unicorn with a percussion horn made a loud sound very like a gong. Two sides could play the game of special noises! There was a roaring cheer from the other ogres.

Clip assumed stallion form and blew a sad note. The other unicorns walked slowly toward him. None looked happy.

The ogres, gruffly cheerful, punched each other roughly on the shoulders and tramped away. They would have a monstrous celebration tonight! The unicorns watched them go without comment.

When the last ogre had departed, Clip assumed hawkform and flew up to the set of flags. Several sharp pecks with his beak loosened the red one. He hauled it clear, and flew with it toward the region of the other flag. The other unicorns followed, making no exclamations, watching for any ogres who might be lagging behind. The ogres had been too stupid to realize that the game had not yet finished, because the dead had not yet returned to life. The Adepts of course would know, but were barred from interfering; they could only watch and grind their teeth. They could not cry warning, because this would be so obvious a foul that their side would forfeit.

Soon Clip reached the spruce tree where the dead ogre lay. He plunged into the foliage and set the red flag at the ogre's ear with the blue one.

The two flags touched. There was the sound of a gong. The casualties came back to life, unicorn and ogre alike. This time the siege really was over, and the unicorns were the victor.

"That be our point!" Neysa exclaimed. "Unicorn point!"

Indeed it was. They had done it for Stile.

14: *Agape*

"I hate this!" she protested.

"There be no other way," Bane reminded her. "For the first game, each side chose its own champion. For the second, each chose the champion o' the other. For this third, each had to compromise. We vetoed their first and second choices, so they vetoed ours; thus thou must bear our standard."

"But against Citizen Tan!" Agape said. "He hates me!"

"Aye, and with reason," he said, smiling. "Was thy body the mare used to tweak his hardware. But this be a game; thou hast merely to play the grid properly, and he can do naught 'gainst thee."

"Oh, Bane, I am afraid!"

He held her, but could not console her. "I would free thee o' this duty an I could, but it be set. The games be e'en; thou must win this one for Blue!"

"I am afraid I will lose!"

"Just remember the strategy: keep it in Mental an thou canst, and in Machine if that be thine option. Then he can not get at thee directly."

"He will find a way!" she said with dire premonition. "Oh, I could just melt!"

"Later, after thou has won the game," he said, smiling. But she was not reassured. She felt singularly inadequate to the occasion. How could she, an alien creature, hope to prevail against a hard-driving malignant Citizen? She wished most ardently that she had never had to return from Moeba, once she had escaped Proton. But that would have meant continued separation from Bane, and from Nepe, and that, too, was intolerable.

All too soon it was time. In the morning she approached the designated console. Citizen Tan was already there, staring at her fixedly. She knew that he did not choose to distinguish between herself and Fleta, and well remembered his pain of the body and pride, years ago, and he had never forgiven those injuries. He was a man bent on vengeance.

"So the amoeba slides in," he said, unsmiling.

She did not answer. She took her place at the console and tried not to shrink too visibly from his gaze.

The screen lighted. She almost dissolved with relief: *she had the numbers!*

She moved her hand carefully, so as to make no foolish error. She touched one finger to 2. MENTAL. There, she had done it! There could be no physical contact between them. She felt as if she had won a significant encounter already. She could not have asked for a better break.

Tan made his selection, as if it were a matter of indifference, and the screen blinked and displayed the secondary grid: 2D. ANIMAL-ASSISTED MENTAL. This meant that they would be playing through animals, commanding them or sending their directives to them by other means. Agape was surprised; she had not thought Citizen Tan to have any interest whatever in animals.

Then she suffered a wash of apprehension: surely he was up to something malignant! Somehow he hoped to get at her physically through those animals. Yet how could he, in the mental category?

Alas, that became all too quickly evident. The definition of "animal" included not only the conventional dogs, cats, horses and such, but also androids of all types, and also the human animal. Thus she found herself playing the primary grid again, this time for the nature of the animal encounter. Bemused, she made what she feared were bad choices, and found herself in the very category she most wanted to avoid: NAKED PHYSICAL, HUMAN ANIMAL. This was a trap of MENTAL that she had somehow overlooked: it reopened everything else. She played the tertiary grid in a blur, certain that disaster was upon her.

Abruptly it ended: they were in Flat Surface Interactive, Human Animal–Assisted, Naked Physical: Surrogate Sex.

"Do each of you understand the nature of the selected game?" the voice of the Game Computer inquired.

"Naturally," Tan snapped.

"N-no," Agape confessed. She only knew it was trouble. How could she have let the Citizen stampede her into this?

"I will explain for the benefit of the one who pleads ignorance," the voice said. "Each player will select an actor of the same sex from the available menu. The actors will be attuned to thoughts sent by their players, and will be responsive to such thoughts if they are not in conflict with the actors' natural inclinations. One player will be designated the initiator, the other the receiver; these designations will reverse at three-hour intervals. The initiator will within the period seduce the receiver—"

"What?" Agape cried faintly.

"And be adjudged the winner of the fall," the machine continued blithely. "If the initiator fails in that period, the receiver wins the fall. Then the receiver will become the initiator and will seduce the new receiver, with the fall similarly determined. For the final period the roles will reverse again. The strictures against force will be relaxed in the final period, so as to ensure a decision. If the initiator does not succeed, the victory will go to the receiver, as the winner of two of three falls."

"What am I to do?" Agape cried in despair.

Citizen Tan said something impolite and very much to the point. He, of course, was enjoying this. He had succeeded after all in bringing her to a sexual encounter, and he intended to have his measure of flesh.

"The setting will be the Commons," the Game Computer said. "Neither actor will be allowed to leave it until the game is concluded, on pain of default. Interference by others will not be tolerated. You will now select your actors, who will be routed to the Commons without being advised of their roles."

"But do you mean real people?" Agape cried. "How can we—"

"A further explanation," the machine said patiently. "The actors will be selected from a pool formed by volunteers that is maintained at a constant level. Each volunteer has been examined and approved, then awareness of this process has been deleted. Only after the game is complete will they understand that they have played their parts. They will be compensated, and of course they will have a certain notoriety because of the significance of this particular game. No onus attaches to them for what occurs. They are real people, but they understood the range of parts available when they volunteered."

"Oh." It was all she could manage at the moment.

"Now you will make your selections. Touch the screen to enlarge a card, and touch SELECT when the card is the one you choose." A pattern of pictures and very fine text appeared on the screen.

Agape nerved herself to glance at Citizen Tan. He was looking at his own screen. It was evident that he was having absolutely no trouble with this. He had probably played this game before. But how could she try to seduce him, or his agent—his actor? Even with her actress? What would Bane think?

She knew the answer to the last question. Bane wanted her to win this game and the tourney, so that Citizen Blue would prevail. Bane loved her, but he was a realist. He would tell her to do what she had to do.

But could she? The very notion of seeking a sexual encounter with another man, even via a surrogate, appalled her. All she knew of this subject she had learned with Bane. Granted the necessity, still she doubted she could do it.

Then she thought of Nepe, captive of the Citizens. Her child. A victory here would bring her back. Now Agape knew that she would do it.

She touched a picture. Immediately it expanded to fill the screen. It showed a beautiful young woman with an expansive halo of black hair, dramatically erect and full breasts, and a confident expression. The text said: NAME: Milda. SEX: Female. AGE: 23 Earth Years. EMPLOYER: Citizen Bliven. ASSIGNMENT: On Call.

Agape read no further. No wonder the woman was beautiful; she was the Citizen's mistress! She was apt to be an easy mark for an amorous serf, because Citizen sex, by most accounts, was demanding and not particularly pleasant for the serf, male or female. The Citizen had to be pleased, at all costs; the penalty for failure was to be fired, and that was bad news on Proton. Thus if a man came who sought sex on an equal basis, the woman should be flattered.

She touched the picture again, and it condensed back to its prior place, surrounded by others. Agape touched a new one.

This showed a relatively homely woman. There was nothing wrong with her appearance; she just was not anything a man would choose to pursue. This one might therefore diminish the male actor's ardor.

Agape realized immediately that her notion was flawed. Suppose a handsome man pursued and flattered such a woman? Unaccustomed to such attention, she might welcome it, and do whatever the man asked in an effort to please him. Agape, as the player, could tell her no, but that might not carry much weight, being contrary to her natural inclinations. She touched the picture again, and it diminished.

The third picture seemed about right: a pretty but slightly older woman with brown hair and brown eyes. She would surely be quite fetching when she smiled, and less attractive otherwise. The legend said: NAME: Deerie. SEX: Female. AGE: 30 Earth Years. EM-

PLOYER: Citizen Tosme. ASSIGNMENT: Foot Massager. INTEL-
LIGENCE: 1.15. CREATIVITY: .95 STABILITY: 1.21.

Agape nodded. This looked very good. Deerie was old enough to
know her mind, especially with a stability quotient twenty-one per cent
above the norm. She had a simple menial job which might be a cover
for "on call" and probably would accede to whatever demand the Citizen might make, but would be no easy mark for anyone else. Female
serfs did not even count Citizen seductions as sex; it was just an involuntary necessity. This was a reasonably smart, unimaginative woman
perhaps halfway through her Proton tenure; she would want to get all
the way through without problems, and take her pay to her home
world. Serfs who made it through could retire quite comfortably elsewhere; the system made it worth their while to undergo this servitude.

But how would this one be if she had to seduce a strange man? Here
that lower creativity score should help: she would accept Agape's bright
notions as her own, not thinking to question them or to develop other
options. Would her age count against her in this respect? Perhaps not,
for she possessed quite comely features and was well proportioned
throughout. Probably she exercised, because she looked physically fit.
That could help if it came to violence—as, unfortunately, it could.

Agape touched SELECT. She would take Deerie as her actress. Citizen Tan, naturally, had long since chosen.

"Go to the two privacy booths indicated," the Game Computer
said. A line appeared on the floor, leading away.

She followed her line, glad that it did not go in the same direction
as Citizen Tan's line. At least she would be away from him physically.

The line led to a glassed-in booth. She entered and closed the door.
There was a comfortable chair. That was all.

She sat in the chair. Immediately the wall before it became a picture:
the Commons, the region of relaxation for serfs when they were not
working for their Citizens. It had many couches and beds, food machines, pools, and screens on which recorded entertainments could be
evoked. It was a pleasant place; she had visited it many times with
Bane, and many more times without him, during his absences in Phaze.
She had brought Nepe here, in the early years before Nepe disappeared; the child had proved to be precocious with the entertainments.
The rule was that serfs were free to do whatever they wished, here,
provided it did not directly interfere with the pleasures of others. They
could indeed indulge in sexual activity here, in full view; those who
did not want to watch were free to look elsewhere. Thus this was the
proper setting for a game such as this.

"Your opponent has the onus," the Game Computer said. "He has therefore been advised of the identity of your actress. Speak cautiously; from this moment all that you say will be conveyed to your actress as soundless thought."

"But—" Agape started.

The picture on the wall jumped, as if someone had reacted. Agape realized that her word had been relayed, and that Deerie had heard in her mind *But—!* Naturally she had jumped; she didn't understand why such a thought had come into her head.

She kept quiet and watched, and after a moment Deerie resumed her motion. Agape realized that the wall-picture she saw was what the actress saw; it moved as her vision did. How this effect was achieved Agape wasn't certain; she had never played this particular game before and never explored this effect. Perhaps cameras on the woman relayed their pictures, and the Game Computer assembled these into a holographic image that duplicated what the woman should be seeing. For it was three-dimensional; it seemed that the wall was glass, and that she was seeing through it into the Commons.

Deerie walked past a mirror, and glanced a moment at her reflection. Agape caught a glimpse of the woman of the picture. The hair was longer now, and the breasts drooped somewhat; how long ago had that picture been taken? But the woman was moving on before Agape could assess the situation fully.

"No!" she said. "Stay and look a moment longer."

The image turned, as the actress responded. She faced back and approached the mirror again.

Agape had spoken involuntarily, but realized that the woman had taken it as her own thought. It was amazing how well this worked! But it would be better to provide a rationale, so that Deerie would not get suspicious.

"I haven't really looked at myself in some time," Agape said. "I would like to reassure myself that I still look respectable."

The woman stood before the mirror. She straightened her back and inhaled. Now her breasts lifted, becoming erect and prominent, and her belly flattened. Yes, she had a good figure; the years had not yet eroded it. "Yes, that's nice," Agape said. "I should maintain a better posture, so as to show myself off to advantage; there is no point in slouching and having others think I am getting old."

Agape's eye was caught by a brightening light to the side. She looked, and realized that the border around the wall-picture contained a series of panels that glowed gently. The brightening one had letters formed by shading: PRIDE. Deerie was experiencing the emotion of pride! That was how the player knew the emotions of the actor; by watching the panels glow.

"Yes, I am glad I paused to take stock of myself," Agape said. "I am reassured."

Deerie lifted her hand to her hair. The brown tresses were pinned back by a comb. She lifted this out and used it to comb out her hair. Because serfs had no clothes, they had no pockets; unless a woman wanted to carry a purse, which was a nuisance on Proton, she had few ways to keep articles with her. Thus the double-duty comb was common.

Deerie formed her hair into gentle inward curls about her shoulders, so that the outline of her face was softened. "Yes, I look better," Agape said. She was becoming comfortable with this mode of communication, and was developing a certain rapport with her actress.

The woman set the comb back into the top of her hair, where it resembled part of a tiara, another nice effect. She walked on through the Commons, evidently going to some particular entertainment.

She came to a bank of food machines and punched for a cup of water. Agape was surprised. Water, when anything at all was available? What kind of relaxation was this?

But then Deerie moved on to an exercise region, and it made sense. She did not want to be burdened with digestion when working out, but water was all right.

Deerie got on the track that circled the region, and began jogging. Slowly she picked up speed, until her breath was heaving. A new panel glowed: EXHILARATION. No wonder she was healthy: her idea of entertainment was to run hard!

"May I join you?" a man inquired, falling in beside her. Deerie jumped, and so did Agape; neither had noticed his approach.

The actress turned her head to look at him. He was a tall, muscular man of about her own age, bronzed and handsome. Evidently somewhat of a professional when it came to physical exercise. "As you wish," Deerie replied noncommittally.

"I have seen you here before," the man said. Though he matched her pace, he was not the least winded. "Frankly, I like your look. Do you like mine?"

Suddenly Agape remembered what they were here for. Citizen Tan had taken a male body, and was out to seduce Deerie! She had to stop this before it got going!

"I don't trust this man!" Agape said. "I don't know him, and I fear his intentions."

But for the first time she encountered resistance. Deerie, as it turned out, was interested in men, and this was the kind she liked. She had no illusions about their interest, but since she wasn't seeking anything permanent, that didn't bother her. She trusted her judgment, not the man, and she deemed this one as a fit companion for an hour's fun. At least, so Agape interpreted the woman's reactions.

"I think he's a sadist," Agape said desperately. "He wants to get me alone and hurt me, and make me cry, and then he will laugh and call me a foolish old maid."

That thought had better effect. "Some other time," Deerie said, and slowed and stepped off the track.

The man looked disappointed, but did not pursue her. He ran on down the track, and in a moment was out of sight.

"You certainly dispatched him, Deerie," another man said.

She looked around. "Oh, hello, Handy," she panted. "What are you doing here?"

"Just thought I'd see how the other half lives," Handy said. "I never exercise myself." He was tall and slender, with a handsome shock of blond hair. "I'm more of a gamesman myself."

"I know," Deerie agreed. "I've seen you play. But you're only twenty-one; when you get to be my age, you'll exercise or sag. Better to start early and stay in shape."

Agape was relieved. These two knew each other, and were friendly, so Handy might serve as a buffer between Deerie and Tan's actor. She should keep them together until the danger passed. "I never realized what good company Handy is," she said for Deerie's benefit.

Handy laughed in response to Deerie's remark, for an instant startling Agape, because it was almost as if he had heard her words. "You may have a point! I would never have taken you for twenty-five!"

"For what?" Deerie asked, startled in her turn.

"I really thought you were my age, but someone said you were older. Maybe they were teasing me."

"I'm thirty."

He laughed again. "I'm not that gullible! Come on, how old really? Twenty-four?"

Deerie studied him. He was young, but a fine figure of a man. "Thirty, really," she said, flattered.

"I don't believe it. But I'm always ready to play a game. Will you bet on it?"

"I'll bet, but you'll lose."

"Good enough. What are the stakes?"

Deerie eyed him, mixed emotions showing on the panels: SPECULATION, PLEASURE, SURPRISE. "What did you have in mind?"

He eyed her back. "You know, I never thought of you this way before, but you're one pretty woman! If you are under thirty, I want your love."

"And if I am thirty, what do I get?"

Handy spread his hands. "I have little to offer. Would you settle for instruction in gamesmanship?"

"No. I have no interest in the Game."

"Then you must name something else. I being a young man with only one thing on my mind, can't think of anything else."

The panels were glowing more brightly. The actress was really flattered by the attention of this young man.

"Exercise!" Deerie exclaimed. "You will run with me ten loops around the track!"

"I'd collapse in two," he said. "You look great running; I was watching you. From in front your breasts jog almost independently of your body, and from behind—"

"Take it or leave it!" she cut in, laughing.

He looked woebegone. "Oh, I'll take it! But I have to win, because I won't look a fraction as good as you on that track, especially after I collapse."

They went to an information screen. "My name is Deerie," the actress said. "I work for Citizen Tosme. How old am I, in standard Earth years?"

The screen flickered. Then the number 30 appeared.

"Oh, no!" Handy groaned. "Wait, let me verify this; maybe this unit's out of whack." He stepped up to the screen. "My name is Handy. I work for Citizen Morely as a furniture polisher. How old am I?"

The numbers appeared: 21.

"And are you sure she's thirty?"

YES.

He sighed. "Well, I'm hung for it." He looked at her again. "Damn, you sure don't look it! Are you sure I can't talk you into my kind of exercise instead?"

Deerie, highly flattered and intrigued, was tempted. "Well—"

"Oh, thank you, you lovely creature!" he exclaimed. He was obviously sincere; he was getting an erection.

Suddenly Agape suffered a shock of suspicion. The first man had desisted immediately, while this one was intent on seduction. His every word was calculated flattery! *Was this Tan's actor?*

She couldn't gamble that he was not. She realized that the fact that

Deerie knew him meant nothing; Tan could have chosen him partly for that reason. And Agape had almost been deceived—if that was the case.

"Too fast!" she said. "I really don't know him that well. I'd better hold him off a while, just to be sure." Because Agape realized that a direct negation might not take, at this point; Deerie's panels were glowing, and among them LUST was gaining brightness. With a man, that one would be the first to glow, while with a woman it might be the last, but it could be very strong in its time, as Agape herself knew. She was not human, but she had emulated a human female for some time, studying the nuances, and when she had learned about sex she had discovered its compulsive component. How she wanted to be with Bane right now! But she was about to lose the fall, unless Handy really was an innocent friend. That seemed decreasingly likely.

Deerie was hesitating, her new thoughts at variance with her growing emotion. Agape jumped in to buttress her side. "He lost the bet! He's just trying to get out of running. He really doesn't care about me; he probably thinks I'm ancient, but he'd rather put up with me than wear himself out on the track."

That got through. The actress was highly conscious of the age differential, which didn't matter for incidental contacts but loomed larger in sexual matters. She did not wish to be foolish. "Hold on there," she said. "I didn't say I would. You lost the bet, remember! I don't think I should let you off so easy."

Handy's erection was now at full mast. "Oh, Deerie, don't tease me like this! You can see I'm not lying. I really do want you!" He glanced down at himself, as if confirming it.

"Every man wants every woman!" Agape retorted. Indeed, she knew that Citizen Tan wanted her, though that was more for the purpose of humiliating her than from actual desire.

"Every man does," Deerie said, speaking the thought. "That is, a man doesn't have to like or respect a woman, he just wants sex wherever he can find it."

Well said! Agape was getting along well with Deerie, or maybe it was the other way around.

"But I like and respect you!" Handy protested.

"Sure you do, joker," another woman said, noting the display. "That's what you said to Jezebel last week, but then you cut her dead."

What a break! Handy had a past, and now that was interfering with his present ploy. *Tan's* ploy! How was he going to explain this?

He tried. "Jezebel was a cow compared to Deerie here. Deerie's the one I really want."

"My best friend—a *cow*?" the woman demanded. "Listen, jerk, I've got three quarters of a mind to take that rod of yours and bend it in half!"

"Like to see you try!" a muffled man's voice came from somewhere. It seemed that the neighboring serfs were catching on to the sport.

"I had better get out of here before it gets embarrassing," Agape said.

At this point, Deerie was glad to agree. She had been flattered and intrigued by Handy's advance, and not at all dismayed by his erection, but she did not want to be a laughing stock. She made a quiet retreat, while Handy was occupied with the other woman.

Agape was relieved. She had survived the first advance. Now she just had to stay clear for the remainder of the period, and this fall would be hers. She couldn't leave the Commons, but she could get involved in something else, so that Handy would have trouble approaching her.

"Let's see, what do I usually do after I exercise?" she asked.

"I go to the pool and exercise some more," Deerie answered herself.

Soon they were swimming. Her location was hardly unknown; it seemed that every woman in the Commons had heard about her episode with Handy the moment it happened. "Good going, girl!" one woman called as she swam by. "They think all they have to do is get it up, and any woman near will leap on!" And, surprisingly, even a few men were chuckling. They liked a good joke as well as the women did, so long as it was on someone else.

Thus it was that the time passed, and Deerie escaped her seduction. Agape had won the first fall!

But now it was the second period, and the onus was on her. The Game Computer confirmed that Handy was the one she had to seek. Her actress had to seduce Tan's actor, or lose the fall. This was the part she hated most.

But she had to do it. She nerved herself, then began working on Deerie, who was sunning herself on the tanning beach. "I guess I wasn't too nice to him. Maybe I should give him his settlement after all."

Deerie, as it turned out, was amenable. She had been turned off the liaison because of the developing embarrassment, not because she disliked the notion. She got up and went in search of Handy.

He was glumly having a drink. Intoxicants were forbidden to serfs, but the convention remained: a person was allowed to decrease inhibitions after imbibing.

She sat down beside him. "Handy, I'm sorry," she said. "I shouldn't have made it awkward for you this morning."

He looked at her. Agape could guess his thoughts. Citizen Tan wanted to curse her, but he was aware that because he had lost the first fall, he would need to win both remaining falls. If he won the second by driving her forever away, he would have no chance to seduce her in the third period. So he had to do it carefully, in such a way as to set up for his next turn. Meanwhile the actor, Handy, unaware of this background, should be quite ready to accommodate her.

"These things happen," he said. "I still think you're a great-looking woman."

Deerie was pleased. She of course did not know what lay behind this day's contact. "Well, you did lose the bet, and I didn't make you run. So if you want to work out your penalty the way you suggested—"

Now it seemed that Tan and Handy had a conflict. Citizen Tan had no intention of having sex, but serf Handy was obviously interested. He was starting another erection. He set aside his finished drink and went quickly to a couch, where he could sit without his condition showing as clearly.

Agape wondered how this kind of game proceeded when the sex occurred in the first period. Didn't that put the female at a disadvantage for the second period, because the male was spent? But she realized that this would be the least of problems; the Game Computer would simply arrange for a sexual restorative to be given, and the man's interest would be at its normal level. It would also be possible to adapt a new set of actors.

"No, I don't care to be embarrassed again," Handy was saying. "You got me all excited before, and then you left me standing in a crowd with my tower on display! Everyone knew I'd been stood up and not laid down. I'm afraid you are only setting me up to do it again."

"Oh, no, Handy, no!" Deerie protested, following him to the couch. "That was an accident! Once the other people came in, I had to go, because I didn't like it that public. But we can go to a privacy booth right now and do it. I promise I'll make it up to you!"

She was doing very well! Handy's erection was growing; he really did want her. But Citizen Tan needed to break this up. "I'll tell you what: let it go for now, and if you're still interested in three hours, then I'll know you mean it. Then I'll do it."

Nice ploy! In three hours it would be Tan's onus again. "I don't think I can wait," Agape said. "He's got me all excited."

Indeed he had. Deerie was now fully committed to the encounter, and hardly needed Agape's encouraging thoughts. "I can't wait!" she said. She was standing beside the couch; she straightened her back and inhaled.

Handy's face was a study, as he warred with the opposing voice in his mind. His body definitely wanted consummation, but the voice was telling him he wasn't interested.

Now was the time to strike. "I know he wants me," Agape said. "But he *is* fearful of another scene like that of this morning. So I won't wait; I will just climb up on him and do it!" Would this work?

It did. Deerie obeyed the thought without question. She practically threw herself on Handy, bearing him back lengthwise on the couch and coming down on top of him. Her mouth sought his for a hungry kiss as her groin rubbed against his.

But her lips found only mush in his. His erection was softening. He had been abruptly turned off! What had happened?

"What's the matter, honey?" Deerie asked, as upset as Agape, though perhaps for different reason. "Here we are all set to do it, and you're leaving!"

"I remembered something," he mumbled.

"My age!" she said, chagrined.

"No, not that! You're a great woman! But I heard somewhere that your employer, he—"

"Citizen Tosme? All I do is massage his feet!"

"And more, when he asks."

"Well, of course. But that's universal; serfs are at the disposal of their Citizens. It doesn't mean anything to me."

"But what I heard—you may not know this—is that because of this, Citizen Tosme has reserved you for himself. Anyone else who uses you will be gelded."

"What?" Deerie was appalled. "That can't be true! I've had numerous—"

"Within the last month?"

"Well, no, actually, I've been busy with my exercise schedule. But—"

"And no one has approached you," he concluded. "Now we know why. I was foolish to—I mean, I just got carried away, and—"

Deerie was completely flustered, and Agape could not get through to her at all. The charge was surely a lie, that Handy would conveniently discover in three hours, but meanwhile he had the planet's best excuse to avoid contact. Deerie herself was all too much afraid it was true; Citizens did that sort of thing when they chose. They did not like to share their sex objects with serfs. Tan had come up with a masterpiece of dissemblance that gave him the complete advantage for the moment.

Agape knew that she had lost her opportunity to win this fall; it would take more than three hours to get her actress settled down. She let Deerie disengage and seek solitude; there was nothing else to be done.

Except to prepare for the final session. Tan's actor would come calling, and this time he would not be limited to words. He would be allowed to coerce or even rape her, and certainly Tan would encourage that. Tan's vengeance was in the making; Agape could have avoided it only by winning this second fall. She had failed, and now the score was even, and there would be hell to pay.

She decided that her best chance was to hide so that he couldn't find her. Since she couldn't leave the Commons without defaulting, she would have to hide by concealing her identity. It would also be better if she were in a crowd; he would be less likely to try rape among people. For one thing, she could scream, and other men would surely come to her rescue. Sex was all right, and could even become a deliberate show, but rape was considered a form of violence by most women and some men. In addition, she could fight. She could put a defensive strategy into Deerie's mind, so that Deerie would understand what to do when the time came.

By the time of the third period, Agape was well prepared. She had caused Deerie to take some dirt from a flower pot and go to a toilet stall, where she rubbed the dirt into her hair and face and torso. Thus she became darker and wilder, looking quite different in the mirror. Her hairstyle was changed too, now being plaited and plastered. It had taken some urging to get the woman to do this, but the persistent thought that Handy had turned angry and intended to humiliate her did the job.

Then Deerie went quietly to a darkened show chamber where a dull holo was being played. She sat on the floor in back and watched as if mesmerized. With luck, she would never be found, and both of them would be spared a horrible ordeal. She was there before the second period ended, so that when the onus changed and Tan/Handy started looking, there would be nothing to see.

But moments after the third period commenced, a shape loomed in the entrance to the chamber. It was Handy—and he seemed to know exactly where he was going and what he was looking for. He must have been watching her all along, anticipating this ploy of hers!

He paused long enough to let his eyes adjust to the gloom. Then he made his way toward her. Should she scream? But he might be searching all the chambers this way, trying to make her identify herself by reacting; she had better keep quiet and hope he passed on by. If he did, then she was on her way to winning.

He did not. His face was contorted; Agape could not guess what thoughts Tan had put into Handy's mind, but it was evident that they had driven the man beyond reason.

"I will scream!" Agape cried.

Deerie opened her mouth—but Handy's hand clapped down on it, stifling her.

"I will bite!" Agape said. But already the man was pulling the woman over, coming down on her, crushing her; she was too disoriented to pay further attention to Agape's thoughts.

But one thing Agape had put into her mind before paid off: Deerie's knee came up, aiming for the man's groin. The blow would have been devastating if it had connected, a definite game winner. But it only struck his outer thigh; he had been on guard against it. Trust a man to know how to rape better than a woman knew how to defend against it! Handy pressed Deerie down flat on her back on the floor, his hand still stifling her, one of his knees wedged between her legs so that she could not clamp her legs together. Her effort to knee him had only put her leg out of position, giving him this opening.

"I will strike him with my free hands!" Agape cried desperately. "I will poke out his eyes! I will hurt him until he stops!" But Deerie was beyond that; terrified, she was retreating into an emotional shell, becoming passive. In fact, she was close to losing consciousness.

"A message for you!" Handy gasped, evidently coached by persistent if meaningless (to him) thoughts. "I owe you this, alien mare!"

"Fight him! Fight him!" Agape cried. "Roll, struggle, bite, resist!"

But Deerie did not. The man positioned himself and began his thrust. The pain began—and Deerie passed out. There was screaming.

The screen went dark. The input from the actress had ended with her consciousness. Agape found herself gasping, her throat raw; she was the one screaming. She was also melting; her lower section was puddling on the floor. Truly, she had been violated.

She had lost the fall and the match, in the worst possible way. Citizen Tan had had his vengeance, on her personally and on Citizen Blue for opposing the Contrary Citizens.

Agape let go, dissolving the rest of the way. In a moment she too was unconscious.

15: *Sirelmoba*

The days on the undersea isle would have been completely delightful, had it not been for their awareness that a great decision was in the making, and that it was going against the Adept Stile and the animals who supported him. Sirelmoba romped with Barelmosi in wolf and human forms, hunting and gathering and eating and sleeping and attempting to mate. They had been unable to complete the last, because she was too young for her first heat, but the urge for it came in cycles and she knew that in due course those cycles would intensify until completion became feasible. Of course once they succeeded, that would be the last of that, because she would enter on her adult stage and would seek a mate elsewhere; her Commitment to Barel, and his to her, would be done. So she was not sorry that they couldn't do it yet, because the trying and failing was a delightful process rife with mystery and hope. Success would end the mystery and promise, and end that aspect of their relationship, and that would have its sadness. So perhaps they were not trying too hard, after all. Actually they were able to go through the motions in human form, but that had no significance; only wolf form counted. Bitches often did it with human men just for sport; sometimes they were even able to fool the men into believing that they were human women. It was a good test of their ability to emulate the conventions as well as the body of that species. They always had a good laugh when the men finally caught on. Sometimes the men laughed too.

The sieges were set up, and the Translucent Adept made a spell that enabled them to see the action as a magic image over the isle. They watched the harpies beat the bats, thanks to the valiant final action of Phoebe. They knew she didn't really want to win, but had to try her best as a matter of honor, and she had done that and brought the victory she deplored. They had seen the 'corns beat the ogres thanks to the stratagem of Barel's dam Fleta, and that was highly gratifying. Barel had been so proud of her!

But meanwhile came the news of the similar contests in Proton-frame. Nepe kept Barel informed, and some of it was very bad. Nepe's rovot granddam—grandbitch?—no, grand*mother*—sometimes she got the various terms confused!—had dueled against the Adept—no, the Citizen Purple, riding dragons, and in the end gone down. It really hadn't been fair, because they were Purple's dragons; naturally they had seen to his victory. Then Nepe's rovot friend Troubot had climbed the glass mountain, throwing water bombs at the lovely bitch Tsetse—oh what fun!—and won the siege. After that Barel had used the bit of magic he was allowed to fashion water balls, and they had re-enacted it, throwing balls at each other in trees. Sirel wondered whether her human form would ever approach the lushness of Tsetse's. Unicorns could assume other forms, and make of them what they wished, so they were always powerful or esthetic or whatever else the 'corn wanted, but werewolves were more limited because both their forms were natural. It was similar with the vampire bats. So she would just have to make do with what she had, and hope for the best.

Then had come the contest between Nepe's mother Agape and the awful Tan Adept—Tan Citizen—wherein they had to make efforts to mate in much the fashion Sirel and Barel had. But there were differences. For one thing, Agape was permanently mated to Nepe's father Bane, so didn't want to do it with Tan. For another, it was a contest, with one wishing to mate and the other opposed, and so they had to negotiate. Barel and Sirel both found this process fascinating. But because there was no heat—it seemed that human beings had some other and less certain mechanism for breeding—nothing had come of it at first. But then at the end Agape must have come into heat after all—perhaps because she was really an alien creature—and Tan had come at her like any male who winded an available female in heat, and done it. In truth, it hadn't looked like very much fun for Agape, perhaps because in acceding to it she lost the siege.

So now the enemy side had won two of the three Proton conflicts. That meant they got the Oracle and the service of Mach or Bane to use it in connection with the Book of Magic in Phaze. There was only one chance to stop them, and that was to have Stile's side win the final siege in Phaze. Then the enemy would not have access to the Book, and would not be able to make the powerful magic that would enable them to prevail in their frame.

And that was why the wolves had to win against the goblins! They were the last good hope.

All of which led to the present need for Sirelmoba to rejoin her Pack. Kurrelgyre needed every wolf for this greatest of sieges, even the cubs!

"So must needs I leave thee, O mine oath-friend," she said tearfully. "But when this be done, then will it change."

"Well I know it, beloved bitch," he agreed, hugging her. "I will watch thine every motion, hoping thy presence dost make the difference."

They separated. She walked to the edge of the isle. "I be ready to go, O Adept!" she called.

Translucent's big water bubble appeared. "Aye, pup; I will conjure thee now to thy Pack."

There was a splash around her, and she felt a wrench. Then the water faded into fog, and the fog dissipated, and she was standing outside of the old palace of the Oracle. The Oracle was no longer there, because it had been moved to Proton-frame, but the palace remained.

She changed to wolf form and lifted her nose to sniff the wind. Sure enough, she caught the mixed scent of the Pack nearby. She loped toward it, and soon was in the circle of wolves.

She trotted up to Kurrelgyre. "Pack Leader, I be reporting for service with the Pack," she growled. In growl-talk it was more of an attitude and sniffing of noses, but the essence was precise.

He growled assent, and dismissed her. This, too, was Pack protocol. Now she was free to rejoin her companions. In a moment she was frisking with Forel (now Forelmo!) and Terel, sniffing noses and tails and growling reunion tokens. Her absence from them had not been long as such things went, but it was her first, and suddenly she felt its impact. It had been fun with Barelmosi, and she had regretted leaving him, but it was fun with her Pack and oath-friends too.

Later Kurrelgyre summoned her for a private conference. He assumed manform, so she assumed girlform.

He asked her about the isle and what she had noted of the activities of the Translucent Adept, and she reported all that she could remember. Then he surprised her. "Sirelmoba, thou willst participate in the strategy session in the morning."

"I?" she asked, astonished. "But I be but a pup!"

"Aye. Thou be not yet grown. In humanguise thou be very like a gobliness."

Her human eyes rounded. Small, like a lady goblin! She might infiltrate the goblin ranks and get the flag!

"Nay, not exactly," he said. "Thou willst try for the flag, aye, but from hiding, while others distract. But an they see thee, then mayhap they will not realize thy nature. This be dangerous; be thou ready to risk it?"

"Aye."

"Come to the session."

"Aye," she repeated faintly.

"Bruit this not about; we fear goblin ears."

"Aye," she said once more.

That was it. Awed by the importance of her mission, she changed back to cub form and returned to her friends. But all she could tell them was that she had been told to report to the strategy session.

The Pack strategy, it turned out, was direct and brutal. The main body of wolves would attack the goblins, attempting to take out as many as possible so that few would remain to defend the red flag. Meanwhile Sirel would circle around behind the flag, hide under a bush, and wait. When she saw an opportunity she would assume girl-form and walk slowly up and take the flag and hide it in her clothing. Then she would walk back the way she had come and hide again, concentrating on concealment rather than speed. If the goblins discovered her, she would assume wolf form and run for it.

Sirel, uncertain, asked what would happen if she got caught. "I mean, who will carry the flag, then?"

The wolves considered. Then they assigned her oath-friends to this mission also: Forelmo would lead, Sirelmoba would follow when he had found a safe way, and Terel would follow her and move up if Sirel were taken out. Meanwhile Terel would mount rear guard. The object of all of them was to remain unobserved, and to do what they had to to get Sirel to the flag.

"Mark well," Kurrelgyre growled, "the harpies used a similar ploy 'gainst the bats; the goblins will be on guard. But by similar token, they will assume we will not be so foolish as to try a known ploy. Ye three will masquerade as goblins, as the harpies could not, and that be the key we hope enables you to succeed. Only small folk can do this; otherwise we would ne'er put a pup at such risk. Now when this session be o'er, come to me, that I may guard you from observation while you practice the goblin ways. Say naught elsewhere."

They were glad to agree, appreciating the importance of secrecy. The Pack Leader had ways of guaranteeing privacy that others did not. If the gobs got any whiff of this, the ploy would be useless; the three of them would be ambushed and dispatched immediately.

After the main strategy was determined, the wolves discussed the likely goblin effort. Goblins were sneaky creatures, sure to come up with bad tricks, and these had to be anticipated. One of the bitches, Homirila, had been at one time a captive of goblins; they had tortured her and forced her to assume woman form as an object for their lust. She had in due course escaped by using her dull human teeth to gnaw through her bonds; the goblins had not expected that. She had returned to the Pack battered in body and spirit, and with an implacable hatred for goblins. But she also had a thorough knowledge of their ways. She had made it a point to range out alone and kill stray goblins, each kill being only a pittance of vengeance, but all she could do to mitigate her malaise of spirit.

Now she explained the likely goblin organization and approach. They would be armed with small spears and clubs, and each would have a knife. Some would have had military training, having served on one of their more disciplined campaigns, and those would be the organizers. They were tough little fighters, fearless in combat, but tended to dissolve into mobs, each intent on grabbing loot for himself. Their females were relatively gentle and often quite pretty in the human style; these would be assigned noncombat duties as far as possible.

The goblins were good at tunneling, seeming to have some magic that facilitated this. It was Homirila's judgment that they would try to tunnel to the blue flag, and draw it under, collapsing the tunnel behind so that pursuit was awkward. But they would surely try any other stratagems they could devise, and the wolves would have to be constantly alert. "Ne'er assume a gob is dead unless you have killed him," she warned. "Bite one and he will scream and fall and lie still—then stab you when you turn away. Stay clear o' any bodies, or dump them in a ditch and guard it. No gob can be trusted, living or dead."

They decided to form a disposal crew that would follow after the fighters, and use spears to stab any dead gobs, then would haul them to a central depot and guard them. That way they would be sure, and not be trapped by gobs feigning death. If they got all the goblins in that pile, fine; then the red flag would be vulnerable.

"I believe we can take them," Homirila concluded, "if we fall not into one o' their traps. Care be the watchword; take time and take naught for granted, and forge a slow victory."

The session broke up. The three cubs remained for their special instruction. This was done by Homirila, who showed them how to fashion goblin garb and darken their manform skins to goblin hue. Forelmo had to practice grimacing, and to add covers to his ears to make them huge and ugly, and fluff his hair out wild to make his head look big enough and put on special shoes that resembled the gross goblin feet. The bitches had less trouble, being much more like gob women, but did have to pad out their shirts to look grown-breasted.

"But will they not know us for non-tribesmen?" Sirel asked. "Their group be not much larger than ours—"

"Three times ours, in numbers," Kurrelgyre said. "They deem three gobs to be equal to one wolf, and it behooves us not to question that, lest they increase the number."

"E'en so," Sirel persisted, "they should know their own, as we do. We know all o' ours, and many o' other Packs, and many 'corns and bats too, and some elves. The gobs be not stupid like ogres."

"Needs must I explain," Homirila said. "Gobs be not like decent folk. They be creatures o' annoyance, ire and hate. They band together because they hate all others worse than they hate other goblins, but it be an uneasy association. All too readily goblin males fight goblin males, and gob women are fair game for erotic pursuit, whether they will or nay. It be a point o' pride that gobs o' both genders have no friends and few acquaintances; all others they detest. Their cubs are cursed into grudging obedience, and leave their dams early as they can. There be no families; offspring be from rape, coercion, deception or, if all else fails, seduction."

"Deception?" Terel asked, morbidly intrigued.

"Gob girls be e'er naïve and hopeful. They want to think that a gob man be decent inside, and that his violence and bad manner be but a show. So when one says he loves a girl, an only she give him a suitable time, she believes, and gives him that time. That may endure till he forget himself and revert to normal, and start hitting her. But by that time she may be gravid. Mostly they bother not; a male simply threatens her with a bashing an she not do for him, or he bash her anyway so she can resist not. Before long the girl comes onto the truth, that there be no good in any gob male, and that be her initiation into womanhood. Thereafter she avoids males when she can, and submits when she has to, that she be not beat on too badly. But by that time, too, she has little use for any other o' her species, and be as isolated as the males. Nay, an ye three look like goblins, and like young ones, none will challenge."

Sirel exchanged glances with Terel and Forelmo. All three were appalled. What an awful curse it was to be a goblin!

But maybe the bitch exaggerated. After all, she had had bad experience with goblins. Still, she was their expert on the matter. They had to hope she was right, so that their mission had a chance.

"Now, an a gob male come at thee—" Homirila said to Sirel.

"But will he not mistake me for one o' theirs?" she asked, hoping she misunderstood the thrust of this advice.

"That be what I mean. He will seek sex with thee, if he be not hard-pressed by wolves at the moment. An it be private, smile at him, let him embrace thee, then stab him in the stomach, thusly." She whipped a knife out from a sheath hidden under her skirt and stabbed upward in a gutting motion.

"But I can do that not!" she protested.

"Aye thou canst, cub! Think o' it as a mere animal kill. Remember, all deaths be for the duration o' the siege only, more's the pity. It be our purpose to dispatch all the gobs we can, that their number be insufficient to defend their flag at the end. E'ery little stab helps!"

Sirel had to acknowledge the validity of that. She had to be prepared to kill creatures who did not seem like animals.

"But an it be public, this be more o' a problem," the bitch continued.

Sirel understood why. If other goblins saw her kill one of them, they would know her for an enemy. But if she did not resist . . .

"Avoid him," the bitch continued. "Sidestep as he reaches for thee. An he pursue thee, flee. This be what the goblin lassies do. Lead him to a private place, then do as before. But an there be no private place, an he catch thee, stare him in the face and say 'What be my payment?' He will profess outrage at the notion, gobs like plundering the wealth o' others, not yielding up their own. Then say 'But Slackjaw paid me with a magic amulet! Be thou not his match?' An he be not diverted by this, and seeks to ravish thee regardless, call to the nearest other male gob and cry 'Canst stand by and watch me be ravished by this dullard, when *thou* dost be the one I hanker for?' Then in the ensuing quarrel, sneak away."

Sirel was impressed and appalled. She realized that if she got killed, she would recover after the siege—but what if she got raped? She wasn't sure that could be undone. After all, she had not yet had her first heat. Her motions with Barel had been tentative and gentle; this would hardly be the case here. A successful masquerade could still put her in jeopardy!

They perfected their costumes, then reverted to wolf form. Now when they changed, they would be complete with costume and knives. They would remain in wolf form until the siege, so that no spy would know.

* * *

Next day was the siege. Kurrelgyre and his senior bitch went out to make contact with the goblin chief. At their return, the action commenced. Several wolves bounded forward, zig-zagging so as to make poor targets. They were met by a number of thrown rocks, but the goblins were no ogres; most of the rocks missed, and those that struck were not very damaging. The wolves landed among them and started tearing flesh.

Meanwhile, other wolves in manform used bows to pick off any goblins they saw exposed. Before long the front region was clear, and the bitches on the body-hauling crew went out to collect the goblin corpses. Sure enough, some of the gobs weren't dead; a bitch got stabbed when she bent over one. Homirila's warning had been apt!

Meanwhile other bitches listened at the ground. Here, too, the warning was apt: in due course they heard the sounds of deep tunneling. It was proceeding at a measured but adequate rate toward the blue flag. Well, there would be a welcoming party when that tunnel broached the surface!

The three cubs saw these activities only in passing. They faded back, pretending to be searching for hidden goblins, but actually working their way out of sight so they could make their long circuit to the rear of the goblin flag. They knew that the goblins' main effort, the tunnel, would take time, just as the wolves' main effort of gob destruction would. They did not have to hurry, only to hide. Still, they felt urgency, lest some surprise cost their side the siege before they had a chance to complete their mission.

They had ranged the terrain in advance, of course, and well knew the lay of it. They had marked the places where goblins could hide. The gobs would be watching for an encirclement, and there were certain key spots for this. These were the tricky ones to navigate.

The first was a ravine that ran from wolf to gob territory. Beyond it was an open plateau leading to the big lake; no cover there. Inside it was a thicketed dirt bank that was so obviously suitable for goblin tunneling that no wolf dared go near it. So the ravine was the route to use—and there would surely be a goblin guarding it. Perhaps two. But not many, because the goblins could not spare a great number for the outlying regions, while the main action was in the center. There was a faint smell of goblin, so the region was suspect.

The pups were prepared. Terel had a small bow, with which she was facile in girlform. She crawled in the brush beyond the bank on the near side of the gully. When she was in place, Forel in wolf form leaped into the gully at its origin and raced straight along its deepening center. If he got through, Sirel would follow. If not—

A goblin popped out of a hole in the top of the bank. He drew back his arm, about to hurl a stone down into the gully.

Terel fired her arrow. It struck through the goblin's back. The goblin collapsed.

Forel continued on down the length of the ravine without other event. It seemed that one goblin was all the enemy had been able to spare for this. Was he truly dead? Sirel wasn't sure, but knew that they would not be returning this way, so it probably didn't matter. She set off in wolf form, following Forel's trail.

The goblin did not stir as she passed him. He was either dead or too canny to move while Terel covered him from behind. Sirel got through unscathed, and joined Forel in the cover of a tree. Forel had sniffed the vicinity and was assured that no goblins were near.

In a moment Terel arrived, having changed back to wolf form and followed their trail. "Dead," she growled. "In hole." Obviously she had verified it, and hauled the gob back into his hole so that the body was hidden. That was good, because it meant that there would be no report of their passage. Of course if another goblin came and found the dead one, there would be a suspicion, but by then it might well be too late.

One hurdle down. The next was a thickly forested section that was sure to be mined with goblins. Indeed the smell was there; goblins would be hiding in several trees, ready to attack any wolf who tried to pass.

Now the three changed to their human forms. They looked exactly like three goblins. They had rehearsed for this too, but Sirel was weak-human-kneed about the ploy's chance for success.

Terel set up in the bushes near the trees, her bow ready. Forel stood and walked boldly toward the trees, making no effort at all to hide. "Hey, any wolves in here?" he called. "I'll bash 'em!"

"Shut up, nut!" a goblin called from the foliage above. "You'll ruin the ambush!"

"Aw, they'll ne'er get this far!" Forel asserted.

Now Sirel walked up. Forel whirled on her. "Hey, that's for me!" he cried, starting toward her.

Sirel dodged behind a tree. "I be coming only to relieve the guards o' the flag!" she protested. "Molest me not, oaf!"

"Ha-ha! What I plan be not molestation, just fun!" He pursued her around the tree.

Sirel fled through the forest, in the direction of the flag. There were assorted chortles from the trees; evidently the ambushers considered this mere good sport. Forel was gaining on her; by the time she reached the cover of the bushes of an overgrown glade, he was almost upon her.

But as they dived into the bushes, they changed back to their wolf forms. They had made it! The ruse had worked! They were through without suspicion.

Could Terel make it also? They waited anxiously.

Soon they heard a commotion from the forest. "Mine!" "Nay, mine!" Then a scream.

Sirel shuddered. Terel had not made it. The ambush goblins, perhaps excited by the notion of chasing females, had pounced on the next one that showed, and Terel had been unable to escape. She must have stabbed one—but there had been more than one, and no chance to play them off against each other. Was Terel dead or raped?

At any rate, their rear guard was gone. Terel had done well, but now they were two. They could not pause for regrets.

The flag was not far ahead. They crept to cover near it and watched.

It was guarded by several goblin maidens. They chatted and tittered and tossed flowers at each other in the manner of maidens everywhere, seeming to have not a care in the frame. But each had a knife in her garter, and there were surely many males within hailing distance. One scream would bring a convergence. Sirel knew better than to try to pass for a gobliness among these; the males overlooked details because of their unbridled lust, but these girls would know. She had to wait for her opportunity.

Time passed. The distant clamor of battle came closer. The goblin defense was understrength, because of the number being used in the tunneling, so it was hardly surprising that the wolves were making progress. But Kurrelgyre was not depending on that to win the flag; he was depending on Sirel. She had to have the patience to do it correctly, and that meant waiting, no matter what else happened.

Suddenly three wolves burst into sight, running for the flag. They had won through! The goblin maidens saw them and screamed.

Then six turf-lids popped up, a goblin head showing in each hole. Six small spears flew at the wolves, who could not avoid them at such close range. All three were struck and wounded.

The goblins scrambled out of their holes, drawing their sharp little knives. The wounded wolves fought, snapping viciously, but each was beset by two goblins, and already bleeding. The action was fierce and brief. Then four goblins and all three wolves lay dead, and the remaining two goblins staggered away, injured.

The maidens went to the goblins, checking the dead and attending to the living.

Then a wolf in manform burst through, armed with a bow. He put an arrow through one goblin, and was aiming at the other when two of the girls leaped at him, their knives flashing. He got the arrow off, and the remaining male died, but then he went down under the stabs of the girls. He changed to wolf form and snapped at them, and both girls screamed as the sharp teeth tore their tender flesh.

Then a third girl ran across with a club. She smashed it down on the wolf's head with all her strength, and he went quiet.

Sirel knew that Forel could have taken out that third maiden with one of his arrows, and perhaps saved the wolf. But that would have revealed his presence, and that was forbidden. He had had to exercise the discipline of his mission, and watch one of his own Pack brothers be killed.

Now only two gob girls remained to guard the flag. Sirel considered. Surely there would soon be replacements for the lost girls, because that flag was important. Now might be her best opportunity.

She assumed her gobliness form and walked toward the flag. "I be here to replace—" She paused, as if just now spying the bodies. She screamed, emulating the manner of the others.

But one of the girls was not fooled. "How came thee from the other direction?" she demanded. "Give me the code word!"

Code word? Sirel had not anticipated this!

The girl drew her knife. "Say it now, or we skewer thee!" These were not, Sirel now knew, quite as innocent or gentle as she had been led to expect. What was she to do?

She drew her own knife. "Say it thyself! I answer not to thee!"

But the second gobliness was approaching from the other side, her knife also drawn. "All answer to us, here. Methinks thou dost be a spy!"

Then the first girl leaped and fell, an arrow protruding from her back. Forel had struck.

Sirel whirled on the other, her own knife flashing. The gobliness, startled by the fall of her companion, was slow to counter, and Sirel's knife plunged into her chest. She sighed and collapsed, looking so woebegone that Sirel felt horribly guilty. She wanted to stop and try to help the girl, but she remembered two things: her mission, and the warning about supposedly dead goblins. She turned away.

An arrow swished by her. Was Forel firing at *her*? Then something touched her leg, behind. She jumped and turned—and found the stabbed gobliness, fallen on her face, her arm outstretched, knife still in hand. Forel had caught her with the arrow as she tried to stab Sirel in the back. She had indeed not been quite dead! She had pretended to be more grievously wounded than she was, so as to put Sirel off guard, and it had worked. Except for Forel's alertness.

Sirel went up to the flag. She climbed the tree and took it down. But as she touched the ground, another goblin appeared. His mouth opened—and Forel's third arrow smashed into that open mouth and through the head.

Sirel tucked the flag out of sight in her clothing. She walked by Forel's bush. "We must go!" she whispered.

"Thou must walk, masquerading," he whispered back. "I will follow concealed and guard thee."

She nodded. It was the best way. She had the flag, but she was not yet out of the goblin region. The longer she could pass for a gobliness, the better.

She walked back toward the region of the blue flag. All around were the bodies of wolves and of goblins; the carnage was horrible. She was glad that this was a siege and not a real battle; it certainly looked real!

A goblin staggered back from the front. "More troops! More troops!" he gasped, seeing Sirel. "They ambushed the tunnel; we took awful losses! All's lost unless—"

"Let me bandage that arm," she said, realizing that she still had a part to play. She bent to rip the material of a dead gob's shirt, to make a bandage. The goblin would not suspect her of being a wolf, this way!

"No time!" he protested. "Got to put in our reserves!"

"The ones guarding the flag are dead," she said. "Wolves broke through. There was a terrible fight, and the wolves are dead, but so are the goblins."

He sagged. "Then all be lost." Then he looked more closely at her, as she approached him with a strip of cloth. "In which case, might as well have some fun." He grabbed for her.

Oops! Maybe she had played it too well. "Wait, let me bandage thee first! Thine arm—"

"Bandage me second," he said, catching hold of her with his good arm, with surprising strength. He bore her back against a tree, crowding close.

Then he sagged. An arrow had sprouted from his back. Forel had struck yet again.

But the delay had been critical. Now more gobs were straggling back from the front. "Hey, look what we got!" one cried, seeing Sirel.

"Change and run!" Forel cried. "I will hold them here!"

She didn't argue; she knew they would catch her, rape her, and soon discover her nature and kill her, in the process stopping her ploy with the flag. She assumed wolf form and leaped away to the side, seeking the cover of brush.

"Wolf! Wolf!" the goblins cried, recovering excitement. "Catch the bitch!"

But the first to start after her was felled by an arrow. The others whirled at this new menace. Much as they liked raping girls of any species, they liked living more. As Sirel reached the brush, she saw them closing in on Forel who, retaining manform, was methodically putting arrows through them. But she knew his supply was limited; he had already expended several in the course of guarding her. There were too many gobs; they would get him and kill him. So it was that Forel sacrificed himself to spring her free, and she had no choice but to accept.

She burst through to the wolf section of the range. Here the gob tunnel debouched. Goblins lay all around, and there was a huge pile of them in the depot; evidently in the end there had been too many bodies for the cleanup crew to drag, so they had been left. A few wolves were licking their wounds, getting ready to resume duty.

She looked to the blue flag—and it was gone! The gobs must have gotten it! But they had not brought it back to their own flag. It must be somewhere in between.

She assumed girlform. "Where be the flag?" she called to the nearest wolf.

He looked at her—and growled. Suddenly all the few wolves of the vicinity were growling, coming for her.

"Wait!" she cried. "This be but a costume. I be no gob girl!" She changed back to wolf form, to prove it.

They relaxed. One of them turned out to be Kurrelgyre. He was wounded, but could still fight. "Didst get it?"

"Aye!" she said, returning to girlform and pulling out the red flag.

"One got our flag, but we killed him," he said. "We were resting, making ready for the final effort. But now, with thy success—" He relaxed, and she saw that his injuries were worse then they had seen at first. He had been putting on a brave show, and was near collapse. "There, across the field," he said, sinking down as he pointed.

Now she saw the dead gob. The blue flag was clutched in his hand. The wolves had not been allowed to touch it, of course, so it remained there where he had fallen. Obviously this had been a near thing!

She reached the body, and extended the captive red flag. Victory!

The dead gob came to life. He snatched up a dagger that had been hidden beneath him and plunged it into her belly. Then, as she fell back, shocked, not yet feeling the pain, he bashed her hand so that the red flag fell out. He jammed the blue flag on top of it! "Victory!" he cried.

The final goblin trick had been so obvious—and it had worked. If only she had remembered to make sure he was dead! She had labored so hard, only to cast it away so foolishly.

The gong sounded. The siege was over—and the goblins had won. The enemy had won two of three sieges, just as in Proton-frame. Sirel's anguish was worse than the pain in her body.

16: *Purple*

Citizen Purple did not waste time performing any jig of joy. He had been planning and organizing throughout, and now with the victories in both frames he had to act with speed and authority. What he did in these few hours could determine the fate of the frames for the next generation.

First he summoned Tsetse. Others had assumed that it was mere lust that had caused him to appropriate her services, but they were only half right. Lust was the cover for her potential usefulness in other respects.

She entered his office, as luscious as ever. "Sir?" she inquired hesitantly. She had been subdued since losing her contest, and he had not reassured her. She feared she would be punished.

"The situation has turned to our favor," he said. "Your little misstep with the machine turned out not to be critical."

"Yes, sir." Now she was almost sure she was about to be punished; she was maintaining as brave a front as she was able, but she was trembling.

"I believe there remains a place for you in this organization, but under probation. You will have to prove yourself."

"Anything, sir!" she exclaimed, pitifully eager. She thought he was going to come up with some new and strenuous sexual activity. All in good time.

"I want you to take a package to Citizen Translucent, for delivery to his hands only, in strict privacy, without delay."

"Immediately, sir!"

"And when you return, bring the child here. I believe you know her personally; she should trust you."

"Nepe? I put her on the shuttle four years ago, when she—" She broke off, realizing that this too might be construed to her disfavor.

He raised an eyebrow. "Continue."

"When she went into hiding," she finished reluctantly.

"So you were involved in her disappearance. It seems fitting that you should be involved in her reappearance. Bring her to me."

"But sir, Citizen Translucent—"

Purple frowned. "Am I mistaken? I had understood that you wished to redeem yourself for past indiscretions."

"I do, sir! But if Citizen Translucent does not release the child—"

Purple waved a hand negligently. "Have no concern. He will not object to your taking her."

"Yes, sir." Greatly relieved, she accepted the package he gave her, and departed with alacrity.

Purple smiled. The package contained a gas bomb that would detonate five seconds after Translucent's contact triggered it. It would render him unconscious for four hours or more depending on his health. Tsetse would be appalled to see him fall, but would realize that she would be blamed unless she made a quick exit. Further, she would have to have protection—which meant Purple himself. So she would have to win his favor by bringing him the brat. Tsetse was certainly going to earn her keep!

Meanwhile, he had to set up for the next stage: possession of the Oracle. Citizen Translucent was slated to take it from Citizen Blue in three hours, but Translucent would prove to be indisposed. Citizen Purple would do it instead.

Soon his various minions were doing their things; Purple had planned for this coup for some time. He had been grudgingly content to let Translucent carry it hitherto, because the job was getting done, but he distrusted the other Citizen's long-range intentions. Translucent was too apt to be generous to his opposition, and that only set up problems for the future.

A call came in. He accepted it immediately, knowing its nature.

Tsetse's face showed. "Sir, I have Nepe. But we are pursued, and I can't get through."

"On the way," Purple said, gratified. His monitor showed that the call was from a privacy stall, the natural place for a woman to hide. This was a matter to cover personally.

He plunged into his transport and barked coordinates. The craft passed through the wall and into the Citizen network.

In moments he was there, opposite the stall. He stepped out—to encounter several android servitors. "Out of my way, vermin!" he snapped.

"But sir, our charge has been kidnapped," one protested. "Our employer's residence was raided—"

"Why do you think I'm here, idiot? I will take care of this matter. Return to your stations."

The androids, confused, could not stand up to a Citizen. They retreated. It would have been another story, had Translucent been conscious, but of course he wasn't. "Tsetse!" he called. "Step across to my carriage, quickly, with the child."

Tsetse emerged, towing Nepe, who looked frightened. They entered his carriage, as a human serf ran up. "Sir, please wait! There has been—"

Purple stepped into the carriage himself, and the door closed. "Home!"

Nepe's eyes focused on him. "You did this!" she flared. "It wasn't a serf revolt!"

So that was what Tsetse had told the child, to gain her immediate cooperation. "Very nice," he murmured.

"You're kidnapping me from Citizen Translucent!" the child continued.

He did not bother to deny it. The girl was quiet, evidently smart enough to realize when protest would be counterproductive.

Soon they arrived back at his protected offices. "Take her to the sport room," he told Tsetse as the carriage door opened. "Keep her happy."

Tsetse took the child by the hand and led her to the room normally reserved for entertainments of a more adult nature. The woman was now as much a captive as the child, because she had attacked a Citizen and would be subject to reprisal the moment she left Purple's protection. The fact that she had not known the nature of the package hardly mattered; she had perpetrated the act. Once Translucent had fallen she had been lost—unless she won her way back to Purple's office and his favor. Yes, this had worked out very nicely.

For the child was a vital key. Translucent's intent had been to utilize Bane and Mach, as before, to establish contact between the frames. He would have returned the child to her parents, knowing that Bane and Mach would honor the terms of the agreement. Citizen Blue had lost, and so had the Adept Stile; the power of the frames was now to be transferred.

But Bane and Mach were unreliable; they had become too assertive, and their sympathy had now been openly given to the other side. They would be seeking ways to reverse the situation, without actually breaking their word. That was dangerous, because in time they might find such a way. Perhaps a potion that would distort the judgment of someone who inadvertently took it. Such things existed; he had used them on others on occasion.

Potion. That gave him a notion. Maybe it would be better to tame the child immediately, so that her word could be added to his when the Oracle was transferred. Yes, that should keep the opposition off balance, until it was too late.

He rose and went to the sports room. Tsetse and Nepe were watching a romantic holo. Interesting, the way the tastes of bright child and not-too-bright young woman coincided.

The holo faded out as he approached Nepe. "I believe it is time for us to come to an understanding," he said. "Let me explain my intent."

Child and woman turned to face him, both attentive, neither relaxed.

"I mean to use you, Nepe, to contact Phaze," he said. "Instead of your father or uncle. I believe you will prove to be a more responsive tool. Are you prepared to cooperate in this?"

The child was forthright. "No."

"Suppose I make you a bit uncomfortable?"

"No good. You know you can't hurt me or even bruise me, because it'll show and you'll be discredited. Nobody respects a child beater."

How delightfully sharp she was! "I do not mean to beat you."

"Then I'll never cooperate!"

"I think you will." Purple walked to a desk, opened a drawer whose lock was coded to his touch, and brought out a round metal device. He raised it so that she could see it. "Do you know what this is?"

"A lethargy box," she said.

"Can you guess to whom it is tuned?"

"Me."

She was bold enough! But of course she had had years of experience with Citizens as "Troubot," the information machine, so had lost her fear of them. All to the good. "You know what it will do to you?"

"Put me to sleep, or just slow me down, depending on the setting. But that's no good; it won't change my mind."

"Allow me to demonstrate how it will change your mind." He turned on the box.

Nepe's small frame sagged somewhat; she no longer had surplus energy, because the field generated by the box depressed her nervous system, sapping her control. The effect was painless and harmless; indeed, such devices were commonly used to facilitate sleeping.

But she still could speak. "I still won't do your bidding, Purp."

Now to throw a genuine scare into her. Because she had seen Citizens in action, she knew how few their limitations were. She would assume the worst. "Tsetse, put her on the desk, on hands and knees."

The woman caught on. "But she's a child, sir!"

He turned a cold eye on her. "You have notions of your own, serf?"

Tsetse swallowed, then went to move the child. She took Nepe by the hand and pulled, and the child walked along as urged. Then Tsetse picked her up somewhat clumsily by the waist and heaved her to the desk. In due course Nepe was on her hands and knees, her bare posterior toward the Citizen.

"You have an idea what comes next?" he asked her.

"Molestation," she said succinctly.

She had indeed assumed the worst—but she did not seem frightened. Citizen Purple had few scruples about the means he used to achieve his ends, but he had never had any sexual hankering for children. He would have to make this a good bluff.

"It is readily avoided," he said, putting a hand on her little buttock. "You can have a perfectly pleasant life here, as long as you cooperate in the matter of the frames."

"My father will kill you as soon as he learns."

"Now how would he learn?" Purple inquired.

"Broken hymen." But her defiance was losing its conviction. Not a moment too soon! He had already played his trump card.

"You will learn that this can be done without touching your hymen," he said, stroking her bottom. "Nothing will show—but you will know, won't you? You won't enjoy it, but you will know."

"Sir—" Tsetse said.

He cut her off with a dark glance. Why didn't the confounded child break?

"I won't tell," Nepe said. "And I won't contact Flach."

It just wasn't working. He would have to try another tack. "Tsetse, orient the camera."

Reluctantly the woman brought the portable holo camera.

"Can you guess to whom this recording will be sent?" he inquired. The child didn't answer.

Well, he just had to hope that the threats had more impact than they seemed to. The child was tougher than he had figured. He definitely wanted her on his team!

"This is merely a warning," he said. "You will cooperate, or you will experience things that please neither you nor your relatives. I want you to think about this until I return."

He turned off the lethargy box and departed.

He closed the door behind him, then went to his main desk. The image of Nepe was on the screen; she was constantly under surveillance. The portable camera was a dummy. Now he would see whether his little demonstration had been effective.

"How can you go along with this, Tsetse?" the child was asking as she climbed down off the desk.

The woman looked miserable. "I can not oppose him. I did not know he was going to use me this way, but I can't stop him. I beg you, do as he says, so he won't hurt you!"

That was exactly what he had wanted her to say. Tsetse, fortunately, was not bright enough to see through his ploy.

"Won't you help me escape?" the child asked, toying with the lethargy box.

"I dare not! Even if I did, everything is guarded! You cannot escape this chamber without his authorization. Neither can I!"

"I thought you'd feel that way," Nepe said. She turned on the box and changed the setting.

Tsetse sagged. Nepe had been smart enough to know that there were a number of settings, and that each person in the vicinity had a setting except the Citizen. She had retuned it to Tsetse.

Purple struck the air with one fist, jubilantly. The child was taking the bait!

Nepe walked around the desk and took Tsetse by the hand.

The woman followed where led, unresisting. "Lie down here," she said, bringing her to the couch. "Sleep. You have no part in this."

Tsetse lay down and closed her eyes. Almost immediately, she was breathing in the regular cadence of sleep.

Nepe had evidently already explored the chamber, for she showed no hesitation. She pulled a light chair to the wall under an air circulation vent, and stood on it. Now she could just reach high enough to catch the grille with the fingers of one hand.

She remained there, the hand clasping the metal strips. Slowly her body dissolved. Her legs and feet became blobs of flesh that were drawn up into the main mass. Her other hand melted into that mass. Then a bolus of flesh moved up the hanging arm and to the grille. It worked its way through. Another bolus rose, passing similarly beyond the mesh.

In due course, Purple knew, all of the child's body would be inside the air tube, and the single hand, left behind, would let go and disappear into the rest. Then the blob would elongate like a snail and travel on up through the tube.

He smiled. Nepe had not disappointed him! Had she really thought he was foolish enough to forget her nature? Rape was of course meaningless to her; she could simply melt her flesh to avoid it, or re-form it intact after suffering any violation. She had played her part perfectly, and now was doing exactly what he had hoped she would. She had responded to his threats by making an effort to escape.

He wished he could remain to watch, but he had pressing other business. Humming, he left the office.

Citizen Blue was at the designated meeting place for the ceremony, with his robot wife and robot son. Blue was in his usual blue clothing, while the other two were naked in the fashion of the serfs they were. Citizen Purple swept in, trailing Citizen Tan. This was all that was required; the holo recording would acquaint other interested parties with the transaction.

"I am ready to do business," Purple said.

"We are expecting Citizen Translucent," Blue said.

"Haven't you heard? He is indisposed at the moment. Therefore this formality devolves on me. You may proceed."

"It is my understanding that he is indisposed because a gas bomb was smuggled into his office," Blue said evenly. "I think we should postpone this ceremony until he is recovered."

"As I recall, you used the pretext of the missing child to cut off our contact with the Oracle before. The child was missing by your connivance. Now you propose to use the pretext of Citizen Translucent's absence to renege on the Oracle again?"

Blue hesitated. It was obvious that he did not like this situation, but could not make more than a token protest, because his side had lost the contests.

"I think we are seeing the falling out of thieves," the robot wench muttered.

"It is not your concern, machine," Purple said, giving her breasts a straight stare. What a satisfaction it had been to beat her in the Game!

Blue did not show his annoyance. "Then we may as well proceed." He turned to face the pickup that was the only indication of the Oracle's presence. "Oracle, are you aware?"

A small hologram appeared: a whirling spiral of light hovering just above the pickup. "I am, Citizen Blue."

"My side held a contest with the Contrary Citizens, the stakes being control of the access to the Oracle and the means to contact the frame of Phaze. The Contrary Citizens won. Accordingly, I am now instructing you, Oracle, to acknowledge the instructions of the Contrary Citizens, whose spokesman is—"

"Citizen Purple," Purple said.

"Currently Citizen Purple," Blue continued. "And to decline to acknowledge my instructions, or those of any who are allied with me. Do you accede?"

"It is an unfortunate pass," the Oracle remarked. "The Contrary Citizens will ruin the planet."

"Do you accede?" Purple demanded.

"I accede," the Oracle said. "I can do only as directed."

"Then you will answer, until further notice directly from me, only to me or to Citizen Tan, who will be working with you initially."

"Citizen Purple and Citizen Tan, logged on," the Oracle agreed. The whirling spiral faded out.

"Now the matter of contact with Phaze," Purple said.

"Mach will serve in that capacity, as before," Blue said. "And Bane, when he is present."

"I think not."

Blue looked at him. "You need them for contact."

"I prefer to use the child Nepe," Purple said. "Her contact is more versatile, and she should prove to be more responsive to our interests."

"That wasn't the understanding!" Mach snapped.

"The understanding was that the means for contact would be provided," Purple responded. "The actual mechanism was unspecified. It therefore becomes an option. I am now exercising that option. The child will be our instrument of contact. Since she is already in our possession, no more need be done. The agreement is complete."

"You beast!" the robot wench cried. She had adopted many human mannerisms.

"I doubt Nepe will work for you," Blue said.

"I believe she will, before long."

"I'm not sure you can even keep her captive long," Mach said. "She has remained with Citizen Translucent because she knew she was part of the stakes; she was to be returned if we won. She did not try to escape because she did not want to interfere with our arrangements. But she has never agreed to be your permanent contact with Phaze. Now she will feel at liberty to make her escape."

"Let me show you her current situation," Purple said. "Oracle, tune in on my office suite and show the child."

In a moment a half-life-sized hologram formed. It showed a bottle containing the head of Nepe. The rest of her was puddled protoplasm.

"As you can see, she is truly captive," Purple said. "I am sure she can not escape that bottle. At the moment the air is good and the temperature comfortable, but there is no assurance that they will remain so. I believe she will elect to cooperate."

"I doubt it," Mach said, with his robotic control of reaction. "She knows that if you hurt her you risk rendering her unable to function. That will do you no good."

"I see that you do not quite understand," Purple said. "Should the child be rendered unable to contact the other frame, you will remain obliged to provide another instrument of contact. It is therefore to your interest to encourage her to cooperate."

They mulled that over. They knew that he would not hesitate to torture the child, and that all he had to do was gradually heat the bottle. Like the spineless creatures they were, they capitulated.

"Put me through to her," Blue said.

"Do it, Oracle."

"Contact is established," the Oracle reported.

"Nepe," Blue said.

The child's head looked up. "Grandpa Blue!"

"We had hoped to have you returned to us at this time. Instead Citizen Purple has elected to use you as his contact with the frame of Phaze. I believe it would be best if you cooperated with him."

"You mean you can't get me out?" she asked.

"Not at present."

She seemed ready to cry. "I'll do it, Grandpa. But I'll escape if I can."

"Enough, Oracle," Purple said, and the hologram faded out. "I believe that concludes our business." He walked out, with Tan following, leaving them to their chagrin.

Now the obvious thing to do was to use Nepe to get the key formulae from the Book of Magic in Phaze and begin aggrandizing his fortune. Wealth was the way to destroy Blue's power. But that would take time, and Blue might well have some nasty tricks left; after all, Mach and Bane were now working on Blue's side. So he would surprise them again, and take Blue out now, a different way. With luck, he would have it done before Translucent recovered consciousness, making his coup complete.

He had made a study of the capacities of the child Nepe, anticipating his need to capture her and hold her prisoner. She was more versatile than most people appreciated. She could assume virtually any form, her substance ranging from liquid of a chosen color to metallic. It took her time to do it, ranging from several hours for a new form to less than an hour for a familiar one. Once she assumed a form, it was stable as long as she chose, while she remained conscious. When she slept, she dissolved into a puddle, exactly as her alien mother did. But she was not identical to her mother; she had robotic ancestry too, and therefore was able to emulate the nature of a machine. That was why she had managed to remain hidden so long; she had fooled them all by masquerading as Troubot and doing an excellent job in the robot's speciality.

Now he had to assume that the child might wait her opportunity, melt down, ooze through a crack, and form into something so remarkable that no right-thinking person would suspect. What would that be? And because he had thought about this a great deal, before capturing her, he had the answer. He knew what she would do, if she had the opportunity.

He never let her out of the bottle. There was air there, valved in under pressure so she could not flow through the tube; if she tried it, she would merely encounter an otherwise sealed tank. Food was put in by an alert robot. She could not escape until she was given greater freedom—such as that required to allow her to assume some more useful form and be interrogated. The enemy would assume that he would waste no time in making use of her ability to contact Phaze, now that her grandfather had told her to.

Instead he brought out a metal sheathing. It looked like the base of a wheeled robot servitor, the kind that transported supplies from one station to another. He sat on its stool and closed it around himself, so that only his top portion projected. From chest upward he was a solid living man; below he was like a wheeled robot. The wheels worked; a motor controlled by his toes propelled the device forward. Of course most of the effect was lost, because his voluminous purple cloak covered everything from neck to floor; it looked as if he were walking, if one did not inspect him too closely.

Now he put out a prepared bulletin, in such a way that it appeared to be unintentional. ". . . don't find her, every serf will be fired with prejudice by morning! What happened to the safeguards?" It seemed to be an internal command that leaked outside his offices.

He made sure he was unobserved, and trundled out in his getup. Once clear of his offices, he made a direct approach to Blue's offices.

No one challenged him, of course; he was a Citizen. But news of his progress preceded him, for when he arrived at Citizen Blue's door, Blue was out to meet him.

"Further mischief, Purple?" Blue inquired tightly.

Purple's eyes flicked up and across, as if checking for something. "We are observed," he said, his voice deliberately tight.

"Of course. Speak your piece."

His voice tightened further. "It must be private."

"I have nothing private to exchange with you."

Purple's hand brushed across his cloak, drawing it up just enough for the metallic base to show. "Quickly, before they know!" he squeaked.

Blue saw the base. He of course knew of the leaked report that suggested Nepe had escaped. What form could she assume that would get her free unchallenged? That of Citizen Purple! But she would have to ride on a mobile machine, to provide mass and height, and cover it over with the cloak. A daring venture indeed!

Blue opened the door panel and let Purple roll in. Inside, the female humanoid robot and the robot son stood. Damn! He had hoped to nab them all at once, the alien and turncoat Tania too. Well, there were the main three, and of course the alien maid Agnes; the others could be covered when they turned up.

"Citizen Purple—in here?" Sheen asked, startled.

"I suspect not," Blue said.

"Is it private?" Purple asked tightly.

"Yes," Blue assured him.

He looked at Mach. "Do you not know me, Uncle?"

" 'Uncle'?" the robot asked, not getting it.

Purple rubbed his cheek, causing the waxy coating on it to crease. He lifted his cloak, showing them all the metal base. He seemed to be human only in the top third.

"Nepe!" Sheen exclaimed, astonished. "You look so real!"

"Where's Mother?" he asked, hoping for one extra bit of information before he acted.

"She's with Tania," Mach said. "Getting some information on—"

"No!" the maid cried, entering the room. "That is not my grand-child!"

Purple looked at her. "What?"

Now Mach turned grim. "If you don't know that Nessie is Agape's elder portion—what we would call her mother—then you are not Nepe. Which means that—"

Purple activated the lethargy box. This was a special one, with simultaneous settings for Blue, Agape, Agnes and Tania, and special modified settings to nullify the two robots. Abruptly all four in the room were without volition.

"Remain here; do not communicate or attempt to leave," he said curtly. "When a call comes from Nepe, you, Blue, will answer it and assure her that you are all right. You will say nothing of your situation." He brought out the box and set it on a counter; they would be unable to approach it. Such a simple, neat device, but so hard to overcome, like a wicker thumb-lock.

Then he departed, closing the panel behind him. It might be days before any of Blue's allies caught on to Blue's situation; they would assume that he was deep in plans for resisting the increasing power of the Contrary Citizens. Any who did approach would be quietly taken out by Purple's watching minions. With luck, by the time Blue got free, it would be academic: Purple would have consolidated his power, and it would be too late for any preventive tricks.

The problem with folk like Blue was that they were too trusting and scrupulous. That was why they had let Purple in without properly verifying his nature. They had not anticipated such a cunning ploy. If only the fool maid from Moeba had not caught on, and forced his immediate action, he might have had Agape and Tania too! Agnes was Agape's parent-half? How had his researches overlooked that? It explained much of the child Nepe's rapid progress in form changing, when she had at one point seemed retarded: she had had expert training from the start. Blue had been cunning too, and it would have been foolhardy to leave him free to work further mischief.

Now for the two missing ones, because otherwise they were sure to go to Blue's residence and be admitted by his monitors. Tania was a cunning wench, and Agape could assume any form; forewarned, they could bypass his minions and disable the lethargy box. It would affect them as they came in range, but that was no good; at the fringe the effect was partial, and they would be able to back away, then send in a robot to turn it off. They would have to be taken out separately, which complicated things, but was necessary.

"Locate Serf Agape and Serf Tania of Citizen Blue's employ," he said to his communicator. "Do not alert them; merely inform me."

In a moment he had his response. "Subjects located at spaceport," Tsetse's voice came. "Aboard ship destined for—"

"Stop that ship!" Purple shouted, causing a passing serf to jump; the serf of course had not heard the communication.

But it was too late. The two females, evidently warned, had taken the most immediate ship out, and it was taking off even as he gave the command. The two had escaped the planet.

Purple suppressed his rage. What did it matter, actually? They could do nothing off planet, and if they returned, he would nab them. All he needed was to be rid of them.

"Monitor all interplanetary calls," he said. "Intercept any relating to personnel allied with Citizen Blue." That would prevent the two from calling in a warning to a Blue ally.

But who had tipped the two off? That person obviously knew, and could take action to free Blue. That person had to be nullified, and quickly.

Citizen Purple headed for home. Here was an early use for the Oracle! Soon he would know the identity of that person, and take him out.

He was half right. Soon he did know, but he could not take him out. It turned out to be a child no older than Nepe, whose residence had a monitor tuned to Blue's residence. This was evidently with the complicity of Blue, a back-up in case of unexpected trouble. It was the residence of Citizen Troal.

Troal happened to be offplanet at the moment, but his son must have picked up the message and immediately alerted Agape.

And the two females had taken that child with them offplanet. That meant he was out of reach—but also no longer a threat. Purple relaxed; the only likely snag was no problem after all. Now he could concentrate on the main effort. There were pressing details to attend to, such as settling with Translucent, who would not be pleased, but who surely would recognize the effectiveness of Purple's actions. If not—well, there was always the lethargy box.

17 : Fleta

Fleta trotted along comfortably, carrying Tania, as they approached the region of the West Pole. She had known of Tania's designs on Bane from the outset, but allied with the Adverse Adepts as she had been, she had not been in a position to protest. After all, Bane had no woman in Phaze, and Tania had once been intended for him, or vice versa, because they were the only two of their generation definitely slated to be Adepts. Tania had been scrupulous about not vamping Mach, so that Fleta had never had cause for a challenge. That was just as well, because though unicorns were proof against most magic, they could not stand against any Adept. She knew it was neither integrity nor fear of her horn that had kept Tania honest; it was the fear of losing her chance at Bane if she ever glanced sidelong at Mach. Tania was unscrupulous but hardly stupid.

Then, gradually, the unexpected had happened. Bane had been proof against Tania's charms, which were considerable (for those who might like that type), but she had not been proof against his. She had fallen in love with him, and in the process had assumed his virtues. Fleta had watched this process with private amazement, but there had been no doubt of its validity. Her own attitude had suffered a corresponding shift from enmity to friendship; she knew pretty closely how Tania felt.

Now they had shifted sides together, and Fleta was glad of that; they would never have to oppose each other. They worked well together, because they now knew each other well, and their abilities were complementary. Fleta could travel readily, while Tania could handle threats. But the question remained: what of Tania? She was doomed not to have her love returned, and Fleta feared she would take a drastic measure: the same one Fleta had taken, when she had seen no future in her love for Mach. Fleta did not want to see this happen, but what alternative was there?

She knew what. She would have to share. There was a precedent for having alternate loves in the frames; Fleta's love was Mach in Phaze, but Bane was available. Similarly, Mach was free in Proton. Tania had changed sides and done good service; she was entitled in each frame to what offered. Fleta just had not yet been able to bring herself to make it official.

Now they were checking on the Translucent Adept, because he had mysteriously declined to attend the ceremony of the transfer of the Book of Magic. Had there been some skulduggery between Adepts? It seemed likely, and the Adept Stile wanted to know, because he much preferred dealing with Translucent. Also, Flach remained on the undersea isle, with Sirelmoba the werebitch, and Fleta hoped to see him. There seemed to be little chance of that, because they were supposed to remain unobserved, but there was always hope. The Red Adept had given them an amulet that would protect them from observation by all except Adepts—but Translucent *was* an Adept. Certainly there would be no way to rescue Flach.

A bat appeared before Fleta's nose. She jumped; she had not seen it approach. Then she recognized its smell. "Al!" she fluted in horn talk.

"Where be thee, O Aunt Fleta?" he piped in bat talk, the pitch so high she could barely hear it. "I see thee not!"

Because of the amulet. She nosed forward and nudged him with her horn. With the contact, he saw her. He changed to boy form, maintaining the touch. "O Aunt Fleta, I used my father's spell to locate thee. He has been enchanted!"

Fleta changed to woman form so quickly that Tania barely had time to dismount. "The Red Adept enchanted?"

"Aye, mare. The Purple Adept did it. Tan, I mean. He got the Book o' Magic, and then—"

"My brother!" Tania exclaimed. "I knew it!"

"Tell us exactly what happened," Fleta said. "Fear not discovery; an thou maintain contact with me, naught be o'erheard."

Alien was reassured. He slowed down enough to give a coherent report. "Purple and Tan came to the Red Demesnes as scheduled, and Stile was there with my father the Troll and my mother the Bat, and they gave o'er the Book o' Magic. Then Stile asked for my friend Flach, thy foal, and Purple said no, he had decided to keep Flach to commune 'tween the frames instead o' Bane and Mach, 'cause a child

be more amenable. He quoted the terms o' the agreement, and nor
Stile nor Red could gainsay him, being much disappointed. Then Stile
departed, and without warning Tan and Purple turned on Red and
together they stunned him so that he fell in deep swoon. My mother
cried out 'gainst this treachery, but Tan stunned her too with his Evil
Eye. Me they saw not, for I was peeking from hiding. Then they
consulted how they would send a goblin garbed like Flach to tell Stile
he escaped, but the goblin would loose a spell to take out Stile and
Bane and all else in the Blue Demesnes, for they thought thee there
too, that no major Adepts be able to oppose Purple's designs. But I
knew thou wast elsewhere, and came to warn thee o' this treachery!"

"But why?" Fleta asked, appalled. "The Adverse Adepts have already won! What need for this?"

"I can guess," Tania said darkly. "Nor Purple nor my brother e'er
trusted Translucent; they wanted to take power from him. They must
have taken him out first, then struck at the rest, so they can rule; an
they had waited, Translucent would have taken control, and been more
generous. So they timed their treachery when none suspected—and
now thy Adepts Red and Stile and Rovot be ensorceled, and mayhap
killed when Purple feel secure. Brown be no match, and we be helpless."

"But we be free," Fleta protested. "We can go and—"

"And be trapped also," Tania said. "They expect that. Be assured
we can stand not against their magic; likely already there be goblins in
search o' us, and our time be measured."

"But one thing—" Alien said.

Fleta glanced at him. "There be yet more?"

"My father gave me an amulet long since, saying an disaster e'er
strike, invoke it. Be this the time?"

"Aye," Fleta and Tania said together.

The boy brought out the amulet, which he wore on a chain about
his neck. It was in the shape of a tiny tube. "I invoke thee."

The tube expanded in his hand, turning silvery. It twisted, so that
the mouthpiece pointed southeast.

They stared at it. "That be a little flute," Fleta said. "What use be
that?"

Alien shrugged; he knew nothing of this.

But Tania's brow was furrowed. "A flute—there was one, once, before our time, when Stile separated the frames. Mayhap—"

"The Platinum Flute!" Fleta exclaimed. "The elves made it, and
keep it now. It—when it be played, it—"

"Brings the frames together," Tania finished. "But only one can play it, and he be long gone from Phaze and Proton-frame. Now, with the frames fore'er parted, there be no use for this. And e'en were it so, what point? The Adverse Adepts rule here, and the Contrary Citizens there."

"This be a mystery," Fleta said. "But surely the Red Adept knew whereof he spoke! Why give Al this token, an it be not the key to aught important?"

Tania nodded. "It be our only hope. Needs must we go where it points, and find the Flute."

"But that will take time, and there be naught!" Fleta protested.

"It be all we have," Tania said grimly. "But mayhap thy dam will know what this portends. She was e'er close to Stile."

Fleta brightened. "Aye! An she had her secret will, I'd be foal o' Stile 'stead o' Stallion! An any know the key to this riddle, it be Neysa."

"But it be far to go, and I can change not my form. An thou wouldst go alone—"

"Nay," Fleta said decisively. "An we meet magic, thine Eye be needful. I will carry thee, as before."

"I had hoped thus," Tania confessed. "Al, change form and stay close; else we can protect thee not."

Then Fleta reverted to 'corn form, and Alien to batform, and Tania mounted. The bat flew to perch on Fleta's head. She started off at a gallop. Fortunately she was rested; they had been proceeding cautiously, and she had grazed recently. However, the amulet of privacy was giving out; they were becoming audible and visible. It might be restored somewhat by another invocation, but that should be saved for an emergency.

She followed the direction indicated by the amulet-flute, deviating only to take advantage of open and level ground. This took her to the Animal Head Demesnes, which was a problem, as they were allies of the Adverse Adepts. Sure enough, a crow-head spied her, and she encountered a line of manlike creatures with assorted animal heads. They were armed with clubs and spears; she would not be able to run that gantlet without getting hurt.

She slowed. Tania sat up tall and Eyed the leader, a lion-head with a magnificent mane. "We be on special business," she said. "Direct thy minions to let us pass, and one to lead us the best way through."

It was that simple. The lion-head, fascinated by the Evil Eye, gestured his minions back. A hawk-head ran forward, leading Fleta, and in a short time she was through what had seemed like a difficult thicket, and facing another open region. "We thank thee, lion!" Tania called as Neysa accelerated.

Tania had already justified her presence, apart from being a friend. Still Fleta could not bring herself to say what she needed to: that her objection to Tania's play for Bane was withdrawn. She was finding herself as foolishly stubborn as her dam!

Fleta could not run forever. In the evening she had to stop. But Al had a suggestion: "An thou be hummingbird, Tania can carry thee, and I can use my night eyes to spy the way through the dark."

"But needs must I also eat," Fleta protested.

"I can find thee sustenance," he said eagerly. "What wouldst thou have?"

"An ounce of nectar would fill my bird belly, but that be hard to come by."

"I will come by it!" he promised. He assumed his batform and disappeared into the twilight.

Soon he was back, hauling something that staggered his flight. It was a leaf cunningly drawn into a bag, and inside it was a pool of sweet nectar.

"How couldst thou harvest so much so soon?" Tania asked. "Each flower has but a trifle!"

"I found a big flower," he said proudly.

Fleta assumed bird form and tried the nectar. It was excellent, and more than she could finish; they had to store the extra for future use.

Then she settled in Tania's tan tresses, and Tania walked, with Al flying ahead. She slept.

She woke at dawn, well rested. She flew up to spy the land, and incidentally loose some droppings; she had not felt free to do that while nesting in Tania's hair.

They were significantly closer to the Purple Mountain Range and to the Harpy Demesnes. Tania had really been exerting herself! Indeed, as she flew back down she saw that the woman was staggering; she had moved as fast as she could all night.

Fleta assumed woman form. "Enough! Thou must eat, and I will take my turn.

"I ate on the way. Al found fruits."

Fleta was further impressed. The bat boy was doing his share too! She assumed 'corn form, and Tania mounted, and Al came in. Now it was evident that he too was tired; he had been all night aloft.

She set off at a trot, following the contour of the foothills of the great mountains. She could tell by their respective postures that both woman and bat were almost instantly asleep. They deserved their rest!

At mid-morning she spied a dragon aloft, for the Dragon Demesnes were just south of the mountains. She hesitated, then decided that prevention was better than risk, and re-invoked her amulet. Then she ignored the dragon, because she knew the amulet shielded her sight, sound and smell from its awareness. She did, however, make sure to tread on hard ground, because any tracks she left would be visible. But this was about the last use she would be able to make of the amulet; its magic was exhausted.

So it went. In two days they reached the Herd where Neysa grazed, and made themselves known to her.

"So we know not what it means," Fleta concluded. "We can fetch the Flute, an the elves yield it to us, but only the Adept Clef can play it—and he be far removed in space and frame, and can join us not."

Neysa considered. "I have thought on such matters before," she said. "I have discussed it with Stile. Finally I made a point, which he in his humor called the Unicorn Point, and we laughed, thinking it lacked relevance. Now methinks he took it more seriously, and this be the reason for Al's amulet."

"A point?" Fleta asked blankly.

"It be this: that the most fundamental force in both frames be the same, and that its difference in the frames be but perception. In Phaze we see magic, and in Proton they see science, but the split between them be illusion. An we knew how, we could do science here, and they could do magic there. It be naught but a—a geis, or what they call a program, a rule that makes it be one way or the other."

Fleta exchanged glances with Tania and Al. All three were baffled. "But science works here not," Fleta said. "And magic works there not. I have been in both, and tried."

"Because of thy mindset, and that o' the frame," Neysa said. "It be the same for all. The geis be unbreakable. But an the frames be merged again, both would work, drawing on either interpretation o' the power o' the basic rock Phazite or Protonite. The curtain between frames be but a window o' awareness, like the screen o' a science computer. Mergence be the answer: that be what Al's amulet means. Only when they be together can the frames be truly at rest."

"But we can merge the frames not, with the Flute here and the Player there," Tania said.

"Methinks Stile could," Neysa said firmly. "An he be ensorceled, thou must do it instead."

"I be no Adept!" Fleta protested. "I be but a mare in want o' her colt, sore beset!"

"Thou dost be more than that," Neysa said. "The frames be already one, an we but perceive it. Since the separation, the parallelism be more, mayhap lacking other way to abate the imbalances caused by the acts o' people. Once there were two Lady Blues, one in each frame, but when the one in Proton died, the other could cross and fill her place. Now with no crossing, the void be filled by another, and that be the Lady Sheen. All the Adepts and most o' the others be parallel, or growing so. The events too: what occurs in one frame, occurs in the other, if not exact, then close. Each contest was won by the same side; it could be not otherwise. Now what thou dost here, thine other self be doing there. If thou canst prevail here, so will it be there, and the way will open. What thou achievest be known in Proton, though there be no seeming contact between thee and the alien. All that thou canst accomplish be double weight. That be the remainder o' the Point."

Fleta knew it was true. She was awed by the realization; the evidences of the parallelism had been there all along, but she had never appreciated them this way. She *had* to succeed!

"But an somehow the frames be merged—what o' the folk?" Fleta asked. "Willst become just one set o' folk for both?"

"Aye."

"But I—"

"Will merge with Agape, methinks. And all others, as their pairs exist. It be a monstrous notion."

"A monstrous notion!" Fleta echoed, intrigued and appalled. She liked Agape, but how could she be merged with her? What then of Mach and Bane—and Tania? Of their triangle?

That was all Neysa would say. Neysa had never been much for words, and once she had made her point—her Unicorn Point—she was done. She was old, and they did not want her to risk the rigors of their mission (or to be slowed down by her: that was unsaid), so they left her at the Herd, pondering her insight. The Unicorn Point—what mixed promise and mischief lay there!

Another day's travel brought them to the spot at which the flute-amulet pointed—and there was nothing there. It was on the slope of the Purple Mountains, in the Elven Demesnes, with nothing but silvery flowers growing. They paused, baffled. First the mystery of the Unicorn Point, then this!

It was Alien who figured it out. "The Flute be underground! The little folk keep it not up in plain sight, and their warrens go ne'er direct. We must find the entrance!"

They quested about, and in due course discovered an elven entrance. Fleta assumed woman form, removed her amulet, and handed it to Tania. "Mayhap this will protect thee aught. I must broach them now. Al and I will do it, while thou dost hide, in case."

"In case what?" the bat boy asked.

"Elves be not always friendly."

He nodded, sobering. Then Fleta knocked at the portal, alerting the elves.

A man appeared. He was about the height of Alien, but considerably stouter. His clothing was the color of platinum, and his skin light blue. "Well, two prisoners!" he exclaimed, drawing his sword. "A fair damsel and a servant boy."

"Nay!" Fleta cried. "We be 'corn and bat, on a mission o' surpassing import!"

"Not any more," the elf said grimly.

Fleta didn't want to have to fight him, but she could not let herself be considered a prisoner. She would have to change to unicorn form, which would be competent to deal with the sword.

Then the elf man turned, startled. His eyes glazed. "Oh, aye," he said. "These be emissaries."

Tania had stepped in. Out of contact with her, Fleta could neither see nor hear her other than dimly; the dwindling power of the amulet was more effective with only one person to cover. Evidently she had touched the elf, and used her Eye to fascinate him. Now, in effect, he was their prisoner.

The elf led them into the passage in the hill. Wan light struggled down so that it was not completely dark, but it remained uncomfortably close. She would not be able to assume unicorn form here; she would be jammed into the walls. At least Al would be able to move; as a bat he could readily handle this region.

They came to a chamber wherein sat an extremely wizened elf, obviously a leader. He wasted no time in amenities. "Thy magic be that o' the Adverse Adepts. Know, O intruders, that we be overtly neutral, but privately we favor Stile and will help thy side not."

Fleta smiled, relieved. "Canst thou be Pyreforge, friend to my foal's grandsire? I be Fleta, and this be Alien, son o'—"

"And thou be helping the wrong side!" he snapped. "Be glad I grant thee the courtesy o' truce, else—"

"Nay, we changed sides," she cried. "Now Mach and I be with Stile, only my foal be captive, and there be enchantment on Blue and Red and Bane, and we alone be free to seek—"

"How can I know that? That Evil Eye—"

"Tania changed too! She be aiding Stile now!"

Pyreforge stared at her. "An thou canst convince me o' that, with her Eye hooded, mayhap my aid be thine."

It took time, but in due course the old elf was satisfied. He turned over the invaluable Platinum Flute. It was in pieces, in a box, but could be readily assembled at need.

"But we know not how to use it," Fleta said. "The amulet guided us here to it, and my dam says we must merge the frames, but—"

"Let me research in my references."

More time passed. The elves gave them bread and water while they waited, treating them with courtesy now that their loyalty to Stile was known. Tania had to give up the fading amulet of privacy and become fully apparent.

"Ah, now I see!" the elf exclaimed as he saw her clearly. "Thou hast the stigmata o' love for Bane! That be why thou didst change sides!"

Tania was taken aback. "Shows it thus?"

"Ordinarily, nay. But thy whole nature has changed, and that be evident. But an the frames merge, what o' thee?"

"O' me?"

"Thou dost love the man o' this frame, who be not with Fleta. Thine other self loves the rovot, who be not with the alien. But—"

"The alien!" Al exclaimed. "My namesake!"

"Aye," Fleta said. "When she and I exchanged, and she were in Phaze, she helped thy parents get together, so they named thee after her. Likewise there be a child in Proton-frame, Mach tells me, named 'Corn, though me thinks I contributed not to that."

"Mine other self!" Al said, pleased.

"As I were saying," Pyreforge continued gruffly. "An the frames merge, so will thy two selves—and there will be one man with one woman. Bane will have the alien, and Fleta will have Mach, all together in one, and none be open for thee. So what o' thee?"

Tania looked crestfallen. "I know not," she said faintly. This was the matter that Fleta had not been able to raise. It was the separation of Mach and Bane that made compromise possible; without that separation, and the two distinct frames, there would be no free man, or free aspect of him.

"Then canst thou labor to merge the frames, an it be possible?"

Tania considered. "I sought to vamp Bane, to win him o'er to our side—I mean the Adverse Adepts—and make a fitting mate for me. I wanted to marry below my station not. But the ploy turned, and he won me to his side, which now be Stile's, and made o' me his creature though ne'er did he touch me. Now must I do what he would have me do, and I would save him though I lose him. I can explain it not else."

"It will do," the old elf said. "Take the Flute to Blue and it will rouse him and enable him to throw off the geis on him. Then will he know what to do."

"There be the answer!" Fleta exclaimed. "To fetch the Flute and bring it to him!"

"Else would we ne'er give it thee," Pyreforge agreed. "An this instrument fall into enemy hands—"

"I will die before that happen," Fleta said, and the air around her rippled.

"Aye," the elf agreed.

Soon they were on their way again, trotting north toward the Blue Demesnes. They passed through the Werewolf Demesnes, but they neither paused there nor made themselves known, for fear the enemy would discover them.

Fleta carried the Platinum Flute, in its box, tied to her barrel. She could feel its latent power, warming her side and lending strength. She knew it could revive Stile!

In two days they were near the castle of the Blue Demesnes. But how were they to get inside? They knew that there would be formidable magic barring their way, and that their amulet would not protect them from discovery here, even if any real strength remained in it.

"Mayhap they be busy elsewhere, not guarding this," Al said hopefully. "I can fly in and spy it out, and if naught happens to me—"

"Aye, go," Fleta said. She did not like putting him in danger, but she couldn't risk bringing the Flute near until she knew it was safe.

Alien changed form and flew low and circuitously toward the castle. In due course he returned. "Tan be there, guarding—but he be sleeping!"

Without a word, Fleta advanced on the castle in her human form. It would have been faster in her natural form, but she didn't want the sound of her hooves waking the Adept. Tania followed. They took advantage of whatever cover they could find.

They crossed the moat and entered the castle. It was unnaturally silent; the animals that usually came for healing were gone, and the normal activities of cooking and working were still. The geis had been laid on it, and it was in effect deserted.

Fleta stepped into the main chamber. There was Stile, sitting frozen, only his eyes alive. His magic involved singing; he could not sing, and so was helpless. Fleta repressed her horror, and tiptoed toward Stile.

"Hold, mare."

She jumped, turning to face the voice. It was Tan, awake! Of course he had feigned sleep, to trick Al and lure them in here; now he had sprung his trap all too neatly.

"Look not at him!" Tania cried.

But it was already too late. The Adept's gaze was on her, meeting her own. The volition drained from her body as his eyes loomed large.

A bat flew at Tan, going for his eyes. But the Adept merely flicked a glance at Alien, and the bat stiffened and fell to the floor, unable to fly. Fleta had some resistance, being a unicorn, but the vampires did not. The boy had done a brave and foolish thing, and now was stunned. The terrible gaze resumed its reduction of her defense; the Adept wasn't even straining.

Tania leaped in front of her. "I will stop him!" she cried. "Take the Flute to Stile!"

But Fleta, tagged peripherally by the Evil Eye, could barely move. She could feel her volition recovering, but the process was distressingly slow. Only her right hand, holding the Platinum Flute, was fully functional; it had not been affected by the Eye. Indeed, it was the source of her recovery; volition was extending along her arm and toward her shoulder. She had thought the power of the Evil Eye was exaggerated; now she knew that her contempt for it had been because of ignorance. Tania had never used it on her, and her respect for Tania was rising.

Meanwhile, Tania blocked off the Adept Tan, countering his gaze with hers. Neither moved; the Eyes were all.

"Dost think to oppose me, turncoat?" Tan inquired with infinite scorn. "Thou canst not, and I will tell thee why. I am the Tan Adept, not thee, and this be not because I be male, but because my power were e'er greater than thine."

Fleta, staring at Tania's back, saw the woman shiver. He was speaking truly!

"Moreover, thou has lost the edge thou hadst," he continued inexorably. "Thou fool, thou didst let Bane turn the worm on thee, draining thee o' thy nerve. Now thou dost be mushy soft, thine Eye weak.''

Tania's body shook. She was losing the contest, and Fleta still lacked control of her legs. She was a unicorn, resistant to hostile magic, but the Adept had stunned her in a moment. If she tried to walk to Stile, she would fall.

"Were thou not my sister, it would go hard with thee. As it is, I will put thee merely to sleep while I deal with these animals. At least thou has done one thing right: thou didst bring to me the Platinum Flute, that else would have been their only remaining threat.''

Fleta jammed the box containing the Flute forward, into Tania's back. "Take it!'' she said. "It will give thee strength!'' She slid the instrument across the woman's back, around her body to her arm, so that she could grasp it.

Tania's body straightened at the contact. The Flute was lending her strength! Despite Tan's brutal words, Tania's power was nearly the equal of his, and she was able to fight back. She took the box, her gaze still locked with that of her brother, and slowly opened it. Stage by stage she assembled the Flute, and her posture showed that she was still gaining strength. At last she held it before her.

Now it was Tan's turn to shake. The Flute made the difference, and Tania was beating him back! Her Eye was becoming stronger than his.

Tan tried to back away, but in a moment came up against the wall. Tania followed, holding the Flute, never relinquishing her gaze. She had to fascinate him, or he would fascinate them all and take the Flute.

Alien stirred. Fleta, almost completely recovered, went to him, picking him up. Her contact helped; he lifted his mouselike head, his big eyes blinking.

Now Fleta was free to take the Flute to Stile—but she didn't have it, and couldn't take it until Tania had finished with Tan. Tania was winning, but it was obviously a debilitating contest; perhaps never before had Eye been opposed to Eye.

At last Tan sank to the ground, his eyes clouding. He had lost; his mind was captive to his sister's. But Tania was little better off. She wavered, and Fleta hastened to support her before she fell. She seemed dazed. Her tan hair glistened with a sheen of sweat, and her eyes were turning bloodshot. Even with the help of the Flute, she had had to give her all in the effort to prevail.

The castle shook. There was a rumble from below. Then the stone floor clove asunder, and the Purple Adept rose through it, buoyed by a waft of smoke.

There was no time for thought. Both Fleta and Alien knew what to do. They hurled themselves at the Adept, Fleta changing to her natural form as she did so.

Purple raised his hand. The floor bucked, throwing Fleta to the side. A jet of purple gas shot out of a fissure and swept Alien out of the air. Both landed at Stile's feet, half stunned. How true it was: ordinary folk had no chance against any Adept!

Now Purple approached Tania as she stood swaying in her sweat-sodden cloak. "I see thou be better talented than we judged," he said. "Now give me the Flute, girl."

Fleta made a desperate effort to protest, but all she could manage was a double note on her horn.

Tania blinked. She looked at Purple, then at the Flute in her hand. It was obvious that she had no way to resist him; her power was spent, while his was strong.

"Thou'rt a pretty thing," Purple said. "Give it me, and I will spare thee punishment, and mayhap take thee for my mistress. I want not to destroy thee." It was obviously no bluff, either way; Purple had all the powers of the deep earth, and he liked women of any type.

Slowly Tania lifted the Platinum Flute. Fleta blew another protest, but could manage no more. There seemed to be no way to keep Purple from his victory.

Alien changed to his boy form. He was too battered to rise, but he could speak. "Play it!" he gasped.

Tania paused. A strange look crossed her face. She was not musically inclined. There was no way she could perform on such an instrument. But she seemed to hear a voice the others could not. She did not pass the Flute to Purple. She lifted it instead to her mouth. She blew.

Then things became strange indeed.

18 : 'Corn

'Corn had been dozing before the holo show when the key began pulsing. Suddenly he was alert; that was the signal for dire emergency!

He turned off the holo—he had seen it before anyway—and held up the key. It was a small flat metallic plaque—a dog tag, his father had joked, though no animals on Planet Proton wore such tags—imprinted with his identity and a secret message. The message could be evoked only by a qualified adult; Citizen Troal trusted his son, but not quite that much. But the pulsing meant that it was time for that message.

'Corn used his father's terminal to run a quick spot trace on all the appropriate adults. This immediately showed the nature of the crisis: of the six on the list, five were marked in red. This meant that they had been in some way incapacitated or compromised, and should not be approached. Citizen Blue, his wife Sheen, their son Mach, his other self Bane, and their maid Agnes—all off the list. Only Bane's wife Agape remained. He had to get to her in a hurry, before something happened to her too!

He borrowed his father's private transport capsule. Citizen Troal and 'Corn's mother, the beautiful Bat Girl, were off planet, on a holiday alone; he might be able to call them, but he knew better than to try. When his key pulsed, it meant not only trouble, but that speed and secrecy were of the essence. Any offplanet call could be monitored, so nothing private was done that way. The same was true of intraplanet communications. But 'Corn had not communicated; he had merely checked a listing without acting. Now he was acting, in the manner he had to.

He set the capsule on Agape's identity and activated its FIND mechanism. It set off, swiftly orienting on the alien female. Soon it caught up with her.

'Corn opened the exit panel and stepped out—right in front of Agape, who was walking down a hall with another beautiful naked woman, Tania. Both women jumped, caught by surprise.

"Aunt Agape!" he exclaimed. "Come into my carriage; there is mischief afoot." She was not really his aunt, of course; she was the mother of his friend Nepe. But for reasons never fully clarified, his parents had indicated that this was an appropriate way to address her.

Agape didn't hesitate. She caught Tania by the arm and both followed him into the carriage. He set the destination for RANDOM, so that no one could readily intercept them.

"Aunt Agape, my key is pulsing!" he said, holding it up. Nothing showed, of course; the pulsing was a rhythmic trace vibration that only he could feel. "This means trouble! My parents are away, so I must act, and you are the only one left who can evoke the message!"

"But what of the others?" Agape asked, alarmed. She could make herself into any form she wanted, but she looked worn and nervous.

"All are marked red. Something has happened to them! I don't dare even go to look; there must be danger for anyone who goes near them."

"My brother!" Tania exclaimed. "I knew it! He's up to mischief, and Citizen Purple too!"

"It must be," Agape agreed. "We were checking on Citizen Translucent, to ascertain why he dropped out of the proceedings. They probably took him out first, then went after Blue and the others after they got the Oracle. We should have known they wouldn't honor any agreements, once they got power!"

"And we are next," Tania said. "Me because I defected, you because you are of Citizen Blue's camp, and—" She broke off, glancing down at 'Corn, as if realizing that the matter was not fit for a child.

'Corn knew what it was, though. He had seen the holo of the game, where Citizen Tan had raped Agape in emulation. He probably wanted to do it in reality too. That was why Agape looked nervous; she knew that her horror hadn't finished.

"But what can we do?" Agape asked. "If the enemy's power is so complete—and it must be the same in Phaze, because of the parallelism—how can we hope to counter it?"

"My key," 'Corn said. "You must evoke it."

"Evoke it? 'Corn, this is not Phaze! We have no amulets here."

"Evoke its message. This is why I sought you. You are the only one left who can do this."

"I? I know nothing of this!"

"Just touch it, please!"

She extended her hand and touched it with one finger.

The key glowed. A picture of a man appeared in its surface: thin, evidently of the older generation. He wore archaic spectacles on his face, and his hair was shading well into gray.

"I don't know this man," Agape said. "Do you?"

"No. But maybe—" 'Corn turned over the key.

There on the other side was a name and address. "Clef, musician," Agape read. "But he's on a far planet!"

"Clef," Tania said. "I have heard that name. Wasn't he the one who played the—the famous Flute, and brought the frames together?"

"That one?" Agape asked, amazed. "I have heard of a friend of Stile's who—who turned out to be the most amazing Adept of all, even though he was just a serf of Proton. But—"

Tania was staring at the picture on the other side of the key. "That must be him. What an elegant man!"

"But so far away! How can he have anything to do with what is happening here?"

"I—I think—" 'Corn said hesitantly. "Maybe—you have to fetch him?"

Agape stared at Tania. "So he can play again?"

Awed, they realized that this could be it. "We need to get offplanet in a hurry anyway," Tania said. "Before Citizen Purple and my brother catch us."

"I can take you to the spaceport," 'Corn said bravely. "Then I can travel around, leading them away—"

Agape put her arms around him and hugged him to her. This was a unique experience, for young as he was, he understood the nature of her beauty. "We can not leave you, 'Corn. You must come too."

"But I am a minor," he protested with mixed emotion. "I can't leave planet without my parents' consent."

"And we dare not call them," Agape said, frowning.

"We'll have to sneak him out," Tania said. "Ship him as baggage."

"But baggage is shipped in the cargo hold," Agape said. "Not pressure or temperature controlled."

"He'll have to be drugged and sealed into a capsule," Tania said. She glanced at 'Corn. "You have the use of Citizen Troal's carriage; can you also authorize his luggage?"

"Yes," 'Corn said, brightening.

"Make out a routing slip in your father's name for one sealed capsule, and an authorization for two serfs to see to its security. We shall be those serfs. The port officials won't question it unless the alarm is already out, and my guess is that Purple will try to make his coup secretly until all opposition has been eliminated. Remember, he's doublecrossing his own, too; Citizen Translucent's personnel will be in an uproar. We'll leave planet together on the first ship out—specify that in the order. This can be done, but it has to be fast."

'Corn took a slip from the papers in the carriage and filled it out. "But how can I be drugged? The moment we go to a medic—"

"I am able to contact the self-willed machines," Agape said. "I have a code. They support Citizen Blue completely."

"Don't make a call!" Tania warned. "They will be monitoring all calls!"

"No call," Agape agreed. "There will be a private access at the spaceport."

They arrived. There was no alarm, so far. Actually, only a few minutes had passed; Citizen Purple was probably still securing his base elsewhere.

Agape paused at a maintenance panel. She tapped on it, then spoke a few words. There seemed to be no response, and 'Corn was afraid she hadn't gotten through. But then a cleaning vehicle rolled up, its lid lifting to reveal a dark interior chamber.

"Get in," Agape said quietly.

"But—" Corn protested, abruptly nervous.

"Do you not know me, friend?" the machine inquired.

"Troubot!" 'Corn cried. Without further protest he climbed in, and the lid closed. He was in darkness, a prisoner, but now he felt secure.

He wanted to inquire how the machines were arranging things, but before he could do so he was unconscious.

He woke, disoriented. Where was he?

Then a lovely female form leaned over him, her arms reaching around his body to draw him to a sitting posture. "You'll be a little woozy, 'Corn, but that will pass in a moment," she said.

"Tania!" he exclaimed. "But you have clothing on!"

Indeed she did. She wore a silken tan dress cinched at the waist by a blue sash, and there was a blue ribbon in her hair. She was amazingly beautiful; the clothing made her look every inch a Citizen.

She smiled. "We're offplanet, 'Corn. You'll have to don clothing too. Offworlders don't necessarily understand about serf nakedness. We have a red suit for you."

"Red suit?" He was still dazed, as much by the changed circumstance as the effects of his drugging. Obviously he had been put under in Troubot—trust his friend to make it easy!—and sealed in and shipped, and now they were—where?

"Red is Citizen Troal's color," she reminded him. "As it is for his opposite in Phaze, the Red Adept. We are at the spaceport at your father's vacation planet; soon he will be meeting us, and we want you to be suitably attired. Then Agape and I will go on to locate Clef."

He let her dress him, bemused. He knew that clothing was worn offplanet, but this was the first time he had been away from Proton and it was hard to set aside the conditioning of a lifetime.

He felt the need to say something, but he didn't know what. So he asked her a personal question. "Tania—if I may ask—aren't you in love with Mach?"

Her work never paused. She was putting socks on his feet, and then shoes. She had evidently had prior experience with such things. "True."

"Then how is it you are friends with Agape? I mean, Bane uses the same body—"

"My love is doomed," she said. "Mach does not love me. No doubt in time I will get over it."

"But didn't he promise—"

"I want his love, not his promise!" she flared. Then, immediately, she apologized. "I'm sorry, 'Corn; I shouldn't have said that. My situation is no concern of yours. I have been foolish in my emotion; see that when you grow up you are more sensible."

"Too late," he said wryly. "I love Nepe, and she loves Troubot."

Tania stared at him. Then she hugged him. "You do understand!" she murmured, and he felt the wetness of tears at his neck. Suddenly he was very glad he had spoken.

Agape appeared, resplendent in a blue dress. It was amazing what clothing did for a person! 'Corn, standing now before a mirror, hardly recognized himself; they were like three different people.

They walked out to meet Citizen Troal. But it was the Bat Girl, in bright red, who came to meet them. He had never seen her dressed before, either; she was the loveliest of all! "Mother!" he cried, and flung himself into her arms.

"Tania and I must go on to find the musician Clef," Agape said. " 'Corn's key indicates that this is our only avenue to reverse the treachery of the Contrary Citizens."

'Corn's mother smiled. "My husband is already contacting him. We shall hold a video conference. Our cottage is about fifteen minutes away."

They rode in the odd conveyance of this planet. It was like a boat, that sailed above a rail set in the ground. Its magnetic suspension was smooth, and as it moved it really did seem to have the buoyancy of a waterborne craft. But even stranger was the landscape through which they rode: *there was no dome!* The atmosphere of this planet was unpolluted; it was possible to breathe anywhere. There were even plants and trees growing as far afield as he could see. As with the clothing: he had known this was the case with many planets, but it was an awesome thing actually to experience.

Made giddy by this new environment, 'Corn was emboldened to ask his mother a personal question. "Why are you called the Bat Girl, Mother, when you don't look anything like a bat?" The oddest thing was that he had never wondered about this before; seeing her in clothing had changed his view of her in more than the physical sense.

She laughed. "Your father named me that! It is because of Agape."

"Agape?" he repeated, startled.

"Some time back, I exchanged places with Fleta the unicorn in Phaze," Agape answered. "In Phaze I was helped by an ugly old troll and a beautiful young vampire. I talked to each, and learned that each was afraid to broach a certain matter to the other: he because he believed that no woman could care for a troll, she because she regarded herself as an animal, having originated as a bat. Because I owed each a debt I could not myself repay, I urged the lady bat to approach the troll."

"But what has that to do with my mother?" 'Corn demanded.

"They did get together, and soon married," Agape explained. "They had a son whom they chose to name after my Proton identity, calling him Alien. Because things tend to be parallel between the frames, something similar happened in Proton, and the happy couple named their son Unicorn, after the person whose body I used in Phaze."

'Corn was stunned. "A troll—a vampire bat—and a unicorn?"

His mother hugged him. "I'm sure your opposite number is no happier about being named after an amoebic alien creature. But we identify strongly with our Phaze counterparts; Phaze is the magic in our lives, even though we can not visit it."

'Corn was silent. Why hadn't he realized this before? Nepe had spoken of her contact with Flach, and his friend Al. Al the alien, 'Corn the unicorn! How obvious, suddenly!

They arrived at the residence. It was a cottage right out in the open, surrounded by flowering trees. But 'Corn was becoming acclimatized to such marvels; they had serious business to transact.

Citizen Troal met them at the door. 'Corn had never thought of his father as a troll before, but now he could see how tall and ugly he was. Of course appearance didn't matter for a Citizen; the most beautiful woman would marry one in an instant, for the sake of the power and comfort of the life he offered. 'Corn had assumed this was the case with his mother; now he knew that there was more to it than that.

"We are tracking the musician," Troal announced. "He should be on the screen momentarily."

Indeed, Clef appeared soon after they entered. He was life size on the wall screen, but the distance between planets caused his image to flicker slightly. He was a man of Troal's age, with a severely receding hairline and the same archaic spectacles the key had shown. "I have not been in touch with Planet Proton for more than a quarter century," he said. "To what do I owe the honor of this contact?"

"Do you remember Citizen Blue?" Troal asked. "Perhaps you know him as the Adept Stile."

"Stile! Yes, of course; how could I forget! He fetched the magic Platinum Flute!"

"We believe he has need for your assistance again."

"There on Proton? But I can not return there; my tenure as a serf concluded, and I am not allowed back. In any event, I have a pressing schedule in this section of the galaxy; we are organizing an interspecies orchestra."

"Your return to Proton may be barred by Proton custom," Troal said. "But events may override that. Citizen Blue is in serious trouble, and there is a suggestion that you are the key to the resolution of his problem."

"I'm not sure you understand, Citizen Troal. My prior service was to enter the frame of Phaze and play the magic Flute at a critical time. Thereafter the frames were permanently separated, it is no longer possible to cross over. Since the magic Flute remains on the other side of the curtain, and only it is capable of re-establishing the connection, there is nothing I can do for you."

"Nevertheless, Citizen Blue evidently believes—"

"I am sorry. I suspect further dialogue is pointless. I am in any event too old to travel such a distance on mere speculation that I might be of some use."

Troal looked baffled. Clef was making sense.

"Sir, if I may talk to him," Tania murmured.

The Citizen shrugged. "Of course. But make it brief."

Tania stepped forward, adjusting her decolletage. "Clef, I be Tania, daughter of one thou mayest have encountered in the Phaze variation as the Tan Adept. Methinks that thou'rt the finest musician o' our time. We believe that thou dost be the only one who can help us save Proton and Phaze from a terrible fate. We know not how thou mayest do this, but we be prepared to do anything required to make it possible. Anything! Please, I beg of thee, come immediately to this planet, that we may explore possibilities."

Clef stared at her. "Of course."

The others watched, astonished, as Tania made a little bow to the screen. Then the connection dissolved.

"What did you do?" 'Corn demanded. "How come he changed his mind?"

She turned to him, a partial smile on her face. Her dress was open at the front, showing most of one breast and part of the other. Her hair was slightly wild. Her eyes seemed enormous—and as her gaze met his, they seemed to grow larger yet, sending an oddly pleasant shiver through him. "You vamped him!" Agape exclaimed.

Tania drew her dress up so that little more than her neck showed, and smoothed out her hair. Her eyes diminished. "It's a talent I have found effective on men other than yours. I prayed for some of what my other self can do with her Eye, and perhaps I got it. It was a desperation ploy."

"But that man is old enough to be your father!" Agape protested.

"And what is wrong with that?" the Bat Girl inquired.

Agape glanced from her to Citizen Troal. "Nothing, of course," she said, embarrassed.

"And you used Phaze idiom, reminding him of what offers there," Citizen Troal remarked. "That was clever of you. I wish I could have seen you as he saw you."

"Not likely!" the Bat Girl snapped. ". . . sir."

They all laughed. 'Corn knew that his mother, perhaps the most beautiful woman of Proton, had nothing to fear from others. Still, the way Tania had looked in that moment—if it had had such impact on himself, a child, what would have been the effect on a grown man? Now Clef's change of heart was no mystery!

Galactic travel was swift, when facilitated by a Citizen of Proton. Within a day Clef arrived.

"I don't want to see him," Tania said, embarrassed. "If I had thought about it at all, I wouldn't have—"

"Clef is a gentleman," Troal said. "Be assured he will treat you as a lady."

"Which I don't deserve!"

But she did meet him, completely demure in a cloaklike dress, and Clef was indeed polite. He had brought his flute—made of platinum but not, he explained, magic, unfortunately. "I would give everything I have dreamed of elsewhere, to be in Phaze again, to possess the magic Flute again," he said. "When you, Tania, perhaps subconsciously, used the Phaze idiom, it reminded me of my longing for it. So my presence here is selfish, I regret to confess. If there is even the remotest chance—" He shrugged.

"We hope there is," Tania said, visibly relieved.

"Citizen Blue must believe there is," 'Corn said, showing his key, which still glowed with Clef's picture. They explained all that they knew of the situation to Clef.

Clef nodded. "So the parallelism has strengthened in recent decades," he said. "That suggests quite strong connections between the frames despite their seeming separation. Perhaps this is because with no way to cross over physically, the force of equalization is channeled to other mechanisms."

"That is our conclusion," Citizen Troal agreed.

"That may mean in turn that something roughly similar to our present meeting is occurring in the frame of Phaze," Clef continued. "Perhaps someone is fetching the magic Flute."

"But how can you play it, when it is there and you are here?" 'Corn asked.

"That is the salient question," Clef said. "But if my friend Stile—or his other self—believes that it is possible, then it behooves us to explore the matter. Perhaps the answer will offer."

"But there is danger for all of us on Planet Proton," Troal reminded him. "Citizen Purple is trying to eliminate all opposition."

"I realize that. But I am in my waning years, and perhaps have relatively little to lose. We must try to consult with Citizen Blue; he is the only one who truly knows how I may help."

"We may be able to sneak a small party in," Citizen Troal said. "My wife and I are watched, so cannot approach the planet, but if others move in by a devious route, it may work. However, the moment you enter Citizen Blue's premises, discovery is inevitable; you will have very little time to act."

"Understood," Clef agreed.

The return was more complicated than the departure, but just as urgent; they knew they had to act swiftly, or it would be too late. If Citizen Purple got well enough established to believe he could afford to kill his captives, what would be left except vengeance and ruin? It was ironic, 'Corn thought, that the Contrary Citizens had already won their contest; had they just honored the agreements, their hold over the planet would have been secure. But victory had been the signal for the falling out of thieves, and now they were hurting each other as much as their opponents.

Indeed, it might have been that internecine quarreling which enabled the foursome to sneak back onto the planet. Citizen was watching Citizen, each nervously guarding his own holdings while trying to grab those of his neighbors. Anarchy was developing. So no notice was taken when a noted musician from a far planet arrived with several sealed boxes of equipment about which he was very finicky. There was also a reaction to local custom. He made a fair scene when leaving the ship: *"Naked?* You expect me to strip stark naked?"

'Corn smiled. He had been revived the moment the ship landed, as had the others, so that they could act quickly. They remained in their boxes, properly naked, ready to push open the unlatched lids and leap out at need. But as long as the ruse remained effective, they remained hidden, listening. 'Corn was sure that Agape and Tania found this scene as amusing as he did. Clef had been a serf, and well understood the rule for serfs; but he was returning as a different man, one who had never before been to this planet. Evidently there had been some details this other person had overlooked.

The spaceport personnel patiently explained about Citizens and serfs. They had been through exactly this sort of scene many times before. They were sorry, but no matter how august the musician was on his home planet, he was reckoned as a serf here, and had to adopt serf ways. He must address any clothed person as "sir" and honor any directive that person gave implicitly; he must seek the sponsorship of a Citizen if he wished to remain on the planet more than a few days; and he must go naked.

"This is an outrage!" Clef fulminated. But in the end, with exceeding reluctance, he bared his old and portly body, for he had an important engagement for which he would not be paid unless he delivered. "But," he assured them grimly, "you have not heard the last of this!"

The personnel did not respond. They had heard it before. Planet Proton was a very special experience, for those who arrived unwarned. Most of the functionaries had had to make similar adjustments when they first came. Clef was allowed to set foot within the dome proper, and his boxes were unloaded.

Shortly later, in the temporary apartment chamber he had rented, Clef opened his luggage. He had used a special monitor to make sure that he was not being spied on. 'Corn and the two women got out. They had passed the first hurdle; now for the second, and critical, one. They had to get to Citizen Blue, and then see how they could help him.

'Corn went ahead, scouting the situation. His hair had been cut and its color changed, and cosmetic tape had been used to change his facial features enough to make him unrecognizable as the boy he had been. His body was thicker; he looked pudgy now, but this was because of a spybeam sensor fitted around his abdomen. Every time he passed a hall monitor, he got a pulse against the skin of his belly, verifying the presence of the invisible beam.

All was quiet in the region of Citizen Blue's complex. 'Corn walked by it without pausing—but the equipment he carried verified the nature of the lock and the people inside. The lock was unchanged, which meant that Agape could enter, bringing her companions with her. Citizen Blue, Sheen and Mach remained there, apparently unhurt, held by a lethargy generator that was tuned to both living people and robots. Citizen Tan was there too, horizontal; that meant he was sleeping at the moment. Excellent!

'Corn completed his circuit, returning to Clef's chamber. "It's clear!" he reported. "Only Citizen Tan is guarding them, and he's sleeping!"

"I don't trust this," Tania said. "My brother is devious, as I am. It could be a trap."

"What choice do we have?" Clef asked. "If we don't go there, we can not rescue Citizen Blue. We shall just have to hope that either they are not expecting us, or that if they are, we can act with greater dispatch than they expect."

Tania nodded. "Sometimes the best way to handle a trap is to spring it," she agreed. "I am expendable; I will try to nullify my brother while you see to Citizen Blue."

"Expendable?" Clef asked, appalled. "I should hope not!"

Tania smiled at him, and he smiled back. Evidently she had after all invoked more than just the memory of Phaze in his mind. 'Corn observed them covertly, hoping to learn something that might be useful in his relationship with Nepe. He knew that Tania wasn't really interested in Clef; she just wanted to be sure he helped rescue Citizen Blue. And, in the process, the one she did love: Mach. Thus she was an excellent reference for the application of sex appeal without emotion.

"In any event," Agape said, "that lethargy box surely has settings for Tania and me and perhaps 'Corn too. We are wearing nullifiers, but our first priority will be to destroy that box."

"I'll do it!" 'Corn cried. "I'll throw it against the wall!"

"Too bad we couldn't get a box tuned to Purple and Tan," Tania said.

They proceeded to Blue's suite. Other serfs were hurrying to and fro; to them the strife between Citizens was either unimportant or unknown. They merely followed orders, whoever was in power. No one paid attention to the little party.

At the panel, Agape didn't hesitate. She put her hand against it, and it slid open, recognizing her. She remained at the panel while the other three quickly and quietly stepped in; then she stepped through and let it close behind.

They filed silently along the short hallway leading to the main room. Tania took the lead, alert for her brother. Clef was next, holding his flute; none of them knew exactly how this instrument could help, but all believed that it related in some significant way.

'Corn saw Citizen Blue, seated on a chair. He was conscious; his eyes moved. But he was unable to move rapidly.

"So the wanderers return!"

That was Citizen Tan's voice! He was awake—and it was indeed a trap!

Then, before 'Corn could react, the heavy hand of lethargy fell on him. He saw Agape and Clef sag; they felt it too. Tan had the box—and it was overriding their nullifiers! Their arrival had not only been anticipated, it had been prepared for. What fools they had been to think it would be otherwise; no wonder their arrival had been without event! Tan had *wanted* them to come here, where they could be captured without commotion.

But Tania was not affected. She whirled and threw herself on the Citizen, grabbing for the box. The rest of them, unable to take similar action, stood in place.

'Corn was facing forward, and could not turn his head fast enough to view the action. Why wasn't there a setting for Tania? Then he understood: she was Tan's twin sister. Her setting would be almost identical to his. If he tried to use the box on her, he would suffer its effects himself. Perhaps he had thought she would not dare return, so hadn't worried about it. Or he had thought she wouldn't dare directly oppose him.

He had been mistaken. 'Corn heard the sounds of their nearby struggle. Tania was female, and smaller than her brother, but she was healthy while he had evidently grown soft in Citizenship. It seemed like an eternity, but was only a few seconds; then the box dropped to the floor. She had beaten him!

No, she had only jarred the box from his grasp. It had not broken; the lethargy remained on them. Tan shoved her away as 'Corn's head slowly turned so that he could see them. She stumbled into Clef.

Tan lunged at her. Tania dodged around Clef. Then, on inspiration, she took the flute from his flaccid hand and held it like a weapon. When Tan reached for her again, she brought it down on his head.

The flute was made of platinum: a beautiful and extremely valuable instrument. Platinum was one of the heaviest of metals. The flute made a most effective club. Tan dropped to the floor, for the moment unable to continue the fight.

Tania stepped toward the lethargy box, ready to smash it similarly, so as to free them all.

Clef managed a protest. "Not with the flute!" The pain in his voice would have been funny if the situation had not been so serious.

Tania nodded. Her hair was wild and she was bruised and shaking, but she had not lost her wits. She tucked the flute under her arm and picked up the box. She found its master switch and turned it off.

Suddenly all of them were free—Blue and Sheen and Mach included.

But before they could do more than look at each other, there was a new voice. "Attempt nothing foolish," Purple said. "I have another box—and more persuasive instruments."

It was of course no bluff. Citizen Tan might have misjudged his sister, but Citizen Purple was more cunning and ruthless. Tania straightened slowly, and the others did not move.

Except for 'Corn. He was at the rear of their column, closest to Purple. He whirled and leaped—

And was felled by a spot lethargy jolt. He collapsed at Purple's feet. Indeed, the man had not been bluffing!

Purple brushed by him, orienting on Tania. "Give me that flute," he said gruffly, "and I may make you my mistress instead of having you executed." He held out his hand.

'Corn, on the floor, was able to move his head just enough to see the tableau. Tania was slowly lifting the flute. Clef was just behind her, chagrined.

Why did Purple want the flute? He had to know it wasn't the magic one! It was valuable, but Purple hardly needed more wealth. The instrument was irrelevant to Purple's interests.

But Purple was no fool. If he wanted the flute, there had to be reason. But what could the flute do, that Purple might fear?

Suddenly 'Corn got a notion. "Play it!" he gasped.

Tania, surprised, looked at the flute she held. She was no musician. There was no way she could do more than tootle on it. But she seemed to understand what 'Corn had realized.

She lifted the flute to her mouth and blew.

There was nothing except a rush of air. She wasn't addressing the mouthpiece correctly. Purple laughed.

Then Clef reached around her and adjusted the flute. He set his hands over hers, each finger guiding one of hers. "Across, not into," he murmured.

"Enough of this foolishness," Purple said, reaching again.

Tania blew again. This time, with Clef's close guidance, she blew a note. Her fingers under Clef's depressed the keys, and the note changed.

The first note was imperfect, yet had a strange quality. The second was better, and stranger. She was catching on, following Clef's cues, making eerie music.

"No!" Purple cried. But she continued to play, with increasing facility, and he did not advance on her.

There seemed to be a light developing around the flute—not a glow, but an ambience. Its color heightened, enhancing its outline. Tania's face seemed to have a double outline, as if she were a holo picture a trifle out of focus. In fact there seemed to be two Tanias, playing two flutes, overlapping.

Then the split images merged. Abruptly the music became intimately compelling. The radiance spread outward, seeming to ripple through the air and the people—and where it passed, they changed, becoming double and then single, then double again, as if swinging in and out of themselves. The air seemed to sparkle and become fresh with the fragrance of a healthy outdoors. Yet the walls of the suite also seemed to be dissolving, and a verdant outdoor landscape was showing through them.

"Now," Clef said. He moved his hands, taking hold of the flute directly. Tania let go, giving it to him. She seemed stunned by what had happened.

The ripple of light jumped inward, as if a bubble were collapsing. The superimposed images faded. But then Clef began to play.

He was a master. All doubt about this was abolished by his first note. His fingers on the flute seemed to glow with sheer competence. Tania stared at him as if mesmerized.

The radiance strengthened, as if a spotlight had focused on the flute. It spread again, slowly; but this time its effects were intensified. It lighted Clef's hands, and they became cleaner, stronger, the fingers more nimble; the discolorations of age faded, leaving the firm flesh of youth. It traveled across his arms, and they filled out, becoming muscular. It touched his neck, which smoothed out, both tendons and wrinkles disappearing. It expanded across his face, shaping it, heightening its animation, strengthening its character. His sparse hair darkened and advanced, thickening. His spectacles now seemed incongruous on so handsome a face.

Tania watched him, rapt. The man was being transformed! His whole body was turning youthful and dynamic as the light bathed it. Agape was staring too, and 'Corn, from the floor; he knew the same thought was in all their minds. How could such a thing be happening, without magic? Yet how could magic be operating, here in Proton?

The globe of light seemed to split. A small intense part of it clothed Clef, while a larger but fainter secondary part of it expanded to enclose them all in its ambience. 'Corn felt it infusing him, changing both his body and his mind in extraordinary manner, both uplifting and alarming him. He saw the others—and each was double, twin images overlapping, but not perfectly. Each was split, yet not harmed, and each looked as confused as he felt. When Tania had played, the outlines of each person had seemed blurred. Now they were distinct, yet dual.

The walls of the suite dissolved again. This time the outdoor landscape assumed full force.

Then they were moving—or the landscape was. As a group they passed through the wall of the suite, and through the walls of the neighboring chambers. There were people in those other chambers, looking startled, but the group swept through them and past them without impediment. 'Corn found himself moving toward a walking serf; then he went through the middle of the man and on, feeling only a momentary drag, as if the air had thickened. *What was happening?*

The pace accelerated, as the music continued. They burst out of Hardom and moved north, like nine figures locked in an invisible ship. Fields and trees passed at a blurring rate, and even hills. They were going somewhere at the speed of a spaceship, without the ship.

A castle loomed on the horizon, a blue pennant flying from a high turret. They shot in toward it, and through its walls.

Abruptly the motion stopped. They were in the castle, and 'Corn's face was near a tuft of grass sprouting from the crevice between two paving stones. But he could not be concerned about that; the travel had stopped, but not the music. Clef was still playing, his whole body concentrating on the effort, as if what had occurred so far were only the preliminary to something greater.

The globe of light touched Tania. The two images of her slid together. Her dishevelment and her bruises were wiped away, enhancing her posture. Her eyes seemed larger, and literally glowing. She had always been a striking woman; now she seemed charismatic. The music was lifting her, making her sway; she was not merely listening, she was *of* it.

Citizen Purple made a noise. His doubled images were also merging. Tania's face turned, her mouth forming a frown. Her eyes seemed to strike out at him—and Purple fell back, reeling as if struck.

That was the Evil Eye! 'Corn had learned of it through Nepe. The Tania of Phaze had it, the ability to hypnotize or hurt people merely by looking at them. But this was Proton!

The light was coming here, bathing him, and bringing with it its strange effects. 'Corn had been amazed by the ghostly traveling; now he experienced a ghostly unity. The thought that had prompted him to urge Tania to play the flute returned, assuming new clarity. This was—

"Aye," he murmured, sitting up.

Aye? That was Phaze talk!

"Aye," his mouth said again. "The flute be doing it." "What's happening?" 'Corn cried, even as he realized the explanation. *He was merging with his other self.*

"Aye," his mouth said a third time. "I be Alien. Thou hast come here to Phaze."

"But this is Proton!" 'Corn protested.

"Nay, methinks it be both. See, the frames be merging, and the folk o' the frames."

'Corn saw it was so. The Proton folks who had occupied the suite of Citizen Blue were superimposed on what must be the Blue Demesnes of Phaze. Somehow the music of the flute had carried them here, where they were joining with their parallel selves.

Yes, as he thought it through, he found confirmation from his other self. Alien—Al—had witnessed the treachery of Tan and Purple, and had gone to find Fleta and Tania, and the three of them had fetched the magic Platinum Flute and come here—and now with Clef playing that Flute, the frames were being brought together. It was overwhelming, yet also sensible.

He looked around him, discovering that the lethargy was gone from his body. Clef was still playing, Tania was still gazing raptly on him, and the others were reacting much as 'Corn himself was. Agape's features were changing, coming to resemble those of

Fleta, Al's thought continued. Her human form was petite and pretty. While, in contrast, the Purple Adept was a mottled and ugly hulk. The man's fat face was twisted in a distorted snarl as he waged some internal war with

Citizen Purple, 'Corn continued. Evidently the two did not like each other much more than they liked anyone else. Probably they were engaged in a no-quarter-given struggle to determine which of them was to control their single body.

Meanwhile, Citizen Blue was coming to life. It seemed that the Adept Stile had been under a spell that the music was abating. But Stile and Blue were not united, and neither were Mach and Bane. What was wrong?

Blue caught 'Corn's eye. "Be not concerned, Al; my body in Phaze be but a golem, and with the mergence I am returned to Stile's." He gestured to the golem, which sat immobile.

Then the man's eyes went glassy, and the golem animated. "On the other hand, 'Corn, I can also assume his body," Stile said. Or maybe Blue; it was difficult to tell which was which. "Because we are one, now, we can not occupy both simultaneously. This was one of the complications that made this a last-resort ploy. Mach has the same problem."

"Aye, and Bane," the living man said, while the robot was still. "But methinks we can live with it."

Agape/Fleta turned to face Bane/Mach. "This could become complicated at certain times," she said.

"Canst not take turns?" he asked.

"An we were an other two, nay," she replied. "But we knew each other well; we have traded bodies before. Now we have the capacities o' both." She demonstrated by melting one hand into a molten lump, then re-forming it. Then she became a unicorn, and a hummingbird, and a woman again.

The Lady Blue stirred. "Welcome, Lady Sheen. Long has it been since we met. Surely we too can share."

The woman went slack and the robot animated. "Surely we can, Lady Blue!"

"But if all of you can cooperate and share so readily," 'Corn asked, "why not Purple?"

Stile/Blue laughed. "For us it be fraught with difficulties, which may belong in the working out. For him it be nigh impossible. This be because we be amicable persons, accustomed to accommodation and sacrifice, while the Adverse and Contrary folk be perverse and greedy, accustomed to yielding naught but under force or threat. We can get along with our other selves; they can not. It be that simple.''

'Corn looked at Purple again. The man's face was mottled and approaching the color of his name as a series of foul emotions crossed it. Purple was evidently unable to wreak mischief on anyone else until he settled his own case.

"But they have the Oracle and the Book of Magic," Agape/Fleta said. "And my child!"

"With the frames unified by the stronger magic of the Flute, neither the Oracle nor the Book of Magic is as important as before," Stile/Blue said. "And as for my grandchild—I will bring him now."

He singsonged a spell, drawing on the immense ongoing magic of the continuing Flute, and disappeared. In a moment he was back with Nepe and a young wolf. "Just as well I did," he said. "They were near the limit of the good air. The Proton pollution has been pushed off the main continent, for now."

Nepe looked around, seeming less surprised than the others. "This is fun!" she exclaimed.

Agape swooped down to gather her up. But Nepe was already changing. "Ugh!" Flach exclaimed as Agape kissed him.

"But then who is the wolf?" 'Corn asked, astonished.

The wolf became a rather pretty young girl. "Sirelmoba," she said.

Flach disengaged from Agape and embraced his bitch-friend. But she changed, and in a moment he was holding Troubot. "Ugh!" the robot exclaimed.

Somebody started laughing. Then all of them were, except Adept/Citizen Purple, who was lost in his own private quarrel. There were certainly things to adjust to! But what a great new situation was opening out: the realms of science and magic merged, both being operative together at last!

"Unicorn Point," Stile/Blue said, looking around. "I see now that the two frames were never meant to be separated, and they shall not be so again. The cities and the creatures of the wild shall learn to coexist. There will be problems, of course; significant ones, such as the matter of pollution. We can't have Phaze atmosphere go the way of Proton's! But what would life be, without challenge?''

"Aye," Neysa said. Then she became Nessie. Now 'Corn understood why Citizen Blue had hired this older alien from Planet Moeba;

he had been facilitating the parallelism, so as to be ready for this mergence, if it came. Flach's granddam, Nepe's grandmother: had one been offplanet at this time, there could have been a bad disruption.

'Corn/Al remembered something. "What of Tania?" he asked. "She did more than anyone to make this possible, and she loves Mach/Bane, and we owe her—"

Fleta/Agape looked up. "It be true. We owe her," she said sadly. "Mayhap she loved power as much as the man, wishing to unite with an Adept or Citizen and so gain back her own, but an we have the debt, needs must we—"

The music of the Flute finally stopped; the mergence was complete. Clef's job was done. Rejuvenated, exhilarated, he lowered the instrument and stood there, smiling and handsome. Slowly he turned to Tania, with a questioning glance.

In two steps she was in his arms, kissing him with a passion verging on ferocity. A light flickered about them.

Now 'Corn appreciated the phenomenal impact the playing of the Flute must have had upon the woman. She had started it, guided by Clef's expertise; then she had experienced the unparalleled magic of his playing. Power? Clef was the leading Adept of the age, because of the Flute. Tania had known that her love for Mach or Bane was futile; now she had discovered all that she longed for—power, Phaze and a matchless man—in Clef. It was true for both Tanias; they had unified cleanly, and evidently had no internal conflicts. The suddenness of her change of love was no more amazing than the magic of the mergence of the frames.

"Come, we have much to do," Stile/Blue said. "Let's hope that folk like Merle are satisfied with their new powers in lieu of other payment, and that our other allies are well off, while the Adverse allies are similarly badly off." He glanced at 'Corn. "Thy folks may remain ensorceled, Al. Needs must we check on the Red Demesnes. Mayhap with 'Corn's folks offworld, there will be a complication we must abate."

"Me too!" Nepe cried. "Come on, 'Corn—let's meet Al's folks!" She ran across and took his arm.

'Corn, dizzy, realized that the prospects were still opening up. Maybe, as with Flach and Sirelmoba, Nepe looked forward to a different partner when grown than when young! He had to admit, things were looking better.

AUTHOR'S NOTE

For those readers who have inquired what happened to the Author's Notes in these novels, an answer: THERE HAVE NEVER BEEN AUTHOR'S NOTES IN THE ADEPT SERIES. But, having established that, here is an exception, because I have a couple of credits to give, an explanation to make, and a question to hedge.

My thanks to "Cutter John" Griffith, whose comments on USENET helped me organize the Adepts; I was having trouble remembering who was which.

Likewise to Thomas A. McCloud, for the Dragon Duel notion and the Add-a-Game device; I adapted from his informative letter to assemble that sequence.

For those interested in structure, yes, it is true: there are eighteen different viewpoints in this novel, one for each chapter. They move rhythmically across the three generations: elder, middle and younger, so that every third chapter relates to the same generation. Also, the odd chapters relate to Phaze, and the even ones to Proton, except for Chapter 6 when Nepe breaks the rule. Nepe is irrepressible!

Now the question that some others will be asking: is this the end of the series? Certainly there remains much to tell, as the kinks are worked out of the merged frames and merged characters. One reader suggested that the Brown Adept be given a romantic interest; indeed it is possible that she has had a richer life than has been seen here. There is also the possibility of a new generation of children with extraordinary science and magic abilities. The rest of the Galaxy can hardly be ignorant of the advantages of magic; an invasion for purposes of ruthless exploitation seems likely. This would of course have to be resisted. So yes, there may well be more, in due course. Don't rush me. I will get to *Phaze Doubt* when I'm ready.